M000317029

WOLF Publishing - This is us:

Two sisters, two personalities.. But only one big love!

Diving into a world of dreams..

...Romance, heartfelt emotions, lovable and witty characters, some humor, and some mystery! Because we want it all! Historical Romance at its best!

Visit our website to learn all about us, our authors and books!

Sign up to our mailing list to receive first hand information on new releases, freebies and promotions as well as exclusive giveaways and sneak-peeks!

WWW.WOLF-PUBLISHING.COM

ALSO BY JENNIFER MONROE

The Sisterhood of Secrets

There is far more for the women at Miss Rutley's Finishing School than an education, for their secretive headmistress will assure her pupils find the happiness they each deserve.

#1 Duke of Madness

#2 Baron of Rake Street

#3 Marquess of Magic

#4 Earl of Deception

#5 Knight of Destiny

#6 Captain of Second Chances

MARQUESS
of
MAGIC

PROLOGUE

Chatsworth, England 1825

Diana, Marchioness of Barrington clutched the letter to her breast and sighed. Received ten days earlier and written in the hand of her former headmistress, Mrs. Agnes Rutley, its message was simple—if possible, return to Mrs. Rutley's School for Young Ladies as quickly as you can.

And so, she heeded the call, just as she had promised all those years ago.

A cool breeze moved the tiny hairs beneath her silk-covered buckram bonnet, tickling her forehead as she gazed up at the building that had been her home twenty years prior. It appeared exactly as she remembered with its ivy-covered white facade and black-trimmed windows. During her four years at the school, Diana had come to understand much.

Oh, she had learned about history, music, and decorum, but it was what she discovered with her many friends that was worth every farthing her father had paid to have her attend the illustrious school. For here was where she was taught about life and all it had to offer.

Turning away from the building, Diana's gaze fell upon the ancient tree where the girls spent a goodly amount of their time. If the weather permitted, she and her friends would sit in the shade, sharing in gossip, dreams for the future, and hope for an everlasting love.

Diana approached the great oak, removed a glove, and touched one of the nine pairs of initials carved into its trunk. There, too, was where the Sisterhood of Secrets had been born. Nine women had come together during a time of desperation, each revealing a deep secret, thus allowing all of them to share in the burdens they carried.

At that very place, they made a pact through the mixing of their blood, a promise to come if any had a great need. Thus, Diana's reason for this visit today.

Although she had kept in contact with some of her friends, others had stopped writing. Life had a tendency to steal a person's time, so she did not blame any of them. Yet, she hoped all would heed the call. After all, a lady was only as good as her word, or so Mrs. Rutley had instilled in them.

Heaving a sigh, Diana recalled her days at the school, the friends she had made, and the experiences she had lived. Oh, to go back and live it again, not knowing how precious those times were. She never realized how much she would miss them now that she was older.

"Now is not the time for regrets," Diana murmured, though she had few. She had someone to see, and judging by the two other carriages, some of her friends had arrived before her.

The door opened before she knocked, and a woman with round, rosy cheeks answered.

"Miss Diana!" Mrs. Shepherd said as she threw her arms around Diana and pulled her close. "I mean Lady Barrington. Let me look at you. I'm so glad you're here, Lady Barrington. Mrs. Rutley'll be so happy to see you. I hope your journey was comfortable."

"It was," Diana said, smiling at the cook. "The roads were as smooth as could be expected, and the weather held. I suppose I could not ask for anything more. And you have not changed a bit, Mrs. Shepherd."

Mrs. Shepherd laughed and patted the silver bun at the nape of her neck. "You're just being kind, my lady. I'm old now. But you, my dear!

Look how beautiful you are! And those blonde curls of yours are as lovely as I remember."

It was Diana's turn to chuckle. "I would not mind a few days reprieve from them, Mrs. Shepherd. They can be a tangled mess sometimes."

Mrs. Shepherd clicked her tongue. "You wouldn't be you without them."

Diana glanced around the familiar foyer and memories came flooding back. Was it through these very windows they had watched the Duke of Madness call out to Julia in the midst of a storm? Had that very spot not been where the old man stood when he came to claim Emma as his bride? Laughter still lived within these walls, as did tears of joy and sadness.

Yet through the wonderful guidance of Mrs. Rutley and the support of one another, the students persevered.

"And how is Mrs. Rutley faring?" Diana asked.

"Stubborn, as always," Mrs. Shepherd replied with a grin. "Quick to give her opinion. And very excited to see you. Miss Julia and Miss Emma are already here. I say you go up there and join them in Mrs. Rutley's bedroom."

With a nod, Diana ascended the staircase, recalling the many times she had made this same trek when she was younger. Often, Miss Theodosia Renwick or Miss Unity Ancell could be found waiting for her at the top.

"Diana, you must come and hear what Louisa has to say!" one might say. Miss Louisa Dunston could be found listening at every keyhole and was always the first to learn what was going on in Mrs. Rutley's office. She was nosy enough for all of them!

The other might say, "Have you heard the trouble Ruth has gotten into today?" Miss Ruth Lockhart was the most adventurous—and the most headstrong—of all Diana's friends. If there was trouble, Ruth was likely the cause of it. After all, it had been she who had produced the pen knife and recommended the blood pact all those years ago.

At the door to Mrs. Rutley's room, Diana paused. Although she was happy to see her old headmistress, she also feared what she would find inside. It would not likely be the vibrant and vivacious woman Diana remembered. That thought saddened her.

Shaking her head, she tapped a knuckle on the door and entered the room, her eyes immediately falling to the bed. Mrs. Rutley was propped up on several pillows, her eyes closed. Sallow skin covered bony arms, and her hair had thinned considerably.

In contrast, the two younger women who sat beside the bed had changed little. Julia, now the Duchess of Elmhurst, was as lovely as she had been with her wheat-colored hair and shining blue eyes. Emma, once the daughter of a baronet, had married the Baron of Rake Street. Lady St. John suited her well and had done little to change her dark hair, button nose, and short stature. A surge of warmth washed over Diana. Oh, but it was good to see them again!

"My friends... no, my sisters," Diana whispered. "It's so good to see you." She glanced at the bed. "How's Mrs. Rutley faring?"

Emma hugged her. "She's resting now. But when she wakes, she'll wish to hear a story. And if you don't mind, Julia and I would like to listen as well."

"A story?" Diana asked. What sort of story could she possibly concoct at such short notice?

She did not have time to consider, for Mrs. Rutley stirred.

Diana hurried to the headmistress's side and took her hand. She may as well have been holding the hand of a skeleton for all the flesh that existed beneath the skin.

"Oh, Diana, I knew you would come," Mrs. Rutley croaked.

Although Mrs. Rutley's gaze was strong—likely the reason Mrs. Shepherd had called her stubborn—Diana could sense the woman's pain.

"Of course, I came," Diana said. "Was that not the pledge we made around the great oak? Were our initials not the signing of a contract of sorts? So yes, I've come to honor that pledge. After all, you taught me that a lady is only as good as her word."

Mrs. Rutley gave a wan smile. "And now that I have you here, I've a request. Although I witnessed its outcome, I wish to hear a story about the great romance you've lived."

Diana gave the older woman's hand a gentle squeeze. Oh, but how the memories came flooding back, filled with admiration, worry, and a myriad of emotions that ended in love. "I would be honored, for it is the story of a marquess rumored to dabble in magic and a young lady who believed the notion of love was dead."

Collecting her thoughts, Diana considered where to begin. Should it be when she and Emma encountered the Marquess of Magic in the bookstore and Diana had promptly embarrassed herself? Or perhaps the day Emma left the school with her parents.

No, neither was the best place to begin.

Smiling, Diana said, "The day Mother arrived at the school, I was certain of two things. The first was that I would never fall in love. The second was that magic in any form did not exist."

CHAPTER ONE

Chatsworth, England 1805

M iss Diana Kendricks' heart was heavy as she hugged her friend and roommate, Miss Louisa Dunston. Like most of the girls who attended Mrs. Rutley's School for Young Women, Louisa was traveling home for the Christmas holiday. Every year was the same. Depending on their age, either the young ladies returned a month later, or they traveled to London to make their debut into society, never to return to the school again.

"Don't worry," Louisa said as numerous voices echoed in the corridor. "I'll see you again soon. Do make note of all the goings-on in my absence. I can't have me missing something important now, can I?"

Diana laughed. Although Louisa was dear to her heart, the girl had a tendency to put her nose where it did not belong. "I'll have a full report waiting for you." She gave her friend another hug. "Now, you'd best go before your parents decide to leave you here."

Once Louisa was gone, Diana went over to sit on the edge of her bed. Like every year since coming to Courtly Manor, she would remain at the school for the Christmas holiday. It had nothing to do with whether her parents could afford to pay the traveling expenses, for although he was not titled, her father was quite wealthy.

No, money had nothing to do with the decision to have Diana remain at school. Although her parents were married, they were apart. And being apart from one another meant they preferred that Diana was elsewhere.

The door opened, and Miss Jenny Clifton poked her head into the room, her long, chestnut braid falling over her shoulder. "May I come in?"

"Of course," Diana replied with a smile. "And why are you whispering?"

"I don't know," she said, joining Diana on the bed. "Out of habit, I suppose. Plus, there is always someone nearby trying to eavesdrop." She smoothed the skirts of her pink and white day dress. "We've an entire month ahead of us, free from any distractions. Do you have any plans?"

Diana shook her head. "I'll likely go into the village a few times, but most of my time will be spent here. Why? Have you something planned?"

"No," Jenny said with a sigh. "But I wouldn't mind going with you to the village for a bit of gazing."

"Gazing?"

Jenny grinned. "It's the proper term for when a woman admires a gentleman from afar. My sister says it's all the rage in London."

It took everything in Diana to keep herself from rolling her eyes. As much as she adored Jenny, the girl believed everything her sister told her, going so far as to say that if a young lady drops a handkerchief in front of a gentleman and he retrieves it for her, he was obligated to court her.

Unfortunately for Jenny, she had tried to do just that last summer, and the gentleman who had picked it up for her had merely grumbled something about clumsy women and went on his way. Despite the fact that Jenny had returned to the school with no prospects, she had insisted that she would try again at another time.

"I'll think about it," Diana said. "The idea of staring at gentlemen holds little appeal."

The truth was, Diana preferred never to meet any gentlemen. Nor marry one, for that matter. She had seen what disaster a marriage could create with her parents. The last thing she wanted was to fall into the same trap.

"It's not staring, it's *gazing*," Jenny corrected. "Besides, it will make for a great diversion. And it's much better than sitting here all day hunched over an embroidery hoop."

"Any proper young lady caught staring—or gazing—will find herself the object of every wagging tongue," said Mrs. Rutley from the doorway, making both girls start. With steel-gray mixed into her chestnut hair, Diana thought her headmistress still pretty. "Diana, your mother is waiting for you in the parlor."

"Thank you, Mrs. Rutley," Diana said, sighing. "Let's talk later, Jenny."

Jenny nodded her agreement and went to leave, but Mrs. Rutley stepped in her way. "I would like you to stay. I received a letter from a certain gentleman. Apparently, you dropped your handkerchief in front of him. Three times, to be exact, and he's concerned about you. Have you been following him around Chatsworth?"

Diana whispered a blessing of good luck to Jenny and made her way downstairs. All her friends had gone, besides Jenny. And Ruth, who was currently closeted in her bedroom. Who knew what that girl was up to?

When she reached the foyer, she said a silent prayer of thanksgiving as Miss Abigail Swanson and her parents exited through the front door.

"I must have some proper food as soon as possible," Abigail was saying with a toss of her red curls "The slop Mrs. Shepherd serves us is not even worthy of a trough. I wouldn't feed it to our dogs."

"We'll see that Mrs. Flack prepares whatever you'd like, my dear," her father said in fawning tones better suited to a toddler.

It was no wonder Abigail was the most obnoxious and spoiled girl who ever existed. Yet what bothered Diana more was that it was Mrs. Shepherd who held the door for them!

"I think your food is perfect," Diana said. "Abigail's opinion does not reflect what the rest of us think."

"Thank you," the cook said. A stout woman, Mrs. Shepherd kept her frizzy, honey-blonde curls under control using a stark white kerchief. "That poor girl's gonna wake up one day and realize how unhappy she really is. When that day comes, I'll bet a month's wages that a flood of tears will follow. Such a shame, it is."

Diana nodded. "At least the trio of terror is down to one."

Abigail's friends, or rather her followers Margaret Tranter and Lydia Gilstrap, left the previous week and would not be returning to the school, or so Diana had heard. Rumors abounded about the reasons why. One said their parents were facing bankruptcy. Yes, both families, which made little sense to her.

The other said they were being forced into marriage. That was much more likely, given the amount of wealth they always purported their families had.

Regardless, the school would be much more peaceful without them. And Abigail would have no lackeys to laugh at her uncouth barbs.

"Thank the good Lord for answering prayers," Mrs. Shepherd said and then winked. "We won't be telling Mrs. Rutley what I just said, now, will we?"

Assuring her she would not, Diana made her way to the parlor. Like the previous years, her mother had come bearing gifts, which sat on the low table between the armchairs and the sofa.

Her mother rose from her seat, the skirts of her traveling dress matching the emeralds in the necklace and rings she wore. "Diana," she cooed, "you're growing into such a beautiful woman."

Diana had inherited her mother's blonde curls and high cheekbones and could only hope to be as lovely as she when she was in her middle years.

"Thank you, Mother," Diana said.

"Well, it appears you've managed without a lady's maid," her mother said. "Did you ask Mrs. Rutley to find you one as I requested?" Bernadine, Diana's lady's maid, had left to get married in September.

"I'm only here for a few more months, Mother," Diana said. "I can manage until then."

Her mother sighed. "I suppose you can. I just want what's best for you. After all, we must do all we can if we're to be noticed by the right people. But I am pleased to see you."

Diana glanced at the door. "So, Father chose not to come again?"

Smiling, her mother took a step back. "You know how busy he is, business and all. I mentioned it in my last letter, did I not? He had to go away, something about a salt mine in Ireland. But come and see all the wonderful gifts he sent you."

Diana bit at her lip to keep her tongue from betraying her thoughts. Her mother knew quite well her father was not away on business, but she would never admit it. That thought only made her heart ache all the more.

Two packages sat on the table. Although they were called "gifts," Diana knew they were nothing more than offerings meant to appease her for his absence. To placate her.

"Are you not going to open them?" her mother asked. "Your father carefully selected them all."

"When will Father be returning home?" Diana asked, tearing away the brown paper from one of the packages. "And when will he come to see me?"

Her mother clasped her hands in her lap. "Diana, you know I've no answer to that. As I said, he's quite busy and cannot arrange his schedule around your wishes."

Diana held up the blue silk wrap embroidered with gold thread. It was beautiful, exquisite even, but knowing why it was gifted to her made her stomach ache.

The next gift was no less lovely. A deep-blue quilted spencer jacket with round buttons lined along the lapel. It would pair nicely with her blue traveling dress.

"Try it on," her mother said. "I'd like to see how it fits. Mrs. Yutes is still using your patterns from this summer, so it should fit well." Her mother insisted their seamstress produce new patterns every year for this exact reason—so her father could gift Diana clothing without her needing to travel home for fittings. "And now the wrap. Oh, yes, lovely! You'll catch every gentleman's eye wearing these."

"Thank you," Diana said, although she felt nothing. Did parents, men especially, not understand that gifts did not heal the hurts they caused? That a father's embrace was worth far more than a new trinket?

Or a mother's hug when their daughter needed love? For so many years, Diana thought her mother the most kindhearted person in the entire country. Whether it be a question of her future or how to treat others with kindness, Diana listened to every word she'd said.

But things had changed in recent years. Now, it was her mother, along with her father, who found herself too busy for her. And losing her mother as a friend and confidante hurt Diana more than she could ever explain. Therefore, she kept that heartbreak to herself.

"There is one more thing," her mother said, handing Diana a long, thin box.

Inside was a gold chain with a sapphire and diamond pendant.

"Here, let me help you." Her mother clasped the chain at the back of her neck. "Very nice. I'm certain you'll find a suitor very soon. You're a very lucky girl. Your father will allow you to choose whomever you want. Is that not wonderful?"

Diana was well aware there were two reasons her father had made that decision. The first was that her elder sister had already married and was now a countess. And as he had no interest in the life of his own wife, what did it matter whom his second daughter married? To him, women were nothing more than chattel. The more he fed them what they wanted, the easier they were to control. That was what hurt Diana the most.

Plus, who was she to receive such expensive gifts when so many others went without? Oh, she was thankful, but they did little to ease the pain she carried inside.

"I'm not certain I'll find a suitor, Mother. The idea of spinsterhood is becoming far too appealing."

Her mother laughed. "What brought this about? You used to go on and on about finding the perfect gentleman and marrying. You must be teasing me."

Diana removed the jacket. "Not at all," she replied. "Why would I wish to marry?"

"Why? So, you can have a happy life. To have children and host parties to show off the magnificent dresses your husband will buy for you. Surely, you still want those things?"

"You mean while my husband is away having an affair under the pretense of business?"

Her mother winced. Diana had not meant for her tone to be so sharp.

"I know about Rosie, Mother," she said, speaking of the lovely maid. "And Mrs. Olster. I know exactly what Father does, and I cannot stand how much it hurts you."

Her mother clicked her tongue in vexation and busied herself with folding the shawl. "I don't know where you've heard such terrible rumors, Diana. Or why you would bother listening to them. Now, enough of this silly talk. I've a bit of money your father gave me to give to you. Enjoy the time away from your studies. Buy yourself jewelry, a new dress, a new hat, whatever you wish. You're young and free. You should be enjoying these days."

Diana placed the bundle of notes on the table and shook her head. So many of her fellow students, like Emma, came from families that struggled. They would have fainted at the sight of so much money! "They are not rumors, Mother. I've seen things with my own eyes. Do you want me to describe them?"

Her mother turned her back on Diana.

"Why do you deny what he does?" Diana demanded. "Are you not shamed that he prefers to be with his mistress than to come to see his daughter? Or even his wife? You cannot honestly say you know nothing about his affairs."

Her mother rounded on her. "Very well, I'll tell you. You're no longer a child I must protect. Yes, your father has had many affairs, and I'm well aware of all of them."

"But does it not hurt you?"

With a snort of derision, her mother replied, "In the beginning, yes. But I've come to accept my lot. He provides us with a fine life, so I turn a blind eye to what he does. In return, I get everything I want." She extended her fingers to show the emeralds set in gold. "At least he has the decency to buy things for me. I didn't choose any of these rings. He gave every one of them to me."

Diana could not stop the single tear from sliding down her cheek. "But why would you wish such a life for me?"

"Because it's far better than being alone," her mother replied. "One day, you'll marry, and if your husband chooses to philander... well, you'll simply have to accept it. But what I won't have is you embarrassing me by becoming a spinster."

Diana's jaw dropped as her mother leaned in and kissed her cheek. Where was the happy woman who once doted over her?

"I'll return in March for your birthday, and we'll discuss then whether you wish to remain here or if you believe you're ready for your debut. At least we're allowing you to decide. Deborah didn't have that luxury."

That meant little to Diana. Her elder sister had never wanted anything else than to be married.

This was not the first time her mother had hinted at Diana remaining at Courtly Manor after her birthday. And Diana knew why. It was the same reason her mother, just like her father, was always in a hurry to leave when they came to visit. For so long, Diana bit her tongue and held back her words of contempt, but she had reached the end of her rope.

"I've asked myself why you never take me with you," Diana said as her mother walked to the door. "Why you prefer me to be here rather than at home. You've found someone else, haven't you? That is why you want me to remain here until summer. I cannot think of any other reason. Unless you simply don't want me around."

At first, Diana thought her mother would not respond. But finally, and without turning, her mother lifted her face and said, "This is the only time during the year that I may search out my own happiness. Do I not have as much right as your father to do so?" Without waiting for Diana to reply, her mother left the room.

Hurt welled up in Diana. So, what she had long suspected was true. Her mother was as disloyal as her father. How could they live such a life? What of the vows they spoke on their wedding day? Did they not understand how much even a moment of infidelity could hurt their children?

Picking up the notes, she counted them. A hundred pounds was far more than any young lady should receive as a gift. And knowing why it was given made it all the worse.

"Diana?"

She turned to find Jenny entering the room.

"Look at your new coat and shawl! They're so lovely!" Then her hazel eyes went wide. "Oh, my! I've never seen so much money! What will you do with it?"

Diana shrugged. "Spend it, I suppose. Although, I'm not sure on what." She smiled at her friend. "Would you like to help?"

CHAPTER TWO

"Dear Lord, give me patience," James, Marquess of Barrington, prayed under his breath. His mother, Ingrid, Lady Barrington, was on another of her monologues about whatever gossip she had failed to share with him thus far, during her short stay at his childhood home of Penford Place.

This was the very reason he had moved from Chatsworth to London several years earlier—to have some semblance of peace. His mother, unfortunately, was not one he could rely on for such pleasures. To her, everyone's business was the business of everyone, and she should be the conduit through which rumors of that business should travel. And for whatever reason, she believed all of them were best shared with her son.

With dark hair speckled with silver and kind blue eyes, James always welcomed her warm smile, for it was a beacon of hope to him. Unfortunately, she used that same smile when gossiping, leaving the listener unable to determine what she might say in any given situation. James stifled a sigh. Her driver waited in front of the house to carry her to her London home, where she preferred to spend her later years.

Country living had never appealed to her. There simply was not enough gossip. Therefore, she had followed him to London the moment her mourning period ended after the death of James's father.

Although James loved his mother, for both she and his late father had loved him unconditionally, her going had not pained him in the slightest. Not when her tongue wagged worse than that of a panting dog!

At least, she had plenty of friends to keep her entertained, leaving James to enjoy some semblance of quiet, even though they both lived in London.

"Then, I learned her son, Sir Timothy," his mother was saying as she smoothed her skirts with the same nervous habit she had always possessed. "You remember him, surely?"

Of course, James did not, but he nodded, nonetheless. If he said he had no recollection, she would then go into an hour-long soliloquy, describing every aspect of the local man's life. And that, before going into what she had learned from Sir Timothy's mother.

"I thought so," she said to his relief. "Well, not only was he caught in a particular situation with a young lady that is all to unbecoming to any gentleman, he also refused to take her as his bride! As a matter of fact, he is refusing to marry at all if you can believe it."

She gave one of her sniffs of disapproval. "He's nearly five and thirty years of age, James. No self-respecting man puts off marriage so long. I've no idea why he keeps delaying finding a wife."

James could conjure several reasons. Chatsworth offered few prospects, for one. Rarely did a gentleman find a worthy bride in such a small village. Not when London was only an hour away by carriage.

Plus, there was always work to keep a man far too busy for courting or other such nonsense. At the age of eight and twenty, between his businesses and the dilemma that had brought him to Penford Place, he had no time to pursue a young lady. He could not imagine it was all that different for Sir Timothy.

That did not mean James had no plans to marry, for he did. Now was just not the right time.

His mother offered him a kind smile. "It's no business of mine to ask why you returned to Chatsworth, James, but you know I'll do all I can if you so need the help."

For all the ways his mother drove him mad with her tales of the *ton,* she was a wonderful mother. Never had she interfered with his life nor forced her opinion on any matter. She trusted his judgment in every-thing, and he could not have appreciated her more for it. He knew she cared and only wanted what was best for him.

If only her opinion of others was as congenial.

"I appreciate you saying so, Mother," he said. "I'll be returning to London soon enough, once matters here are resolved." Then to make her smile, he added, "You'll have to tell me more about Sir Timothy the next time we're together."

He sighed. The fact she shared all her gossip with him was his own fault, specifically for the very reason that he always made similar requests. Yet he did not have the heart to ask her to stop. If she did not have her tittle-tattle, she would have nothing.

As expected, she beamed at his request. "I look forward to it," she said as she rose from her seat. "Oh, before I forget. I would like to make one request for the day you choose a wife."

James frowned. His mother had never interfered in such matters. Why did she wish to do so now? "Yes?"

"Do make sure she's not just any bride, James. If the Barrington line is to continue, I would suggest that you choose a young lady who comes from a family of handsome people." She grimaced. "I don't know what I would do if I was forced to endure an ugly grandchild like Lady Ann must." She spoke of Lady Ann Mosley, one of his mother's closest friends and fellow talebearer.

James doubted the child was anywhere near as ugly as his mother claimed. Granted, his eyes were spaced oddly, but his mother likened the poor babe to the offspring of gargoyles.

"Are you saying that if the woman I choose has an extra arm and eye, I must refuse?" he teased.

His mother chuckled. "You know very well what I mean."

"Indeed, I do, Mother, and I'll keep it in mind when I start playing the suitor."

"Good," his mother said before kissing his cheek.

He walked her to the door where Baldwin, his butler, waited with her wrap and hat. He was the thinnest man James had ever seen with a hawk-like nose and a long chin, giving him a profile that resembled the moon.

As she tied the ribbon of the hat beneath her chin, his mother gasped. "I nearly forgot! Lady Honora told me last week about a terrible rumor that is circulating about Miss Amelia."

James nearly swallowed his tongue. Miss Amelia Lansing was the daughter of Nelson and Joanna, Viscount and Viscountess of Stanton, and she and James had been friends since they were children. Her family lived in Larkston, a village ten miles from Chatsworth. Their fathers had shared in several enterprises over the years, which allowed James and Miss Amelia to spend hours together when they were younger. Yet as wonderful as their friendship was, and as much as their parents would have celebrated their union, neither had romantic notions toward the other.

"Oh?" James said, pushing a nonchalant tone into his voice that he did not feel. "Is her stay in Paris not going well?"

His mother waved a dismissive hand. "Oh yes, quite well. It's just that Lady Honora received a letter from her last week. It seems that" —she leaned in closer and lowered her voice as if someone nearby would overhear—"Miss Amelia is with child, and Lord Evans is the father!"

James sighed with relief. Known for his many affairs, Baron Evans had fathered several children and claimed none. But the idea he had anything to do with Miss Amelia was outrageous. "I find that highly unlikely."

Taking a step forward, his mother placed a hand on his arm. "My son, I've inquired of my closest friends, and from what I've learned, Miss Amelia has been, shall we say, promiscuous as of late? She's taken on more than one lover!" She gave a dramatic sigh. "How do I break such terrible news to her mother? I must say, I did not see this coming. And from Miss Amelia of all people!"

"I'm sure she's enjoying Paris and most certainly *not* with child," James said, although his heart pounded with worry. His mother might have bouts of misinformation about insignificant points, but rarely was she wrong about something as serious as this. "Do you truly believe the young lady you wished me to marry would put herself into that sort of situation? And with Evans of all people? Tell Lady Stanton that she has nothing to fear. Any rumors floating about are likely unsubstantiated. After all these years, surely Miss Amelia would not be so foolhardy."

"No, I suppose not," his mother said, pulling a glove onto her hand. "But why would anyone concoct such a terrible lie?"

"Because people enjoy a good story, even if it's at the expense of another. Or rather, *especially* when it is. I imagine Miss Amelia rejected the advances of some gentleman, and he chose to retaliate. That is the only thing that makes sense."

His mother nodded and patted James on the arm once more. "It's a shame the two of you never married. What beautiful grandchildren I would have now."

James kissed her cheek, choosing to ignore yet another roundabout way to bring up his bachelorhood. "I'll see you soon, Mother."

"I'm leaving," she said with a laugh. "There is no reason to rush me out the door. Oh, and Baldwin, please don't repeat what you just heard. The last thing this family needs is gossip being spread around about us."

The butler gave her a diffident bow. "Of course, my lady."

Once the carriage was trundling down the drive, James returned to the house and closed the front door. "That was close," he said, wiping sweat from his brow. "I feared she would never leave."

"Indeed, it was close, my lord," Baldwin said. "Shall I pour you a drink for your nerves?"

"It would take the entire bottle to calm me," James said with a chuckle as he pulled on the black gloves he always wore whenever he left the house. "No, I believe I will go to the bookstore in Chatsworth." He leaned in closer to the butler and added in a whisper, "Unless you know a way to make problems disappear."

"If I knew, my lord, I would surely say. You're under a great deal of pressure for a man of your age. You deserve to purchase a new book. Doing so always gives you a reprieve from whatever is bothering you."

James sighed. "I've no one else to blame. I brought this stress upon myself with the choices I've made." He clapped the butler on the shoulder. "Thank you, Baldwin. For all you've done for me."

"It's been a pleasure and an honor," Baldwin replied, beaming. "I'll see your carriage brought around, my lord."

As James watched the butler walk away, he considered that truer words could not have been said. Baldwin had done so much for him over the years and had become James's closest confidant. If it were not for him, James was unsure how he would be able to handle his current troubles.

Donning his overcoat, James headed out to the garden. A snip of cold filled the air but not overly so. The limbs of the trees were barren, and the flowerbeds were devoid of any color. December could be so dreary without snow to cover the ground.

Making his way past the short, wooden gate, he walked through the open field behind the house. His destination was the guest cottage on the other side. Inside was a problem not even his magic could make right.

When James was a child, he had always been obsessed with the art of illusion. After successfully making a coin disappear at a party, several of his father's friends had bestowed upon him the moniker of Marquess of Magic.

Yet, just like all rumors, although his acquisition of the name was rooted in innocence, the story of how he had acquired the name changed over time. One rumor said that he dabbled in witchcraft learned from a coven. Another said he had made a pact with the devil.

Although his magic was nothing more than sleight of hand and illusion, there were times when he wished he truly could work magic. Perhaps he could use it to change the past. Then he could take back a particular choice he had made. A choice with horrible consequences.

Smoke rose from the chimney as he approached the cottage. A small single-story stone building, it was just large enough to provide privacy for one or two people. And privacy was certainly called for now.

A face appeared in the window and then disappeared. A moment later, the door opened, and that same smiling face greeted him.

The woman before him was pretty with her brown hair hanging in waves down her back. Her doll-like face would have made any man look at her twice. She was his friend. And more so the secret he had been hiding.

"James?" Amelia said, using his Christian name as they did when they were alone. "Is anything wrong?"

James smiled. "No. She's gone. Are you well?"

"Oh, yes." She grimaced and her hand went immediately to her swollen belly. "He kicks often, as of late. And keeps me up at all hours, though I don't mind." She said the last with a sad smile.

There was no reason to speak of the rumor his mother had just conveyed, for James knew it was untrue. Or at least a part of it was— Lord Evans was not the father of Amelia's child.

His eyes lingered on her stomach far longer than appropriate for any gentleman, but he could not help himself. A shiver coursed through his body. Amelia had changed much. Gone were the fine clothes, replaced by simple dresses. A woman had been paid handsomely to travel to Paris under Amelia's name. She was tasked to send pre-written letters to various people in England every few weeks, especially Amelia's parents.

Lies and deceit had been plentiful but sadly necessary. For any unwed lady carrying a child would be cast aside easier than a man with the plague. And being the daughter of a viscount would only make the scandal worse.

"Please, come in," Amelia said. "I've just started the fire."

James glanced around, frowning. "And where is Prudence?" he asked, referring to her lady's maid. "Surely, she should be the one building the fire. After all, you assured me you needed no help because she was here to see to your needs."

"I sent her to bed. She was up until late for me again and was exhausted." She offered James a smile. "I'm not so helpless I can't manage without her for a few hours."

Although Amelia was nearly five and twenty—and carrying a child while having no husband—she did not allow her circumstances to weigh her down. James could not help but admire her tenacity.

"I'm going into Chatsworth," he said. "Is there anything I can get you while I'm there? I plan to stop by the bookshop. Is there any particular book you would like me to purchase for you? Or perhaps something from the bakery?"

"Oh, I need nothing," Amelia said. "You've provided me with everything I need and more." She smiled at him. "I'm in your debt."

James snorted. "That's untrue. I'm only doing what is right. After all, I'm responsible for the child."

The babe was not his, of course, but he had introduced Amelia and the man who had fathered the child. Although most men would deny the fact if they had been in the same position, he felt the part he played made the situation his responsibility. After all, she had trusted him, and he had failed her.

When Amelia went to argue, he put up a hand to forestall her. "No more arguing. Now, I've made inquiries. We should have a solution before the child is born."

Amelia had made the decision to give the baby away, hoping to find a couple unable to have children of their own. The choice had been a painful one, but she had thought it best for everyone involved. Because she was adamant, James had sent word to a woman who promised to find a family for the child.

"James, what you're doing for me, no man would do, titled or not. And I thank you." She wiped at her eyes.

James noticed the larger Amelia's stomach grew, so did her bouts of tears. Once, James had thought she was in pain and had offered her a glass of brandy. She had refused with a laugh. And rightly so. He had no idea women in her condition could be so weepy.

"I'm only doing what is right," he said. "As always, if you need anything, anything at all, inform Baldwin."

"I shall," she said. Then she lifted herself up onto the tips of her toes and kissed his cheek. "Thank you, again."

With a nod, James headed outside and made his way to the front of the house. Once the carriage was trundling down the drive, he leaned back and closed his eyes.

The child was not due for another two months, but he still hated to leave her alone. He had seen she had the most comfortable environment he could give her. Once the child was born, it would be placed in the home of a loving family.

They had to continue to take care, of course, for he could not allow his name—or that of Amelia—to be ruined forever.

CHAPTER THREE

"Gifts are nothing more than a form of bribery," Diana said as she and Jenny descended the stairs. "A way to appease someone after he or she has wronged another."

Jenny snorted. "How so? I would love to receive more gifts."

Diana pulled on her coat. "Oh? And what about these? 'If you're good, you'll get a toy.' Or 'I'm sorry I was unable to see you. Here, have this lovely pin.' And my favorite. 'Thank you for allowing me to call. I've brought you a lovely bouquet of flowers.' It's all a ruse to make the receiver do what the giver wants."

Mrs. Rutley emerged from her office. "Your father wrote," she said, handing Diana a letter. "I received one, as well. I believe I already know what yours says."

"But Mother only left an hour ago. Why did he not send it with her?" Then she dropped her gaze. She knew why. Her parents had lied and were now living apart. They saw no reason to inform one another about their plans, even when she was involved.

With a sigh, she slid a finger beneath the seal and unfolded the letter. She skimmed the first few sentences. A friend of her father would be calling on her. Make a good impression. The usual short and direct words he spoke aloud conveyed in writing. All business and no heart.

With a shake of her head, Diana slid the letter into the pocket of her overcoat. Her father had no interest in her life, and now he was sending a gentleman to call on her? The idea was revolting.

No, that was unfair. Perhaps this was just what she and her father needed to repair their broken relationship. It was worth a try, anyway.

"Are you all right?" Mrs. Rutley asked.

"Yes," she lied. The truth was she was far from all right. But how did one reveal that she despised her father? "We should be going. We'll be back long before dark."

With her arm snaked through that of Jenny, they walked away from Courtly Manor. Diana's heart was heavy. Yet another Christmas spent without her family. Why was her father so aloof? Why should she trust him with his selection of gentleman callers? Did all men have affairs and then send their daughters gifts to alleviate their guilt?

No, of course not. The Duke of Elmhurst, Julia's fiancé, was not like that. Nor was Baron St. John, the man Emma was going to marry. Perhaps they had found the only two men who were true gentlemen.

Or had her father been an honorable man like the duke and the baron when he and her mother married, only to become unfaithful later? If so, the chances of Emma and Julia becoming like her mother were great. But Diana hoped it was not the case.

From her first day at Mrs. Rutley's School for Young Women, Diana had known that men could not be trusted. The other girls spoke often of one day marrying and the wonderful lives they would lead. Diana had joined them, for she did not have the heart to dampen their dreams. Deep inside, however, she knew all roads after marriage led to heartache.

Jenny wore her usual smile, one that said that everything in the world was right. How could she carry on like that? How Diana wished she could be as optimistic about life as she once had! After watching her parents grow further apart with each passing year, she came to the conclusion that marriage was not the fairy tale she had once believed. No, it was a prison one was forced to endure. For her, it would be a life sentence when she had committed no crime.

"Are you sad you're not returning home for Christmas?" Diana asked.

A horse and rider passed them, the horse's hooves kicking up flecks of mud. The snow from a recent storm had melted for the most part, but some remained where the sun could not hit it—such as beneath a cluster of trees or in the shade of a large bush.

"A little, I suppose," Jenny replied. "My parents say they're extremely busy, but I know they would rather not have me around. It's why I was sent away to school instead of being instructed by a private tutor."

Diana nodded, for what Jenny said was likely true. Many fathers could afford private instruction from the comfort of their homes, but few wanted the responsibility of having a daughter.

Boys were another matter altogether. Having a tutor far outweighed sending a son away, for they could put to practice what they learned on matters of the estate. And when they were old enough, they would then go to university. What could girls offer? A newly embroidered handkerchief?

"Well," Diana said, tightening the grip on her friend's arm, "I'm glad you're here. And today, we'll have fun! In fact, over the next month, we'll have so much fun, even our parents will be jealous!"

Jenny laughed. "I like that idea."

Chatsworth was a small, quaint village that touted several shops on its main street. Granted, it was not London, but it was large enough for the girls to enjoy themselves.

"Shall we begin by doing a bit of gazing?" Jenny asked, looking around them.

"Gazing?" Diana asked.

Jenny nodded. "It's when you spend time watching what people do. But especially men, so as to catch their eye. I know! Across from the millinery is a pub. We can watch the men coming and going. I'm sure we can attract the attention of more than a few of them."

Diana shook her head. What had come over her friend? Over the last month, Jenny did all she could to be near any gentleman she could find. Even if Diana agreed to this outrageous notion, catching the eye of men stumbling out of a pub would not have been her first choice.

"How about we go into the shops and spend some money first," Diana said. Upon seeing Jenny's frown, she added, "And if by chance you see a gentleman, you may look. But don't stare. Mrs. Rutley already warned you that staring is very unladylike, did she not?"

Jenny gave a sad nod. "I know she's correct, but what's a young lady to do with all these handsome gentlemen about?"

Diana glanced around them and laughed. Handsome men? What handsome men? A man with a silver mustache that matched his hair rubbed a hand on his rather large stomach. Another stumbled across the street, nearly colliding with a carriage parked alongside the foot-path. Yet another man yawned, showing no more than four teeth.

"Nonetheless, we'll behave as Mrs. Rutley expects us to behave," Diana said, holding Jenny tighter. "Come, let's go before *we* become the objects of gazing."

Unfortunately, the cobbler had nothing that caught their eye, nor did the jeweler or the millinery. But the dressmaker's shop was abuzz with life. Women flipped through the many books of plates, others commenting on the variety of new ribbons, and clerks—all women—retrieved various fabrics and documented orders for their customers.

Jenny gasped and pointed at a particular plate. "This dress would look so lovely on you. I say you should put in an order. You'll be the envy of everyone in the village."

"Indeed, it is beautiful," Diana said with a sigh. "But I don't want it. If you'd like to have one made, however, I'd be happy to pay for it."

Jenny closed the book and turned to Diana. "What's wrong? You've found nothing thus far, and that's not like you. I thought you wanted to spend all your money."

Glancing around them, Diana motioned for Jenny to follow her outside where fewer ears could listen in on their conversation. "Do you remember our vow beneath the tree and how we all shared a secret?"

Jenny nodded. "How can I forget?"

"Well, although I've suspected my father has been having affairs, Mother confirmed it today. Being uncertain had allowed me to hold to the possibility it was untrue, but now I've been reassured that all men are bad."

"Surely, you don't believe that, do you?" Jenny asked. "What about

Emma? Or Julia? Even Mrs. Rutley has mentioned the joy of falling in love."

"Well, Julia and Emma aren't yet married, are they? So, we don't know for certain their marriages will end happily. And Mrs. Rutley, for all her wisdom, never remarried, did she? Have you not wondered why?"

"But I overheard you speaking to Mrs. Shepherd about a certain marquess. Perhaps he's different."

Diana snorted. "I admit I had hoped to gain his attention, but I've given up on that notion. In fact, I'd prefer to die than to ever see him again!"

The gentleman, rumored to dabble in magic, was handsome. When she had seen him at the bookshop on one of her many visits to the village, she felt as if she were walking on the clouds. This man would be different, she had been sure of it.

But she had ruined any chances of catching his eye.

Jenny frowned. "What happened? It must have been terrible. Your cheeks are redder than the beets Mrs. Shepherd served at dinner last evening."

Diana bit at her bottom lip. "Swear you'll never tell a soul. I'd rather run away and live in a cave than to have anyone else know!"

"May I burn in the pit of Hades if I tell anyone," Jenny said fervently.

Diana gasped. "Jenny! Where did you hear such a saying?"

Jenny shrugged. "Ruth."

"Of course," Diana said. Ruth was lovely, to be sure, but she was prone to mischief. She also gambled, and her choice of words were those a lady should never even consider entertaining.

"Well, you should not repeat everything you hear," Diana said as they drew near Mistral's Booksellers. "Now, follow me. I'll tell you exactly what happened." When Jenny gave her a huge grin, Diana added, "Remember, you're not to repeat any of this to anyone!"

"I already promised I would not," Jenny said.

As they entered the bookshop, Diana surveyed their surroundings. Tall bookcases filled with books ran along each wall. In the middle of the shop were cases the height of a man, and they ran toward the back of the shop.

"Good afternoon, ladies," Mr. Mistral said, smiling at them as he sorted through a stack of books. He wore the same brown cap he always did to cover his balding pate. "If you're wanting the latest fashion magazines, I've just received a new shipment."

"Thank you," Diana said, "but we'll be looking around for now." She grasped Jenny by the arm and pulled her down the middle aisle. "He's a very nice man, but he'll ramble on and on if you let him."

She led Jenny to the last row of bookcases, peeked around the last case, and sighed in relief upon seeing no one. "Have you heard of the Marquess of Magic?"

"Who hasn't!" Jenny whispered, tugging at the long braid that hung over her shoulder. "I even know how he earned the name."

Diana was impressed. "Do you? I've often wondered but have been too afraid to ask. So? Tell me!"

"Up until two years ago, he lived here in Chatsworth. I heard he kissed a woman but had no true interest in courting her. Unfortunately for him—and for her, I suppose—she fell in love with him. To this day, she refuses every suitor who calls because she only wants him."

Diana frowned. "And? What does that have to do with magic?"

Jenny clicked her tongue. "Don't you see? She fell under his magic spell! I've heard that about a dozen more, and all of them chose to become spinsters rather than marry anyone other than the marquess."

"I heard a very different story," Diana said. "I heard that he's using magic to make himself appear far younger than he truly is. He's nearly fifty but looks more like he's thirty!" She shook her head. "That, of course, is mere speculation and likely gossip based on no facts. Mrs. Shepherd, however, told me about him, so I simply had to come here to find him. That is how Emma and I ended up here searching for him."

"And?" Jenny asked, clearly enthralled with Diana's story. "Did you find him?"

"I did," Diana replied, grinning widely. "And before you ask, he is devilishly handsome." She sighed heavily. "But what does it matter now? I made a complete and utter fool of myself."

"How so? Did you stumble over your words?" She gasped. "Surely, you didn't bat your eyelashes too much at him!"

"No, of course not," Diana replied. "But it was far worse than that. When he caught me staring at him, I grabbed the nearest book off the shelf without looking at its title." She looked through the various tomes until she encountered that very book. "Yes, this is the one."

Jenny read the title, and her eyes widened. "*Mating Rituals of Ancient Men?* Oh, Diana, of all the books you could have grabbed!"

Diana gave a sad nod. "The marquess ridiculed me, and for good reason! I've never been so embarrassed in all my life." She pressed the book to her chest and thought about the marquess. "To say he's handsome does not truly capture him. There is a... a mystery about him that piques my curiosity. If he whispered in my ear that I had made a fool of myself, I would not care. Though, having him so close to me would have had me reeling!" She sighed again. "But what does it matter? I scared him away that day."

She nearly snorted. What did it matter, indeed? Why would she, a woman hoping to live her life in spinsterhood, want any man giving her his attention? What a waste of time for both of them!

"Well, if it isn't Miss Kendricks."

Diana turned, let out a stifled cry, and dropped the book. The Marquess of Magic—the very man of whom she had been speaking—stood smiling down at her. Was it possible he was more handsome now than he had been the last time she saw him? His short, blond hair had a wave to it that enhanced his sharp jawline. He wore all black, from head to foot, as well as his hands. She struggled to breathe as she looked into his eyes, which were the color of chestnuts. His nose was straight and regal.

Swallowing hard, Diana considered the warning about which Jenny's sister wrote. Something about men having the ability to command with their eyes. At first, she thought the words foolish, but now...

"Indeed," Jenny said, breaking the tension between them. "Her name is Miss Kendricks."

The marquess smiled, and Diana's legs nearly gave way. "What brings you into this fine establishment, Miss Kendricks?" he asked, a twinkle in his eye. "Are you here to purchase the same book you were looking at the last time we encountered one another? Or are you buying it for another friend?"

With well over thirty pounds in her reticule, Diana imagined hiring a carriage, heading north to Scotland, and never returning. Her friends and Mrs. Rutley would stand around the tree, wondering how Diana could put herself in the same predicament twice. For generations, the tale of her foolishness would be told to every young girl as a warning to keep a good eye on what she was doing.

Her cheeks burned with embarrassment as the marquess picked up the book from the floor. "Such an interesting title, don't you think? Do you mind if I look through it?"

Unable to bring forth a single word, Diana shook her head and then nodded. What had he asked?

"I must say, Miss Kendricks, I've heard women are advancing in many areas, but I would not have believed this would have been one of them if I had not seen it for myself."

Jenny took a step forward. "Women are making all sorts of advances in society, my lord."

"Indeed," the marquess said. "I just never imagined any lady would be interested in this particular subject." He closed the book and had the audacity to wink at Diana and whisper, "Would you like me to purchase this for you?"

"No!" Diana blurted before getting herself back under control. "That is, thank you, my lord, but I don't want that book."

"Really? Then why have I found you with it not once, but twice?" He placed the book in her hands. "I'll admit that I was disappointed the first time, but twice is devastating." Diana's breath caught in her throat as he leaned in close and again whispered in her ear, "I would recommend making such purchases in secret, Miss Kendricks. If not, you'll have few prospects. This type of reading may send away any potential suitors. But fear not, I have no plans to go anywhere."

Diana prayed Jenny would find a bucket of water to pour over her before she leapt into this man's arms.

Rather than doing so, however, she reached all the way down into her toes to summon what little amount of courage she could muster. Which disappeared like a droplet of water on a hot skillet when his cheek brushed hers. How dare he be so intimate in such a public setting! And his smell! If she could bottle his scent, she would fill the air with it.

"I pray you do not," she managed to say, her lips trembling, "for I would never forgive you."

She clamped shut her mouth. What had made her say that? What did he think of her?

Glancing at the book, she realized he could not think worse of her by this point.

"And as to this," she said, lifting the book, "I can assure you, it's not for me."

The marquess had an amused look on his features. "Are you meaning to blame this on your friend? Again?" He turned to Jenny. "Is this true? Are you the one wanting the book?"

"No," Jenny squeaked.

Diana let out a frustrated sigh. How could a woman go from wanting to touch a man's face in one instant and wishing to strangle him in the next?

"My lord, if you'll allow me to—" When he raised his hand, she shut her mouth.

"Please, Miss Kendricks, let us depart without any more excuses."

The embarrassment that had consumed her now turned to anger. Marquess or Master or whatever of Magic, no one embarrassed her thrice!

"I'm not making excuses, my lord. I wish only to state the facts."

"And that, too, is an excuse," he said, cutting off her words. "If I may make a suggestion, Miss Kendricks? Either purchase this book or leave it be. Why torment yourself?" With a chuckle, he placed the book on the shelf. "Good day to you both," he said, dipping his head and strolling away.

Diana turned to Jenny. "What have I done? I may have to run away so I never encounter him again!"

"Don't act too hastily," Jenny whispered. "I say you should remain here."

"Why?" Diana demanded. "I've every reason to leave. Twice I've met him, and both times have ended in failure!"

Jenny gave her a wide grin. "There must be a reason the marquess was here, too. And if we remain, we just may learn why!"

CHAPTER FOUR

Encountering Miss Diana Kendricks for a second time sent a mischievous streak through James, and he could not understand why. For some unknown reason, he could not resist relaxing propriety and teasing the young lady. Let the tongues wag. He was enjoying himself.

Teasing was one thing, however. What on earth made him give her the impression that he would be remaining in Chatsworth? All he wanted to do was return to London and his life away from this village.

He paused. What had made her say that his leaving would be unforgivable? They were not acquainted, or barely acquainted. It was not as if they had designs on each other! What had them speaking as if they were kindred spirits? Or lovers? The idea was ludicrous at best!

Yet, the way she had thrust out her chin and defended herself did nothing to stop him from continuing with the banter. If anything, her reaction, paired with her deep blush, had goaded him as easily as his friends had in his youth. Her blue eyes were full of innocence, igniting a primal need in him. Whispering in her ear had him inhaling her sweet feminine fragrance. Jasmine had always appealed to him.

Miss Kendricks was a perfectly crafted masterpiece; one a man could admire all day long. He would not have minded running his fingers through her thick blonde curls or kissing her plump and pouty lips. Just thinking of them stoked the fire within him. He had been tempted to kiss her right there in the middle of the bookshop. So much so that he had to take a step away from her, lest he gave into temptation.

In the next aisle, James stared at the various titles without seeing them. His thoughts were elsewhere. More precisely, they were on Miss Kendricks. Her face was perfection. High cheekbones, a perfectly sculptured nose, and a heart-shaped face were forever burned into his mind.

A man in a pub once referred to a woman as a ravishing beauty, and James had disregarded the comment as the words of a drunkard. Now, he reassessed that description, for Miss Kendricks satisfied that definition perfectly. And it had nothing to do with the fine clothes she wore. Something deep inside her radiated from every pore.

This was a woman with whom James could share in conversation over a glass of wine. He had no doubt she was well-read and would hold her own. Yet, would he be interested in the same subjects as she? After all, the book she had been holding on both occasions of their meeting was suspect at best.

Was she ashamed to purchase such a title and therefore went to the bookshop to read a chapter a day? That was a logical conclusion for being found in public holding a scandalous book. Society could be fierce when it came to women's choices in reading. That did not mean he was not curious as to why she would choose a book in that particular subject.

A burst of cold air made James turn to see the two young ladies exit the store.

Perhaps we'll meet another time, he thought, a smile playing on his lips.

With a shake of his head, he returned to the previous aisle. His reason for coming into the shop was to choose a new book for Amelia. She had read through nearly every book he had in his personal library over the last few months, and he wanted to purchase something to make her happy.

After all, was there any greater expression of friendship than the presentation of a gift?

He took a book off the shelf and flipped through the pages. Inside were numerous plates on the latest fashions for women, some even in color, and James knew Amelia would enjoy it. He then moved on to where books on magic were displayed, but he found nothing of interest that he did not already own.

At the counter, Mr. Mistral pushed his round spectacles back up his long, straight nose and said, "Good afternoon, my lord. Have you made a selection?"

"I have, indeed," James said, placing the tome on the counter. "I believe it will be quite enjoyable."

His heart nearly burst from his chest when a gloved hand reached out and took the book in hand. "*Women's Fashions in Paris Since the Dawn of the New Century*," Miss Kendricks read, her voice filled with amusement. "I agree with your assessment, my lord. This book will bring you *many* hours of pleasure." The corners of her lips twitched. Oh, but this young lady was a pixie!

"This is a gift for—" He clamped shut his mouth. He nearly had blurted out Amelia's name!

"Please, my lord, let us depart without any more excuses."

James had to force himself not to gape. She had used his own words against him! Not to mention that his pride was bruised. Most people treated him with reverence. None would have spoken to him in such a way.

That did not mean he did not enjoy it, not when it came from such a lovely creature.

When the proprietor chuckled, James turned and glared at him. The man cleared his throat and turned away, but James did not miss him hiding a smile.

When he turned back to Miss Kendricks, she was gone.

"There is no reason to wrap it," James said as Mr. Mistral reached beneath the counter. "I'm in a hurry."

With the book pressed against his side, James hurried out of the shop and looked left and right in search of Miss Kendricks. She had bested him at a duel in banter, and he could not have that! Not with her. Scanning the pedestrians, he finally found Miss Kendricks and her companion, laughing together beside a man selling roasted chestnuts.

When he approached, both women stopped their laughter and stared at him.

"Miss Kendricks, if I may have a moment, please."

Miss Kendricks grasped her companion by the arm, flashed him a wicked smile, and hurried away.

James was stunned. What woman ran from a marquess? How dare she! Surely, society was on the brink of disaster when a woman was so inconsiderate toward a man of his station.

The man selling the roasted chestnuts chuckled. "Ye scared 'er away," he said, his red hair matching his cheeks. "It musta been some argument. Women are difficult at the best of times, I'll tell ye. If ye come 'ome drunk, they'll never forgive ye. They'll even bring it up to ye, years later, no matter 'ow much ye tell 'em yer sorry. Me wife's used it against me for fifteen years! Not that ye've been drunk, sir. I don't mean nothin' 'bout it. Just tellin' ye the way of things."

With an annoyed glance at the chestnut vendor, James went after the two young ladies. They entered a shop, and he hurried his step, pushed open the door, followed them inside, and stopped. Two dozen eyes stared at him in horror. One woman pulled her young daughter close to her. Then it dawned on him where he was.

He had been so intent on confronting Miss Kendricks, that he entered the shop without looking at the signage. It was not just any shop. Mrs. Newberry's dress shop was a female sanctuary, one that no man, let alone a marquess, entered without a woman dragging him inside, and rarely then.

If Mrs. Newberry only supplied dresses, that would have been one thing. Yet she also offered other items of a more intimate nature. Or so James's mother had told him when she asked him to wait outside when he was younger. And judging by the looks he was receiving now, the women there would defend their sacred ground at any cost.

He looked at Miss Kendricks for help, but she merely batted her eyelashes and smirked.

"Well played, Miss Kendricks," he whispered when she approached him. "Well played, indeed."

Miss Kendricks grinned. "Admit that you've been bested by a woman, and I'll be happy to aid in your escape."

James chuckled. "Bested by you? I'm afraid that will never happen."

"Then there is nothing I can do. I'm sorry for your fate."

Fate? What did she mean by fate? Before he could ask her, a woman of perhaps thirty, with wheat-colored hair pulled back into a severe bun at the nape of her neck, walked up to them. "Good afternoon, my lord," she said with a distinct French accent. "I am Mrs. Newberry. We've missed seeing your mother since she moved away. Do send her my sincerest greetings."

"I'll do that," James said. From the corner of his eye, he could see Miss Kendricks grinning.

"Is there anything with which I can assist you?" Mrs. Newberry asked. "Are you here to collect something for Her Ladyship? I don't recall having received any orders, but perhaps one of the assistants failed to inform me."

With his eyes locked on Miss Kendricks's blue ones, James replied, "Thank you but no. I was in search of a friend who said she would be here. Maybe I missed her." He smiled at Miss Kendricks. He *would* win this battle!

To his shock, however, Miss Kendricks winked at him and then turned to Mrs. Newberry. "I'm afraid that Lord Barrington is quite shy and is only making excuses. I'm the friend for whom he was searching, and I know exactly what he wants." Before James could respond in any way, she reached for the book he was carrying. "Will you show him the latest fashions from Paris? He's taken quite an interest in that subject as of late."

Mrs. Newberry's brows jumped. "Your study of fashion is most welcome here, my lord. Come. Allow me to show you what we have to offer. We may not be as à la mode as London, but we do try to keep with recent trends."

James closed his eyes. He had been bested again!

"You may look through the books without fear, my lord," Miss Kendricks said. "Is that not correct, Mrs. Newberry?" She leaned in closer to the dressmaker. "Perhaps the latest in petticoats would interest him." She laughed and exited the shop.

"I really must be going," James said to Mrs. Newberry before pushing past the gaping women. Once outside, he glanced around in search of Miss Kendricks, but she and her companion were nowhere to be seen.

Even if he did find them, he was reluctant to follow them. Who knew where they would lead him next!

Despite his recent embarrassment, James found he hoped to see Miss Kendricks again. If nothing else, he wanted to gaze into her blue eyes, for the feeling it brought him took away the worries he had in life.

And it would allow him the chance to balance the scales in this strange battle they had begun.

CHAPTER FIVE

Taking a deep breath of cool afternoon air, James thought
about his encounter with Miss Kendricks earlier that day. She
seemed to have taken residence in his head, and he did not
object to her being there. He enjoyed her lovely teasing, to be sure, but
it was her smile, her beauty, and her laugh, which was as sweet as her
voice, that had him mesmerized.

"What are you thinking about?" Amelia asked as she walked
beside him.

James chuckled. "Nothing of consequence," he replied.

They had taken the stroll for her health and for the sake of fresh
air. With no guests arriving at Penford Place for the foreseeable future,
James was able to take strolls with Amelia without concern for anyone
catching them unawares.

"How is the child faring?"

"He has kicked me only twice thus far today," Amelia replied with a
laugh. "I must be doing something right."

He led her to a bench to retrieve the present he had left there.
"Today is special," he said, "because it's your birthday. This is for you.
My apologies for not having it wrapped."

Amelia's eyes went wide as she took the book in her hands. "Oh,

James, this is a marvelous gift! But after all you've done for me, I cannot accept it."

He smiled down at her. "Don't say that. If anyone in this world deserves a gift, it's you."

With a nod, she opened the book and flipped through the pages, her smile expressing what she truly thought of the present. "I'll cherish it always," she said. "Thank you." She kissed his cheek. "Again, I'm fortunate to know you."

"It's I who am fortunate," he said, offering her his arm once more. "But enough of such talk. We would not want me stumbling over my pride."

Amelia laughed, and they continued their walk.

Once again, Miss Kendricks appeared in his mind. Perhaps if he returned to the bookshop next Saturday, they would cross paths again. He stifled a chuckle. Would she be reading the next chapter of her book?

"I tire earlier every day," Amelia said as they approached the front of the guest cottage. She opened the door. "Will you come inside and stay for a few minutes?"

Amelia led him toward the kitchen, but before he entered, Prudence, her lady's maid, walked up to them. Nearing her thirtieth year, the maid was a tiny woman with dark-brown hair and eyes. And like Amelia, she always wore a smile.

"Good afternoon, my lord," the maid said, bobbing a curtsy. Then she turned to Amelia. "I'm off to the village, miss. May I bring you anything?"

"I don't believe so," Amelia replied. "Enjoy your time alone."

Assuring her mistress that she would, Prudence curtsied again and left.

"You're fortunate to have such a trustworthy lady's maid," James said, pulling out a chair for Amelia.

"And like you, she has been a wonderful source of support as a friend." She walked over to the cookstove and placed a kettle atop it.

James shook his head. "Don't make me—"

Amelia clicked her tongue at him. "I'll make us some tea, and I'll not hear a word of argument about it. I've learned to do much for myself these last few months, just you wait and see."

Knowing it would be useless to argue, James watched as the woman stoked the fire in the cookstove.

Amelia and her parents had moved away when he was nine, yet they continued to call whenever they returned to Chatsworth until he moved to London.

Over the years, he and Amelia had stayed in touch, either meeting in London whenever she was visiting there or corresponding in writing. They could talk about anything from trivial matters, such as Amelia finding her favorite flower the columbine in a field, to issues of great importance.

He recalled one particular incident over which they still laughed. Not long after Amelia had moved away, James had developed a fascination for one of the maids at Penford Place. Given his young age at the time, he wrote to Amelia to tell her about his plans to marry the woman.

Amelia had replied that Peggy was far too old.

She's nearly thirty, James! she had written. *And she's not nobly born. Your parents will never allow it.*

Then she went on to tell him in no uncertain terms that he was to stop his nonsense.

You'll find the right woman. Just be patient.

Although James did not love Amelia, not in the romantic sense, he cared for her like a sister. And he always would.

He shook his head, bringing his thoughts back to the present as Miss Amelia poured him a cup of tea. Glancing at her protruding stomach, he stifled a grimace. A perfect friendship ruined by a single mistake that he had inadvertently caused.

"Here we are," Amelia said as she lowered herself into the chair he had pulled out for her. "You went quiet again. I'll ask only once more, what is on your mind?"

"A young boy who was prepared to ask a maid to court," he said, making Amelia laugh. He could always make her laugh, and he enjoyed doing so. "Oh, how naive I was. I was so certain that the son of a marquess could court whomever he chose."

Amelia laughed, adding a drop of milk to her tea. "You were very naive and still are," she said. "Oh, don't give me that look, James. You were so young then. I'm just thankful our parents remained such good friends. Much like us." She dropped her gaze, and James was sure she was hiding her shame. "It doesn't matter."

"Everything will work out for the best," James said. "You've made it this far and will not fail. Not like I did today."

"What's this?" Amelia said, her teacup halfway to her lips. "Has the marquess lost at cards again?"

James snorted. "That I could endure. No, this was a young lady, Miss Diana Kendricks. I attempted to best her in a battle of wits for the second time, but I was not as successful this time around."

He went on to explain what had happened. When he finished, he had hoped for sympathy from his friend. Instead, he was met with giggles.

"Oh, James, I must say," Amelia said, her face reddening as her laughter grew. "That must be the funniest thing I've ever heard! But I realize now, I gave you the wrong advice."

His eyebrows rose. "What advice is that?"

"About the maid all those years ago," she replied, grinning. "You should have courted and married her. That would have saved you the mortification you must be feeling now. I'd say the probability of you leaving bachelorhood has declined by at least forty percent!"

James could not help but join in her laughter. Amelia could match wits with the best of them!

"I appreciate the tea, but I must go." James rose and kissed her cheek. "I'll see you again soon, I'm sure."

Bidding her farewell, he returned to the house through the back door. On his way to the study, he heard a familiar and unwelcome voice coming from the portico at the front of the house.

"My dear man, I'm hurt. Why are you not allowing me entry into my friend's home?"

"His Lordship has asked—" the butler began to say, his voice filled with outrage.

"It's all right, Baldwin," James said. "I'll see him. And please find

Mrs. Bunting and tell her to serve dinner an hour earlier than usual. I've much work to finish this evening."

The butler bowed. "Yes, my lord." And he hurried away.

"Hello, Stonebrook," James said, putting out his hand to the red-haired and freckled man. A few inches shorter than James and the son of a baron, Mr. Peter Stonebrook, heir to the Forthington barony, would come into a great deal of money once his father died. If he did not spend it all first. To him, everything—and anyone—could be bought. One of the many things James despised about him.

"How are things, old friend?" Stonebrook said in that same jovial tone he always used. Old friend was a poor choice of words, for they'd only became acquainted two years earlier in London through a mutual friend.

"What brings you to the area, Stonebrook?" James asked. "And more specifically, to Penford Place?"

"I've business in Chatsworth," Stonebrook replied. "So, I thought I'd call while I was here." He glanced past James. "Well, aren't you going to invite me in?"

For a moment, James considered sending the man away. Stonebrook was not his friend. Not anymore. He was now an acquaintance at best, and James would have preferred to have nothing to do with him. Yet sending the man away would raise suspicion, which James did not need.

The purpose for James returning to Chatsworth was to escape everyone in London he knew. Including Stonebrook. Seeing the man at his front door did not sit well with him. Calling unannounced was simply rude and only made matters worse.

But there was that nagging voice reminding him that he could do nothing to bring suspicion down on Amelia or Penford Place.

"I suppose work can wait," James said, feigning a smile. "Please, come in. Would you like a drink?"

Stonebrook glanced around the lavish foyer. "You've a very nice home, Barrington. At least compared to others I passed on my way here. I've been to Chatsworth only twice, but this is my first venture outside of the village."

"What brings you here?" James asked again as he led Stonebrook into the drawing room. "Are you purchasing some land?"

James prayed it was not the case.

"No. I'm hoping to find a woman with whom I may entertain myself. Or perhaps even marry if she works out. I've a friend in London who has two daughters. One is married, but the other resides here in Chatsworth, so I've come to call on her. She's not an aristocrat, but her father's a very wealthy man. I'm hoping to have him connect me with several gentlemen willing to do business with me."

"Have you met her yet?" James asked, handing Stonebrook a glass of brandy.

"Not yet, but I will later today. I'll see if she passes my criteria. If so, I'll soon have control of her father's purse strings, so I can empty his purse into my coffers. It will certainly make me far wealthier than most men in my position once Father's gone."

James gritted his teeth. He knew very well what sort of "criteria" Stonebrook had in mind and how he would go about testing this poor young lady. Stonebrook was a great manipulator.

Two years earlier, they had agreed to trade a pair of horses, one for one. What James learned was that the true Stonebrook was a liar and a scoundrel, leaving James dumbfounded when he was given a horse so old, Moses likely rode it. And Stonebrook had shown not a drop of remorse for his attempt to swindle James.

"I hope you find happiness with this woman, whoever she is. But perhaps you should leave certain matters until after marriage. That is the right thing to do, after all."

Stonebrook laughed. "Happiness? I'm looking to find a woman who can warm my bed and produce an heir. Happiness is found in sports and games of chance, certainly not marriage."

James took a sip of his brandy. If circumstances were different, he would be in agreement. At least about his need to find a bride. His idea of choosing the right woman was far different from that of Stonebrook. Yet there were too many problems with Amelia to even consider beginning such a search.

No, perhaps later, once she returned home. Then he would find a woman to marry. Perhaps even Miss Kendricks. But for now, he had to take care of Amelia's situation.

Besides, what young lady would allow a potential suitor who hides away an unmarried pregnant woman to call on her? To reveal such a dark secret, he would have to trust her greatly, and right now, James found trusting most people a struggle.

"I plan on taking her to the theater this evening," Stonebrook was saying. "The one that is run by the charity."

"There is only one in Chatsworth," James said. He frowned. "I didn't realize you had an interest in theater."

Stonebrook snorted. "Hardly. I went earlier to purchase tickets and made a generous donation. The man running it assured me he would see me recognized for my charitable gift."

James feigned a smile, but inside, he wished to tell the man how pathetic he was.

"Tell me, Barrington. Why did you leave London?"

"I'm sure I mentioned that this is where my family home is," James said, turning the glass in his hand. "You are here, are you not? Sometimes a man wishes to return home for all sorts of reasons. Memories, perhaps. And one must return from time to time to see to the estate. All I know is that I find the solitude gratifying. It allows me to work in peace without numerous interruptions from callers."

"Interesting," Stonebrook said, absently tapping the side of his glass. "Have you seen anything of Miss Lansing?"

"Miss Lansing?" James said. He took a gulp of his drink, the brandy burning his throat. "No, not lately. Last I heard, she had left for Paris. Did you not know?"

Stonebrook smirked. "I did. However, Lady Barker traveled there recently. And you know what? She saw not hide nor hair of Miss Lansing. As a matter of fact, no one recollected seeing her there at all."

Lady Emily Barker, the younger daughter of the Earl of Sidrickton, was so much of a gossip, James would have thought his mother had taken a vow of silence in comparison.

"You know as well as I that Lady Barker has a propensity for all sorts of tales, Stonebrook. Since when have you taken an interest in gossip? I imagine Miss Lansing prefers to be left alone, likely away from the likes of people such as Lady Barker." He shrugged. "Or maybe she met a man and eloped. Either way, I wouldn't know."

Stonebrook chuckled. "I doubt that. But I would not be surprised if you know exactly what she's up to. You two are close. And it has nothing to do with the fact you've said as much. I've seen it. The way you speak to her and..." He leaned forward. "The way she looks at you."

James's jaw tightened with every word Stonebrook said. "I don't know, nor do I care, what Miss Lansing is doing in Paris," he said, rising from his chair. "Her life is not mine to lead."

Stonebrook barked a laugh as he, too, stood. "A woman has a particular look when a man pleases her." He clapped a hand on James's shoulder. "Most men wait many years, until they are old and gray, before making good use of their female friends. But that is not the case with you and Miss Lansing, is it? Do tell, Barrington. After all, men and women cannot simply be friends. It's unnatural."

"Don't speak of Miss Lansing in such an indecent manner," James snapped. "We are friends and nothing more."

Rather than being cowed, Stonebrook beamed. "Admirable, I must say. But I cannot blame you if you wanted to move beyond friendship. Miss Lansing's quite pretty. Surely, you've considered enjoying what she has to offer at least once? You don't mind if I pour myself another, do you?" He walked over to the decanters without waiting for James to respond.

James tried to control his rage. He knew what Stonebrook was doing, but he would never divulge the whereabouts of Amelia.

"I've no time for rumors better suited to women working on their needlework," James said.

Stonebrook set down his glass and turned to look at James. "My apologies. You apparently care for the young lady. My jesting was not meant to anger you. But if you do happen to hear word of Miss Lansing, or if you learn where she can be found, do let me know."

"I doubt I'll learn anything."

"You mustn't keep her to yourself," Stonebrook continued. "You must share women, especially one who looks like her." He downed the measure of brandy in one gulp. "Well, I must go before it gets too late. We'll speak soon."

James did not respond. If he had his way, they would never speak again.

As they walked to the door, Stonebrook stopped and said, "I say, why don't we dine together some evening?"

"My schedule is rather full," James said. When Stonebrook arched a doubtful eyebrow, James added, "But perhaps dinner can be arranged. Where shall I send word?"

"I'm staying at the local inn," Stone book replied. Then he grinned. "If all goes well with this young lady on whom I plan to call, I'll be visiting Chatsworth more often in the coming months."

James gave an unintelligible grunt before closing the door on Stonebrook. He let out a sigh and turned to find Baldwin entering the foyer.

"What shall we do about him, my lord?" the butler asked. "I don't trust him in the slightest. What if he tries to harm your good name?"

"I'll entertain him and then send him away for good," James replied. "If he learns that Amelia is here, all our plans will be for naught."

"Perhaps you should consider moving her now rather than later. It's far too risky for you. You should put yourself first, my lord."

James shook his head. "If I do that, what kind of man will that make me? Don't worry, Baldwin. One way or another, we'll fix what I've done."

Although he heard himself say the words, James's confidence behind them was waning. Hiding a pregnant woman was no easy task. And having those with loose tongues so close, those such as Stonebrook, was a risk indeed. A single whisper could ruin a man forever.

And Stonebrook would do far more than whisper.

CHAPTER SIX

Gossip rarely appealed to Diana. To her, speaking about others when they were not there to defend themselves was despicable. Everyone deserved the opportunity to set straight anything said about him or her.

Yet standing beside Jenny and Esther, the assistant cook to Mrs. Shepherd, Diana could not help but to want to hear more. After all, Esther was discussing something her cousin overheard, and that cousin was employed by the Marquess of Magic. Therefore, she had good reason to listen to what the girl had to say.

A tall, bony woman, Esther was the same age as Diana, with honey-blonde hair and deep-blue eyes. The maid was so thin, Diana wondered if she ate anything she and Mrs. Shepherd prepared in the kitchen.

"Now, you have to understand," Esther was saying as she rolled out the dough on the counter between them, "when a man's as handsome as him, every woman's gonna be looking, aren't they? Well, Judith worked for him both here and in London, and she says he's been seen out and about with a few ladies, but he rarely sees them more than once. Maybe twice."

"Why do you suppose that is?" Diana asked, unable to help herself.

Esther shook her head. "For reasons ladies like yourself shouldn't be hearing or speaking of. Mrs. Rutley'd have my head for repeating what I've heard, not to mention that Mrs. Shepherd would beat me silly."

Was Esther implying that Lord Barrington was a scoundrel? Well, Diana wished to know for certain. "I heard it has something to do with why he's called the Marquess of Magic. Jenny heard a rumor that he has put women under his spell with a single kiss. Is that what you've heard?"

Dusting her hands, Esther sighed. "That's what they say. Supposedly, women he's kissed walk around lost in love and hoping to find him again."

"See!" Jenny said in a harsh whisper. "I told you! Dozens of them."

Esther nodded. "But there are loads of rumors about him. Like he wears them black gloves to cover all the burns on his hands from mixing potions. But Judith, she says he's a good man. Treats his servants with respect, says he even spends time with them if you can believe that!"

Diana was uncertain what to think of that statement. To treat a servant kindly was one thing, but to spend time with them was most unlikely.

"I can see you don't believe me," Esther said, pounding a hand into the dough again. "What if I told you a secret that'll convince you?"

Jenny's grin nearly covered her face. "I won't say anything, I promise! I may enjoy a bit of gossip, but there are some things I never repeat. Especially if I've vowed not to do so."

Esther glanced at Diana, and she nodded. "Yes, do tell. We won't repeat it, we promise."

Dusting her hands once more and leaning over the ball of dough, Esther said, "Right, then. It's said that the marquess drinks and dances with the servants. Proper parties and all-like."

Diana could not help herself. She laughed. "I'm sorry, and I mean no offense to you or your cousin, but a marquess who invites servants into his home for drinks and a dance? That's as likely as a carriage driving itself without the aid of horses. It just doesn't happen."

Some of the tales the girls told were absurd, but this was far more than that. She was more likely to believe he made magic potions than that he danced around with servants.

"I never said in his home," Esther said with a scowl. "Whenever he visits his estate, Penford Place here in Chatsworth, he joins the servants in the stables every Saturday at eight. Judith says he provides them with the drink and even dances with them." She tucked a strand of blonde hair back under her mob cap.

Diana had no time to consider any of this as footsteps warned her only moments before Mrs. Shepherd entered the kitchen.

Esther, always aware, said, "I'm so glad you enjoyed yourselves at the shops, misses. I'd best be getting back to work."

"And what are you two doing here?" Mrs. Shepherd asked, a hand on her hip.

"Bothering Esther again," Jenny replied. "We're leaving now, however."

"Well, hurry along, then. Esther's got dinner to prepare. She doesn't have time for chitchat."

Motioning to Jenny, Diana led her out of the kitchen and to the empty corridor.

"What do you think?" Jenny asked. "Is what Esther said true?"

Diana frowned in thought. "I don't know. A marquess who attends parties hosted by his servants? I've never heard of such a thing. I suppose it's plausible, but really? Don't you think the tale is a bit fanciful?"

Jenny pulled at her braid. "You may be right," she said. "Or you could be wrong." She glanced over her shoulder. "Maybe we should go and see for ourselves. We know when and where. How difficult can it be to find Penford Place?"

Diana worried her bottom lip. Although she had embarrassed herself in the presence of the marquess twice now, she did find him handsome. And mysterious. What fun it would be to investigate whether this particular rumor, the one about a party in the stable, was true!

Yet leaving the school that late would require a good excuse. Then again, even if she found one, did she truly wish to know the truth?

An image of the marquess came to mind. He was leaning in and whispering in her ear. The sensation of his breath on her neck had been exhilarating, and for some odd reason, her legs had gone weak. Perhaps seeing him again would be worth the trouble if she were caught.

"Let me think of a way for us to go," Diana said as they walked toward the foyer. "Mrs. Rutley isn't simply going to allow us out after dark without good reason."

No sooner had the words left her mouth than the headmistress walked toward them.

"Ah, Diana, I was just looking for you," Mrs. Rutley said. "You've a guest, the gentleman about whom your father wrote us."

Diana sighed. She had completely forgotten. "Oh yes, of course."

Jenny leaned in and whispered, "Let's hope he's handsome. You'll tell me when you're done, won't you?"

"Of course," Diana replied.

Jenny walked away, and Diana looked down at her day dress. "Do you think my dress is appropriate?"

"You look wonderful, as always," Mrs. Rutley replied. "Now, come. He's been waiting for ten minutes already."

Remembering the man Emma's parents had sent for her, Diana said a silent prayer as she followed the headmistress to the drawing room.

Please, God, don't let him be an old man!

To her relief, the man who awaited her was not old. He was not handsome, but also was he not ugly. In his mid-twenties, he was tall and slim. His red hair was combed up in the latest style, and he wore a friendly smile on a very freckled face.

"Mr. Peter Stonebrook," Mrs. Rutley said, "may I introduce Miss Diana Kendricks."

Mr. Stonebrook took a step forward and bowed. "Miss Kendricks, what a relief it is to finally meet you."

Diana's eyes widened. "A relief?"

The young man laughed. "My apologies. I didn't mean it the way it sounded. Your father often brags about you so much, I feel as if I already know you."

Diana's heart warmed. Her father bragged about her? Perhaps he truly did care after all. "I'm pleased to hear it, sir," she said.

Mrs. Rutley led her to the couch and they sat. "Please, sit," she said.

Mr. Stonebrook took the chair across from them. "Thank you. Whenever your father mentions the school you attend and the fact that you excel in all the lessons you're taught, I'm reminded of my own schooling." He let out a small chuckle and dropped his gaze. "My apologies. I tend to speak far too much about my school days. But they were so enjoyable, I cannot help myself."

Diana smiled. He was kind and humble. Two very good characteristics in a man. "Please, I'm eager to hear more."

With a smile, Mr. Stonebrook said, "Everything I learned enthralled me, especially Latin. I understand you've learned some Latin, at least according to Mrs. Rutley."

"I have," Diana replied. "As well as French. I must admit I prefer Latin. *Gallica difficile est mihi*."

Mr. Stonebrook chuckled. "Indeed. French is difficult for me, as well. Then again, I've never studied it myself. That could be why I struggle."

They laughed, but then an uncomfortable silence fell over the room. Diana had been trained in the etiquette of conversing, but for some reason, her brain was doing little to help her conjure any ideas for discussion.

Thankfully, Mrs. Rutley asked, "What brings you to Chatsworth, Mr. Stonebrook?"

"Several things, really. Meeting Miss Diana was one of them, but I also heard the owner of the inn wishes to expand and is in need of an investor. Yet, I'm not one to think only of myself. I also hope to donate money to the Chatsworth Theater. A village wishing to give its people the opportunity to dabble in the arts is a worthy cause. But unlike those on Drury Lane and Covent Garden in London, these smaller theaters struggle at the best of times. And what's better for the residents of Chatsworth than a way to entertain themselves?"

A wave of hope washed over Diana. Decent men did exist in the world! And this man was one of them. "How wonderful that you think of others before yourself."

Mr. Stonebrook snapped his fingers. "I nearly forgot. A troupe is performing this Saturday. If I may be so bold, I would like to ask if you would like to accompany me? With a chaperone and the permission of your headmistress, of course."

Diana turned an excited look on Mrs. Rutley. "May I?"

Mrs. Rutley smiled. "Your father has given permission for Mr. Stonebrook to call, so I see no reason you cannot attend."

"Wonderful," Mr. Stonebrook said. "I'll have my carriage come for you at half-past five on Saturday. The performance begins at six. It won't be as grand as those in London, but it should be entertaining."

"Indeed," Diana replied, clasping her hands in front of her. "I look forward to it."

Although her smile was broad for such an excursion, it fell when she took in Mr. Stonebrook's gaze. For a moment, she thought she saw a glimmer of lust behind those brown eyes. And deceit?

Diana had seen the same look before. Last year in the village a man had bumped into her. She was certain it had been intentional because his eyes lingered on parts of her body they should not have. Not an hour later, she passed the tailor's shop where she overheard him saying the most inappropriate things. About her!

The question was, would Mr. Stonebrook be as inappropriate?

No, she was judging him before getting to know him. Plus, whatever she thought she had seen was not as blatant as the man in the village, for the look was gone so fast, it likely had never been there in the first place. Her imagination had gotten away from her, was all.

And why should it not? The marquess had teased her relentlessly about that blasted book. That did not mean all men were as glib as he.

Mr. Stonebrook stood. "Then, Saturday it is. I look forward to our time together, Miss Diana." He took her hand and kissed the knuckles. "Until then."

When Mrs. Rutley returned from walking him to the door, Diana sighed and said, "What a respectable gentleman! I somehow believed that Father would send someone dull and boring, but he's much better than I expected."

"We'll see," Mrs. Rutley said, making Diana frown. "Jenny will accompany you as your chaperone. Miss Thompson is away for the next month, and Mrs. Garvey is in Wales visiting her ill sister."

Diana was relieved. Both women were paid chaperones. Miss Thompson was nice enough, but she tended to spend a great deal of time talking. And Mrs. Garvey was a stickler for decorum. So much so, if she had her way, Diana would be leashed to her wrist.

Mrs. Rutley placed a hand on Diana's arm. "Although your father sent this man—and understand that I don't doubt his judgment—I expect you to keep your wits about you. Too often, the words we wish to hear are not those we need."

"Yes, Mrs. Rutley," Diana replied. "I'll be careful. May I go tell Jenny?"

Nodding, the headmistress said, "I'll be away this evening, so it will be only you three girls at dinner. Do make sure Ruth behaves."

Diana could not help but laugh. "I'll do my best," she said.

Stopping first at Ruth's room, Diana knocked on the door and entered. Ruth sat on her bed, a newspaper splayed open before her.

"What are you reading?" Diana asked as she joined Ruth.

"Have you any idea the number of notices asking for men to work on the ships?" Ruth asked. "To think they can sail to foreign lands. What adventures they must have! And here I am preparing for a life of servitude. It's simply unfair!" She pulled back a stray strand of red hair. "Perhaps I'll search for a captain who's in need of a young wife. I don't care what age he is or his appearance as long as I can sail with him."

Diana clicked her tongue. "You're preparing to live the life of a married woman, perhaps even a lady, not to sail with some drunk captain looking for a bride."

Ruth snorted. "As I said. Servitude."

Tired of arguing, Diana said, "Mrs. Rutley will be gone this evening, so it will only be you, Jenny, and I at dinner tonight."

A mischievous grin crossed Ruth's lips. "Then I believe I've plans after dinner. Several people have requested my presence."

Would Ruth never stop getting into trouble? Not likely. Well, Diana loved her friend and needed to do what she could to keep her safe. Even if she had to lie.

"Mrs. Shepherd already warned me about you," Diana said. "She's promised to check in on you every fifteen minutes. I would mind your-self if I were you."

Ruth grumbled something Diana could not hear and returned to her newspaper.

Diana left the room and went to her own. Jenny lay in bed, holding a bottle of perfume.

"Well?" Jenny asked, sitting up and giving Diana an expectant look. "Was he old? Was he handsome? Oh, I bet he was ugly."

"He's most definitely not old, and he is... plain. I don't mean to be uncharitable, but I would certainly not describe him as handsome."

"Are you saying that the marquess is handsomer, then?"

"No doubt," Diana said before she could stop herself. She covered her mouth. "What I mean to say is, if they stood one beside the other, they would be judged as very close. But the marquess would win by a small margin."

"You're lying! Now, out with it. The truth. Which man do you prefer?"

Diana fell onto her back on the bed and sighed. "The marquess," she replied grudgingly. "He's the type of man any woman would prefer. You've seen him. Tall and handsome. I imagine he hides very fine arms beneath that coat of his. Arms that could hold me all evening. Mr. Stonebrook is not terrible looking, but he's nowhere as handsome as the marquess. I will say he's sweet and one whose company I'll be enjoying this Saturday evening."

"Saturday? What's happening Saturday?"

"We have plans to go to the theater in Chatsworth. And you're to chaperone."

Jenny clapped her hands together and laughed. "Tell me everything!"

Diana did as she bade, Jenny asking question after question about Mr. Stonebrook.

"Yes, he will become a baron when his father dies."

"Yes, he seemed genuinely kind."

"No, he did not seem the type of man to become improper."

It was the final question that gave Diana pause.

"What about the party at Penford Place? Do you not still want to see if the rumors are true?"

"I do," Diana replied. "But how can we attend both events in one night without getting into trouble?"

Jenny pulled on her braid. "It will take careful planning. Every detail must be perfect. Any misstep will have us imprisoned in our rooms for the rest of next term."

"The theater begins at six. I imagine the show will not last more than an hour, two at most. The marquess joins the servants at eight, yet Mr. Stonebrook will be responsible for us and is expected to have us back to the school after the play ends. And we certainly cannot request he take us to the stables..."

Jenny began pacing the small space between the beds. "Then we must devise an excuse to leave Mr. Stonebrook at the theater once it ends. But it must be something he's unable to argue with, or something so terrible that he inquires after us with Mrs. Rutley."

Diana nodded. "Yes, that is true. But what can we say?"

For several moments, they fell silent, both in their own thoughts.

"I've an excellent idea!" Diana said. "Listen closely, for I'll need your help to see it through."

CHAPTER SEVEN

Diana spent the majority of Saturday afternoon preparing for her outing with Mr. Stonebrook. After rejecting ten dresses of varying styles and colors which now lay strewn across her bed, she finally decided on a pale-blue-and-white striped gown with a wide blue ribbon around the high waist. Over it, she wore her new spencer jacket. White gloves and a wide-brimmed straw hat trimmed with blue lace and a blue lace daisy finished off the look.

At least the unruly curls would be hidden beneath the hat! There were times when Diana wished she had Louisa's lovely flowing golden locks or Emma's pleasant dark waves. Putting up with all these curls could be such a bother!

Most of the girls at the school spent hours with a hot iron to achieve what Diana had naturally. There had to be a way to make her hair more like theirs. At least hats were still in style to hide what she had!

Checking her reflection in the standing mirror, Diana had to admit the effect was pleasant. She had never been one for powders or rouge. Her natural coloring suited her just fine. Although, she did pinch her cheeks to give her a slightly blushed look.

"Are you ready?" Jenny asked, her chestnut braid wrapped around her head rather than hanging over her shoulder as she preferred. "You look lovely. I would bet everything I own that Mr. Stonebrook will be unable to take his eyes off you."

Diana was sure she would have no need to pinch her cheeks again. "And look at you! That dress really brings out the green in your eyes." Jenny's eyes were hazel in color, and the tiny green wreaths printed on her white dress did help the green specks to be more pronounced. Her bonnet had a large green feather and a green ribbon that she tied beneath her chin.

Mr. Stonebrook was already in the foyer speaking with Mrs. Rutley when Diana descended the staircase ten minutes before he was meant to arrive. He looked up at Diana, and she was pleasantly surprised when his eyes went wide, then his smile broadened.

"Good evening, Miss Kendricks. You look lovely. I didn't realize I was so early, but I see you're ready. I'm pleased."

Diana curtsied. "May I introduce Miss Clifton?"

"It's a pleasure to meet you, Miss Clifton," Mr. Stonebrook replied.

Jenny's cheeks reddened. "Likewise, Mr. Stonebrook."

"Well, shall we be on our way?" Mr. Stonebrook asked. "We may be a bit early, but that will give us some time to chat before the play begins."

"I would like that," Diana replied.

Bidding Mrs. Rutley goodbye, the trio headed to the waiting carriage. A lantern hung on hooks on either side of the driver's perch, but the gibbous moon in the otherwise clear sky lit the road quite well. Diana was glad for her new coat, for the air was chilled. At least it was not frigid.

The inside of the carriage was beautifully crafted with plush brown cushioned seats and gold-etched designs on the white ceiling. Diana sat beside Jenny on one bench, and Mr. Stonebrook sat across from them.

"I hope you had an enjoyable week since we last spoke," Mr. Stonebrook said. His smile was polite, and he did not leer as some gentlemen did. That eased Diana's worries.

"Since we've no lessons, it was pleasant. We've been spending our days relaxing. I've come to realize I've no idea what to do with all my time. And you?"

Mr. Stonebrook laughed. "I wish I had time for leisure. Each passing day seems to keep me more occupied than the one before. But the last thing a young lady such as yourself needs is to hear a man grumbling about his work."

Diana could not help but smile. "I don't mind in the least, Mr. Stonebrook. Tell me, do you attend the theaters in London often? I'm hoping to see as many performances as I can during my first Season."

He smiled. "If I were not so busy, I'd attend every show possible. Though, I must admit, if you were in London, I'd have reason to forget about it altogether."

Diana's cheeks heated at the compliment. She had to admit, he was much different than she'd expected, especially given that her father had sent him. Perhaps her father cared more for her than she thought, for Mr. Stonebrook was a kind, attentive man. He may not have had the dashing good looks of the Marquess of Magic, but he made up for it in solicitude.

Only a dozen or so people were in attendance at the theater, many of them far older than Diana's parents. This did not surprise her, however. The building that housed the theater was small and had seating for fifty people at most. How they remained open in the village had always been a wonder, but she was glad she had the distraction. Also, a majority of the villagers had likely seen this particular play, which had opened the previous week. Now, they would be able to enjoy the show without the crowds. Or as crowded as it could be, anyway.

The foyer was small and sparsely decorated. Several chairs lined the walls for those who preferred to sit while waiting. A vase filled with purple hellebores, pink heather, and winter jasmine sat on a table in the middle of the room. The dark, well-worn carpet made the space seem smaller than it was.

"We have seats in the balcony, but I'm afraid it's nothing like what we would find in London where we would have a private box. Here, the theater reminds me of a church, and the balcony is a shared space."

Diana smiled. "I'm sure wherever we sit will be wonderful."

The lower level of the theater consisted of two sections, each containing five rows of four seats. The balcony, which looked directly down at the stage, also had two sections but with only two rows of four seats each.

Diana stared down into the lower level and was glad to be where she was. The balcony offered individual cushioned chairs, whereas the seating below was nothing more than pews with short planks to separate each seat. And those seats were uncomfortable. She knew that firsthand.

"Now that we are here, Miss Kendricks," Mr. Stonebrook said as he sat to Diana's left, "I must admit that I'm feeling... awkward."

Diana frowned. Awkward? Was she so boring that he felt uncomfortable in her company?

"If you'd like to leave, we can," he added.

"What about our situation makes you feel awkward, sir?" Diana asked. She prayed it was not her. Was she not good enough for him? That had to be it. He would become a baron upon the death of his father. She was nothing more than the second daughter of a wealthy merchant. What had she been thinking, accepting his invitation?

Oh, yes, her father had insisted. Perhaps she was being melodramatic. Then again, she was not one to fall for such sensationalism. She was far too sensible to give in to hysterics.

"As you mentioned, this is not London," Mr. Stonebrook replied, a blush creeping over his face. "I should not have suggested bringing you to a place that is so far beneath you."

Diana frowned. Had it not been he who had made the comparison? No, perhaps it had been she, for the sad expression he wore said as much.

"This place is... charming," she assured him. "I'm sure the play will be, as well. After all, they traveled from London, or at least that is what the playbill says. We'll be so lost in the story that we'll not even notice our surroundings."

He smiled at her. "Well, if you're comfortable here, I see no reason we cannot stay." He leaned in close and whispered, "Thank you. You've eased my worries considerably."

Diana smiled at him, and he blushed again and looked away.

Perhaps he was handsomer than she first thought. His profile was not as pronounced as that of the marquess, but she could tolerate looking at him.

She chastised herself. What reason would she have for comparing this man with one she had only met twice? And for only a few moments. Mr. Stonebrook was attentive and concerned with pleasing her. That said much about the gentleman he was. She found his company thus far pleasant and could imagine spending time with him again.

Turning her attention away from him—she did not wish to be accused of gazing—Diana looked down as a man walked out to the middle of the stage.

"Ladies and gentlemen!" he said in a booming voice that filled the small theater. "Thank you for visiting the Chatsworth Theater. We do hope you enjoy the troupe's rendition of *For the Love of a Servant Woman.*" He placed a hand over his forehead as if to shade his eyes. "Before we begin, may I ask Mr. Peter Stonebrook to stand?"

Mr. Stonebrook reddened to his ears. "Oh, no! I do hate having attention drawn to me." Yet he stood, nonetheless. The few attendees who sat in the lower level turned to stare up at him.

"The Chatsworth Theater has been hoping to make improvements on the building for some time, but we've lacked the funds to do so. Now, however, thanks to a sizable donation from the future Baron of Forthington, we now have the necessary funds to see our little theater become the artistic endeavor we've always hoped it to be." He gave a diffident bow. "Thank you, sir."

Diana smiled at the polite applause from the other audience members. Mr. Stonebrook adored the theater, enjoyed learning languages, and was a generous man. He was everything any young woman would want in a potential suitor.

Any young woman but Diana, that is. No matter how hard she tried, she could not seem to get Lord Barrington out of her mind. Something about him made her strangely giddy, as if she had consumed an entire bottle of sherry.

Not that she had ever done that, of course. A quarter of a bottle had her dropping into bed in the midst of a spinning room and rising the following morning with an aching head.

Needless to say, the Marquess of Magic had somehow put a spell on her, and she was uncertain what to do about that. After all, rumors followed him around like a puppy searching for its mother. Tonight, she would learn if those rumors were true, even if it meant risking being caught doing so.

Truth be told, Diana would do anything to see him again. And that only complicated matters.

The theater grew dark, and soon the play began. It was the story of a servant and her master, who fell in love and dreamed of a life together.

At times, Diana was laughing uproariously at their capers. At other times, she sat in apt silence on the edge of her seat. She felt a bond with the servant woman, Daphne by name, for she feared what would happen if she and the man she loved married. Would their happiness endure? Or would she and the Earl of Holverling be torn apart by a world that loathed love?

The latter was her deepest fear and what drove her to hoping for spinsterhood. Would her husband, whoever he might be, remain faithful to her? Or would he promise her the moon only to give her its reflection on the water? Was that not how her parents lived? Their marriage was an illusion, a reflection of what it could have been. And she hoped never to be forced to endure such a life.

Unlike the popular tragedies of the day, by the end, the characters married, vowing to love one another. Forever. Neither died. Neither was forced to marry another. Instead, they married and set off toward a life of adoration for one another.

"Well, that was much better than I expected," Mr. Stonebrook said as he stood to join Diana and Jenny in the applause. "It was a surprisingly excellent performance, and the story was lovely. If more people treated one another with respect, they would be happy, and the world would be a better place."

Diana stared at him, stunned. "I believe the same. It pleases me to know gentlemen such as yourself still exist in a time when love is set aside for position and greed."

As she had expected, the play lasted just over an hour. There was no need for grand performances that lasted hours, not in Chatsworth. That was better left for late nights in London, where theatergoers could enjoy a bit of time together after the performance ended. Few villages catered to late-night revelers. Or at least no places a proper young woman would enter.

As they made their way outside, Mr. Stonebrook offered Diana his arm. "The main protagonist, Horace, reminded me of a servant I once employed. He asked permission to leave his position so he could marry and become a blacksmith."

Diana raised her brows in surprise. "Oh? And how did you respond?"

"I told him that few are fortunate enough to find love, and he should not waste such an opportunity. I'm happy to say, I received a letter from him three months ago, and he has found success in both business and marriage."

"What a wonderful story!" Diana said. "Thank you for sharing that with me."

Diana was enjoying herself so much that she nearly forgot she and Jenny had other plans.

"Are you all right, Miss Kendricks?" he asked.

"No. Well, yes. You see, we've a carriage waiting at the home of Miss Clifton's cousin. We had already accepted her invitation weeks ago—it's a celebration of sorts."

"A birthday celebration," Jenny piped in.

Diana nodded. "Indeed. Well, as you invited me to the theater, Miss Clifton's cousin was willing to change the time of her celebration. It's only a few of her closest friends, so she had no difficulty in rescheduling. I do hope you understand."

Mr. Stonebrook frowned. "I wasn't aware. Would you like my driver to follow you to make sure you arrive there safely?"

Diana shook her head. "Oh no, that won't be necessary. The house is not far. The only reason I requested the carriage was so we have a way to return to the school. We certainly could not walk after dark now, could we?"

"I would rather die than have that happen," Mr. Stonebrook said.

"Well, I'll say farewell now, then. May I make just one request before we part?"

Diana nodded. "Yes, of course."

"May I call on you again?"

For a moment, Diana could not respond. Although Mr. Stonebrook was kind, she did not feel the same attraction she had for Lord Barrington. Yet the evening had been enjoyable, and more importantly, seeing this man again would please her father.

He brags about you! she reminded herself. That thought made her feel warm and cozy inside.

"I would like that, Mr. Stonebrook," she found herself replying. Allowing him to call did not mean they were courting. There was nothing wrong with sharing conversation over a cup of tea.

"You've no idea how happy that makes me, Miss Kendricks," Mr. Stonebrook said. "Your words warm my heart, for they are exactly what I hoped to hear." He dipped his head. "Good evening to you both."

Diana watched him get into the waiting carriage. Once it was gone, she turned to her friend. "Oh, Jenny, what a wonderful man he is! Have you encountered such an attentive and kind man?"

Jenny smiled. "Not in some time. Do you still want to see what we can learn about the marquess? We can go back to the school instead if you've found a new gentleman to entertain you."

"Oh no, we're still going to Penford Place," Diana said as a hired carriage pulled up beside them. "I would like to know the truth about Lord Barrington. But we must be quick. If we return to the school too late, we may raise Mrs. Rutley's suspicion, and we can't have that."

"I agree. And whatever we see, we must repeat to no one."

Diana laughed. "Do you think we'll witness some sort of unspeakable act? Surely, he's more of a gentleman than that. Even if he is annoying."

But she could not help but pause. Perhaps returning to the school was a wise decision. Yet, there was a mystery surrounding the marquess, and Diana wanted—no, she needed!—to find out what it was.

CHAPTER EIGHT

J ames pushed aside the ledger in which he had been working. After an early dinner alone this Saturday evening, he had busied himself with work in an attempt to distract himself from the chaos that was his life.

Not only did the arrival of Stonebrook consume his thoughts, so did Amelia. Anyone with any wits about him would recognize how foolhardy and dangerous it was to hide her on his estate. Yet here he was, doing just that.

He employed few servants at Penford Place. After all, who would they serve once he returned to London? Those who remained full time could be trusted, but that did not mean word would not leak out about her whereabouts.

Perhaps James should do as Baldwin suggested and send her away. There were plenty of homes that would take a woman in Amelia's condition and be discreet. She could convalesce until her time came to have the baby. Once the child was born, he would be placed in a home with a loving family, and Amelia would return to her life as if none of it had taken place.

She already spoke French as well as any native, and as she continued to practice every day, her abilities would only grow. Perhaps not as greatly as if she had gone to France, but well enough to convince everyone she had not remained in England.

James sighed. No, he could not send her away. How could a man claim to care for a woman only to rid himself of her at a time when society deemed her an embarrassment? Or unclean. Improper. There were a thousand words to describe a woman who carried a child out of wedlock, and James rejected every one of them.

Then there was Miss Kendricks. She was so lovely; he could not rid her image from his mind. Twice he had teased her, and twice she had challenged him, filled with pride. What she had done to him at the dressmaker's shop, and the smile she wore while doing it, made her all the more alluring.

What had made him tease her this last time? Being in her presence seemed to melt away his worries, giving him a sense of being rewarded. But rewarded for what? Harassing her for her choice in reading material? Although, he had to admit, that particular subject stumped him.

Would she consider allowing him to call on her?

He chuckled and shook his head. What a foolish thought. She was not even from a titled family. Not that he cared about such things, of course, but he still had expectations to fill.

"The Marquess of Magic?" he mumbled aloud. "More like the Marquess of Foolish Notions."

"If you'd like my opinion, my lord," Baldwin said from the doorway, making James nearly jump out of his chair, "I prefer the former to the latter. The latter does you no justice."

James laughed and glanced at the mantel clock. "It's getting late. Are you not joining the others?"

"No, my lord. I find as I become older, the thought of sleeping becomes more enticing than drink and music. Is there anything I can do for you before I retire for the night?"

"I don't believe so," James replied.

The butler gave a bow and withdrew, leaving James to stare at the closed ledger. He could not look at another entry, not tonight. Too many mistakes happened when one tried to work, once tiredness had settled over him.

As he returned the ledger to the shelf, a shadow fell over him, and he turned to find Amelia entering the room.

"Baldwin said you were alone," she said. "It seems your name remains safe for another day."

"I thought you would be asleep," James said, walking over to stand before her. "You must be terribly tired."

Amelia shook her head. "I slept earlier, far longer than I planned. Then I remembered there is a grand party tonight in the stables. I would attend, but my lady's maid is occupied, and I have no chaperone. Perhaps, I can have a fine gentleman escort me to keep me safe. Are you acquainted with any?"

James frowned in thought. "As a matter of fact, I do. But I must warn you. He's known to be far quieter than a man of his standing ought to be, and he prefers to watch rather than participate. You may find his company dull. But if you're willing to accept his shortcomings, he would be happy to act as your escort."

Laughing, Amelia said, "I'd be honored. Even under those conditions." She placed a hand on his proffered arm, and they made their way to the foyer where he donned his overcoat and customary black gloves.

Every Saturday night, the servants gathered in the stables, where they shared in drinks, stories, and a bit of music. James did not attend every Saturday—not when he had to travel an hour to get to Penford Place—but he did try to go whenever he was in residence. His father had given his blessing long before James was born when several of the staff requested to throw a party for one of the maids' birthdays.

Since then, it became a regular occurrence, and James would not stop them for the world. They worked hard and deserved a bit of diversion. And it was far better for them to enjoy themselves on the estate than at the pubs or the gaming hells in Chatsworth.

They kept their celebrating to the stables and never allowed it to carry over when they returned to their responsibilities. If anything, they worked all the harder and were far more loyal because of it. Which proved handy when he had secrets to keep as he did now.

"Do you remember the first time we attended the servants' party?" James asked.

Amelia laughed and her cheeks reddened. "How can I forget? One moment you had me sneaking out of my room, and the next I see you holding a bottle of brandy and offering me a drink. To this day, I'm thankful we were not caught!"

James joined in her laughter. He was twelve at the time and had known for years what occurred in the stables every week. Despite his father's warning to stay away, his curiosity had gotten the best of him, and he decided to join them. Amelia and her parents had been staying at Penford Place for the week, so he had asked her to join him, not knowing what they would find.

"We mustn't!" she had argued. "Have you any idea what Mama and Papa would say if they caught us with the servants? They would tan my hide." She had rubbed her bottom in remembrance of the last time her parents had punished her for whatever infraction she had done previously.

"You worry too much," a twelve-year-old James had argued. "Nothing'll happen to us. You know it."

She had sniffed at him. "Maybe not, but what if they dismiss all the servants? Then who'll clean the fireplace and serve dinner? Tell me that! You'll be left to do all their work, including seeing to the horses. Is that what you want?"

Ignoring her, he had sneaked down to the stables and peeked through a window, and she had reluctantly followed.

And to this day, James found the atmosphere enthralling.

The sound of music reached his ears long before they arrived at the stables, returning him to the present.

"If we'd been caught, Mother would have locked me in my room until I was of age," James said, laughing. "I may still be there today if it were not for you."

"I'm sure you would have found a way to convince your mother to release you long before then." She paused. "Listen. It sounds like Alfred is playing tonight."

The sound of a fiddle told James that she was correct. Alfred Unders worked in the gardens and could play any song requested of him, despite the fact he never learned to read music. Others sang if the call rose. The few windows glowed orange from the light within.

James pulled open the stable door. Stalls ran around three of the walls, each with its own window. His father had always wanted to be different from others.

"One long corridor is far too common," he had said when James was but a boy. "I want to build something original, something that looks nothing like all the others. A grand building that will be the envy of all our peers!"

And so, he did. The new design meant extra work for the stable hands. Gone was the luxury of a front and back door to air out the building, which meant putting in more effort in keeping the place clean and as free of barn odors as possible. But why complain? Especially now the staff had a place to celebrate together.

Crude chairs made from old brown crates lined the walls between the stall doors. Three black barrels served as makeshift tables to place one's drink. Or something to lean against as a tall stable hand was doing. One corner was devoid of a stall and held various tools, including spades, brushes, and brooms. In the middle of the open area was what James deemed the "servants' ballroom."

In the opposite corner from the tool area stood Alfred, a man of fifty with wild brown hair and eyebrows to match and a fiddle beneath his chin. Scattered around the room were a dozen servants, all handpicked by James to remain at the estate. He knew every one of them by name and had spent time building trust with them.

How? One might ask. By sneaking out of the house and attending their great parties regularly since he was fifteen years of age. Now, he could attend anytime he wished without fear of his parents' wrath. It was one thing to allow your staff to hold parties in your stable, but quite another to participate!

Although James joined them occasionally in a song or in one of the country dances, his enjoyment came from watching them. Even after a long week of work, they had such energy, held such glee. They were nothing like the *ton*, and that only made his time with them all the more pleasant.

Not once had any of them revealed that he attended when he was in residence, nor did their demeanor change once the party was over.

Outside of their Saturday-night fun, they showed him the diffidence befitting a marquess.

"My lord. My lady," eighteen-year-old Linda Beasley said, smiling as she walked past with two cups in her hand. Gone was her mob cap and the uniform typical of her position as chambermaid. Now she wore a simple green and blue dress, her brown hair hung down her back, and a smile covered her face.

Although James trusted every man and woman here, servants had a tendency to gossip. Therefore, he had introduced Amelia as Mrs. Triton, the wife of an associate, who had come to convalesce at his home while her husband was in America on business. It had been because of her station as "Mrs. Triton" that easily explained her residence in the guest cottage rather than the house in which a titled person might stay.

"You are most kind to allow me use of your guest cottage, my lord," she had said in the presence of several maids upon her arrival. "Prudence is a quite capable cook and her cleaning abilities sound. There is no need to have your maids do extra work on account of me."

And thus, "Mrs. Triton," having saved the staff extra labor, was brought into the circle of trust for Saturday-night parties.

"Here now," James said, placing a hand on a chair that looked sturdy. "Sit. You really should rest."

Amelia laughed. "Am I your donkey to order about?" She included a wink, which said she was merely teasing. Smoothing her skirts, she added, "The fabric is far different from what I'm accustomed to, but I've come to appreciate it."

They had agreed that bringing yet another person into their trust was imprudent, that included a seamstress to alter her dresses as her body changed. The last thing they needed was to give Mrs. Newberry fodder for her gossip.

"Nor should you go off purchasing fabric for me," Amelia had insisted. "That in itself will have tongues wagging."

"I can send one of the maids—"

Amelia had clicked her tongue in vexation. "And what would a maid be doing with fine muslin or cotton fabric? No, I'll use whatever is on hand. Prudence is deft with a needle, so I'm sure she can make the necessary adjustments to what I brought with me."

Unfortunately, she had not brought any of her lovely dresses and gowns but instead had packed whatever Prudence could find amongst her father's staff. That meant clothing far different from that which she was accustomed.

"I'll return to my regular clothing after the baby is born," Amelia had insisted. "There's no need to ruin perfectly good clothing that would be of no use to me once I've returned to myself again."

This had turned out to be a wise choice, for now Amelia fit in well with the other servants. Not that James had many callers, but it did add another layer of protection in case one of his nosy neighbors learned he was in residence.

He could trust few members of the *ton*. Too many might see through the ruse of Amelia as his cousin. It was one thing to hide the truth from the servants and quite another to hide it from his peers. His peers were less likely to take him at his word.

James smiled. "You'll be back in your old clothing soon enough. Life will be much better, you'll see."

Amelia nodded and looked down at her stomach. "As long as the child has a loving home, that is all that matters."

The sadness in her voice twisted his heart. "I'll find one soon," he said for what felt like the hundredth time. "I promise."

Leaving Amelia to enjoy the party from her chair, James went to stand at his usual place against the wall. The music had gone from a slow ballad to a lively country dance. The servants talked and laughed, all so much more jovial than even the best parties thrown in England by the aristocracy.

James began to relax. Those of the lower class enjoyed themselves just as much as the *ton*. Rather than wine, however, they drank ale of dubious origin. A blanket covered a mound of hay to make a makeshift table that held the various foodstuffs each had brought with them. They came together every week to celebrate life, bringing with them whatever "luxuries" they could contribute. More than once, James had offered to provide food and drink, but each time he was refused.

"No offense, my lord," Paul Klipper, the head stable hand, had said, "but this is our time. Let us provide for ourselves."

It was not said in disrespect but rather with dignity. That, in turn, had filled James with pride, for it meant his employees were well-paid and happy with their lot.

Then something caught James's eye. Linda gave Alfred a sly grin. The two had grown close over the last few months, and this smile only solidified his suspicion. Perhaps the two would marry.

This, of course, drove James to a realization. Although he had called on a handful of ladies, none had held his interest. If he could find that one special woman—after this situation with Amelia was resolved—he would then marry. Most gentlemen preferred to wed after they reached their thirtieth birthday, anyway. No one would give it a second thought if he waited a little longer.

Laughter brought James back to the present. Alfred was playing a lively tune that called the others to the middle of the room to dance. James clapped to the beat as brown-haired Donald Corleon, one of the young footmen, began to sing.

Laughing with the others when the chorus was done, James removed his coat, rolled up the sleeves of his shirt, and joined the other revelers.

Unlike similar dances performed by those of his station, this dance was livelier and required whatever foot movement a dancer preferred. There was no need to practice and memorize a particular step or to concern oneself with a misstep. When dancing with these people, James could be whoever he wished to be at that time. And it was freeing!

Red-haired and freckled Judith Stevenson walked up to him. "May I join you, my lord?" she asked as she curtsied.

He smiled and replied, "Why, of course, my lady." His half-bow made the onlookers laugh with glee.

With her back facing James, Judith lifted her skirts to reveal white-stockinged ankles. Hopping from one foot to the other, her skirts rose higher with each step until her thighs showed.

This was not the first time he had seen this dance, for many of the younger servants enjoyed its steps. But if any of his peers were to witness such scandalous behavior, he would have been chivvied out of town.

Well, they might not have been that forthright, but the rumors would have been outrageous.

He could hear them now.

"Did you see how provocative that girl was? I'm sure he's opened his bed to her on more than one occasion!"

"I couldn't agree more," another would say. *"He's likely to get himself into trouble if he's not careful. It's one thing to bed a servant and quite another to announce it in public in such a scandalous way!"*

"Achoo!"

James came to an abrupt halt and looked for any sign that one of the revelers had sneezed. No one seemed to have noticed. He, however, was always on alert, even when enjoying himself as he was now. Asking one of the servants to do so would mean one would be left out of the fun, and this was their time. *They* included *him*, not the other way around.

A horse whinnied in one of the stalls, and James peered in that direction, frowning. A cool breeze whipped past him, and he glanced at the door, but it was still closed.

Then his eye caught a movement in the shadows of something much too small to be a horse and too large to be a dog. Someone was hiding, and he would find out who that someone was!

CHAPTER NINE

T he long drive that led to the home of the Marquess of Magic was dark, despite the glow of the moon overhead. Diana had instructed the driver to wait on the main road as she and Jenny alighted from the carriage. She had paid him handsomely to be sure he would keep her secret.

"Don't you want to go?" Jenny asked when Diana had not moved more than a few feet past the main gate. "If you'd like, I can go look and report back what I see."

"No," Diana replied. "It's not proper for a young lady to be out walking alone after dark." She nearly laughed. They had left propriety at the entrance to the theater in Chatsworth ten minutes earlier! "Nor should she lie or sneak away to an estate uninvited. Oh, Jenny, what are we doing?"

Diana felt torn. Her actions tonight went against any sense of morals, but she could not help herself. Lord Barrington fascinated her. Plus, did she not have the right to learn for certain whether the rumors about him were true? Why trust the wagging tongues of the gossip-mongers when she had a way to learn the truth for herself?

Oh, who was she fooling? Every night, she lay in bed recalling their encounter at the bookshop. He had smelled so... masculine. She would never look at a lemon the same again. And the feel of his hot breath in her ear had sent pleasant shivers through her body. His whisper resounded in every dream.

"Don't worry," Jenny said, reaching out and taking Diana's hand in hers. "There are women who've done worse, I'm sure. My sister told me she heard of a baroness whose husband was away for a month. Apparently, she fancied one of the footmen, so she arranged for him to come to her room under the pretense of—"

"We'd best hurry before it becomes too late," Diana snapped. The last thing she wanted to hear was the indiscretions of a baroness! What she was doing was not as bad, but it was close enough to make her skin pebble and the hairs on the back of her neck stand on end.

"I just hope we don't see anything revolting," Jenny said. "I've heard what men do when they've had too much to drink." She gave an exaggerated shiver, but judging by the smile she wore, Diana was sure Jenny had seen many things no lady should discuss—privately or in public.

"We're here to put this rumor to rest and return to the school once we have," Diana said in attempt to rally her confidence and push away the image Jenny had created. "Do you honestly believe that debauchery is taking place? I bet there won't even be a party. What we'll find instead is nothing more than the stable hands seeing to their duties before going to bed for the night."

Penford Place was made of red brick. It was a large, square, three-story building with two wings on either side and a one-story addition Overall, it was plainer than she had expected, given it belonged to a marquess. Where were the grand parapets and tall towers of the castle he should have had? What a disappointment!

Her thoughts went immediately to Lord Barrington. Was he inside reading the book he had purchased on Paris fashion?

She grinned. He had learned rather quickly that he could not best her in a battle of wits. Especially after he had followed her into Mrs. Newberry's shop! Granted, he hid his embarrassment well that day. But why would he purchase a book clearly intended for a woman? Perhaps she would convince him to explain the next time she saw him again.

"Diana, listen," Jenny said in a harsh whisper, breaking Diana from her thoughts. "Do you hear music?"

Diana strained to hear. "Where is it coming from?"

"I think the stables," Jenny said, her eyes so wide, the moon glinted in them.

"No! Surely not!" Diana said.

Jenny grasped Diana's arm and pulled. "Come on! Let's go find out!"

Diana nearly laughed again. Anyone would have seen them scurrying bent-back across the open expanse of perfectly trimmed grass if he had peered outside, so bright was the moon. There were no shadows in which to hide nor clouds to cover the moon.

Please, don't look outside! Diana prayed silently in case the marquess was indeed reading indoors. Not that there was any indication he was indeed inside.

"How will we see inside?" Diana whispered. "We can't go to the door. Someone will see us for sure, and Mrs. Rutley will murder us when she's told we were found sneaking around in the dark."

Jenny was moving her upper body from left to right, peering toward the stables. "Look, we can see from there." She pointed to a place along the outside wall. "Well, let's not stand here all night. We've investigating to do!"

The music grew louder as they scampered to one of the windows and peered through the bubbled glass. Inside, she could see a stall with a black mare and, beyond that, the glow of several lanterns.

Jenny pulled on the window, and it opened with ease. "We can climb in through here."

What am I doing here? Diana asked as Jenny dragged over a crate. They had no business spying on the marquess. How he spent his time was his affair and not hers. What right did she have to confirm the rumors? And what difference would it make whether they were true? Perhaps it was an innate desire to see the marquess again.

Yes, that had to be it. He was different from most men, for he made her feel alive. Yet, that made no sense. They had only met twice —three times if one counted the dress shop as a separate occasion— and only for a few moments each time.

Her breath turned to vapor in the air as she crawled through the open window and dropped into the stall. The top section of the stall door was open, allowing them the perfect view of the revelry.

At least a dozen servants were present. The violin player was an exceptionally thin man with brown hair in need of combing. Beside him stood another man, much younger and with blond hair, clapping and stomping his feet. An extremely pretty woman with her hand resting on her swollen stomach and several other women of varying ages laughed and drank with their male counterparts. The mood was festive, to be sure.

So, the rumors about the Saturday-night parties were true. But where was the marquess?

The man alongside the violin player leaned over and picked up a mug off the floor. Then he threw back his head and downed whatever was inside, and given the grimace the followed, it was not likely water.

He wiped his mouth and began to sing.

I met a young lady
  Down by the creek.
  She wore just a shift
  And had a great deal of cheek.
  Later that night
  I found myself unable to sleep.
  Then I realized I knew the reason why.

The rest of the servants joined in for the last line.

"A woman don't like a man who sniffles and cries!"

Laughter and cheers filled the place.

Diana turned to Jenny. "This is so wonderful!" she said in a harsh whisper. "What a lovely way for the servants to spend their time. I've never seen anything like it."

"Neither have I," Jenny said. "Diana! Look or you'll miss it!"

Diana returned her gaze to the party and gasped in shock. Out of the shadows emerged the marquess, devoid of his coat and with his shirtsleeves rolled up to his elbows.

Was it wrong to find a man in such a state of undress handsome? No, he was more than handsome. He was alluring. Her cheeks burned as she admired the fit of his breeches, and his arms were as muscular as she had imagined. Then to her utter shock, he joined the others and began to clap his hands in time with the music.

The rumors were true! Diana was both confused and enthralled by what she was seeing. It was ludicrous and improper, yet if she had the chance, she would surely join him. He was enjoying himself immensely, she was certain.

When a woman with wild red hair and a pretty smile walked up to Lord Barrington, Diana covered her mouth to keep from gasping aloud. But when the two began to dance, a spear of jealousy pierced her heart.

The woman lifted her skirts, exposing not only her ankles but a great deal of leg as well, and lifted each leg in turn. Then the marquess moved behind her, hopping from left to right on either side of her, much to the delight of the onlookers.

"How scandalous!" Jenny exclaimed. "A servant dancing with a lord is one thing, but like this? It's quite another. What do you think?"

Diana was unsure how to take in the scene before her. She had no right to feel jealous. She and the marquess barely knew each other. Yet jealous she was.

Or was this proof of the other rumor she had heard? Did he work his magic to get women to fall in love with him with a single kiss? And was this woman one of them?

The thought of dancing in this manner with Lord Barrington brought heat to her cheeks. And unlike the other thoughts, this time they brought about a giddiness she had not expected. To be so open, and so close to Lord Barrington, would be most welcome!

"Jenny," Diana whispered, excitement for what they were witnessing filling her, "do you think—"

She was unable to finish her sentence as two things happened at once. The song the violin player had been playing slowed and came to an end, and Jenny crinkled her nose as if she were ready to cry.

Yet cry she did not. Instead, she let out a sneeze so loud, surely it would have woken everyone from Chatsworth to London.

"I'm sorry!" Jenny gasped. She pulled on Diana's arm. "Come on! We'd best go before they find us hiding here!"

They hurried to the window and crawled through. How they managed to do so without a crate, Diana did not know. Perhaps her fear had given her wings. Outside, she lowered herself to the ground and turned to leave, only to collide with a solid mass. A mass with arms that grasped her by the waist.

Diana let out a choked cry as she looked up into the face of the Marquess of Magic.

"Well, well, Miss Kendricks. Of all the people I would have expected to spy on me, you would not have made the list."

"My lord," Diana gasped at him. Shadows partially concealed his features and, for reasons unknown, only made him all the more alluring. Her breath came in short gasps, and she found herself wishing he would tighten his grip on her.

Have you gone mad? she chastised herself silently. What was wrong with her? Mr. Stonebrook would not have taken such liberties. It was not as if she had fallen and needed to be caught before tumbling to the ground!

"We were not spying," Diana said in a clipped tone.

"Oh? Then perhaps you can explain what you *were* doing?" Lord Barrington released his hold and took a step back. "Come now. I would like an explanation if you please."

Diana racked her brain for any explanation, any excuse that would make sense, yet none came. Feeling defeated, she said, "Would you prefer the truth?"

"I think it would be best, yes."

With a sigh, Diana said, "I've heard certain rumors about you, my lord. Rumors that you dance with your servants—among others." The last she added as an afterthought. There was no need to expand on what those other rumors were. "I admit that my curiosity got the best of me, and I wanted to see for myself if it was true."

She waited for the scolding she was sure to come. After all, she had sneaked onto his property to spy! She prayed he would not tell Mrs. Rutley, for the headmistress would never trust her or Jenny again.

Rather than scolding her, however, Lord Barrington laughed. "I see. And from whom did you learn this little secret of mine?"

"I... I cannot say, for it was told to me in the strictest confidence,"

Diana replied while Jenny, at the same time, said, "Esther, the kitchen maid at the school, her cousin Judith is employed by you."

Diana closed her eyes in horror. If she could have stepped on her friend's toe to make her be quiet, she would have!

When she opened her eyes, the marquess was frowning.

"Is there no one I can trust?" he said in a voice so quiet Diana was sure she was not meant to hear. He sighed. "Never mind. I'll speak to her later. For now, I must know what other rumors you've heard about me." He raised a gloved hand. "Perhaps the reason I wear black gloves?"

Diana shook her head. The last thing she wanted was to repeat what she had heard about him dabbling in magic. She would hate to see him hanged. He was far too handsome to die.

"Witchcraft, my lord," Jenny offered.

Diana groaned. Why did the girl not learn to hold her tongue?

Lord Barrington arched an eyebrow. "Is that so?"

Jenny nodded, her eyes wide with excitement. "Oh, yes. There are all sorts of rumors that you practice the dark arts. I, for one, find it fascinating. Would you be willing to work a spell for us tonight? I promise never to tell a soul, and I know Diana would keep it to herself, as well."

The marquess heaved a sigh. "I may as well be truthful, too," he said. "The rumors are true."

Diana's stomach fell. As much as she enjoyed hearing that he could do magic, she never believed it was true, not really. As long as she believed thus, she could allow herself to dream. Now she could have nothing to do with him. And that was unfortunate.

Lord Barrington laughed. "The looks on your faces are worth more than any estate I own!" he said. "I do *not* practice witchcraft. Let me show you why I wear these gloves." He removed one and moved his hand into the light that came through the window. The skin was red and blotchy. "When the weather is too cold, my hands hurt and become irritated. Nothing seems to help. Perhaps it's an odd ailment, but there it is. The gloves are to protect my hands from the cold. I sometimes even wear them in the house during the winter months."

Feeling silly and perhaps a bit childish, Diana said, "My apologies for spying on you. And for paying heed to the rumors. I really should know better. Few are true. I'm sure Jenny is sorry, too. I can assure you we've never repeated anything we heard about you, nor will we say anything about what we've seen tonight."

"I'm not worried, nor would I be surprised if you did. Why would I expect anything else from a woman who reads *certain books*?"

The way he smiled at her lit a fire inside her, and she narrowed her eyes. So, he wished to duel with her again, did he? Very well, she was not afraid of him! Her arsenal was far better equipped than his!

"Well, I would not expect any less behavior from a man who reads books on women's fashion."

A small wince was all the evidence that her words had pricked him. "Bold words for a woman so beautiful," he said.

Her throat went dry. How was it that Mr. Stonebrook saying such things had no effect on her? Yet when the marquess said very much the same, her heart fluttered and the air in her lungs disappeared.

"I must admit we've found ourselves in a particular dilemma, Miss Kendricks. You've caught me in a situation out of which I cannot explain myself."

"Then the dilemma is yours, my lord. Not mine."

He chuckled. "Is that what you believe? Perhaps you've already concocted an excuse for why you were found on my property after dark?"

Diana swallowed hard. "I'll not say anything, my lord. And neither will Jenny. We've both vowed to keep this to ourselves."

The marquess studied her for several moments and then nodded. "I believe you. Now that you know the truth about me, I'm curious about you, Miss Kendricks."

Straightening her back, Diana jutted out her chin. "I can assure you I have an impeccable reputation, my lord. You'll hear no rumors about me."

"Not yet," Lord Barrington said. "But there is the issue of you leading a gentleman into a dressmaker's shop..." Then he winked at her!

Diana was unsure why, but she enjoyed this banter immensely! She could go for hours in a duel of wits with this man.

"The question would not be why I led you there, but why you chose to follow me."

His laughter warmed her chilled body. She could listen to his laugh forever. "Very good, Miss Kendricks. You've a very sharp tongue. I suppose we should continue this conversation at a later time. Perhaps over dinner?"

"I'd like that," Diana said without hesitation. "When?"

"Tuesday at five," the marquess replied. "I'll send my carriage to collect you and your friend."

"You know where I live?" Diana asked, taken aback.

"Of course. You attend Mrs. Rutley's school. When we met three weeks ago, I overheard your friend here. Miss Clifton, I believe? She said something about your headmistress being devastated if you dropped a handkerchief in order to gain a man's attention?"

Despite the dim lighting, Diana could see Jenny's cheeks redden, and she slid her arm through that of her friend. "Miss Clifton was aware that you were listening in on our conversation and thus her reason for concocting such a silly tale. Perhaps you should learn not to eavesdrop." She punctuated her words with a firm nod.

"Oh, I've learned a lesson, Miss Kendricks," Lord Barrington replied as he took a step toward her.

Diana trembled. Not from fear but with something she could not name. Finding his eyes, she whispered, "And what is that, my lord?"

He placed a gloved hand against her cheek. "That real magic may truly exist, for I find myself under your spell."

CHAPTER TEN

Time was sluggish as Diana waited for Tuesday to arrive. The carriage was not due for another hour as she sat at her vanity table while Jenny carefully placed another pin in Diana's hair.

"For a woman who's proclaimed to have no interest in marrying, you're being very fussy over your hair."

Diana gave her friend a glower. "Just because a woman wishes to look her best does not mean she has an ulterior motive. I'm just undecided which style to wear." Seeing Jenny's frown in the reflection, she added, "You don't believe me?"

"I don't doubt *you* believe what you've said, but I don't think it's the truth."

Now it was Diana's turn to frown. "That makes no sense."

Sighing, Jenny placed her hands on Diana's shoulders. "You accompanied Emma to the bookshop specifically to search out Lord Barrington. Don't argue. You know it's true. Then you did it again with me. After that, you chose to go to his estate to verify rumors you had no business verifying."

Diana gaped. "At your insistence!"

"And now you're having dinner with him," Jenny continued, clearly ignoring Diana's accusation. "Which would be well enough if the previous encounters had not been so suspect. I saw how you interacted with him at the bookshop and outside the stables. You were grinning like a fool both times, and I doubt you remembered to draw breath!"

With a sigh, Diana said, "Yes, you're right. But can you blame me? He's not only handsome, but he also has this air of mystery surrounding him. It's a kind of... well, magic. I find myself drawn to him." She turned and gave Jenny an earnest look as she remembered him touching her cheek and the sensations it conjured. "Do you think I've fallen under his spell?"

"Perhaps," Jenny said, shrugging as she slid another pin into Diana's hair. "And if he's a good man, what is there to fear?"

Diana sighed. "That he'll be just like every other man I've known. Or worse. But truth be told, I've considered giving up my desire for spinsterhood. *If* the marquess proves to be a decent man. And if he asks me to court him."

"There is only one way to learn the truth," Jenny said. "And tonight will be the perfect opportunity to do so. Now, your hair. Tell me you like what I've done, or I'll be forced to pull out every pin in frustration."

Diana laughed and looked this way and that at her reflection. She had brushed her hair dry rather than allowing it to dry on its own, which had relaxed many of the curls. Then Jenny had piled it high atop her head, adding more than a dozen pins, each tipped with a silver butterfly whose body was made from a diamond. All gifts from her father when he had been unable to see her because he was away.

"It's wonderful," Diana said. "Your skills are far better than mine."

"Well, I would give anything to have your lovely curls," Jenny said, pulling a glove over her own hand. "Why you insist on brushing them out is beyond me."

Diana laughed. "And I would love to enjoy even a few moments of not having to deal with my curls. If I could have your hair, I'd not allow it to sit in a braid all day."

Jenny frowned. "You can't mean I should keep it loose. I'd be forced to spend hours dealing with a tangled mess!"

Mrs. Rutley and Mrs. Shepherd were in the foyer, their heads together and speaking in hushed whispers when Diana and Jenny arrived. The headmistress and the cook had been friends for many years, and Diana wondered what sort of discussions they had. Mrs. Rutley glanced up at Diana, whispered one last thing to Mrs. Shepherd, who hurried away.

"You look beautiful," the headmistress said. "Are you ready for this evening?" Both girls nodded. "You'll have a lovely time, I'm sure. Lord Barrington is a decent and respectable gentleman. I imagine you'll enjoy his company."

"Oh, you know him?" Diana asked in surprise. Why had Mrs. Rutley not mentioned this before? Then again, it was a small community. Why would she not be acquainted with most residents in the area?

"Not well, no, but I've heard many good things about him from people I trust."

"I have a question, Mrs. Rutley," Diana said. "And it concerns... well, gossip that has been circulating about the marquess. I'd rather not repeat what others have said, for it's far too embarrassing, but have any rumors about him come your way?"

Mrs. Rutley pursed her lips. "One day, when you leave here and find your place in society, you'll hear all sorts of tales about many people. Sometimes, the stories are such that few can help but repeat them. What you must do is consider why a particular rumor exists and what consequence it holds for you. If it will not affect you, ignore it, for what business is it of yours? You're old enough to know that most gossip has few roots of truth, which means it is likely untrue. But if you can be affected by what you hear, then I recommend you consider the source before passing judgment."

Diana nodded slowly. "So if I were to, say, have a romantic interest in Lord Barrington—which I do not, I assure you—but if I did, his actions could be hurtful to me. Am I correct in saying so?"

"If they are true, then yes," Mrs. Rutley replied. "If they are not, you've nothing with which to concern yourself. But as you've no romantic interest in the marquess, or so you've said, it makes little difference either way."

"Let's pretend I did," Diana said. "How would I go about learning the truth? I can't outright ask a gentleman about these particular rumors I've heard, can I? After all, he could choose to lie."

Mrs. Rutley took Diana by the hand and smiled. "Let your heart guide you, my dear, for it will always reveal the truth."

Diana kissed Mrs. Rutley's cheek. "Thank you."

As she and Jenny donned their coats, a knock came to the door. When Mrs. Rutley opened it, Lord Barrington stood on the other side. He wore his black gloves and hat and a dark overcoat.

Diana thought about the foolish rumors that surrounded him. It was all so silly! In fact, it was so much so that she let out a laugh before covering her mouth to stop it.

Lord Barrington raised a single eyebrow. "It appears I've just missed the telling of a joke."

"Not at all," Diana said, pretending to cough into her gloved hand. "Just a light tickle in my throat is all." What she wanted to do was crawl into a hole and hide. "May I introduce Mrs. Rutley, the school's headmistress."

The marquess dipped his head. "I've heard wonderful things about your school, Mrs. Rutley."

"I'm pleased to hear it, my lord," the headmistress replied. "I take great pride in guiding young ladies, preparing them for their lives ahead. It may seem unconventional, but I believe in educating women in areas beyond needlework and posture."

Lord Barrington glanced at Diana and smiled. "Indeed. I've seen this firsthand. Miss Kendricks and I met because of her love of books."

Diana's eyes widened. *He wouldn't!*

Thankfully, he did not mention the title of the book with which he had caught her. "If you're ready, Miss Kendricks and Miss Clifton, the carriage awaits."

With a nod and suppressing a smile of her own, Diana walked past the marquess onto the portico. Jenny followed next.

"I've asked the cook to prepare lamb for dinner," the marquess said. "I believe you'll enjoy it. Mrs. Bunting has been cooking for the Barrington family for thirty years."

He offered her his hand and helped her into the carriage. Once they were all seated, he continued, "I would like to speak to you, Miss Kendricks, concerning my behavior as of late."

"Oh?" Diana said in surprise.

"I've unmercifully teased you since our first meeting. A marquess simply does not act so... familiar with a young lady he does not know." He chuckled. "I could not explain why I felt the need to share in banter with you if I were asked to do so."

Diana grinned. "Then perhaps I should apologize, as well. After all, I did nothing to stop you. Instead, I joined in. Sometimes a bit of banter is a welcome distraction, wouldn't you say?"

He laughed again. "I suppose so. Now, we had an agreement concerning the sort of conversation in which we would participate. We agreed to discuss motives. Therefore, I'd like to begin now, if I may. What did you mean by embarrassing me at the dress shop?"

Placing a hand to her chest, Diana gave him an innocent look. "But, my lord, all I was doing was shopping. It was you who followed me. When I noticed your shocked expression, I only wished to be of aid. After all, you did have a book on fashion in your hands."

"A gift for a friend," he said, although he grinned as he said it. "Please, don't make me beg. Why did you put me in that situation?"

It was as if Diana had known this man her entire life. He was cordial and funny, and she felt comfortable in his presence. And it was for that very reason she decided to tell the truth.

"Our first encounter at the bookshop was not by chance," she said. "I was curious about you, you see. When you noticed me staring at you, I reached for the closest book without reading the title. I mentioned that encounter to Miss Clifton, so we returned to the bookstore so I could show her exactly what had happened. Unfortunately, you encountered me again, with that very same book in my hands."

"So, the first time was by chance," Lord Barrington said, wearing a mischievous grin. "But the second was not?"

"As I was saying," she said firmly to silence him. "I refused to be bested, so when I saw you had entered Mrs. Newberry's shop, unaware where you were, I used that moment to strike back."

The marquess threw his head back and laughed. "I must say, you've marvelous skills in the art of verbal warfare, Miss Kendricks. You had already bested me at the bookshop, and in doing so, you humbled me. But I was doubly so by your actions at the dressmaker's shop."

"Then you're not angry?"

He smiled at her. "Not in the least. For the first time in a very long time, I was happy and without worry. And it's all because of you."

Although the conversation remained lighthearted, Diana was curious about that statement. How could a marquess be unhappy with his lot? And how on earth could she be responsible for changing him so drastically?

Yet had she not had very much the same reaction upon meeting him? Had their interactions not ignited a part of her that had lain dormant for far too long?

He also makes me happy, she thought with surprise. And pleasure.

When they arrived at Penford Place, Diana was pleasantly surprised that the interior was far more lavish than its plain exterior. Despite the fact that Lord Barrington was not in residence often, the house was well-maintained, which said much about his staff.

Diana had heard tales of servants becoming slovenly when their masters were away. Her father had given the sack to footmen and maids after he learned they were skirting their responsibilities when the family had gone on holiday. Clearly those in the employ of the marquess did no such thing. If allowing the help to have time alone to spend as they wished made them more resolute, she would see hers enjoyed those same luxuries.

"We'll be in the library, Baldwin," Lord Barrington said once the butler had taken their coats. "Find us there when dinner is ready." He turned to Diana. "I believe you'll find my collection of books fairly boastable."

Diana raised an eyebrow. "Boastable? Are you certain you've read any of them?"

He laughed. "Yes, well, perhaps it's not a true word, but I do find it fits the occasion. Follow me."

The hallway down which they walked was lined with paintings of what Diana suspected were former Marquesses of Barrington.

They arrived at a closed set of double doors. "My home is over a hundred years old," the marquess said. "Reading has always been a favorite pastime for each Barrington who has resided here. In fact, they preferred it to many of the favored activities of men of the *ton*.

With a sense of grandeur, he flew open the door and stepped aside. "After you."

If Diana had been enthralled upon entering Penford Place, it was nothing to compare to how she felt upon entering the library. "You've more books than any bookshop I've encountered," she said, filling her voice with the awe she felt.

Indeed, every wall was filled floor to ceiling with shelves of books. The bookcases were so tall that one needed a ladder to reach those on the upper shelves. In the middle of the room lay a red-and-gold rug upon which sat two chairs, a small sofa, and a low table.

"Now you know why I frequent the bookshop," Lord Barrington said. "Contrary to what others may say about me, I'm there to add to my collection."

Diana walked over and touched the crimson spine of one of the tomes. "Most people are foolish," she said offhandedly. "I rarely believe rumors. Doing so is a waste of one's time."

"Hearing that pleases me more than you can know," the marquess said. His smile was warm. He walked over to a particular shelf. "These are all about the art of warfare, a subject of which I've become quite knowledgeable. Those," he pointed to the shelves above, "pertain to the sciences, and the ones at the very top are business related. They are the driest, which is why I moved them so far out of reach."

Diana could hear the pride in Lord Barrington's tone as he pointed out each genre—fiction, history, philosophy, and even architecture.

"And now, I'll show you where I house the books that have been known to cause the *ton* to revolt."

"Oh?" Diana asked, glancing at an astounded Jenny.

The marquess grinned. "Indeed. I may even be banished from England if my peers learn I possess such tomes."

"Perhaps..." Diana swallowed hard. "Perhaps it would be best if you not show them to me, then, my lord. I mean... is the subject appropriate for a young lady?"

She had heard rumors of books that included the foulest language and men and women copulating, with explicit illustrations to boot! She had no interest whatsoever in seeing such rubbish. Maybe coming tonight had been a mistake.

Allow your heart to keep guiding you. It will reveal the truth.

The marquess chuckled. "Judge for yourself, Miss Kendricks."

Reluctantly, Diana joined him before a particular shelf.

"These are books on the art of magic," he said. "Some instruct while others have been touched by great magicians and now are true articles of magical powers." He removed one of his black gloves and pulled a book from the shelf. "This one contains a hidden drawing of a horse. Tell me what you see." Holding the book flat in one hand, he riffled the pages with the other.

Diana's eyes went wide. "I see... a white horse standing in the middle of a river, rising onto its rear legs." She reached over and turned a page. "But that is nothing more than a series of drawings on the corner of the pages. That's not magic."

"Once again, your mind serves you well, Miss Kendricks," Lord Barrington said, smiling. "That is not magic. But this is." He frowned and stared at some distant point behind her.

Diana and Jenny glanced over their shoulders.

"I thought I heard Baldwin," the marquess said. "Silly me. Well, it doesn't matter. Now, allow me to show you my magic." He stretched his neck, moving his head to one side and then the other. Then he took a deep breath and exhaled, slowly blowing on the book as he riffled the pages once more.

To her surprise, the horse moved again, but this time he was brown rather than white, and its head touched a blue sky while rear legs disappeared into tall, green grass.

"That's impossible!" Diana explained, Jenny echoing the same at her side. "How did you do that?"

Did magic truly exist? She would have said it did not—could not—if she had not seen it with her own eyes!

"Would you like to look?" he asked, holding the book out to her.

Diana took a step back. "I... thank you, my lord, but I'd prefer to keep my distance from that." Who knew what sort of magic it would do to her if she touched such a book!

With a laugh, Lord Barrington said, "Magic cannot harm you, Miss Kendricks. Not my kind of magic, anyway. But if it eases your worry, I can assure you the book is not cursed, nor is it dangerous in any way. I purchased it in London only last year."

"But you said it was touched by a great magician," Diana said. "Are you saying that great magicians reside in London?" She would have thought such men preferred exotic places, like India or China.

The marquess chuckled again. "Storytelling is a part of the act," he explained. "There are no great magicians. It's all an illusion."

Diana frowned. "But that makes no sense. What you just showed me..." She shook her head. "I'm confused and feel so foolish."

"You should not," he said. "Here, allow me to demonstrate." Lord Barrington riffled the pages, and the picture of the white horse in a stream moved. "Now, while you were distracted, I did something."

"Distracted? We watched every move you made."

Jenny gasped. "When you stared behind us! We looked away, too."

"Exactly right, Miss Clifton. While you looked away, I merely flipped over the book like this." He turned the book to the back cover, which looked like the front, and riffled the pages again. This time, the brown horse moved.

"I feel tricked!" Diana said, laughing. "Yet at the same time, I find it fascinating." Then a realization hit her. "Your name! The Marquess of Magic. You were not given that name because you study the dark arts nor because you kiss women and then disappear. Rather it's because you're a master of illusion."

She was so excited that her words tumbled out quickly. It took her tongue a moment to tell her mind what she had said. It was no wonder Lord Barrington was laughing!

"I'm sorry. I didn't mean to—"

"You've nothing for which to apologize, Miss Kendricks." Lord Barrington replaced the book on the shelf. "As a child, I performed my first illusion using a coin. A friend of my father anointed me the Marquess of Magic because I was so deft at making the coin disappear, and it has remained since."

"Be that as it may," Diana said, "repeating such terrible rumors is unbecoming, my lord. Especially to the very man to whom they pertain. I do hope you don't think poorly of me." She readied herself to be asked to leave.

Instead, he smiled. "Miss Kendricks, you only repeated what you heard. We all do that from time to time. I'm sure your intentions were not ill. I hope that by showing you this simple illusion you'll no longer believe such terrible things about me."

"I assure you, my lord. I've never thought ill of you, but I'm pleased to know the truth."

"Then I'll no longer be annoyed by the woman who bested me in a dressmaker's shop. In fact, I would be honored to call you my friend."

Diana's cheeks heated. "I would like that."

"Good. And now that we are friends, I say we address ourselves less formally." He turned to Jenny. "As Miss Kendricks' chaperone, will you approve such a step away from decorum?"

Jenny's grin answered before her words. "Oh yes, my lord. I see no problem there."

Lord Barrington grinned. "Then you'll refer to me as simply Barrington, and I'll address you as Miss Diana and Miss Jenny. If you don't mind, of course, Miss Clifton."

Jenny was red to her ears. "Not at all, my lord."

"Barrington," he corrected. "And are you in agreement, Miss Diana?"

A pleasant shiver ran through Diana's body as she said, "Indeed, I am, Barrington."

Her heart was aflutter as she wondered about the day she could address him simply as James.

She paused. Jenny had been correct. The man did cause Diana's breath to catch. When her eyes locked on to his, for the first time, Diana wanted a man to kiss her. But not just any man, rather the one standing before her. The man who was both handsome and kind with a spirit that was soft and welcoming.

"My lord," the butler said, startling Diana from her revelry, "dinner is served."

"Thank you, Baldwin." Barrington rubbed his gloved hands together. "Shall we eat and share in conversation as friends do?"

Diana swallowed hard as she placed a hand on his proffered arm. Oh, she could remain at his side forever!

CHAPTER ELEVEN

Dinner was perfect, made more so by the conversation James shared with Miss Diana. Everything about the young woman enthralled him, from her opinions on various topics to the way her cheeks turned a shade of crimson whenever he smiled at her. He could have stared at her forever.

"After the sleight of hand with the coin," he was explaining as the trio withdrew to the parlor, "I purchased my first book filled with all sorts of illusions. Then another, and then another. Despite the irritation on my skin, my hands move quickly."

"It's all so fascinating," Miss Diana repeated for the dozenth time. "Who do you believe was the greatest magician? And does he still live?"

James smiled. "No, *she* died some years ago."

"She?" Miss Diana asked, her eyes wide.

"Indeed. Clara Moonlight, a pseudonym, of course, but she is rumored to have been the greatest." He walked over to a bookcase that sat along one wall, the only one in the room. "Now, I would like to show you one last illusion." He picked up a candelabra and handed it to her. "We'll be needing this."

Miss Jenny leaned forward and narrowed her eyes as if trying to read the titles. "Do these books contain more magic?" She appeared fearful of touching them.

"No," James replied, "but the bookcase itself does. Do I have your word—and I do mean both of you—you will keep what I'm about to reveal to you to yourselves?"

"Of course," Miss Diana replied.

"I'll not say a word," Miss Jenny agreed, her eyes nearly covering her face.

Pressing down with his foot on a hidden lever located on the bottom shelf, James slid the case to the right.

Miss Diana gasped. "It's a hidden room!"

"It's far more than a room," James said, grinning as he took the candelabra from her. "It's a secret passageway. Follow me."

He led the two young women into the passageway, which was as tall as the room they had just left and just wide enough to walk through, without his shoulders touching the walls.

"When my grandfather's father, Phillip Barrington, commissioned this house to be built, he insisted on having the secret passageways included without them being added to the building's design."

"You mean there are more?" Miss Diana asked in surprise.

"Oh, yes," James replied. "And he never explained his reasoning. Some have conjectured that he was involved in illicit trade and used them to hide contraband. Or he used them as a way to escape if the authorities converged on the house. Others say they were meant to be used by the servants as a means of navigating the house unseen. But none of those rumors were true. It was his love of magic that made him build them."

"Do you mean to say that every room has access to the passage-ways?" Diana asked.

"Indeed. All except the dining room and those rooms used for stor-age. Which proves he was not hiding contraband, not if he could not reach the places items would be stored." He came to a stop and moved aside a small piece of wood attached to the wall. "Now, look through here."

Miss Diana closed one eye, leaned close to the wall, and then laughed. "It's the drawing room! Jenny, you must look!"

As she took a step back to make room for her friend, Miss Diana inadvertently pressed herself against James, and his heart began to thud in his chest.

"My... my apologies, my lord," Miss Diana said, her voice breathy.

"No need to apologize, I assure you," James said with a shaky laugh. Even in the dark passageway, he could smell her lavender soap overwhelming his senses. And his thoughts.

"I can see the sofa and the fireplace..." Miss Jenny was saying. But James ignored her. Only Miss Diana filled his notice.

Before he knew what he was doing, he placed a finger beneath her chin and lifted her head. Candlelight flickered in her innocent blue eyes, and that urge became primal, primitive. Without thinking, he leaned down and pressed his lips to hers. Her lips were soft and tasted of grapes from the wine she had consumed at dinner.

A deep yearning inside him burst forth, not lust but rather a true sensation he had never experienced before. Passion, hunger, desire, a myriad of sensations filled him. Yet what made it all the more exciting was how Miss Diana expressed them in equal measure.

Although he could have kissed her for hours, rational thinking returned. He pulled away reluctantly, and she sighed.

"That was lovely," she whispered.

"A maid just entered the room!" Miss Jenny said as she pulled away from the wall. "May we look at another?"

Thankful she had not witnessed his impropriety, James nodded. "Of course. Follow me."

For the next twenty minutes, they meandered through the passageway, stopping at each peephole to look into another room. Each had its own hidden door—the back of a wardrobe in a bedroom, a long mirror attached to the wall in another—and he showed them every one of them.

"How many have been shown these passageways?" Miss Diana asked. "They cannot be very secret if everyone knows about them."

James laughed. "I have few callers, and of those, I choose only those I'm certain I can trust to see them."

When they stepped back into the parlor, Miss Jenny walked over to a table and picked up a book. "May I look through this book, my lord?"

she asked. "It's about the fashion of the Tudor period. The wide skirts have always fascinated me."

"By all means," James replied. "It belongs to my mother, but you're likely to get more enjoyment out of it than she has."

Jenny frowned. "Does she not enjoy the subject?"

He shrugged. "She left it behind, did she not?"

Smiling, Jenny walked over to one of the armchairs and sat in it, the book in her lap.

When James was sure Miss Jenny was otherwise occupied, he lowered his voice and said, "I wish to apologize for earlier. I cannot explain my actions, and I'll do my best not to act so improperly again."

"There is no need to apologize," Miss Diana replied, her voice as low as his. "I imagine it's just another part of your magic. At least, it felt magical to me."

That beast inside him roared again, and he had to muster all his strength not to pull her into his arms once more. To discover the woman she was would be a marvelous exploration!

"Why are you here in Chatsworth?" she asked, breaking him from his illicit thoughts. "Will you not be leaving for the Season soon?"

He wanted to tell her the truth. It was one thing to share the secret passageways but quite another to trust someone he had just met with his true secrets. Stonebrook had betrayed him within months. Perhaps he could be honest with her once he knew her better. Now, however, was far too risky.

"I'll have to miss this Season, I'm afraid," he said. "I've some pressing matters I must attend to." Seeing a frown form on those beautiful lips, he added, "But if I were to attend, I'd wish to enjoy it with you."

"Oh?" she said, the frown dropping and a smile taking its place. Her cheeks turned a delectable pink.

James considered all he had endured over the last few months. Not subjecting himself to the obligations of the London Season for the time being had eased his worries somewhat. In the past, he had received the many invitations to various balls and dinners. For a moment, he allowed himself to imagine enjoying himself with Miss Diana at his side.

"Yes, indeed," he replied. "I'm sure you would wear the finest gown, one that would complement your blue eyes. To have a lovely creature such as yourself beside me would be an honor. I would claim every dance with you for myself. If any man were to speak to you, I would have no choice but to interrupt and send him away. And in between all that, I would find time to buy you the most wonderful pieces of jewelry. Perhaps a gold necklace with a blue sapphire to match your eyes."

Spoiling this woman would make him so very happy!

As she looked up at him, his heart thudded in his chest once more. Her eyes were the color of a summer sky.

"I don't need *gifts* to spend time with you, my lord."

James had to take a step back at her icy tone.

"Although I can appreciate whatever dilemma keeps you here, I do wish you the best in resolving it.

Confusion filled his mind. What had he said that was wrong?

Then it dawned on him. He had offended her in the worst way! She believed he wanted to *pay* her to be with him!

"I... I only meant that in jest," he said, saying the first excuse that came to mind. A terrible excuse, but once spoken, he could not take it back. "I meant no offense, I assure you! But if you were on my arm, there would be nothing that I would refuse you." Her frown deepened, which in turn, made his frustration grow tenfold. "I only mean that you deserve nice things. Is that not what every woman wants?"

"It's getting late," she said stiffly. "Jenny, we should be going."

James reached out and grasped Miss Diana by the arm. "We were having a lovely evening, but it's clear I've disappointed you somehow."

"Not at all, my lord." Her tone could have ironed the wrinkles out of a shirt. "It's just that Mrs. Rutley will worry if we're not home early."

She looked down at the gloved hand that gripped her arm, and he released her. She gave him a small smile and walked out of the room.

James followed the young ladies to the foyer, where Baldwin helped them into their coats. What he wanted to do was escort them all the way back to the school. After what had just occurred, however, he was unsure if she would accept his offer to do so.

He understood how he offended her initially, but his explanation should have cleared up any misunderstanding. Yet she remained aloof.

Once she was seated on the bench inside the carriage, he leaned forward and said, "May I call on you later in the week? Perhaps Friday?"

"I don't know if Mrs. Rutley will allow it, my lord," Miss Diana responded, her cool tone still in place. "But you are welcome to make the request. Though I must warn you, my schedule is quite full."

James nodded and closed the carriage door. As it trundled down the drive, he drew his coat in tighter. There was something about that young woman, something magical, that made him feel alive.

The kiss they shared had been wonderful. The idea of going to London made her smile. Yet the offer of a gift had offended her? It made little sense.

He sighed and returned to the house. Perhaps this was for the best. After all, he had his hands full with Amelia.

CHAPTER TWELVE

"Would you like me to send for a rug maker, my lord?" Baldwin asked James. "I believe I can find one willing to call from London."

James turned and scowled at the butler. "Why would I need a rug maker?"

"Forgive me for saying so, my lord, but you've been pacing the room so much over the past two days that I'm afraid the one you have is wearing thin. And once the rug is gone, you may want to consider getting your shoes resoled."

Despite his frustration, James could not help but laugh. "Is that your way of saying that I'm spending too much time worrying?"

Baldwin gave him an affronted look. "I would never presume to be so forward, my lord. But you have been a bit out of sorts, far too much for a man of your age. Perhaps I can offer you a drink to help ease your nerves."

"Yes. And then I'd like to seek your advice."

The butler gave him a nod before going to the decanters to pour the brandy.

James took a seat as he waited.

"Now, my lord," Baldwin said as he handed James his drink, "what is it that troubles you?"

"It's Miss Kendricks, the young lady who came to dinner two nights ago. I've never met a woman wiser or more beautiful. And although it may seem silly, it's as if I've known her all my life rather than the few short weeks since we met in the bookshop."

"I don't believe it's silly, my lord."

"But it is! I know nothing about her, and yet I feel this way? It makes no sense, whatsoever!"

Baldwin sniffed. "I've known you since you were born, my lord. Yet I don't know everything about you."

"You know what I mean," James snapped.

"I do," the butler replied. "Are you saying that you'd like to become better acquainted with the young lady?"

James balanced the glass on his knee. "Partly. The problem is, I offended her. Now I'm worried she may never allow me in her presence again." He sighed. "No, I'm sure of it."

Baldwin nodded. "I see. I'll not ask you how you offended the young lady, but how egregious was the offense?"

"It depends on which offense you mean," James said with a sigh. "The first she claimed caused her no harm." That was the impromptu kiss, and he was not certain she had absolved him of his forwardness despite her words to the contrary. "The second made her leave with proclamations that she was unavailable for the foreseeable future." That happened after he spoke of having her on his arm for the Season, and how he would lavish her with gifts. Which offended her more—being on his arm or the gifts—remained to be seen.

"Perhaps you can send her a letter," the butler offered.

"It's a thought to consider," James said. Miss Diana had referred him to her headmistress. Why, then, would he expect her to even open, let alone read, any letters he was to send?

"That is a dilemma, my lord. But at least you'll be given the opportunity to have your say."

James waved a frustrated hand and downed his brandy. "How can I do that if I don't know what the problem is in the first place? I cannot work out what went wrong in a letter, Baldwin. Written words can be easily misconstrued. It would be best if I met with her in person."

"May I speak freely, my lord?" Baldwin asked, his hands clasped behind him.

"Of course. After all, I'm seeking advice. Let's be as if we were friends sharing in drinks at a pub. I must have the truth, no matter how much it hurts."

Baldwin took a deep breath as if preparing himself for battle. "You and I have had varied conversations in the past, my lord, and have shared in a variety of subjects. As far as I know, I've never offended you. Is that true?"

James eyed the butler. "No, not yet. Go on, out with it."

Shifting on his feet, Baldwin inhaled again. "You've a young lady who is with child hiding in the guest cottage. That alone is enough to monopolize a man's time. But now you wish to pursue Miss Kendricks, and after you've sworn off calling on anyone until the issue with Miss Lansing is resolved. Am I correct in saying so?"

James understood the butler's point. "Indeed. I could not have said it better myself."

"Then you have... how does the saying go? Perhaps you've bitten off more than you can chew?"

Derisive laughter bubbled up inside James. "You're an astute man, Baldwin. As for Amelia, I can handle that situation without Miss Kendricks learning of it. I'll simply have to keep them apart."

But was it worth the risk? If Miss Diana learned about Amelia, James would not blame her if she chose to flee and never see him again. An image of Miss Diana came to mind, and he knew he could not be apart from her.

"I'll continue calling on Miss Kendricks. If she allows me to do so, that is. If I do choose to become a suitor, or if we moved toward courtship, it would happen well past the birth of Amelia's child." He grinned at the butler. "The truth is, I wish to seek Miss Kendricks's company because it's far better than yours."

Baldwin chuckled. "I would hope so, my lord. What fun would it be to spend time with me? I'm a fossil of a man. But I believe you've more than an interest in the young lady's company. I see the way you look at her, my lord, and there is more there than even you recognize."

James frowned. "I'm not seeking to bed her, Baldwin."

That affronted look returned. "No, no, my lord! I don't mean *that*! But you do have a romantic interest in her. I'm sure of it."

"Your sight has become as poor as your hearing," James said with a cynical laugh. "I admit that I find her captivating, but it's a little early to consider the possibility of marriage."

It was not as if James was against marriage, for he had long desired a suitable companion. But he and Miss Diana knew too little about one another. Yet their attraction was strong. No, it was powerful.

The butler walked over and took James's empty glass. "My eyes do not fail me, my lord. I've seen this before. With your parents."

"My parents?" James asked, surprised. "My parents despised one another!"

"They did, but not in the beginning, my lord," Baldwin said as he poured another measure of brandy. "Before they married, your father sought out your mother. One would have thought they would be happy forever. Or at least content."

Although they never argued in his presence it was not until his later teen years that he began to grow suspicious. During his early years, they had provided a happy life for him. Whether it was trips to London, journeying to the coast, or even simple walks around the estate, he had no doubt they adored him. They had given him a wonderful childhood of which many children could have only dreamed. Learning they despised one another had come as a shock.

Theirs had been an arranged marriage, agreed upon by his grandparents, years before his parents were old enough to know better. With his father's passing, whatever reason they'd held grudges had died with him.

"What happened?" James asked, accepting the glass. "I must admit, seeing them grow apart always concerned me. But how could something so wonderful turn into two people unwilling to even look at one another?"

Baldwin shrugged. "I don't know much about matters of love, my lord. Perhaps I'm mistaken and they never loved each other. Whatever they had, though, they lost within the first few years of marriage. It was a pity, really, for a hut filled with happiness is far better than a castle without." Then Baldwin offered a smile. "Regardless, my lord, they did love you. Whenever I saw the three of you together, they were at their happiest. You all were."

"Thank you, Baldwin. I, too, look back with fond memories of the three of us together. It's as you said, they were at their happiest. No one could counterfeit that."

"I could not agree more, my lord."

As he sipped at his brandy, James wondered what had happened between his parents. Yet he pushed it aside for now. He had other, more immediate issues that needed his attention. And that included his desire to see Miss Diana again.

As Baldwin headed to the door, James stood. "What do you suggest I do about Miss Kendricks? I would like to make things right between us. Should I seek her out or leave her be?"

Baldwin turned to face him. "Frankly speaking, my lord, if you don't approach her to learn what went wrong, I believe you'll regret it."

"But what if I do and she rejects my offer of apology? What then?"

"Then you'll know for certain if she is the one for you, my lord," Baldwin said. "One way or another, you'll know, and that will save you —and the rugs—from ruin." And with that, the butler dipped his head and withdrew.

James smiled. Baldwin was always the best source of advice.

Was it true that he had feelings for Miss Diana? How could a man be so full of desire for a woman in such a short time? Not the physical desire that had him kissing her in the secret passageway but a desire to be close to her, to know more about her. The way she looked at him and her sharp wit were magical.

An image of his mother ignoring his father came to mind. Or was it his father who refused to acknowledge the existence of his mother? Either way, many dinners were spent in utter silence. Would he and Miss Diana travel down that same path? Miss Diana would make a wonderful friend. That, he had already determined. But would an attempt at romance put an end to that friendship?

Well, he would not find the answer in the bottom of his brandy glass. What he needed was to write and request to call on Miss Diana. If she refused to listen, at least he would have cleared his conscience, and he could rid himself of any embarrassment he had caused her. Yes, that was what he would do.

As he rose, Amelia entered the room, making him start.

"I'm sorry to bother you, but may I speak to you a moment?" she asked. James nodded and rushed over to help her to a chair. "I know my presence here must remain secret, and I would never want to threaten that. But remaining in the guest cottage has become so mundane. I'd like your permission to go for a carriage ride. Doctor Humphreys says it should be safe as long as I don't travel far, and I promise to keep the curtains closed." She gave him a small smile. "I don't mean to sound ungrateful, for I truly am, but—"

"I don't blame you for wanting to go out," James interrupted. "But I cannot help but worry that someone will see you."

Amelia nodded and dropped her gaze. "I understand."

James considered her dilemma. Her situation was difficult enough but being unable to leave was as bad as being a prisoner. Even if her prison offered luxury.

"How about this," he said, placing a hand on her arm and smiling. "I've pressing matters to which I must attend. Matters of business. But I'll free up my schedule in, say, three days, so we can take a carriage ride together. Now, we'll have to stick to the country. No traveling to the village. Can you agree to that?"

With a wide smile, Amelia replied, "Oh yes, thank you. And we won't have to be gone long. The baby will not appreciate the bumpy roads. Nor will I, for that matter." She rubbed her lower back with a laugh.

"I'll make sure we only take the good roads," James said. "Now, if you'll excuse me, I have a letter to write."

He helped her stand, and she kissed his cheek. "Thank you. For everything."

James nodded and made his way to the study. He did not like the fact that Amelia had to hide, but soon the baby would be born and all would be set to rights.

And if he was able to right the wrongs with Miss Diana, as well, the next few months would be all the better.

CHAPTER THIRTEEN

hy is it men believe women can be treated like chattel? Diana wondered as she lay staring at the ceiling above her bed. Dinner with Lord Barrington had been magical, and when he kissed her, the world erupted around her, nearly sending her body asunder. She had felt so alive for the first time in her life while struggling to comprehend the emotions that had risen in her soul.

To know he wanted her at his side during the Season sparked her imagination, for that suggestion could only lead to courtship, could it not?

Yet, his interest was not simply to have her at his side. No, he wished to parade her about like some trophy. A prized mare to make his peers green with envy. At the moment she came to accept that the possibility of marriage could be a pleasant thought, it came crashing down around her ears.

The offer of gifts had stung her. Just like her father. Just like every other blasted man who walked the earth, who believed women could be bought, Lord Barrington had proven he was no different.

Despite this catastrophe, the curiosity as to what burdens he carried still tickled the back of her mind. Granted, they had known one another a short time, but Diana had to admit his unwillingness to confide in her saddened her.

"Mrs. Rutley asked me to remind you that Mr. Stonebrook will be here soon," Ruth said from the doorway. She frowned and walked into the room. "You look miserable. What is troubling you?"

Diana sighed and sat. Upon Diana's return from dinner four days earlier, Mrs. Rutley had informed her that Mr. Stonebrook would be calling on her today. After what had taken place at Penford Place, Diana came close to asking the headmistress to send word that she was unavailable. Yet, Mr. Stonebrook was pleasant enough company. *He* did not offer to pay her for her time!

That did not mean she would give up spinsterhood for him. "Mr. Stonebrook is nice enough, but I don't wish for his company."

Ruth sat on the edge of the bed, not caring the skirts of her pink day dress bundled beneath her. "It's quite easy, Diana. Just tell him you don't wish to see him once he arrives. Or I can tell him if you'd prefer."

The sly grin Ruth wore made Diana shake her head. "My father wants me to allow him to call, and the last thing I want is one of his letters informing me that I've disappointed him when he learns I've sent away Mr. Stonebrook." She sighed again. "Even if I do meet with him, I can't help but wonder if it will be enough to please my father. Nothing I do seems to make him happy."

But he does brag about you, even if you don't hear it, she reminded herself.

Ruth leaned forward. "You've two men calling on you. Is that not what you wanted?"

"Of course not," Diana said indignantly. "Oh, but what does it matter? All men are the same." She absently picked at a piece of lint on her blanket. "I wanted nothing to do with any man, but after my encounter with Lord Barrington, I changed my mind. Then Father and his request that I speak to Mr. Stonebrook..." Her sigh was the heaviest yet. "I should have been resolute in my decision."

You've become a silly goose, Diana Kendricks! she chastised herself. All these sighs were better suited for half-witted, lovestruck women. No one could describe Diana in such a sentimental way! Not until today.

"I'll marry one day," Ruth said. "But not some fancy marquess. My husband will be the captain of a ship!"

"But why a captain? Why would you want to spend your life bobbing around the world on a ship?"

Ruth grinned as she pushed back her red hair. "To take me away on adventures, of course. I've heard all sorts of stories about America. Maybe I'll go there. And Theodosia and Unity want to go with me, too."

Theodosia Renwick and Unity Ancell attended the school with Diana, and they were two of the nine women who were a part of the Sisterhood of Secrets. Although Theodosia was taller than Unity, both had brown curly hair and large brown eyes and considered themselves twins, despite the fact they were not related.

As far as Diana was concerned, all this talk of travels and adventures was all nonsense. Men would always stand in the way of any woman hoping to have their own life. Every day, a woman's hopes and dreams were pulled down and buried by one man or another. It was sickening!

But who was Diana to do the same to Ruth?

"Just you wait and see," Ruth was saying. "I'll live a life only found in books. You may come if you'd like."

Diana laughed. "Thank you, but I've no desire to travel. I would be happiest living in a flat or a cottage alone. Not even my parents would care if I chose such a life."

Then a thought came to mind. "Ruth, why don't your parents come to see you?"

Ruth's smile fell, and Diana regretted asking the question. Ruth never spoke of her family or her life outside of the school, and no one had ever seen her parents. There had to be a reason, but it was not for Diana to interfere in someone else's business.

Regret filled Diana. "I'm sorry. I should not have asked."

Standing, Ruth pasted a smile on her lips. "We should go downstairs. Would you like me to act as your chaperone? I've no idea where Jenny is."

"That would be lovely," Diana replied as she snaked an arm through that of her friend.

Ruth stopped at the door and turned to face Diana. "Since we're in the Sisterhood, I'd like to share a secret with you."

Diana grinned. "I'd like that. And you know you can trust me. If you want me to keep whatever you say to myself, I shall."

Ruth nodded. "My parents don't care a fig about me."

"I know you feel—"

"It's not what I feel, Diana. It's what I know. But please, don't tell the other girls."

"I promise I never will," Diana said.

As they descended the main staircase, Diana saw Mrs. Shepherd speaking with Mr. Stonebrook.

"I'll go fetch her... oh look, here she is."

Diana gripped her skirts and curtsied. "Mr. Stonebrook. And this is my very good friend, Miss Ruth Lockhart."

He responded with a bow and a smile. "A pleasure, I'm sure. I appreciate you allowing me to call on you."

"Would you like some tea?" Diana asked. "I can have a tray brought up."

"Actually, I was thinking that we could go for a short stroll," Mr. Stonebrook said. "The sun is shining, and it's relatively warm for this time of year." He turned to Mrs. Shepherd. "If that is acceptable, of course."

Mrs. Shepherd stood with her arms crossed beneath her breasts, that stern expression on her face she always wore when one of the girls had a gentleman caller. "As long as Miss Ruth acts as her chaperone, I can't see why not. Just be sure to wear a wrap. This is December. Relatively warm is still cold. We don't need any reason for you to want to keep her warm now, do we?"

Ruth covered her laugh with a cough, but Diana stared in horror at the cook. "I'm sure Mr. Stonebrook will be more than a gentleman, Mrs. Shepherd. Won't you?"

"On my honor," Mr. Stonebrook replied.

Diana could not read his reaction to Mrs. Shepherd's comment. He had proven to be a kind soul, and the last thing she wanted was for him to be offended by the overprotective cook.

The air was indeed chilled, but not frigid, as they walked out to the portico at the front of the house.

"How was your time in London?" Diana asked as they began their stroll.

"Busy, as usual," Mr. Stonebrook replied. "My mind tends to wander when I'm there, often with thoughts of being in the company of lovely young ladies such as yourself."

Diana did not miss Ruth rolling her eyes but said nothing. She did not want to draw Mr. Stonebrook's attention to that fact. "That's very kind of you to say."

"I spoke to your father again," he said. "He's very pleased I'm enjoying your company and asked me to send you his best."

His best? What an odd thing for her father to say. Not once had he ever sent such a message, either in his own hand or by word through someone else. Perhaps allowing Mr. Stonebrook to call on her had made him see the young lady she now was. Maybe she had allowed her anger to blind her to what her father truly felt for her.

They neared the tree where Diana and the others made their pact.

"Miss Kendricks, you seem distant today," Mr. Stonebrook said. "Is there anything wrong?"

"She's just fine," Ruth said before Diana could respond. "She's just tired is all. We didn't sleep well last night on account of Jenny's snoring."

Diana forced a small smile. "Will you excuse us for a moment?" she asked as she gripped Ruth by the arm and pulled her a few steps away. "What are you doing?"

"There's something about that man I don't like," Ruth said in a harsh whisper. "I can't place what it is exactly, but I don't think he's as nice as he pretends to be."

"How can you say that?" Diana demanded. "I was there when the Chatsworth Theater applauded his generosity. Now please, no more comments from you!"

They returned to Mr. Stonebrook, and Diana gave him an apologetic smile. "Forgive my rudeness. We had a few matters to resolve. But it's all settled now."

Mr. Stonebrook chuckled. "No forgiveness needed," he said, offering his arm. "Let's continue our stroll."

They walked toward the path that led to the back gardens, a corridor of sorts between the side of the school building and a hedgerow wide enough for three people to walk unhampered.

"I must admit, Miss Kendricks, I've thought of you often this past week." He glanced at her. "Am I being too bold in saying so?"

His words were kind, and any other woman would have taken them as romantic. Yet Diana did not. As much as Lord Barrington had hurt her, he was like a constant itch in the back of her mind. But she did not want to make Mr. Stonebrook feel awkward.

"It's not bold at all," she replied. "I, too, have thought of you."

When his smile widened, she stifled a groan. Why had she lied? Well, not lied outright, for he *had* entered her mind, just not often. If she were completely honest, she would have said rarely.

"Then I'm glad I spoke up," he said. "You must understand, when a man is in the presence of a woman such as you, he can become very... nervous."

Diana came to a stop in front of the stable. "What do you mean?"

"You're an intelligent and lovely young lady. I find it remarkable that you'd allow someone like me to call on you. After all, women tend to find me... shall we say, unappealing?"

Diana's jaw dropped in shock. "Mr. Stonebrook, I find gentlemen such as yourself quite admirable. Whatever horrible things other women may have said about you, I can assure you they are untrue. Those women are the ones who are unappealing."

He took a step closer and gazed down at her. "Are you saying that I am desirable to women? That you might consider a man like me as a possible suitor?"

Diana's breath caught in her throat, but not in the same way it had when Lord Barrington stood so close to her. Then she had wanted to move even closer to him. Now, she wanted to take a step back.

"Well, yes, I suppose so," she said, confused at his question.

"A woman like you is like a rare gemstone. Many men search their entire lives for it, but only a select few will ever appreciate it. Thank you for allowing me to appreciate you, Miss Kendricks."

His words were flattering. Too flattering. She had made a mistake in encouraging him and had to rectify the situation. And soon!

"I'm thankful to have a friend like you," she said, emphasizing the word "friend."

He stared at her for several moments, his features devoid of any emotion whatsoever.

"I should be going," he said, a sudden smile blossoming on his lips. "I'll send my card soon so we can do this again. If you'd like to, that is."

Did she wish to have him call on her again? If the decision were hers, she would have said no. Yet if agreeing pleased her father, it would be well worth the short stroll. It was not as if she would be dining with him. Plus, the marquess was no longer a part of her life, not after what he had done. What could it hurt to agree?

"Yes, that would be lovely," she said. "I find your company enjoyable." Enjoyable was a bit much, but she did not despise the time they spent together.

"I promise you'll find many things about me enjoyable, Miss Kendricks," he said in a husky tone. Was there an underlining meaning to his words? "Until next time." He took her hand and kissed her knuckles. Then he gave Ruth a small nod. "Miss Lockhart."

Diana walked with Ruth to the portico and watched as the carriage pulled away.

"He's sweet," Diana said. "I can't imagine the two of us falling in love, but perhaps we can be friends. What do you think?"

Ruth shook her head. "He wants far more than friendship, Diana. I'd beware of him if I were you."

Diana gaped. "Are you implying what I think you are?" She clicked her tongue. "Mr. Stonebrook has been nothing but kind. Not once has he shown any sign of impropriety."

"If you say so," Ruth said, shrugging. "But whatever you do, choose either him or the marquess. Managing two men will become much more difficult as time moves forward."

CHAPTER FOURTEEN

A fter too many hours inside, Diana always found the gardens of
the school a lovely place to be alone with her thoughts, and
today was no exception.

Since returning from the home of Lord Barrington, she had kept
busy with various activities in an attempt to ignore her feelings for
him, but to no avail. No matter how hard she tried, she could not push
him from her thoughts. Even while strolling with Mr. Stonebrook, the
marquess had appeared in her mind without invitation.

Vapor escaped her mouth, and she pulled her wrap tighter to ward
off the cold. How had she gotten herself into this mess? What had
happened to her desire to run her own life? Spinsterhood would allow
her to do just that. As if she were a ship on the ocean driven by a
wayward wind, Lord Barrington had burst into her life, changing the
course of her future forever.

Yet, the kiss they shared had been as much of an illusion as that
which the marquess had performed with the book. It had been unex-
pected, thrilling, and had sent her heart to pounding as it had never
done before. Never would she have thought a single kiss would have
changed her, but it had. In one breath, she had been willing to give
into the storm that was Lord Barrington.

But now she lay bobbing in the ocean, her sails hanging. Because he had wanted to buy her time. Buy her interest. Buy *her*. Why did men believe all women had to be bribed to get what they wanted? Oh, he had said his offer was done in jest, but she doubted he was telling the truth.

"There you are, Diana," Mrs. Rutley said, startling Diana from her thoughts. "I thought you were upstairs with Jenny and Ruth."

"I needed some time alone," Diana said. "I'm afraid my mind is muddled."

"Is that so?" Mrs. Rutley asked. "This wouldn't have to do with Mr. Stonebrook, would it? Or perhaps your thoughts are on Lord Barrington. Is there anything I can do to help?"

Diana sighed. "I don't know. Mr. Stonebrook is pleasant enough, but if he never called again, I would not be disappointed. Dinner with Lord Barrington was wonderful, and I was pleased to learn that many of the rumors surrounding him are untrue. Yet, I also learned he's no different from any other men." She turned to the headmistress. "Are men all the same?"

Mrs. Rutley chuckled. "In some regard, yes. But you must be more specific if I'm to help."

"Lord Barrington said something that upset me," Diana replied. "So when he asked if he could call again, I made excuses. Now I'm torn. I want him to call, but I don't." She blew out her breath in frustration. "Oh, Mrs. Rutley, I've no idea what I want!"

Mrs. Rutley's brow knitted in thought. "I think you should allow him to call. Perhaps you should give him a chance to explain himself. I'm sure whatever he said, whatever upset you, can be resolved if you'll simply listen."

Diana considered this advice. Perhaps Mrs. Rutley was right. Plus, if they were able to meet again, she would be able to ask him certain questions that had been tugging at her thoughts.

"Yes, I'll go now and write to him."

Mrs. Rutley smiled. "There is no need. He's already here. Why don't I have him join you out here? I'd be happy to chaperone if you would like." She turned away without waiting for Diana to respond.

Diana stared wide-eyed after the headmistress. Lord Barrington was here? What had compelled him to call without sending a card first? She glanced down at the simple blue day dress she wore. Why could she have not chosen the green and white dress? Or even the yellow with the printed white daisies?

Well, nothing could be done about it now. The sound of footsteps had her straightening her posture. Lord Barrington walked beside Mrs. Rutley, who stopped several paces away to give them some privacy.

"My apologies for calling without sending word ahead, Miss Diana," the marquess said. "And on a Sunday, no less." His cheeks were red from the cold, which said he had likely come by horse rather than carriage.

Diana jutted out her chin. "You're here now. What can I do for you?"

"I must admit, I've been unable to sleep since our dinner together. You left my home upset about something. I would like to right whatever wrong I did."

Diana sniffed. Would he propose to offer her more gifts? Or would he offer some sort of excuse for his behavior? "I'm listening."

"From time to time, everyone finds him or herself caught in one sort of difficulty or another. And we usually bring it upon ourselves. I surely did."

"You mentioned you were working through troubles. Are they so great?"

Lord Barrington nodded. "Unfortunately, yes. But I don't wish to place my burdens upon you." He shifted on his feet. "It seems I perturbed you with my talk of spending time together during the Season. May I ask why?"

For a moment, Diana considered sharing what was on her heart but chose not to do so. "Like you, I keep my troubles to myself." If he did not wish to trust her, why should she trust him?

"But I must understand what I did wrong if I'm to not do it again."

"One day I'll tell you. But today is not that day."

He sighed. "Well, whatever I said, I can assure you that I need nothing more than to have you at my side. Perhaps one day, we'll both be willing to share our secrets. When we've come to know one another better."

Heat scorched her cheeks. "I hope so."

"I will tell this as a way to open negotiations. I made a terrible mistake, and I'm doing what I can to correct it. But spending time with you has eased my distress. I find your company enlightening, and I cannot imagine any other woman with whom I'd like to spend time."

"I find your company welcoming, as well," Diana said, the warmth spreading to her insides.

They stood staring at one another for several moments, the silence speaking volumes.

Unable to resist, Diana gave a nervous laugh. "You're not here to offer me gifts again, are you?"

Lord Barrington studied her for a moment. "So, it was the mention of gifts that sent you fleeing. If that is the case, my answer is no. I'm here because the thought of never seeing you again is agonizing. We became friends, and I would not want to lose that."

His words were like a healing salve on her wounded soul. "I must admit, despite my words to the contrary, over the last few days, I had hoped you would call. When I'm with you, it's as if we've known one another for years rather than weeks."

He took a step forward and took her hand in his. "Miss Diana, I would like nothing more than to enjoy your company. You've no other suitors occupying your time, have you? If not, I'd like to call again, so we can perhaps build up that friendship we share."

Should she mention Mr. Stonebrook? No, he was not a suitor. Her reason for allowing him to call had nothing to do with a possible future with him and everything to do with pleasing her father.

"There is another gentleman," Lord Barrington said, dropping her hand.

"No, not at all," Diana replied with a smile. "I was just wondering when you plan to call. If only to outwit you again."

Lord Barrington threw back his head and laughed. "Well, we'll just see about that, Miss Diana. But in the meantime, I would like the chance to get to know you better."

"As would I," Diana said.

Why did her mind suddenly return to the kiss they had shared? It was strange, but although she had thought him like other men, he was not. How she knew that was unclear, but she *knew*. It was as Mrs. Rutley said. Her heart told her all she needed to know.

"Why don't you join me for dinner again on Thursday?" Lord Barrington asked. "I can discuss it with your headmistress if you would like."

"I would," Diana replied. "And I'd like to see another of your illusions. I enjoy watching you perform."

The marquess grinned. "That can be arranged. I must go, but I'll see you soon. Goodbye, Miss *Diana*."

Hearing him say her name made her legs go weak. And as he walked away, she sighed.

"Goodbye, James Barrington," she whispered. Oh, but his name tasted wonderful on her tongue!

"I feel as if I'm ebbing and flowing with the tide," Diana said as she sat with Jenny and Ruth on her bed after explaining the conversation she and the marquess shared. "When he spoke of attending the Season together, my heart threatened to touch the heavens!"

She did not dare bring up the kiss. Jenny would have been beside herself if she learned they had found a way to circumvent her vigilance as Diana's chaperone. Not to mention how angry she would have been that Diana had kept such news to herself!

"Then you should allow him!" Ruth said. "I'd be happy to join you."

Diana shook her head. "No, he's made it clear he's unable to attend this year. Which makes no sense."

Jenny frowned. "That confused me, too. Why offer and then say he cannot go?"

"I've no idea," Diana said. "All he'll say is that he has a problem he must rectify. But I find I believe him. And trust him." She sighed. "I want to be happy, not end up like my mother. And I feel he can do this for me."

Ruth stood from the bed, walked over to the vanity table, and began looking through the many bottles of perfume Diana owned.

"What I'd like to know is why an eligible bachelor, especially one of his station, wishes to avoid the Season. There can only be one reason."

"What would that be?" Diana asked. When Ruth refused to answer, she said, "Come now, you must suspect something."

Ruth heaved a heavy sigh. "Men like this marquess are rogues. It wouldn't surprise me if he has a dozen women believing they are the only one for him. I'd wager he's convinced them of it by offering a fake courtship. Maybe that is what brought him here. They've learned the truth, and he's hiding from all those women."

Diana shook her head. Had Ruth not accused Mr. Stonebrook of having ulterior motives, too? And all based on rumors. "Lord Barrington is trustworthy," she said. "I'm sure of it. He revealed certain secrets to Jenny and me."

"It's true," Jenny piped in. "Secrets so great they could ruin his name. A rogue would not be so open." That was taking what he had shared much too far, but Diana was not going to point it out.

Ruth snorted. "Have you considered that maybe he told you that to build just enough trust you'd be unwilling to call into question his motives?" She waved her hand dismissively. "If he's inviting you to dinner, what's the harm?" Then she placed a thoughtful finger to her chin. "But don't you have another man showing an interest in you? How goes the saying? '*It is only prudent never to place complete confidence in that by which we have even once been deceived.*'"

Diana laughed. "My, listen to you quoting Rene Descartes. Mr. Twilling would be proud." Mr. Twilling was the tutor who instructed the pupils in history and philosophy. Never a drier man had Diana encountered in her life!

"Well, it's true," Ruth said. "Lord Barrington is keeping secrets. Even you admitted it."

"Just because he keeps secrets does not mean he's being deceptive," Diana said. "After all, we've only recently become acquainted, so we're allowed to keep back certain information." She nibbled on the tip of her finger. "But he did ask if I had another suitor, and I chose not to mention Mr. Stonebrook. After all, we're merely friends." She shrugged. "Perhaps I should have."

Ruth laughed. "Maybe my previous advice was much too hasty. Perhaps there's no need to worry. After all, neither man has asked you to court. I say you continue allowing Mr. Stonebrook to call so your father is happy. If anything comes of it, you can tell Lord Barrington to take a swim in the Thames! The same goes for seeing Lord Barrington. The loser will simply be sent away."

Diana could not help but join in with the laughter.

"Well, I would like to rest before dinner," Ruth said as she walked toward the door. "Just think about what I've said." Then she was gone.

Jenny turned to Diana. "Well? What do you plan to do? Do you think it's wise to allow two men to call on you?"

The question was valid. "The truth is, I enjoy being with Lord Barrington far more than Mr. Stonebrook. And I don't believe he's a rogue. Although—" She clamped a hand over her mouth.

Jenny laughed. "Do you honestly believe I didn't see what happened in the secret passageway? I'm not blind, you know. I just chose not to stare." She leaned in closer, her eyes sparkling. "Was it wonderful?"

Diana nodded. "Very much so! I don't think I've ever experienced anything so beautiful."

"And what about Mr. Stonebrook? Has he kissed you? You really should have something with which to compare your kisses."

"Jenny! I'm no hussy!"

Jenny clicked her tongue. "I never said you were. But I'm curious what you plan to do about Mr. Stonebrook, given your interest lies with Lord Barrington."

"I've no idea," Diana replied. "He wishes to call on me again, and I suppose I'll allow him. It's what Father wants. I'll simply have to make it clear that we're to be nothing more than friends."

Jenny rose and offered Diana her hands. Diana allowed her to pull her up from the bed. "I cannot believe it," Jenny whispered. "You've two men vying for your attention. The reasons make no difference, but how exciting that there is a duel taking place."

"A duel?"

"Indeed! They don't know it yet, but each is doing all he can to charm you. Only one can emerge victorious, and it's you who will decide the victor. It's all so romantic!"

Diana smiled. "I already know who the victor is," she said. "I'll allow Mr. Stonebrook to call on me as a friend for Father's benefit. But my attention will be on seeing more of Lord Barrington. And making myself happy. This way, I win."

CHAPTER FIFTEEN

After a lovely visit on Thursday, James gained permission from Mrs. Rutley to call on Miss Diana again two days later. Saturday dawned gray and foggy, but it did not stop him from collecting her late that morning. If all went well, the fog would lift and the day would clear. Or so he hoped. Yet the threat of bad weather would not prevent him from seeing Miss Diana today.

Exiting the vehicle, James walked up to the portico of Mrs. Rutley's School for Young Women and rapped twice on the front door. A moment later, the door opened to Mrs. Rutley herself.

"Good morning, my lord," she said. "Please, come in from the cold. Diana will be down soon."

"Thank you, Mrs. Rutley," James said as he walked past her. "And it's not too cold, at least not yet. It would not surprise me if we got more snow before the end of the month." He stopped to study the headmistress. "Mrs. Rutley, do I know you?"

She gave him a polite laugh. "We've spoken on several occasions if that is what you mean."

Frowning, he said, "No, it's more than that. I've a feeling that we knew each other as more than acquaintances at some point in my life. Perhaps when I was younger?"

Growing up in Chatsworth, he would have likely encountered Mrs. Rutley at one function or another, or even in the village itself. But he could not shake the feeling of familiarity.

Mrs. Rutley waved a dismissive hand. "You know what life is like in a village. Everyone knows everyone else, even if they don't truly *know* them. I'm sure we've heard whatever rumors are floating around about each other. Gossip makes us feel as if we know more about a person than we truly do. May I offer you some tea while you wait?"

"No, thank you." He looked up and nearly choked on his words as his gaze fell on Miss Diana at the top of the stairs. His chest ached from the pounding of his heart. Oh, but she was beautiful!

She wore a pale-pink walking dress with bows down the front and tight sleeves that puffed at the shoulder. The neck was lined in fur, which matched the fur on the hand muffler she held. But it was her smile that radiated most.

Her friend, Miss Jenny, followed behind, her green dress muted in comparison. Or perhaps James simply did not take as much notice of the chaperone as he did Miss Diana. Beautiful was not enough to describe her, for she was far lovelier than any woman he had ever encountered.

"My lord," Miss Diana said, dropping into a curtsy when she reached the bottom of the stairs.

Miss Jenny followed suit. Or so James thought, since he could not take his eyes off the playful smile Miss Diana wore as he bowed.

"It's wonderful to see you again, Miss Kendricks," he said. "We shan't be long, Mrs. Rutley. Is there any particular time they should be returned? A function they must attend?"

"We've nothing scheduled for today, my lord," Mrs. Rutley replied. "I trust both of my girls will be safe in your company, so please, enjoy the day. Don't worry about any particular time."

Once they were outside and the front door was closed, Miss Diana glanced over her shoulder and said in a whisper, "I've never seen Mrs. Rutley so carefree with anyone as she is with you. Even with the pupils she is not so."

James smiled down at her. "Perhaps you're her favorite," he said, grinning. "A headmistress cannot admit when she prefers one student over the others. I would think you should receive preferential treatment."

He handed first Miss Diana and then Miss Jenny into the carriage and took a seat across from them. Again, he could not take his eyes off her. When she pulled a gloved hand from her muffler to brush back a long curl that had fallen loose, such a desire came over him that he clenched the side of the bench.

"What are you staring at, Barrington?" Miss Diana asked, her voice filled with amusement. The fact she had remembered to use a more familiar address made his skin feel warm.

"You, Miss Diana. I'm just pleased to see you again."

She smiled and he found it the most wonderful thing he had ever seen.

"Have you done any reading as of late, my lord?" Her smile took on a mischievousness he chose to ignore.

"Not much," he replied. "I've been far too busy helping... a friend." He nearly had said Amelia's name! This was a risky topic, and so he chose to change it. "Have you gone anywhere since the last time we met?"

"Oh, no," Miss Diana blurted. "I remained at the school and went nowhere. Nowhere at all. With this weather, there was no reason to leave."

What an odd response, he thought. Or rather what an odd way *to* respond. She reminded him of a child creating a story to hide a secret from her parents. But for what possible reason would she be creating an alibi? Perhaps it was his near blunder about Amelia that made him see what was not there.

He pushed aside his silly suspicions and said, "I thought we would visit somewhere different for our outing today. A place you may have likely visited, or at least seen often, but not from the perspective we'll see it today."

It was not long before the carriage came to a stop, and the trio alighted. They were on a less-traveled road surrounded by forest covered in fog.

"I would like to show you a bridge," he said. "But it's not just any bridge."

Miss Diana took his proffered arm. "I don't believe I've been here before. What road is this?"

"This was an ancient road that passed through several of the smaller villages. It's been out of use for years since people stopped traveling between Chatsworth and Spelling."

Miss Diana frowned. "Spelling?"

James smiled. "Yes. Two hundred years ago, it was a tiny village for miners—more an encampment than a village, really. When the nearby mines closed down and the miners left in search of new positions, Spelling fell into ruin. Over the years, the few stone buildings there were dismantled, and the stones used for new buildings. When the people were gone, the forest grew up and around what remained."

It was not long before they arrived at the bridge. The stone structure connected the banks of a shallow ravine where water once flowed but was now taken over by grass. Just wide enough for a cart to pass over, the bridge had waist-high gray stone walls on either side. Down the center of those walls was a layer of onyx.

"How lovely!" Miss Diana said breathily as she ran a gloved hand across one of the black stones.

James removed one of his black gloves and placed his hand on one of the stones. "Touch them without your gloves."

She gave him a quizzical look but did as he bade. "It's smooth," she said with a smile. "Unusually so." Then her eyes went wide. "There's an etching of a horse here." She moved to the next stone and squatted, her hand moving over the smooth surface. "And an archer." She moved to the next. "This one is a man with a broadsword!"

Miss Jenny walked over to the opposite wall, exploring the stones there. "There are more over here," she said. "When were these drawings made, my lord?"

"I've heard anywhere from four hundred years to a millennium ago," he said. "I tend to believe they are older than they are newer."

Miss Diana rose. "Do you know who created them?"

"No one knows for certain," he replied. "But it's said that they tell stories about the people who once dwelt here. They were skilled craftsmen from all sorts of trades. Many were weaponsmiths who created weapons for Edward the Elder."

Without a second thought, he reached down and gathered her hand in his. Her skin was as smooth as the stones, and a sudden urge to protect her came over him. "Most of the etchings depict a man in battle using the weapons created by his kinsmen. But there are several that do not."

Hand in hand, he led her to the middle of the bridge. "The women also depicted their lives here," he said, pointing to three stones much larger than those on either side. On it was an image of a group of women looking toward the sun. The one in the middle was a gathering of children, and the last was a group of men facing the east.

Miss Diana squatted once more and placed her hand on the etching of the men. "Are they leaving for war?"

James nodded. "Legend says that war came to this area. The King's army was off fighting along the eastern coast, leaving those in this area unprotected. So, the men took up the very weapons they had crafted for their king and set out to defend their homes and those they loved." His eyes locked on to those of Miss Diana. "Choosing to fight in order to protect a woman must bring about a great sense of honor."

"It must be wonderful to be valued so highly," Miss Diana whispered.

It was as if time froze for them as they gazed into one another's eyes. Nothing existed in the world except Miss Diana and the very bridge on which they stood. The sun broke through the boughs above, warming the air around them.

James realized he would have fought every battle to keep this woman safe.

"*Oof!*" As a pin pricking a bubble, the moment was gone as Miss Jenny stumbled over a loose stone.

James cleared his throat and walked to the far side of the bridge. "This completes the story."

One stone depicted an image of a man and a woman facing one another, and the next, the last stone before the bridge ended, was of a man with his back to the woman.

"I don't understand," Miss Diana said. "After all he did for her, he leaves her?"

James shook his head. "This one here"—he pointed to the drawing of the couple facing one another—"is known as the confession stone. Some say the two people are confessing their love while others say they are confessing secrets they had been keeping from one another. That way, if he dies in battle, their souls will be cleansed. Rumor says if anyone wishes to make a confession, they may do so here without fear of repudiation."

"What a beautiful story," Miss Diana said. "And did the men return? I do hope so."

"That I cannot say," James replied. "But since we are here, I would like to make a confession to you."

He paused to gather his thoughts. He could not reveal that he hid a young lady in his guest cottage. She would be gone soon enough, anyway. But he did wish to confess the new feelings that had risen inside him since he and Miss Diana had spent more time together. Yet, how did he do so without sounding foolish?

"Do you recall when I said that I've not been happy for some time now?"

Miss Diana nodded. "I do."

"What I've come to realize is, when I'm with you, I *am* happy. The worries in my life do not go away, but they do feel lighter." He shook his head. "I don't mean to say that my lot is terrible, for it is not. But it's much better with you in it. One day, I hope to share more with you."

"I look forward to it," Miss Diana replied. "And thank you for bringing me here. The bridge, the story it tells, it's all so very special. And I believe the woman on this stone also made some sort of admission. Therefore, in order to keep with tradition, I'll make a confession to you, too."

Diana had not been sure what to expect from their outing, but it certainly had not been a beautiful bridge that told such a wonderful story. Yet it was more than that. The words Lord Barrington spoke made the moment all the more magical. She did not begrudge him his secrets, for they were not in a place to reveal all, but a need rose for her to share one of hers.

She wanted to tell him about Mr. Stonebrook and her need to appease her father by allowing him to call. No, that would have to wait. Plus, he would be gone once Diana made it clear she had no interest in anything beyond a simple friendship.

Until then, she would enjoy the warmth of the affection her father showed by way of Mr. Stonebrook. Some men simply were unable to express their true feelings in the presence of women, but her father boasting about her said that he cared for her far more than he had ever expressed to her.

Another reason for deciding not to speak of Mr. Stonebrook was because sharing about another man in such a romantic setting would be a slap in the face to the many women who had once stood here. After all, it was not as if he were a suitor. Therefore, she chose another secret to share with him.

"Before you and I became acquainted, my plan was to become a spinster. My parents are unhappy in their marriage, and I've seen so many other couples like them. So, while my friends talked about their future husbands and the life they hoped to lead, I dreamt of being alone."

Although the cold touched her cheeks, Diana felt a pleasant warmness as they held hands. Not for the first time, new emotions burst into being; emotions she could not identify but enjoyed.

"After spending time with you," she continued, "I see the possibility of a new journey beginning, and I no longer want to be alone. I now have a hope that, as the months ahead of us unfold, we'll grow closer."

Lord Barrington grinned. "What a relief! I feel the same. Have we gone mad developing feelings for each other in such a short time, do you think?"

Diana shook her head. "I don't see what we share as madness in any sense of the word. And I must admit that I look forward to seeing where this road leads us."

The dreams she had held so close to her breast now seemed like they belonged to another person. Was it common for a young woman to change her outlook on life so quickly upon meeting a man? Diana suspected it was not, but regardless, that was what had occurred. For Lord Barrington made her feel alive and had given her hope for a life far different from that which her parents shared. Somehow, her heart had accepted him as its guardian, just like the men who had left for war on this very bridge.

"I'm pleased you chose to share that with me, Miss Diana," the marquess said. "I may not be in the same type of war in which the men who created this bridge were, but I am in a battle of sorts. Now however, I'm much more confident that I'll return safely. And it's all because I know you'll be there waiting for me."

Diana thought her legs would give way, and she found herself wishing he would kiss her. Unfortunately—or perhaps, fortunately for propriety's sake—Jenny had returned from her perusal of the stones on the other side of the bridge.

"These are astounding," Jenny said. She walked over to the edge. "And the view is stunning."

Lord Barrington leaned in and whispered, "I've noticed that when it's cold, the tip of your nose reddens."

Diana gasped and touched her nose. "It does not!"

He chuckled. "It does, but don't worry. I think it's delightful. Just as is everything about you."

If Jenny had not been nearby, Diana would have leapt into the marquess's arms and made him kiss her! "Well, when you tease me," she whispered back, "your eyes twinkle. I do find it attractive."

The sound of unusually loud footsteps, followed by a cough, made Diana pull her hand from his.

"I could not help but overhear the story you told about the etchings on the stones," Jenny said with a wide grin.

"And what is your opinion about the legend?" Lord Barrington asked. "Do you believe there is any truth to it?"

"Oh, I've no doubt it's true, my lord. The Romans once saw onyx as good luck. They added it to their weapons or hung it from a chain before battle. Midwives believed it helped in childbirth. In some lands, these stones would be considered as precious as any emerald."

Diana could not help but stare at her friend. "Where did you learn all this?"

"My father has an extensive library," Jenny said, grinning widely. "Why? Does it surprise you that I'm well-read in history?"

"I should say it does," Diana said. Not once had Jenny given her any indication that she knew anything beyond the rubbish her sister told her.

Lord Barrington said, "I have to admit I've learned something new today." He glanced around them. "We should be going before the fog thickens. I thought it would have dissipated by now."

Indeed, the sun had disappeared behind a bank of low-hanging clouds, adding a significant chill to the air.

Back in the carriage, Diana listened as the marquess shared more about the bridge. Everything he said enthralled her, and she had to clasp her hands to keep from applauding his knowledge.

That night as Diana lay in bed, she found her mind on the marquess. He was perfect in every way! What they felt for one another would grow over the coming months, she was sure of it. It was destined to become something special, something she never thought she would have.

Then a sudden thought came to mind that made her sit upright. Despite her desire to please her father, it was about time she put an end to Mr. Stonebrook and his calls. Doing so would be tricky, but she could not have him getting the wrong idea about them. Even if it meant once again disappointing her father.

CHAPTER SIXTEEN

The air was frigid as Diana, Jenny, and Ruth walked to Chatsworth for their usual Saturday outing. A weak sun made every attempt to reach past the clouds, and when it did manage to appear, a burst of warmth hit them only to disappear when the clouds once again won over.

They had gone into Mrs. Newberry's but found nothing of interest, so they walked over to peer through the window of the cobbler's shop. Lady Maria Grandle was inside talking to Mr. Repington, the cobbler.

"I bet she's gossiping," Jenny said, her breath fogging the window. "Mrs. Rutley warned me that if I don't stop my gossiping, I'll turn out just like her."

"How so?" Ruth asked. "Does gossiping make you become an old lady with iron-gray hair and a stooped back? Because that's exactly what Lady Grandle is." She sighed. "It's a shame she's in there. I was hoping Charles would be available to chat."

Diana arched an eyebrow. "Charles?" she demanded at Ruth's familiar address for the cobbler's son, who had taken a shine to Ruth. He was always willing to do all sorts of favors for her, and Diana feared what her friend promised in return. "Why do you wish to pursue a cobbler's son? He's not a captain, Ruth."

Ruth sighed. "That's true. I suppose flirting with him is a waste of time."

Diana wanted to cry with relief. Had Ruth seen reason? Perhaps her mischievous ways would finally come to an end!

"Captains can be found near a pub," Ruth continued. "Or anywhere near Rake Street. I'll go there." And without waiting for Diana and Jenny, she hurried away.

"Oh, that girl!" Diana said. "Why can't she behave herself?"

Jenny patted Diana's arm. "Don't worry. Ruth never gets into too much trouble."

"Only because she's never caught!" Diana snapped. Well, she was not Ruth's keeper, despite the number of times she had tried to be. At some point, her wily friend would either change her ways, or trouble would find her. "I've done all I can to guide her. But she'll be held accountable for her actions one day. I just hope she's not hurt too badly."

As they walked past the tailor's shop, Jenny came to a stop and grabbed Diana by the arm. "I've something I wish to say."

"Oh?" Diana asked as she turned to face her friend, who wore such a sad expression, she looked ready to weep. "What's wrong? Does this have to do with Ruth? Oh, surely she hasn't gotten into trouble already!"

"It's about time I act my age," Jenny said, reaching into her reticule and pulling out a handkerchief. "I'm nearly eighteen, and I've come to realize that the advice my sister gave me about dropping a handkerchief to gain a man's attention is pure nonsense."

Diana smiled. "And what brought about this sudden burst of brilliance?"

"Ruth and the trouble she's likely to bring on herself. I've seen how you, Julia, and Emma behave like ladies, and you have all found decent gentleman. There's no need to play games to catch a man's attention."

"Oh, Jenny, I'm so happy to hear you say this. It really is very mature of you." She wrapped her arms around herself and shivered. "I say we return to the school and ask Mrs. Shepherd to warm us a cup of chocolate. It's far too cold to be out today."

"And what about Ruth?"

Diana frowned. "Do you honestly think she would return with us if we went in search of her?"

"No, I don't suppose she will," Jenny replied.

As Diana turned to head back from where they came, however, Jenny said. "Wait." She squeezed the handkerchief in her hand. "It's about time I put my sister's ways behind me for good. From this moment on, Miss Jenny Clifton will act as she should." Then she tossed the handkerchief over her shoulder and brushed her hands together. "There. And good riddance."

Diana slipped her arm through that of Jenny, and they began the trek back to Courtly Manor.

They had not taken five steps, however, when a deep voice said, "Excuse me, miss."

They turned to find a man walking up to them. Imposingly tall, he was in his late twenties with a broad chest, square jaw, dark-brown eyes, and deep-brown hair beneath his round hat.

Diana gaped. She knew who this man was. Known as the Earl of Deception, vicious rumors circulated that Nicholas, Lord Dowding, used people for his own gain, to the point that many lost everything in the end. On his cheek was a pale scar that was said came from the blade of a man who tried to exact his revenge for what the earl had done. Although Diana dismissed most rumors, this one she believed, for he wore a sly look that said he was up to no good.

"Yes?" Jenny squeaked.

"It appears you dropped your handkerchief," Lord Dowding said. "It is yours, is it not?"

Diana knew Jenny had enough common sense to deny ownership of said item, for most of the rumors she had heard came from Jenny herself.

"Th-thank you, my lord," Jenny said. "It does belong to me. How can I ever repay your kindness?"

Did she bat her eyelashes? Diana considered slapping the girl!

"I'm uncertain at the moment," the earl replied. "But one day, I'll think of a way. How will I send word, Miss...?"

"Clifton. Miss Jenny Clifton. I attend Mrs. Rutley's School for

Young Women. And whatever you request, I'll be more than happy to oblige."

"Whatever I request, you say?"

Jenny gave what Diana considered a lovestruck grin. "I promise. You'll find that I'm a lady who does all she can to keep her word."

Oh, the irony of it all! For all the times Jenny had used the handkerchief and failed, it had to work on the Earl of Deception. Worse still, she had promised to oblige him with any request he made. To thank him was one thing, but it was quite another to be in his debt.

"I've no doubt you will." He tapped his hat. "Until next time, Miss Clifton."

"Yes, until then," Jenny whispered, followed by a heavy sigh as the earl walked away. "Oh, Diana, he's so tall! And handsome. I bet he's very strong."

"He may be all those things, but you've forgotten one."

"What is that?"

Diana glanced about to make sure no one was nearby. "He determines a person's future with the stroke of a pen! And it does not always end well. In fact, it rarely does!"

Jenny covered her mouth. "I forgot! I've no idea what came over me. I looked into his eyes, and all reason fled!"

"Some men have that effect on us," Diana mumbled, for she had felt the same in Lord Barrington's company.

"Oh, Diana, what am I to do?" Jenny wailed. "I told him I would do anything he asked. What if he wishes to call on me?"

"Call on you?" Diana asked as she grasped hold of Jenny's arm. "Pray he forgets about it altogether. Because if he does not, you'd best hope his request will not cost you your future!"

CHAPTER SEVENTEEN

Over the next ten days, Lord Barrington had called on Diana twice. They were drawing closer, becoming better friends each time they were together. They laughed, shared snippets of their lives, and discussed their hopes and dreams. Diana found she looked forward to each call with greater anticipation than the previous.

Today, however, it was not the marquess who sat across from her and Jenny but rather Mr. Stonebrook. This was the first time he had called since she decided not to see him anymore, but she had yet to devise a plan for how she would inform him of this decision. After all, doing so would upset him. And her father.

Especially her father.

Mr. Stonebrook had collected Diana and Jenny with the promise of a surprise. Although the idea appealed to her, she could not push away the guilt of then having to explain that she no longer wished to see him again. It would be in very bad form.

"When I was in London," Mr. Stonebrook said, breaking Diana from her thoughts, "I found you on my mind at every turn. I could barely contain my excitement of returning to see you again. And now that I'm here, I cannot be more pleased to be in your company once more."

Diana wrung her hands in her lap. "Thank you."

What more could she say? She would not lie and reply in kind, for even in his presence, she found it difficult to keep her thoughts on him. Lord Barrington occupied every waking moment, so there was no place for Mr. Stonebrook.

Her companion must have sensed this, for he frowned and said, "I've a feeling this outing is an inconvenience to you. If you'd rather return to the school, we may."

He brushed a wave of red hair from his forehead, and Diana offered him a smile. How many women of her standing would have been elated to have a wealthy gentleman like Mr. Stonebrook call on them? Likely many. Perhaps knowing this would make what she had to do easier.

But looking at him, she could see her father smiling at her, telling all he encountered how proud he was of her. No, it would not make it easier.

"My apologies, Mr. Stonebrook. I've been preoccupied as of late. I admit that I cannot wait to see what surprise you have waiting for me."

Oh, why was she such a coward to speak the truth?

"I'll admit that my schedule has been full, as well. With the Season approaching and the expectations of my peers..." He sighed. "Just be thankful you'll not be forced to attend."

What a curious statement, she thought. Aloud, she said, "Are you saying if you could avoid it, you would?"

Mr. Stonebrook nodded. "Indeed."

"May I ask why?"

"For the simple fact that other women do not compare to you, Miss Kendricks. And I speak not only of your beauty, which you possess in great quantity, but also your intellect. I'll be forced to endure poor conversation and put on an amused air when what I'm enduring is boredom. I'd prefer to be alone."

Diana frowned. "Do you mean alone for the Season?"

He leaned forward. "Please don't consider me odd, but I've a dream to one day live in the country, in a place so far removed from society it would make Chatsworth seem large. I'd spend my days reading, riding across the countryside, or perhaps even penning a story. I'm weary of the fierce competition the *ton* places on its members."

He leaned back into the bench. "All I need is a woman at my side who enjoys such a life, one I admire, and who makes me feel alive. That would make my life complete." He sighed heavily. "The problem is, I've yet to meet such a woman. And I fear I never will. Most prefer the busy life London has to offer."

Diana understood all too well what he meant. She, too, had hoped for a life where she could do as she wanted without the need to please someone else. That had meant a life alone.

Then she met Lord Barrington and that all changed.

"I once thought the idea of marriage as a form of punishment," she said. "Especially if I was forced to marry a man who was boring. I must admit that the idea of living in a cottage in the country has appealed to me quite often."

An image of she and Lord Barrington living alone, far away from everyone, made her smile. The size of the house did not matter as long as she was with him. Life would never be boring, then.

"Would you?" Mr. Stonebrook asked.

"Most definitely," Diana replied. "To spend time reading together, to discuss whatever subjects that come to mind..." Her smile widened at the thought of Lord Barrington kissing her again. "Oh, yes, it would be a wonderful life, indeed."

When she caught sight of Mr. Stonebrook's grin, Diana knew she had made a mistake. He believed she was speaking of him!

The carriage slowed, and Diana wished she had taken his invitation to return to the school.

"Well, Miss Kendricks, if you ever wish to escape, you're more than welcome to join me in my humble cottage for wine and reading. And don't worry. I won't tell anyone that you wish to do so. It will be our little secret."

An odd feeling came over Diana at hearing these words. Why did she get the sense that his motives were sinister? Perhaps it came from listening to Ruth too often.

"I'll keep that in mind, sir," she replied, giving him a small smile. "But you'll need a cottage first before I can accept that invitation."

He barked a laugh, and she was reminded of how Lord Barrington's laugh soothed her. Only because Mr. Stonebrook's did not. It did not make her feel uncomfortable, per se, but it neither gave her that pleasant tingling down her spine.

"You're right about that," Mr. Stonebrook said. "Lest we find ourselves in a field with only a blanket for covering from the weather."

This had them both laughing as the carriage came to a stop. Mr. Stonebrook alighted and handed down first Diana and then Jenny. Before them sat the remnants of an ancient church. The building still stood, but the windows were missing and large patches of weeds and moss covered the damp stones.

"I imagine you're wondering why we've come here," he said.

Diana nodded. "Well, yes."

"I'll explain while we walk," he said. "But the ground is slippery, so allow me to escort you."

Taking the arm he offered, Diana walked beside him, Jenny following behind. They climbed a set of stone steps built into the small hill in front of the entrance to the church.

"Two nights ago, a gentleman told me about this place, and I had to see it for myself." He pushed the large wooden door. It groaned with annoyance at their trespassing.

"It looks like it's been abandoned for some time," Diana said, looking around the empty nave. "There are more leaves inside than out."

Indeed, several trees had grown up where the stone flooring had cracked and separated. The roof was gone, allowing them to see the sky. Decaying leaves, broken branches, and piles of stone where the walls had fallen filled the space. Although its previous beauty was now dulled, it was special in its own right.

"I've a reason for choosing this location," Mr. Stonebrook said. "A church is where one goes to make confessions, and I have a confession I would like to make to you, Miss Kendricks."

Although Lord Barrington had said very much the same thing during their visit to the bridge, rather than being excited, Diana's heart now leapt in alarm.

"Do you recall when I said that your father boasts about you often?"

Diana heaved a sigh of relief. What she thought he would say, she was not sure, but this was a topic that pleased her.

"I do. Hearing it made me very happy. You see, he's never admitted that he speaks highly of me outside of my company. Nor *in* my company, for that matter. Typically, he sees me as either a disappointment or simply in his way. Or so I believed until you shared with me that it was untrue."

Mr. Stonebrook sighed. "I feared as much. When he told me about you, I have to admit I didn't believe him. You see, because I'll eventually take over the barony, many fathers do all they can to convince me that their daughters are perfect for me. What I soon learn is that they are nothing as their fathers described. You, however, are the exception."

He took a step closer, and Diana swallowed hard.

Please, don't try to kiss me!

"What I've found is a young woman who far exceeds my expectations. Her mind is sharp, and her beauty captivates me."

"Sir," Diana said as she willed her heartbeat to slow. This needed to end now! "Twice today you've commented on my beauty. I think you should stop."

"But I cannot," he replied as he took another step closer. "I wish to say it a hundred—nay, a thousand!—more times. You've a rare beauty, Miss Kendricks, and therefore, I confess that I was a fool for doubting your father. My eyes have shown me that women such as you do exist."

His closeness was suffocating. "Though I appreciate your kind compliments, I think—"

"*Latet enim veritas, sed nihil pretiosius veritate,*" Mr. Stonebrook whispered.

Truth is hidden, yet nothing is more beautiful than truth.

In any other situation, she would have found the Latin phrase wonderful. Now, however, it only made her uncomfortable. For she had not been truthful.

Well, it was about time she was. "Since you've spoken your truth today, I'll share mine. You've been a perfect gentleman. Whether we are sharing in conversation or you're taking me to a place such as this, I've been well pleased. Yet, I've a confession to make."

He placed the back of his hand on her cheek, and the misgivings from earlier intensified. She was making a complete mess of things! Why did she not speak her mind outright and clear the air in one go?

Diana glanced over to see Jenny studying a warn tablet that hung on the far wall, oblivious to the conversation taking place with the young woman she was meant to chaperone. Diana willed her friend to look her way, but to no avail.

"I can no longer hide my feelings for you, Miss Kendricks," Mr. Stonebrook was saying. "I admire you greatly and resisting any longer would be a sin."

"Mr. Stonebrook, I appreciate you saying so, but I cannot—"

Her words were interrupted when he pressed his lips to hers.

Although the setting was perfect, the kiss meant nothing. It was not as if it was appalling, but it lacked the power those of the marquess had over her. She may as well have been kissing her arm for all the effect it had on her.

Placing her hands on his chest, she pushed him back. "Mr. Stonebrook, I'm a woman of propriety and don't engage in such conduct."

"I don't know what came over me," Mr. Stonebrook said. "You consume my thoughts, Miss Kendricks, and I'm like a man drunk on wine whenever I'm with you."

Something was not right inside her. No sensation of floating above the ground came over her. Nor did a fire erupt in her belly. Instead, she was planted firmly on the ground. And chilled to the bone from both his closeness and the damp air around them.

Unsure how to respond, Diana said, "I appreciate you taking me on this outing, sir, but I really do need to tell you something."

"Let's explore for a moment before we leave," he said. "Then you may share whatever you wish."

With a frustrated sigh, she took his proffered arm, and they walked through the interior of the building. It was not large, but it likely had sat perhaps a hundred people in its day. At the far end was a raised dais where the priest would have stood. Fragments of stained glass lay scattered across the floor beneath the remains of its frame.

"Your father will be very pleased when I tell him how well we are getting on."

Diana found it difficult to concentrate on his words, so heavy was the blanket of guilt that hung over her.

You're a coward, Diana Kendricks! A terrible, good-for-nothing coward.

Although she and Lord Barrington were not courting, she felt as if allowing Mr. Stonebrook to kiss her was a betrayal. The notion was silly, of course, but the guilt remained long after they returned to the carriage and were on their way back to the school.

Jenny waited patiently on the portico while Diana attempted to talk to Mr. Stonebrook once again.

"At the church, I wished to tell you something."

He smiled at her. "If you're worried that your father will disapprove of us, I can assure you he will not. I received word from him just yesterday, encouraging me to continue to call on you. He said it makes him very happy knowing we get on so well."

Diana was taken aback. "Did he?" She would have to write to her father to explain that Mr. Stonebrook and she were not compatible. Hopefully, he would understand and agree that the best course of action would be to have them stop seeing one another.

Yet now, she found herself in a new dilemma. If she dismissed Mr. Stonebrook before writing to her father, what would happen to the newfound relationship she and her father shared? For so long, she had vied for his acceptance, and now that she had it, was she willing to take the chance of upsetting him?

No, she could not. Therefore, once again, she was unable to do anything but delay requesting that Mr. Stonebrook not return to call on her.

"I... I should go inside now," she said. "We'll speak later."

"Are you sure there is nothing you wish to say?" Mr. Stonebrook asked. Was it her imagination, or did his smile seem as if he knew something she did not?

"I'm sure." She turned and hurried to join Jenny.

They watched as the carriage pulled away, and Jenny said, "Well, what do you think of Mr. Stonebrook now?"

Diana sighed. "He's kind, and one day, he'll make a woman very happy. But that woman cannot be me. Let's go inside. I've a letter to write to my father."

Finding she had no writing paper, Diana went to Mrs. Rutley's office in search of some. She opened one of the desk drawers and frowned at its contents. A knife, a children's wooden top, a set of dice, playing cards, and other trinkets one would not expect for a headmistress. Perhaps they did not belong to Mrs. Rutley. More than likely she had confiscated them from her students, Ruth in particular. She could see Ruth with any number of those items.

In the next drawer, Diana found the parchment she sought and placed it on the desktop. For a moment, all she could do was stare at the blank paper. What could she say? Mr. Stonebrook had been a way to appease her father, but asking to no longer encourage the man would only make her father angry. Were her feelings worth more than the shred of relationship with her father?

Worrying her bottom lip, she considered her parents. Although she was certain her mother loved her, Diana had always had doubts that her father did, as well. Not once could she recall him saying he loved her. Or even cared two figs about her.

Drenched in sadness, she took the quill in hand and dipped the nib in the ink. This letter was necessary, but she was reluctant to write it. What if this broke that thin strand of thread that connected her and her father? And if she did not, what would that mean for her future? It was all so very confusing!

"You look out of sorts, Diana," Mrs. Rutley said as she entered the room and closed the door behind her. "What is troubling you?"

Diana sighed heavily. "It's my father. Why does he not love me as much as he obviously does my sister? Why must I be the one to please him without receiving any of his affection in return? I want to tell him what will make me happy, but I'm afraid he'll only become angry, and we'll lose what little love we have for one another."

"Come and sit beside me and tell me what brought this on," the headmistress said.

Diana took one of the two armchairs in front of the desk. "Mr. Stonebrook is a very nice man, but I've no feelings for him. I would like to have him stop calling on me, but if I say so, Father will withdraw from me more than he is already."

"And what makes you think your father does not love you?"

"The countless gifts he lavishes on me are nothing more than a way to appease me," Diana said. "Why is it that men feel the giving of gifts can compensate for the hurt they impose on us?" Her jaw tightened in anger. "The only reason he sends me money is so I can land a gentleman like Mr. Stonebrook. With Father, it's all about his contracts. He cares nothing for me nor what I want."

Angry tears rolled down Diana's cheeks as Mrs. Rutley pulled her into an embrace. It had been a long time since Diana had wept, and doing so felt good. "I'm sorry for crying, Mrs. Rutley. I'm trying to be strong, I truly am. But it's just so hard sometimes."

Mrs. Rutley brushed back a long curl over Diana's ear. "Diana, the strength of a woman does not lie in whether she cries. It lies in the obstacles that lay before her, and how she approaches each challenge. Now tell me, does your dislike of Mr. Stonebrook have anything to do with your feelings for Lord Barrington?"

"It's not that I dislike Mr. Stonebrook, but nor do I like him. He's nice enough, but I've no feelings toward him at all. But Lord Barrington? What we share is far different. We grow closer every time we're together, and I see a path ahead that says we'll only grow closer."

"And why is that, do you think?"

"It's... well, I cannot say exactly, but he needs time to resolve a problem he has. He's assured me that when it's done, we can move forward with a more serious relationship." She blew out her breath. "Oh, Mrs. Rutley, what do I do? I don't want Mr. Stonebrook calling again, but Father wishes for me to allow him to do so. I must get rid of him, but short of kissing another man in public, I'm at a loss as to how to do that!"

Mrs. Rutley pursed her lips for a moment. "I rarely believe that lying is appropriate, but you must have an excuse to refuse Mr. Stonebrook's calls. If you do so often enough, his interest in you may wane."

"That is true," Diana said, knitting her brow in thought. "But how can I avoid him if I'm not allowed to lie?"

The headmistress smiled. "You'll tell him the truth—that you've been punished for arguing with a member of my staff. Unfortunately, you've been forbidden to go on any outings for an entire day. I'll decide which day, and if it happens to be the very one he planned to call, there is not much you can do about it."

Diana frowned. "But I've not argued with anyone."

"It appears you're doing so right now, Miss Kendricks," Mrs. Rutley said in a stern tone. Then she winked. "Now, the first time he requests to call, we'll allow it. We'll devise various excuses sprinkled throughout after that. By doing so, your father will remain happy, but Mr. Stonebrook will grow weary of the game and will thus move on to another young lady."

Throwing her arms around the headmistress, Diana said, "Oh, thank you!"

"Of course. And if you find yourself struggling with this situation in the future, don't keep it to yourself. I'm always here to lend an ear."

Diana wiped her cheeks with a handkerchief. "Yes, I know, Mrs. Rutley. And thank you so much."

As she left the office, Diana wondered how a headmistress could love her students more than their parents did. If it were not for Mrs. Rutley, Diana did not know what her life would be like.

Then a thought came to mind. She had yet to spend the money her father had sent her for the month. Rather than spending it on herself, she would use it to make someone else happy.

And she went in search of Jenny to ask her opinion about her idea.

CHAPTER EIGHTEEN

E very moment spent with Miss Diana surpassed every moment
before, and James found himself admiring the young woman
all the more. Their conversations ranged from what the *ton*
expected from him to his love of magic. But it was times like this,
when he listened to her speak of herself and what interested her, that
he fell under her spell.

He had collected her and her companion, Miss Jenny, from the
school this early Friday afternoon so they could peruse his library and
choose a book to borrow. Then they were to have dinner together
after.

Bringing her to Penford Place again was foolish, he knew. Yet as
they would be inside the main house, and he had asked Amelia not to
leave the cottage until the start of the festivities in the stable, the
chances of Miss Diana learning about Amelia were low.

He despised keeping this secret, but every excuse to explain
Amelia's presence fell flat to his ears. It was far easier to say nothing
and wait for the inevitable day when the woman—and her unborn
child—were gone. Then there would be no need for explanations at all.

As Miss Diana spoke of her love of horses, James could not help
but appreciate the lovely blonde curls that hung down to her shoulders

beneath her large green bonnet. Or how smooth her skin looked. How plump her lips were. With each day they spent together, his admiration for her grew.

Although he had not kissed her again since that day in the secret passageway, the temptation had not waned. Rather it had increased, causing a longing he struggled to contain, and he turned away lest he was caught staring.

"But I've other new activities that I'd like to pursue," she was saying, her cheeks turning a delectable pink as she pulled closer the parcel wrapped in brown paper on her lap. "And I believe you can help me in this endeavor." Her gloved fingers strummed the top of the parcel, and she laughed. "You're worse than a child, Barrington."

"Am I? How so?"

"I can see the curiosity for what I have here," she said. When he glanced at Miss Jenny, Miss Diana added, "And don't look at her. She won't tell you, either." She gave a mock sigh of exasperation. "Oh, very well. I meant to wait until we were seated in the library, but here. You may open it now."

He took the parcel and, for a moment, had a feel of regret for not having a gift in return. But how was he to know she would be presenting him with something? He pulled on the string, unwrapped the parcel, and inside was a book. "*The Art of Juggling,*" he read aloud. "I don't have this book. How did you know I was searching for it?"

Miss Diana shrugged. "I made inquiries at the bookshop. Do you like it?"

"Very much so," he replied. "I'll cherish it always." He set the book on the bench beside him. "Now, what are these new interests you have? Are you saying you would like to learn to juggle?"

She laughed. "No, but I would like you to teach me another illusion."

"Another illusion, eh? Well, you would make a fine apprentice. But you must never reveal to anyone how the illusions are done. No great magician does."

Her smile warmed his heart. "Then it will be our little secret."

The carriage came to a stop in front of Penford Place, and James helped the women alight. When they entered the foyer, Baldwin was waiting.

"Good afternoon, Miss Kendricks, Miss Clifton," the butler said as he took their coats and bonnets. Then he turned to James. "I'm sorry to interrupt while you have guests, my lord, but I'm afraid I've urgent matters that need your immediate attention."

James nodded and turned to the young women. "I hope you don't mind making your way to the parlor alone. I'll join you in a moment."

Miss Diana smiled. "Not to the library? I see. You're afraid we'll pocket one of your books if you're not there to supervise us."

"No, of course not," James said. "If you'd rather—"

Her laugh made his skin pebble in a way far too pleasant for mixed company. "I'm only teasing. We'll wait for you there."

Once she and Miss Jenny were gone, James returned his attention to the butler. "So, what trouble has come to visit this time?"

"There are two matters, my lord," Baldwin replied. "One of which I fear is quite troublesome."

James sighed. "Let's begin with the less troublesome, then."

Baldwin bowed and handed James a letter. He immediately recognized his mother's seal.

Sliding his finger under the seal, James unfolded the parchment and began to read. "It appears Mother has some news that cannot wait. She'll be arriving Wednesday next and plans to stay until the end of the week."

What sort of gossip will she be bringing with her? he wondered. Perhaps she would announce that she and Lord Telcott were marrying. A widower with silver hair and a pleasant demeanor, James found he liked the old viscount and would be pleased if they wed.

"And the other matter?" James asked.

"Mr. Stonebrook called while you were away, my lord. He asked that I remind you that you owe him a dinner."

James stifled a groan. He had hoped to keep the man at bay until Amelia was gone, but if he waited too much longer, he would arouse suspicion. "I'll write and invite him to come on Sunday. Inform Mrs. Bunting."

Then, hopefully, he'll never return!

"Very good, my lord," Baldwin said with a bow.

James made his way to the library where he paused at the door to observe Miss Diana without her knowing. Oh, but she was a gorgeous creature! Her brown silk dress lacked embellishments, but that only added to her allure. It was as if she had been created by the hands of a sculptor, and life had been breathed into her by the gods themselves.

"I apologize for the delay," James said as he entered the room.

"Not at all," Miss Diana said, smiling. "May Miss Jenny borrow one of your books?"

"Yes, of course," James replied. "Would you like me to show you anything in particular?"

Miss Jenny shook her head. "No. I can manage. I won't be long."

When she was gone, James turned his attention back to Miss Diana.

"Well?" she said. "Which illusion will you show me next?"

Placing the book she had given him on a nearby table, he replied, "We'll begin with the simplest." He removed his gloves and reached into his pocket. "Come closer and watch." As she stood beside him, her fragrance and presence caused his heartbeat to increase. "Do you see this coin?" he asked, pushing away the huskiness in his voice.

"I do."

"Watch carefully." He closed his left fist around the coin. "I'm going to magically send the coin to my right hand." He moved an open right hand first over and then under the closed fist. "This magic comes from ancient times, when the Greeks had to hide their riches from the Romans during the first century." He then clasped both hands into fists and grinned. "The question is, was I successful in hiding my riches from you? In which hand was the coin when I started?"

Miss Diana narrowed her eyes at his fists and pointed at the left. "This one."

He opened his hand. It was empty. Then he opened the other, and there lay the coin.

"How wonderful!" she exclaimed. "How did you do that?"

"Allow me to show you. But you must remove your gloves first." He waited for her to do so. "Now, the trick is to make certain the coin fits into the space between your middle finger and your index finger." He slowed down the well-practiced movement. "The key is to have your audience focus on the story, so they are less likely to notice when you drop the coin from one hand to the other. Like this."

With slow, deliberate movements, he ran his open right hand above and below the left, allowing the coin to drop into his right hand. "And that is all you must do. Remember, the art of illusion is all about keeping your audience's attention on too many things at once, so they are less observant. It takes practice, but I imagine you'll be able to do all sorts of magic in no time." He handed her the coin. "Now, you try."

She took the coin from him and stared at it. "What do I do first?"

He took hold of her hand. It was smooth and soft, and he savored the feel of her skin against his.

During her first attempt, she dropped the coin. "That did not go well," she said, laughing.

He picked up the coin and handed it to her again. "Remember, slowly at first. Just practice the movements." He placed his hand beneath hers, once again delighting in the touch of her skin.

At first, he moved her hand, showing her where the coin was to sit, how it would drop. Then he allowed her to do it with his guidance until she was able to do the entire movement on her own.

"I did it!" she said, her voice filled with glee.

James laughed. "So you did." When her blue eyes met his, his breath caught.

"Thank you for teaching me," she said.

When she batted her eyelashes, a flame erupted inside him. A longing to pull her into his arms overtook him. "I can no longer fight this," he whispered, and before he knew what had come over him, he was kissing her.

Their lips performed magic he never thought possible. It took everything in him to pull away. He wanted nothing more than to keep her close, to kiss her whenever he chose. But now was not that time.

Miss Diana tilted her head and looked up at him. "Why is it we follow our hearts, and yet you still hide something from me?"

Was he so obvious? "I don't want to hurt you," he whispered. "I long to have you near me, but I must keep my distance. For now. I want so much for you to understand."

"I do try. I find that when I'm in your arms, I feel safe."

She gave her pouty lip a playful bite, and the beast inside him roared again. He pulled her in his arms again, and this time, the kiss was urgent, a need that had to be filled.

The echoes of footsteps made them take a hurried step apart just as Miss Jenny entered the room. "I found the most interesting book," she said with such enthusiasm that James could not help but laugh, Miss Diana joining him. "What? Why are you laughing?"

James knew full well that what Miss Jenny said had no humor at all. Rather it was the nervousness he and Miss Diana shared at nearly being caught in a kiss that made them laugh.

Thankfully, Miss Diana had the sense to calm her features and ask, "What book did you find?"

James let out a relieved sigh as they discussed the book of poetry Miss Jenny had chosen. For a moment, he imagined properly courting her with her father's permission. Diana deserved such an honor. His situation with Amelia had him delaying a relationship with any woman, but as he watched Miss Diana laughing with her friend, the idea of righting their situation was not as distant as he once believed.

Miss Jenny sat in a chair beside the roaring fire and opened her book. Miss Diana joined James.

"She seems content," he said. "I'm glad she found something to enjoy."

"Jenny is a wonderful friend and one of the most unselfish people I know." She looked at him, a shy smile on her lips. "I'm glad her curiosity in books allowed me some time alone with you."

James had to fight the urge to kiss her again. "Do practice the illusion I taught you, and I'll teach you more later."

Miss Diana glanced in the direction of her friend, who now had her nose buried in the book. "I hope my success is rewarded with another kiss."

Their conversation turned to more practical matters, and soon, he was telling her about the most recent correspondence with his mother.

"I do hope she remarries," he said. "She's been very lonely since my father passed." Then an idea came to mind. "You must meet Mother. I know she'll adore you. Come to dinner on Wednesday."

"I would like that," Miss Diana said.

"But I must warn you. She does tend to gossip. You may find your-self wishing you had declined this invitation."

She laughed. "Don't worry. I can handle a bit of gossip. You forget that I attend a girl's school. Gossip is everywhere. But I do hope she sees what a perfect couple we make." Her eyes widened. "I mean friends! Your mother will see what great friends we are!"

Her cheeks were so red, she looked as if she had spent too much time in the sun. But he understood her meaning, for they were compatible in so many ways. And once he saw to the woman living in the guest cottage, he would consider a more serious relationship with the young lady before him.

Yet as he looked down at her lovely features, he wondered if it would not be best to reveal this secret to her now.

"Miss Diana," he began, but then he stopped. No, it was far too risky. "I believe you and my mother will get on well," he said instead. "And if there is any way to repay you for agreeing to meet her, please, don't hesitate to ask."

She grinned. "I can think of one form of repayment," she said, her eyes twinkling.

"Name it."

"I'll dine with your mother if you promise to take me to the servants' party tonight."

Panic surged through James. How could he possibly make such an agreement? Amelia would be present, and although he could request she not attend, he did not want to do so.

Blast it! This situation with Amelia was becoming more difficult with each passing day! Now, Mr. Stonebrook was to come to dinner this Sunday, his mother would be visiting from Wednesday through Friday, and Miss Diana wished to join in the festivities with the servants.

"Surely you have better ways to spend your time," he said, knowing full well the argument was moot.

She frowned. "If you would prefer I don't attend, I can find another way to spend my evening. Although, it will be less entertaining."

Not wanting to arouse her suspicion, he said, "Very well, you may attend. But I must ask that you show your best decorum."

She grinned. "Very well, I agree to your terms."

As they sat speaking of the days ahead, James found his mind returning to the complications that were overtaking his life. The last thing he wanted was for anyone to find Amelia anywhere near the estate. Therefore, he made a decision. It was time to ask Amelia to leave.

CHAPTER NINETEEN

After what had been a lovely dinner, and now bundled in their coats and mufflers, Diana followed Lord Barrington out to the portico, Jenny waiting nearby. The kiss they had shared could have warmed her for several weeks, but now a strange uneasiness had settled between them. Perhaps she should not have made her request.

"I cannot help but feel I've made you uncomfortable, my lord," she said as she peered toward the stables. "I suppose it was silly to ask you to take me to watch the servants dance."

His chuckle had a nervous tinge to it. "No, there should be no problem. It's just that I want to protect you is all."

"Still, I know asking is unladylike. But you must understand, after seeing how much you were enjoying yourself, I found myself wanting to join."

He frowned. "Never say you're unladylike, Miss Diana. Your demeanor surpasses those of the titled women with whom I'm acquainted."

Her heart fluttered at his words, and she smiled as she placed a hand on his offered arm. As they walked toward the stable, she could not help but allow her mind to wander. What would it be like if they began courting? With the amount of time they spent together, they practically were, so it would be much like it was now. Or so she imagined.

As they drew closer to the stable, the sound of music filled the air, and the magic of the night bloomed.

"I've never met a gentleman like you," she said when they stopped outside the stable doors. "You're kind and adventurous, and you have this wonderful love of magic. You're a gentleman above all others."

He smiled as he bowed. "Then it appears our friendship is no illusion, Miss Diana. We're compatible in so many ways, given in how many areas of life we are alike."

Diana's cheeks burned despite the chill in the air. The idea they were compatible in any way was enough to make her heart want to burst through her chest.

Lord Barrington opened the doors, and she and Jenny entered. The area was alight with several lanterns. The same man she had seen before played a fiddle, and a blanket lay over a pile of hay filled with all sorts of prepared food. The woman with red hair who had danced with Lord Barrington was off to one side chatting with two other women, her laugh loud and boisterous.

Then her eyes fell to the pregnant servant, who sat to one side reading a book.

Diana thought it strange. She would never begrudge a maid for reading, but what she found interesting was her coat. It was far better made than those the other servants wore, as was the wrap over her shoulders. How did one of her station afford such nice things?

It's no concern of yours, Diana Kendricks! she chastised herself. When had she become a judgmental shrew?

The red-haired woman walked over to where two men sat. "Get outa them chairs, boys," she snapped. Then she walked over to Diana and Lord Barrington. "It's good to see you again, my lord. We've some chairs for the ladies, too." She pointed to where the men had been sitting only moments before.

"Thank you, Judith," Lord Barrington said.

Ah, this is Esther's cousin, Diana thought.

The marquess grabbed a third chair. "Have a seat," he said.

Diana sat to Lord Barrington's right, and Jenny to his left, when a man carrying a bottle of spirits stumbled toward the fiddle player.

"I've got a few words fer you all," he said in a voice that carried around the open space.

"He's Stephen," Lord Barrington whispered. "He sings quite well, but because of his love of the drink, he tends to either forget the words or he mixes them up."

Having Lord Barrington so close made Diana feel warm. And protected. From what, she did not know, but whenever he was with her, she felt like no troubles could ever come her way.

Stephen stumbled and nearly fell, and Diana joined the others in laughter.

"The servants seem to have a high regard for you," she whispered as the fiddle player picked up his instrument and began playing.

"This is their time, and yet, they allow me to join them," he said. "And have for many years. I have a very high regard for them, too."

Stephen raised his bottle, took a rather long drink, and then wiped his mouth on his sleeve. Then he began to sing.

'Twas on a cold winter's night
  My love broke my heart
  For what is love, if it's hidden away?
  The game we played was but a charade.

Diana's heart ached as the man continued his song, the story simple yet beautiful. It was as if he spoke of her and Lord Barrington, for although they were certainly not in love, she did care for him. And like the pair in the song, they acted a charade that they had no secrets from one another. Was his ballad an indication of the end she and Lord Barrington would endure? For the lovers in the song separated, never to join together again.

"Enough with the woeful songs!" Judith shouted. "Let's hear something more cheerful."

Everyone clapped their hands in agreement, and the music increased in tempo.

"I must return to the house for a moment. Will you be all right here alone?"

Diana laughed. "I'm sure I'll be safe enough," she said with mock annoyance.

After the marquess was gone, Diana leaned over and hissed, "Jenny!" But her voice was drowned out by the enthusiasm of the revelers.

Then to her shock, Jenny leapt from her chair, lifted her skirts, and joined in the lively dance, not caring when her stockinged leg was out there for everyone to see!

"Mrs. Rutley will kill the pair of us when she learns about this," Diana mumbled. She stood, debating whether she should put a stop to Jenny's brazen behavior.

No, Diana thought, *let her be. What harm can she do?* They had left all sense behind the moment they entered the stable, so a dance could not add much more to their shame.

"Don't worry," a voice said from behind her. "No one will say anything."

Diana turned as the pregnant woman sat beside her.

"I can see that you're worried," the woman said. "But you shouldn't be. She's safe here."

"Yes, you're right," Diana said with a sigh. "I just didn't expect her to join in with such... enthusiasm." She glanced down at the book the woman held. "You can read?" Her breath caught in her throat. "I'm sorry. I didn't mean it like that. It's just that I know few servants who prefer reading to dancing."

"Servant?" the woman said, frowning. "You think...? Oh yes, of course. A literate servant is a rarity, and when one chooses this type of pastime, it does cause a bit of controversy."

Diana had not expected to hear such an educated tongue. Perhaps the woman was even better read than Diana first believed.

"What are you reading?" Diana asked.

The woman smiled and showed the cover. "A book on Paris fashion. It's quite good."

Diana's heart skipped a beat, for she had seen that book before. It was the very same book Lord Barrington had purchased that day in the bookshop. He had said it was for a friend, but instead it was for a servant?

"What an interesting topic," Diana said. "Did you purchase it at Mistral's?"

The woman pulled back the book. "It was a gift," she said. Then she jutted her chin toward the dancers. "Are you enjoying yourself thus far?"

"Oh, yes. It's been quite enjoyable. Barrington... or rather His Lordship is a wonderful host."

"Indeed, Lord Barrington is a great man," the woman said with a wide smile. "Oh, it appears your friend has tired out already. I'll leave you to your reveling. It was nice chatting with you." And she walked away.

Jenny, who had finally lowered her skirts, dropped into the chair the woman had just vacated. "That was the most fun I've had in my life!" she said, gasping for breath. "You should try it."

Pushing aside the woman and her book, Diana smiled at Jenny. "I don't think so. But I must admit, the idea is tempting."

Soon, Diana joined in with the clapping. When a man in gray trousers and black suspenders began hopping to the quick tune, nearly treading on the toes of his dance partner, she, too, laughed.

Then she gaped as Lord Barrington returned to the dancing, clapping together the black-gloved hands he had not been wearing earlier as he lifted his legs in time to the music.

Jenny leaned in and whispered, "You should dance with him! It would be great fun."

"I don't know," Diana replied. "I would feel silly. It's too embarrassing. What would he think of me? And if word got out, I'd never be able to live through the shame."

"The lord of the estate doesn't seem to be embarrassed," Jenny said. "And his servants don't seem to think it odd he joins them."

Diana sighed. "I suppose it could not hurt."

With great trepidation, she rose and walked over to where the marquess was dancing. Lifting her skirts, she closed her eyes and allowed the music to take over her.

Soon, she was lifting her legs and kicking out her feet, hopping from left foot to right, while the servants clapped around her. Lord Barrington moved in closer, smiling broadly down at her.

A sudden realization came to Diana. They were not in London, and this certainly was not an elegant ballroom. Yet she danced with a man for whom she cared deeply, and that was all that mattered. He was mysterious and wonderful.

As he danced around her, their eyes met, and Diana understood that her feelings for him had grown. What they shared was much more than friendship. It was not love, not yet, but whatever it was, it was lovely and she wanted it to last forever.

What had started as a means to catch a glimpse of the infamous Marquess of Magic had led Diana to admiring him beyond belief. Now, she wanted nothing more than to share her feelings for him.

"You seem to be enjoying yourself," Lord Barrington said as he circled her once more.

"I am," Diana said with a laugh. "But I do hope the song ends soon. My feet are not accustomed to so much work."

He grinned at her. "Don't worry. I'll catch you if you fall."

If her cheeks were not hot enough from the exertion of dancing, they were at his words!

The song finally came to an end, and he led her back to their chairs. "So, does the Season seem as appealing as it once did, now that you've experienced a lively servants' dance?"

Diana shook her head. "If I were to spend the Season here with happy servants and you, I would never want anything else."

"I'm tempted to agree, for if you were at my side, what more could a man possibly want?"

With a throat as dry as an arid land, Diana found herself unable to respond. She wished to reveal her feelings for him but preferred to do so in a more intimate setting.

A new song began, and other dancers joined in the fun. Diana glanced to where the pregnant woman had been sitting, but the chair was empty.

"I'm curious about your servant," she said, still clapping to the music.

"If you mean Judith, you've nothing about which to worry. I spoke to her about her gossiping, and she's promised to keep a better hold on her tongue."

"No, not her. I mean the one with child."

He gave her a confused look. "Who?"

"The one who sat over there." She pointed to the empty chair.

"Oh, you mean Mrs. Triton," he said, chuckling nervously. "She's not a servant. Why did you think so?"''

Diana frowned. Something was amiss. If the woman was not a servant, why had she not corrected Diana? His attempt at a casual response sounded forced, which only made her more curious about the woman. "I assumed by her dress she was a servant."

Lord Barrington smiled. "I believe she has had trouble finding a suitable dress to accommodate her changing condition."

Diana considered his response. Perhaps the woman was embarrassed. Rather than correcting Diana's mistake, she had just played along. Yet that did not feel right, either.

They seemed to be dancing around the subject of the mystery woman, and she wished to learn the truth.

"I was just thinking how beautiful she is, bringing a child into the world. Who is she?"

"Her husband is a man with whom I do business. He's gone to America on business, so she's staying in the guest cottage until he returns, which should be soon.

The explanation was sound, but she could not shake the feeling that he was not telling the entire truth. But the music overtook her again, and she pushed aside the worries. Now was not the time to be concerned with anything but enjoying herself.

"We really should get you back to the school," he said after listening to two more songs.

"Yes," Diana replied. "We can't have Mrs. Rutley growing suspicious now, can we?" She smiled. "But in all honesty, I'd rather that we could stay here forever. I've had a thoroughly enjoyable evening. Dare I say it's been magical? Yes, I dare say it because every moment with you is magical."

"Have no doubt that I feel the same while I'm with you," the marquess said. "For it's rumored that the greatest magicians of the past were able to cast a spell over anyone they wished. And I'm most certainly under yours."

CHAPTER TWENTY

Since the party two nights earlier, James could not rid his mind of Miss Diana. Teaching her the coin illusion—the very one that had earned him his moniker as a child—had been one of the most enjoyable things he had done as of late. Yet it paled in comparison to his time spent with her in the stable.

That shared experience had pulled them closer. Intimately so. Seeing her flushed face from the exertion of the unfamiliar dance paired with a grin had given him a feeling he was unable to shake. Nor did he wish to do so.

The inability to name what he felt for her confused him. On one hand, he wanted to pull her into his arms and kiss her, never to release her again. To have her forever near him, to see her lovely face, hear her laugh. To simply be in her presence.

He was no fool to believe he loved her, for did such an emotion truly exist? All magic had a solution of which only magicians were aware, a secret that said it was all an illusion. Was that what this was with Miss Diana? An illusion? Or was it a true spell, one that could not be undone?

Whichever it was, it gave him a sense of elation he had never experienced before. As if he had no more worries in life. Miss Diana had proven to be a great magician, for not only could she make a coin disappear, but she could also ease his troubles.

The sound of voices in the foyer made James rise from his seat. Stonebrook was scheduled to arrive for dinner this evening. Hopefully his last before leaving Chatsworth. If James was not certain Stonebrook would have ousted him for hiding Amelia, he would have sent him packing after the first time the man called.

But Stonebrook would soon become a baron, and what was currently his father's estate offered a great deal of trade that interested James. If keeping the door open to several lucrative agreements meant being forced to endure the man's company for a single dinner, James was willing to suffer in the short-term. If luck was in his favor, James would be able to get what he needed and then sever all ties with one Peter Stonebrook.

"Let's get this over with," James mumbled as the door opened. Then he forced a smiled as he welcomed his guest. "Good evening, Stonebrook."

"Good evening," Stonebrook said, taking James's hand and shaking it. "Thank you for having me."

"Brandy?" James offered.

"Yes, please," Stonebrook replied, taking the seat James indicated. "I must say, this dinner is long in the waiting, Barrington. Were you avoiding me? You're not involved with a woman about whom I know nothing, are you?"

James forced a laugh. "No, of course not." He was not about to tell this fopdoodle about Miss Diana. It was not as if they were good friends having a discourse about their lives. Tonight was perfunctory and nothing more. Yet there was no sense burning the boats before crossing the water. "Work and preparations for my mother's visit have been taking up a great deal of my time."

"Pity it's not a woman," Stonebrook replied with a chuckle. "I've been calling on a lovely young lady as of late. Quite beautiful, in fact."

"Is this the same woman you mentioned earlier?" James asked as he handed Stonebrook a glass. "The one whose father sent you to her?"

Stonebrook snorted. "You make it sound as if the man ordered me like some servant, which I assure you he did not. But even if he had, it would have been well worth the trouble. This woman must be the loveliest I've ever encountered. An innocent and delicate creature who'll not remain so for long if I have my way."

"Then you've designs to bed her?" James asked in disgust. He felt sorry for whomever this woman was.

"What else would I do with her?" Stonebrook asked. "And the best part is that she believes I'm some charitable gentleman who is also a secret poet." He shook his head. "But I'll not lie, I've considered calling the whole thing off. It was that blasted kiss."

James arched a brow. "A kiss? How would a kiss cause you any problems? Is that not the first step in reaching your goal?"

Stonebrook waved a dismissive hand. "It should be, but not this time. Something changed after I kissed her, not in me, of course, but with her. She's given me all sorts of excuses not to see me, and I admit it's drawn my ire. Women don't just stop allowing me to call without a good reason. This one was a bit naiver than I thought, I suppose."

"It appears your trickery failed," James said, pushing down the glee that filled him. "At least you've plenty of women to choose from in London."

"Not like this creature," Stonebrook sighed, tapping a finger on the rim of his glass. "She's a true prize. Well worth the sport. And there are other ways to win. I've written her father, asking to speak with him. Whatever this girl is playing at, he'll put a stop to it in no time."

James relished the burning sensation the gulp of brandy brought him. Although Stonebrook was a scoundrel, nothing James said would dissuade him from his course. What was it about this particular young lady that had him so obsessed? "I'm sure you could land another young woman. Why this one?"

Stonebrook frowned. "What do you mean?"

"You seem to be going to great lengths to win her over, playing this charade of a man of charity and what not. What is it about her that keeps you on the pursuit?"

With a sigh, Stonebrook rested his glass on a knee. "If this were any other woman, you would be right, for my efforts to win her trust do seem to be in vain. But I've never encountered a young lady as lovely and virtuous."

"So, you're in love?"

To this, Stonebrook threw back his head and laughed. "Love? Of course not. It's the thrill of the conquest that holds my attention." He leaned forward. "Her father has no time for her. I've seen this first-hand. Yet whenever he mentions her, his eyes light up." His grin nearly cut his face in half. "I've a feeling she knows her father would be disappointed if she dismissed me, thus the reason for the excuses. But I've no doubt I can convince him to order his daughter to make time for me. Then I'll bed her."

James could not help but scowl. "And what? Leave her?"

"Not at all. I'll marry her."

"That makes no sense. Why not marry her first?"

Again, Stonebrook laughed. "Not knowing if I'll enjoy her before I'm forced to spend the rest of my life with her?"

"And I imagine her father's money plays some part in all this, as well."

"I'll admit, he is wealthy," Stonebrook replied. "But my interest lies in the idea of having such a lovely woman I may parade about on my arm. Men like you will be jealous."

James bit his tongue. If this man knew how beautiful Miss Diana was, he would not be speaking so assuredly.

"But for whatever reason, the girl has no interest in me," Stonebrook said, frowning. "It's easy to see that." Then he grinned again. "But that's all a part of the fun, is it not? The ultimate hunt!" He rose and walked over to pour himself another drink but paused as he glanced out the window. "Now, that's strange. Why is your butler carrying a tray to the guest house?"

James leapt from his seat and hurried to stand beside Stonebrook. Indeed, there was Baldwin with what only could have been a food tray.

"Is Miss Lansing here?"

James's throat went dry. "I told you, she's in Paris."

"I don't believe you, Barrington," Stonebrook said. "But what does it matter? Your face says it all." He lifted his glass as if to toast. "You risk much in hiding a pregnant woman, you know."

"I'm well aware of the risks in everything I do," James said, the anger in him rising. "And you and I shall *not* discuss Miss Lansing."

Stonebrook finished off the last of his brandy and placed the empty glass on the windowsill. "You're far too protective of that woman," he said. "Are you planning to raise the bastard child? Do you think she'll tell her future husband about it?"

"You're overstepping, Stonebrook," James growled.

Stonebrook ignored him. "Once the child arrives and her figure returns, many men will want to indulge themselves with her. Perhaps I should call on her—to comfort her, as well."

With a roar that came from the pit of his stomach, James grasped hold of Stonebrook's coat. "You'll not dare to even look her way!"

"Get your hands off me," Stonebrook said. "Release me at once, I say!"

"If you speak a word of her whereabouts to anyone, I'll see you silenced. You may become a baron one day, but I'm a marquess. I've an extremely far reach and deep pockets. Who do you think has more influence, you or me?"

Stonebrook gave no indication James's threat concerned him. "Don't worry. I'll say nothing about the harlot you love and have secreted away."

Before he knew what he was doing, James pulled back his arm and struck Stonebrook in the stomach, making him double over with a resounding, "*Oof!*"

"You'll regret that, Barrington," Stonebrook gasped. "Don't think I'll forget what you've done!" Clutching his stomach, the man ran for the door.

"Not a word, Stonebrook," James called out after him. "If I hear even an inkling that you've said anything, I've connections with men who are more than willing to retaliate in ways you'd never expect!"

Stonebrook came to a stop at the door and turned around. "Why should I say anything?" he asked. "I'll gain nothing by it. It will be your own foolery that will destroy you in the end. And when it does, I'll rejoice, for the Barrington name will be ruined forever."

Once Stonebrook was gone, James balled his hand into a fist and slammed it on the table beside him, sending his empty glass crashing to the floor. The threat would have been enough to silence the man, but James had to go and strike him!

Worse still, James had to do something about Amelia. Stonebrook had been right about one thing. If anyone learned she was there, his honor would be ruined forever.

CHAPTER TWENTY-ONE

Early Monday afternoon, Diana clutched at her knotted stomach as Jenny brushed her hair. The cause of her worry was in the letter she had received the day before from Mr. Stonebrook requesting to call on her today. No, insisting that he call on her. She had been putting him off long enough, he had said in his correspondence. If she rejected him again, he would simply have to speak to her father.

And that, she could not have.

"It's about time I put an end to this farce once and for all," Diana said. "But how shall I do that without upsetting my father?"

A light rap on the door made Diana start. "Yes?"

The door opened, and Mrs. Rutley entered. "May I speak with you before you leave?" She looked at Jenny. "Alone, please."

Jenny nodded and left the room.

"Is everything all right, Mrs. Rutley?" Diana asked, that knot in her stomach tightening.

"Indeed it is, Diana. Here, sit with me." She patted the place beside her on the edge of the bed. "Does this outing worry you?"

Diana sighed and looked down at the letter. "He's kind to me, and I don't mind his company. But it's about time I explained the truth to him. Father is a dear for sending him to me, but I despise making excuses at every turn. It's unfair to him. And to me."

Mrs. Rutley smiled. "Does this have anything to do with Lord Barrington, per chance?"

"Perhaps," Diana said, her cheeks heated.

The headmistress's eyebrows rose. "Do you believe he wishes to court you?"

"I cannot say for certain, Mrs. Rutley. I promised to keep it to myself, but I see no harm in telling you what little I know. He has family issues to see to before moving forward with any courtship He's not said what those issues are exactly, but they seem very important."

"I see," Mrs. Rutley said.

Diana turned to her headmistress. "Why does life have to be so complicated?" she asked. "It's as if my life is a sea of the unknown."

Mrs. Rutley chuckled. "Oh, Diana, you'll learn soon enough that life is oftentimes filled with the unknown. None of us know what the future holds. Tomorrow is mysterious enough without adding the days, months, and years that follow. I'm not saying you should not be prepared, but what you cannot do is be overly worried about it. Prepare as best you can and be flexible enough to work with what is thrown at you."

Diana laughed. "You make it sound like I'll be heading into a storm."

"Storm, calm, one never knows, my dear. Prepare yourself for both and neither will come as a surprise. Now, Mr. Stonebrook is waiting for you downstairs. Are you ready?"

"I am," Diana said. She placed a bonnet on her head, white with pink roses and a deep-pink ribbon to match her walking gown. She had no idea where they were going, but he had said they would take a stroll. Therefore, she wore a pair of white leather, heeled half-boots.

She donned her gloves as they walked down the corridor that led to the stairway. "Oh!" she gasped. "I forgot my coat." She hurried back to her room to collect a fur-lined pelisse, a gift from her father during a trip to France. This was the first time to don it. A fitting item for an outing with the man her father had also sent to her.

Upon entering the foyer, Mr. Stonebrook smiled at her. "Good afternoon, Miss Kendricks," he said with a bow. "I'm so pleased to finally be given the chance to see you again. I must admit I wondered if you were only coming up with excuses to stay away from me."

"If Miss Kendricks would do as she's asked," Mrs. Rutley replied with a frown, "I'd have no reason to restrict her outings as a form of punishment."

Mr. Stonebrook arched an inquisitive eyebrow. "What's this? Are you saying that this lovely young lady has a rebellious nature?" He seemed amused by this.

"I've no such thing," Diana replied. But when Mrs. Rutley gave her a pointed look, she added, "Well, perhaps I do. But if I wish to remain awake reading until the late hours, I should be allowed. Don't you think so, Mr. Stonebrook?"

He laughed. "I do, indeed, Miss Kendricks. I would never deny your wish to read for as long as you'd like. But as you're in the care of Mrs. Rutley, perhaps keeping to her rules is in your best interest. And mine. Shall we?"

Diana nodded and motioned to Jenny, who was waiting behind Mrs. Rutley.

Soon, the trio was well on their way.

"Where are we going, Mr. Stonebrook?" Diana asked.

"There's a lovely park in Chatsworth through which we can take a pleasant stroll. Now that we're no longer within the hearing of your headmistress, why don't you tell me what you were really doing? I know women enjoy reading, but to be doing so to the point you must be disciplined seems a bit excessive."

With a nervous laugh, Diana said, "That was only one of the reasons I had to refuse your offers to call, Mr. Stonebrook. I've also been occupied as of late. I'm afraid my studies were waning before the holiday began, and Mrs. Rutley warned me that she would send me home if I didn't show an improvement."

"I can't imagine you not excelling in your lessons," Mr. Stonebrook said with a small smile. "You're far too intelligent from what I've witnessed.

"It's very kind of you to say so," Diana replied.

When they arrived in the village, the carriage came to a stop at the entrance to a large park. Diana and the other students had been there on several occasions. The gardens at Courtly Manor were beautiful, but a change of view was always welcome.

Mr. Stonebrook offered his arm, which she took, Jenny following behind them. "I'm pleased to know that you've not been ignoring me," he said.

Diana stifled a sigh. "As I said, I've been unavailable." This was like contending with a disgruntled child!

"I know," he said, "but I can't help but wonder if you see my company as too boring."

A tug of guilt played at her heart. She might not find him interesting, but that was no reason to insult him. "You're not a bore, sir. I assure you. I find you quite knowledgeable in many subjects, which makes for many enjoyable conversations." That may have been stretching the truth just a bit.

An uncomfortable silence settled around them. Perhaps accepting this invitation had been a mistake. It felt as if she were here just to placate Mr. Stonebrook. Or her father.

"You may be truthful with me, Miss Kendricks," he said finally. "I'll not be angry. I just wish to know if you've decided you no longer welcome my company."

Diana's heart skipped a beat. How did he know? Well, she had hoped to break off this... whatever this was. What better time than the present?"

"I've enjoyed our brief time together, Mr. Stonebrook, I truly have. But I've no romantic notions toward you. Would it not be better if you were free of me so you could pursue someone who sees you as more than a friend?"

Mr. Stonebrook flinched. "It's just as I feared. I find a woman who is both beautiful and intelligent, and I've driven her away."

"I assure you—"

He held up a hand to forestall her. "What's brought on this change of heart? Do you think me unworthy of someone like you? I may not be a baron yet, but one day I shall be. And my estate is wealthy enough to offer whatever your heart desires."

"I've no interest in marrying a man for his money, Mr. Stonebrook," she said sharply.

"No, I suppose not, given how you were raised. But if this is what you want, I'll contact your father and inform him." He shook his head sadly. "I had envisioned us together in London, going to every party imaginable. The Season is the perfect opportunity for ladies and gentlemen to become better acquainted. Their futures are often decided by their parents."

"That is true," Diana said, unsure what his point was. "Or so I understand. I've yet to attend a London Season, but I'm aware of what takes place there."

Coming to an abrupt stop, Mr. Stonebrook turned to face her. "I believed you and I would be those people, but I see now it's not meant to be."

"I'm sorry," Diana said. "But I do hope we can remain friends."

He shrugged. "If that is all I'm allowed, then I'll settle for friendship." He smiled at her and took her hand in his. "I suppose I should return you to the school. And don't worry, I'll inform your father."

"My father?" she asked, taken aback.

"But of course. He's been happy that I've been calling on you. But don't worry, I'll explain to him that we've parted ways."

Diana bit at her lower lip. "He'll not be pleased with me. If I may ask..."

"Yes?"

"Will you tell Father that the decision to remain friends is mutual? He'll be extremely aggrieved if he believes that I made the decision against your wishes."

The smile Mr. Stonebrook placed on his lips made Diana shiver. "He won't be aggrieved once I've spoken to him, Miss Kendricks. Thank you for giving me... no, for giving *us* a chance."

"And thank you for understanding," Diana said, a sense of relief rushing through her. "But as for Father, perhaps I should write to him—"

"No, allow me to contact him first. If your letter were to arrive before I've had the chance to speak to him, he may be more upset than necessary."

Diana considered this and then nodded her agreement. He lifted her hand to his lips and kissed her knuckles.

"Let's get you back to the school before Mrs. Rutley believes we've run away together."

Diana could not help but laugh as he walked her back to the carriage. Soon, they were on their way.

Now Diana had two reasons to smile. First, Mr. Stonebrook had taken her rejection far better than she had anticipated, and they would remain friends. Second, she could now focus her attention on the marquess.

And *that* she looked forward to with great anticipation!

CHAPTER TWENTY-TWO

The logs in the fireplace crackled as James sat beside Amelia in the drawing room of Penford Place. Across from them sat Mrs. Susanna Helstrom, gray-silver hair platted into a single braid that hung over one shoulder and soft wrinkles around her eyes that deepened when she smiled. The woman specialized in the placement of newborn babies in the homes of families unable to have children of their own. And she did so discreetly.

Yet, she was not smiling now.

"What brings you to Penford Place?" James asked.

Mrs. Helstrom shifted in her seat. "This is not easy for me to say, but the family I mentioned before, the one interested in taking your child? They've found another young lady and have decided to wait for her child."

James glanced at Amelia, who wore a sad expression. "What does that mean?" asked Amelia. "Are you saying my baby will go to an orphanage?"

"Not at all," Mrs. Helstrom replied. "There are plenty of families willing to take on newborn babies. It's the older children who we're unable to find homes for. I've been in contact with a couple who are very near your age."

"How wonderful!" Amelia said. "What can you tell me about them?"

"All I can say is that he's a knight who comes from a very respected family. He and his wife have been unable to conceive, thus the reason for contacting me."

"And their names?" Amelia asked. "Where do they live?"

Mrs. Helstrom shot James a concerned look, and he turned to Amelia. "We've talked about this. You can never know anything about the family who adopts your child. It's in the best interest of everyone involved. All you can do is trust that Mrs. Helstrom will find the baby a good home."

Amelia placed a hand on her protruding stomach. Had she changed her mind?

"Is there anything wrong?" Mrs. Helstrom asked, her voice filled with soft concern. She asked a hefty price for her services, but James could not have imagined a kinder and more accommodating woman.

"No," Amelia replied. "But I can't help thinking that I'll never see this baby grow to an adult. See his first steps. Hear his first words." A tear rolled down her cheek, and James handed her a handkerchief. "Thank you. You must think me a simpering child. I know this is what is best, for who knows what sort of life I could give him if he remained with me. He'll be forced to endure the shame of being born out of wedlock. No man will want to marry me, my parents will shun me, and the child will be the one to suffer. I feel him moving, a living being inside me, but I must do what's best for him. Knowing that does not make it any less difficult." She glanced at James. "At least you've found a way to keep him from being placed in a foundling home, I suppose."

"The right choices are often the hardest," Mrs. Helstrom said with a warm smile. "But I can assure you, the child will be loved."

A wave of guilt crashed over James as he watched Amelia dab the tears from her cheeks. It was his fault she was weeping. And with child.

"Now," Mrs. Helstrom said, returning to her serious demeanor, "shall we discuss the arrangements. Will you give birth here or elsewhere?"

"I've made arrangements to bring a midwife here," James replied for Amelia. "One from Cornwall who has no ties to the area and is willing to be discreet. I'll be setting her up with a cottage not far from here."

"What will happen when the baby's born, Mrs. Helstrom?" Amelia asked.

"When your time draws near, the couple who will be taking your baby will stay at an inn close by. You understand why I can't tell you where exactly, don't you?"

Amelia gave a sad nod. "I do."

Mrs. Helstrom left an hour later, and James felt much better. Amelia, however, was not taking any of it well.

He took her hands in his. "Oh, Amelia, if I could have done more to take away this burden—"

"No, don't say it," she said. "I know you mean well, but this child is not a burden. No child should be considered as such, for they are all gifts. It's just that this one will be a gift for a woman unable to have her own. Is that not a beautiful thing?"

James smiled. "It truly is," he replied. "Come. Let's have some more tea, and we'll discuss our plans for Mother's arrival on Wednesday."

Mr. Peter Stonebrook had a knack for recognizing when someone was lying. Or if they were omitting information he wished to know. He considered both as villainous and more so a personal insult if they did so to him.

When Miss Kendricks had informed him she no longer wanted him to call, he knew it was because of another man. Which man, he did not know, but he would find out. Not to challenge him to a duel— Peter had never been a very good shot—but rather so he would know to whom he would flourish his winnings when he took her for his bride.

If Miss Kendricks believed he would allow her to get away so easily, she had another think coming. He had his plans, and no woman would stop him from seeing them fulfilled. What she thought made little difference.

He had met and bedded many women. In the beginning, that was all he desired with Miss Kendricks. But during their second time together, a thought had occurred to him. .

Why bed her one night when he could have her for the rest of his life? Or hers. If she became tiresome, he could find a way to dispose of her and see her replaced by a younger version. But until then, he would enjoy having her on his arm to flaunt in front his peers.

He would not roll over like some lap dog. If she thought he would simply honor her request of no longer calling on her, she was quite mistaken. Her disregard of him only made him more determined.

The carriage came to a stop, and he opened the door without waiting for the footman. The large home belonging to Mr. Samuel Kendricks should have been a part of a titled estate, which said much about the man's coffers. Another reason Peter hoped to marry the daughter.

Not that his estate was struggling, but that did not mean he could not add to its wealth in creative ways. This would be just like any other business proposition, only they would be discussing the trade of the man's daughter rather than a mine.

When Mr. Kendricks had first contacted Peter about calling on his daughter, Peter had been certain the girl would be ghastly. After all, beautiful women did not need their father initiating calls. Peter had been pleasantly surprised upon his arrival at the school.

The butler who answered the door was a short man with a mop of silver hair. "Mr. Stonebrook," he said as he bowed. He took Peter's hat and coat. "Mr. Kendricks is in his study. Please, follow me."

"Ah, Stonebrook, come in," Mr. Kendricks said as he stood behind his desk. "That will be all, Mitchell. Please, have a seat. I've a meeting I must attend soon, but your letter sounded urgent. What can I do for you?"

Mr. Kendricks was in his middle years with a mix of silver and blond hair combed to one side in an attempt to hide a large balding area on the top of his head. His daughter resembled him around the eyes and nose, but his cheeks were rounder.

"I've come with word about your daughter, sir."

"Is Diana all right?" Mr. Kendricks asked. "I've not received word from her or Mrs. Rutley that there are any problems."

Despite the man's performance, Peter did not believe he had any true concern for his daughter. Like most men of his station, he used his daughter to entice gentlemen, much like offering an apple to a horse. Then they jumped at the chance to get their grubby hands on the wealth of titled men.

In the past, when the subject of the daughter rose, Mr. Kendricks had nothing but complaints for his younger daughter. Which was why Peter was no longer concerned Miss Kendricks would belong to another man. Mr. Kendricks would give his daughter away if he could.

"Miss Kendricks is well, sir," Peter replied. "And I'm so pleased that you asked that I call on her. I find her company pleasing, one which I would not want to lose."

Mr. Kendricks frowned. "Then continue calling on her," he grumbled as he filed away a paper. "I've told you and Mrs. Rutley that you may."

"Well, that is partly why I'm here," Peter said. "I spoke to Miss Diana, explained my intentions for coming today, and, well, I would like to court her."

Mr. Kendricks frowned. "And she's agreed to this?" he asked. "Not that her opinion matters, of course, but her mother's given her some silly notion that she has a say."

Peter paused. A man who cared nothing for his daughter was one thing, but to have one who believed his daughter could make decisions for herself was quite another.

But before Peter posed his lie, the father said, "Of course she does, or you wouldn't be here. If she's in agreement, then you have my blessing."

"I appreciate it," Peter said, smiling. This was much easier than he could have ever anticipated!

"And if you intend on marrying her, all the better. Then I'll not have to pay for her final year of schooling. If you need, I'll send her a letter stating my approval."

Peter could not believe his luck! This had been the easiest transaction he had ever made. "Would you mind writing it now? I'm planning on returning to Chatsworth today, so I can deliver it myself if you would like."

The man snorted. "That would save me the time of posting it." He took out a piece of parchment and scribbled on it. Then he salted, folded, and sealed the page. "There you are."

"Thank you," Peter said, taking the letter in hand. "And I can assure you—"

"I don't mean to be rude, but I really must get to this meeting. I can't be late."

Peter offered the man his hand, ignoring the lack of formal address. He could take care of that little bit of oversight once the daughter was his. "Of course. And I'll see myself out."

Once back in the carriage, Peter allowed himself to relax. He had now secured the most beautiful woman in the country and had established the opportunity to trade with a very wealthy man.

Yet one challenge remained.

Lord Barrington and Miss Amelia Lansing. Two people who could destroy what he had built if they chose to reveal their secret.

CHAPTER TWENTY-THREE

"Have you been practicing the illusion I showed you?" Lord Barrington asked of Diana as they sat in the parlor of Penford Place, Jenny as Diana's chaperone.

They arrived an hour earlier at the marquess's behest, which came in the form of a letter the previous day imploring Diana to call. "An urgent matter," the letter had said.

Unlike Mr. Stonebrook's requests, Diana had accepted. If it were up to her, she would see Lord Barrington every moment of every day.

They had spent that first hour discussing a variety of topics—where they would like to travel, how they enjoyed spending their summers, favorite books they had read and the like. Now they were on the inevitable subject of magic.

Diana straightened her back with pride. "I have, my lord," she replied to his question.

"Then you must perform it for me!" the marquess said. "I've been looking forward to seeing how much you've improved."

Rising from her seat, Diana placed the coin in her hand. "This coin was given to me by my grandfather," she said, her palm open as she recited the story she had concocted as a part of the illusion. Devising her own tale had been as delightful as practicing the sleight of hand itself. "It was given to him by a tribal leader in the deepest jungles of South America."

She closed her left hand into a fist around the coin, sliding the coin between her fingers as he had taught her. "What makes this coin unique is the curse that was placed upon it." She waved her right hand first above and then below her closed fist, dropping the coin as she had been practicing. "For if the coin is stolen from the tribe rather than given as a gift or in trade..." She closed her left hand around the coin again and put both fists out in front of her. "It will disappear, to be returned to the tribe once again."

"What a clever story," Lord Barrington said.

Diana gave a nod of gratitude. "Now, which hand had I placed the coin, do you remember?"

"In the left," Jenny replied.

"Do you believe my story that my grandfather was given the coin?" Diana asked. "Or did he steal it instead?"

The marquess tapped his chin. "I believe you've spoken the truth, Miss Kendricks."

"If that's the case," Diana said, "the coin will still be in my left hand. Let's see if you're correct."

She opened her left fist. It was empty.

Lord Barrington barked with laughter. "So, he stole it?"

With a flourish, she opened her right hand. "My grandfather was no thief, my lord," she said with mock indignation. "The coin is right here!"

Jenny clapped her hands together excitedly, and Lord Barrington beamed with pleasure.

"Well done, Miss Diana," he said. "I must say, that was very well done. You've clearly been practicing. My advice is to continue doing so. Then your act will be flawless."

Diana pursed her lips, although she was not angry in the least. "Are you saying that I did not fool you?"

"As I'm another magician, fooling me is very difficult," Lord Barrington replied.

"And what about you, Jenny?" Diana demanded.

Jenny's cheeks turned pink. "It was very good, Diana, but I'm afraid I saw the coin drop. But only because I knew the trick, too, I'm sure!" Her voice was apologetic.

"I'm well aware that I must continue to practice, Jenny," Diana said with a laugh. Then she smiled at Lord Barrington. "Is there another illusion you can teach me, my lord?"

"As a matter of fact, there is," the marquess replied. "But we must go to the stable for your instruction."

"The stable?" Diana asked, sliding the coin into her reticule.

"Can you make a horse disappear?" Jenny asked, leaping from her seat. "I'd very much like to see that!"

Lord Barrington barked a loud laugh. "No, but I can do something better."

Once everyone was bundled in their coats and mufflers, they went outside and made their way to the stable. The wind was cold, and dark clouds filled the sky, threatening rain.

When they entered the stable, Lord Barrington approached a young man with coal-black hair that Diana recognized from the Saturday party, although she did not remember his name. The marquess said something Diana could not hear, and the stable hand nodded and hurried away.

"I've a feeling he wishes to speak to you alone," Jenny whispered. "So, I'll go and pet a horse or two." Her grin had a mischievous glint to it as she hurried away.

Some chaperone you are, Miss Clifton! Diana thought amusedly. Not that she minded, of course. Having time relatively alone with the marquess was quite appealing. Even if it was improper.

"My apologies for the delay," Lord Barrington said as he joined Diana.

Diana smiled. "No need for apologies. But I'm curious as to what illusion you wish to perform for me this time."

And will it include a kiss for its finale?

The marquess removed his black gloves, placed them in the waist-line of his breeches, and put out his hands. "Do you see anything?" he asked, turning his hands from palms down to palms up.

Shaking her head, Diana said, "Besides your hands, no, I see nothing."

"I believe what we share is something magical," he said, rubbing his hands together. "In the short time we've come to know one another, I've developed feelings for you I never believed possible. You've brightened my life. You're a flower that blooms on a winter's day like today." He reached up and touched her cheek. When he pulled back his hand, he held a daisy.

Diana gasped as he handed her the flower. "How wonderful!" she exclaimed. "And thank you. It's lovely."

"*You* are lovely, Miss Diana," he said.

He looked down at his hands. "I've struggled with trusting people as of late. Even you, although you've done nothing wrong. I'm doing all I can to work through my problems, and I ask for your patience."

"Of course," Diana replied. "You have my patience." *And anything else you request of me,* she added silently.

When he smiled down at her, Diana thought her legs would give way. What a wonderful smile he had!

"Despite these problems," he continued, "I've brought you here to ask for the honor of courting you. That is, if you'd like—"

So excited was Diana that she spoke over him. "Yes! I would love nothing more! And since you've shared with me, I would like to share something with you. Remember when I became angry when you mentioned buying me gifts?"

"I do."

"I know you meant the gesture as a way to show me that you care, but I've learned that gifts can be used to placate people. My father would rather spend his days with his nose buried in his ledgers or in the company of whomever can connect him to the next big enterprise. He never has time for me. He prefers to give me gifts than to cancel a meeting, even if it's a day of celebration. In essence, everything he gave me was nothing short of a bribe, a reward of sorts, to make me love him. Love cannot be bought, yet that is how I feel. Bought and paid for with every gift he gave me when I would have settled for a kind word or a loving embrace."

Tears long suppressed trickled down her cheeks, and the marquess pulled her into his arms. He held her until she no longer wept.

Then he was kissing her, an urgent, fervent kiss that said everything Diana wanted to hear. A fire erupted inside her, and she wanted nothing more than to remain there with him forever.

But alas, it came to an end, as all kisses must.

"I promise I'll never attempt to buy your love," he whispered, his voice husky. "Do you believe me?"

Diana nodded, for any words were stuck in her throat.

"Good. For I've a gift for you, one I promise is not a bribe of any kind." He took a step back and called over his shoulder, "You may bring her in, Arthur."

The dark-haired man appeared, leading a white mare.

"Miss Diana, this is my gift to you."

Diana was stunned. "She's beautiful, my lord. But why?"

Lord Barrington took the reins from Arthur, who dipped his head and stepped away. "You mentioned your love of horses, so I thought that once we marry, you'll need your own."

Diana's heart soared so high she could have touched the moon. How could she have even considered spinsterhood? The idea now seemed silly to her, for she wanted nothing more than to be with this man. The very man she loved.

"Are you saying we'll marry?" she said, teasingly.

"Is that not what courtship leads to, Miss Diana?" he asked. "If I had my way, we'd marry tomorrow. But I'll settle for courtship until the problems I mentioned are dealt with. I would like us to enter our life together free of troubles."

"I cannot wait," she whispered.

"Nor can I."

As Lord Barrington walked away to return the horse to its stall, Diana thought of the lovely surprise she had received. And lovely it was. Yet she could not shake a particular worry.

Although she had confided in him about her concerns for the receiving of gifts, he did not reveal to her what troubles burdened him. How could they enter into marriage free of troubles if he kept secrets from her? And had he not said he struggled with trusting others, her included? Trust was a cornerstone of marriage, or so thought Diana. Without it, it was just another contract. And contracts had no need of love.

Could she enter into an agreement that left her no happier than her parents? Oh, but how she wanted to say she could!

CHAPTER TWENTY-FOUR

J ames pinched the bridge of his nose. His mother had arrived at
Penford Place with a fresh collection of rumors. For the past
hour, he had endured stories of unfaithful wives, thieving
servants, and drunken fights. His mother meant well—or so he
told himself—but she was far too interested in the affairs of others.

His thoughts drifted to Miss Diana and her impending arrival later
this evening for dinner. Although he had informed his mother of his
request to court the lovely young woman, he had also asked her in no
uncertain terms to keep the information to herself.

And he trusted she would. As much as she enjoyed the sharing of
tales about others, any pertaining to the Barrington name had no business being repeated. Or so she had said on many occasions.

Yet, as he considered his future with Miss Diana, a tug of guilt
pulled at his heart. If they were to marry, why did he not trust her
enough to tell her about Amelia? He had no reason to keep the information from her, yet he had done so, nonetheless. Plus, he had lied
when she had inquired about Amelia the night of the servants' party.

What would Miss Diana think if he explained the situation to her?
Not that he was concerned about himself but rather for Amelia and

her current condition. Most women would look on her with scorn, think ill of her, and thus James, as well.

No, it was not a risk he was willing to take, not when Amelia's problem—his problem—would soon be resolved- without anyone learning the truth. Or at least not anyone who mattered.

"I don't care if her parents are of the landed gentry," his mother was saying, breaking him from his thoughts. "There are women of better substance and who come from better families. One would not purchase a dog of poor stock, so why would it be any different when choosing a bride?"

James had been so lost in thought, he had missed about whom she was speaking. If he were to inquire, she would only become frustrated with him. And did he truly care enough about her gossip to inquire?

"If the couple is happy, then it should make no difference," he said. "And while we're on the subject, are there any other couples you would like to mention? Yourself perhaps?"

His mother set down her cup. "Whatever do you mean?"

James smiled. "I've heard you and Lord Telcott have become rather friendly as of late. Is that not the big announcement you wished to share with me in person? That you and he are getting married?"

She gave him a blank stare. "Lord Telcott? Heavens no. He's a friend and nothing more. I'm doing something far more important. I meant to wait and announce it at dinner, but I suppose now is as good a time as any."

"Go on," James said.

"I'm going to the Continent for a year."

This was not the news James had expected to hear. "Whatever for?" he asked. His mother had said on more than one occasion that she had no reason to ever leave England.

"I've become friends with several other widows. We meet to play whist and to share in a bit of gossip."

James doubted that "a bit" was the accurate term but chose to not speak that thought aloud.

"We've discussed how we spent our lives raising our children and taking care of our husbands. Now that we no longer have either responsibility, we've decided we deserve to spend our time as we wish.

You enjoyed your Grand Tour, so why can we not have one of our own? Although, we'll not be taking three years as you young gentlemen tend to do. And we'll be limiting our travels to Paris, Rome, and Venice. We're far too old to see more than that. If Lord Telcott finds himself in one of those great cities, we may share in a meal, but that will be the extent of our time together."

"I think it sounds wonderful, Mother!" James said. "We must host a party before you go. I'm sure you'll not leave until spring, so what do you think about next month?"

His mother laughed. "There's no need for that, my son. Plus, who would attend? Most of the *ton* will already have gone to London by then."

"There are a few of us left," James replied dryly. "I think it would be great fun..." He clamped shut his mouth. What was he thinking? He could not host a party with Amelia in the guest cottage! Yet there was no recanting, for his mother was all smiles at the idea despite her words of refusal.

He could not take any chances, so he would have to send Amelia away for a few days. That would take away the risk of anyone encountering her in her current state.

"Very well. If you feel the need to throw a party, who am I to refuse a celebration in my name? Now that that's settled," his mother said, "I've another matter I would like to discuss with you. You know I don't like to pry into your life, but you are my son, so I must ask."

James gave her a guarded smile. "Go on."

"I told you about the rumors surrounding Miss Amelia, did I not?"

"You did."

"Well, Lady Godwin whispered in my ear that her daughter, Anna, told her that she heard it on good authority that you and Miss Amelia are close."

James laughed. "We've always been close, Mother. Even you're aware of that fact." His mother arched an eyebrow, and James's eyes went wide. "Oh, you mean..."

"Indeed, I do," his mother replied.

An all-too familiar pounding began behind James's right eye. "You of all people should know those are nothing more than rumors, Mother. Surely, you think better of me?"

"Of course I do, James. But you know how the *ton* enjoys gossip. I'd like to know who's spreading these lies. And why? Have you angered someone as of late?"

An image of Mr. Stonebrook came to mind. "I'm not sure," he replied.

"I explained to Lady Godwin that her information was inaccurate. Miss Amelia is as pure as new-fallen snow and would never give into such temptation." She stood. "I don't understand why women enjoy repeating these terrible lies."

James gaped. Did his mother not see that she had done just that? "Are you going to lie down?"

"I am. I look forward to meeting Miss Kendricks this evening. The fact that you seem to care about her as much as you do says we'll get along well."

Once his mother was gone, James hurried to the foyer. Baldwin arrived at the same time. "Get me my coat," he said to the butler. He glanced up toward the top of the stairs to make certain his mother was not there. "The rumors concerning Miss Amelia have increased, and now I've become mixed up in it all. We both know who's behind them."

Baldwin helped James with his coat as he said, "I was quite good at boxing in my younger years, my lord. If you need me to use those skills with Mr. Stonebrook, I'd be happy to lend you my services."

James smiled. "I appreciate your offer, but I see no reason to resort to violence. This will all be over soon enough." He sighed heavily. "Or at least I hope it will be." He glanced at the stairs again. "If my mother comes downstairs before I return—"

"I'll say you had to speak to Mrs. Bunting about tonight's dinner," the butler finished for him.

"Good man," James said. "I should not be gone more than an hour."

He slid on his gloves as he walked through the house and out into the garden. The wind stung his cheeks as he made his way to the guest cottage. He had requested of Amelia that she remain inside while his mother was in residence, and she had readily agreed. She did not want news of her condition getting out any more than James did.

He knocked on the door to the cottage, and Amelia herself answered.

"James? Is everything all right? Your mother hasn't learned I'm here, has she?"

James shook his head. "Not yet."

"Come inside."

As he walked past her, he noticed for the first time that she was bundled in a coat and had a muffler tied around her neck.

"I asked you not to go outside while Mother is here," he said, unable to keep annoyance from his tone. "If she sees you—"

"But I've not been outside," Amelia said as she lowered her head. "I would never put you in such a precarious situation. I'm only dressed this way because I'm cold, and I knew a fire would only draw her suspicion."

It was then that he realized how cold the inside of the house was. "Oh, Amelia, I didn't mean for you to freeze to death. And I didn't mean to snap at you. I'm just under a great deal of stress with Mother being here at such an inconvenient time."

Amelia's eyes misted. "I'm sorry for putting you in this situation. It's not fair that you should suffer. Perhaps I should leave." She moved over to a chair and sat. "My feet hurt, my back aches constantly." She sighed. "I don't mean to complain. Forgive me. What news did your mother bring?"

"You've a right to a fire and a comfortable home," James said, taking the seat beside her. "Mother says she's heard that you've not gone to Paris. And they've included me in the rumors."

"I'm so sorry, James."

"We'll just have to be careful and—"

"No," she said, pushing herself to her feet once more with great effort. "This has gone on for far too long. I've been thinking and have decided that I should find somewhere else to live until the baby is born."

"But where will you go?" James asked. "I see no reason for you to leave."

But had he not come here to have her do just that?

Not for the remainder of her time, he argued with himself. What he wanted was for this to be over!

Amelia smiled. "There is every reason to go," she said. "You and Miss Kendricks don't need an unwed expectant mother getting in your way. It's time you focused your attention on her and your future together and not on me."

"Miss Diana doesn't have to know. This matter is our business, not hers."

"You can't enter into a courtship with me hanging over your shoulder," Amelia said. "And since you would prefer she not know, the only other option we have is for me to leave. You've too much going on as it is to worry about whether the wrong people find out about me."

"But I've got obligations to fulfill. Responsibilities I must see to."

Amelia shook her head. "That's not true. The child is not your concern."

"But it is!" James said. "All this started with me, and I'll see it to the very end."

Wiping tears from her cheek, she said, "What you're doing for me is very noble, and it shows why we've remained friends for so long. If you think it safe for me to remain, I shall. But I urge you to reconsider my offer to leave. Either that or tell Miss Diana about me."

"Remain for the time being," James said. "But I must ask you to go away for a few days next month, just after Twelfth Night. I completely lost my mind today..." He went on to explain about his impromptu offer of hosting a party for his mother.

"I see no problem with that," Amelia said. "It will be nice to have a change of scenery."

James went to the fireplace and began building a fire.

"What if your mother notices the smoke?"

"I'll tell her I've a friend staying here," he replied. "I'll not have you suffering in the cold."

Once the fire was lit, he stood and dusted his hands.

"This young woman, Miss Kendricks," Amelia said. "Do you love her?"

The question caught James off guard, and he frowned.

"You can tell me," she insisted. "I need to hear something beautiful."

James contemplated this question and said, "I care for her, yes. But I'm not sure I would call it love. Not just yet, anyway. She's always on my mind, and when I'm away from her for any amount of time, I find myself longing to be in her company."

"It's just as I suspected. You're in love with her. You just aren't aware of it at this point."

"I don't know if that's true," James said with a nervous laugh. "I care for you, as well, but that's not love."

Amelia let out a laugh. "Though neither of us consider the other in that way, do we? It's why we've always been friends and shall remain so."

James frowned. "I'm not sure what you're trying to say."

"What I'm saying is that you've something beautiful with this young woman. Don't use an excuse, even me and my situation, to delay telling her how you feel. What you have with her is clearly special, for you've a glow around you whenever you speak about her. You must tell her everything. Hold nothing back. She'll understand."

James sighed. "You've always been far too intelligent for your own good. I'll most certainly think on your advice. Now, move in closer to the fire and get warm. And no more of this nonsense of not wanting to build a fire."

She smiled. "If you insist. But do be careful. And do as I suggest."

"I'll take your advice into consideration," he said.

Whether he acted upon it was another thing altogether.

~ ~ ~

The mantle clock showed it was ten minutes to six as James made his way to the foyer to await the arrival of Miss Diana. His mother was waiting for him, looking lovely in her peach-colored gown.

He looked forward to seeing Miss Diana again, and as promised, he had given careful consideration of the advice Amelia had given him.

What she had said was true. The time had come when he would tell Miss Diana the truth about everything—what he felt for her and the secret he had been keeping in the guest house. They could not enter into a courtship while holding back important information. It was not right.

Baldwin opened the door, and Miss Diana and her chaperone entered.

"Miss Kendricks," James said with a bow. "Miss Clifton. I trust your journey was comfortable?"

"Indeed, it was, my lord," Miss Diana replied as Baldwin took her coat. She wore a lovely gown the color of goldenrods with brown embroidery on the bodice and along the bottom hem. Her hair was pulled into a high chignon with two perfect curls hanging on either side of her face. The crimson in her cheeks from the cold heightened her beauty. Never had he thought her so lovely.

"May I present my mother, Lady Barrington. Mother, this is Miss Diana Kendricks and her chaperone, Miss Jenny Clifton."

His mother walked up to Miss Diana. "You are a beautiful creature, my dear," she said in gushing tones. "And your gown! So lovely. Did Mrs. Newberry in Chatsworth make this for you?"

"No," Miss Diana replied. "My mother had it commissioned in London but I've had few opportunities to wear it."

James could not help but notice that something was not quite right about her smile. Tension radiated off the younger woman like heat from a fire.

"Dinner is ready, my lord," Baldwin said. "Would you like to sit now or wait until you've had some time in the parlor first?"

James glanced at the women. "Shall we go straight to the dining room?"

"Yes, let's," his mother replied. "I don't know about anyone else, but I'm famished."

His mother walked ahead, speaking to Miss Jenny and allowing James to walk with Miss Diana

"Is everything all right?" he asked, leaning in close to whisper.

"We must speak alone later," she replied. "There is something that has been bothering me, and I've a number of questions I would like to ask you."

James nodded. "I, too, have something I'd like to share with you. I'm sure we can find a way to have a few moments alone after dinner."

Once they were seated at the table, the footman poured the wine.

"Mother, I'm not sure if I told you that Miss Kendricks and Miss Clifton attend Mrs. Rutley's School for Young Women in Chatsworth. Were you aware they are taught Latin and history there?"

"You don't mean Mrs. Agnes Rutley, surely," his mother said. "She should not be training any women, not after what she's done."

"Done?" James asked, confused. "What has she done?"

His mother turned to their guests. "Are you aware that your head-mistress was once married?"

"Of course," Miss Diana replied.

"You may not have been told," his mother continued, "but her husband died under the most unusual circumstances. Many of the townspeople believe it was murder, but there was never any evidence to say so. She was not married a full year when he had a terrible fall. How convenient that she now resides in the very estate he owned."

James frowned. What had come over his mother? Gossip had always been a favorite subject of hers, but she usually knew when to hold her tongue.

"Mother," he said, fighting to keep his tone cordial but firm, "I'm sure these young ladies would prefer not to listen to rumors about their headmistress, especially at the dinner table. I suggest we speak of more pleasant matters and end this unnecessary and clearly unsubstantiated gossip at once."

"My apologies," his mother said with a sigh. "My intentions were not to spoil your meal."

Miss Diana only smiled in response.

"So, you've studied Latin?" his mother continued. "Have you learned any other languages?"

James took a sip of his wine, relieved that the conversation had moved on to more pleasant topics. Miss Diana courteously answered each question his mother asked and asked a few of her own. Apparently, she had not been offended by his mother's question. Regardless, he would speak to her later about her choice of topics.

What concerned him more was the anger behind her words. What had Mrs. Rutley done to offend his mother so? Surely it had nothing to do with the possibility of murder, not one that was never proven.

By the time the meat course was served, James was once again enjoying himself. He could not help smiling at Miss Diana eating a morsel of roasted chicken or a bite of potato. Why was he fascinated by everything she did?

He had his suspicions but would not mention them to her just yet.

"So, I understand that you and my son met at the local bookstore," his mother said. "Is that correct?"

"Indeed, my lady," Miss Diana replied. "His Lordship was perusing books in the same section as a friend and I."

To James, that day seemed so long ago. It was strange that a single encounter could develop into what it was today. And Miss Diana was as lovely today as she had been before. No, more so!

As the plates were removed, James could not have wished for a better evening.

"Shall we have coffee in the drawing room before you go?"

"I would like that, my lord," Miss Diana replied.

Although he had enjoyed their dinner together, James was determined to speak to Miss Diana concerning Amelia. Plus, he was still curious what she wished to share with him.

As they made their way to the door, his mother walked over to the window that overlooked the garden, a puzzled look on her face. "Why is there smoke coming from the chimney of the guest cottage, James?" she asked. "I was unaware you had anyone staying. Why did you not ask them to join us for dinner?"

"Just a friend," James said. Then he said the first name that came to mind. "Mr. Peter Stonebrook, a man I know from London."

His mother frowned. "I don't believe I'm acquainted with any Stonebrooks, though the name seems familiar. Who's his father?"

"It doesn't matter, Mother," James said, glancing at Miss Diana, who had gone so pale she would have disappeared if the walls had been white. "Come. Baldwin will already have the coffee brought to the drawing room. We wouldn't want it to go cold."

As his mother passed him, she leaned in close and lowered her voice. "I wish to speak to you for a moment alone if possible."

He turned to Miss Kendricks and Miss Clifton. "Ladies, Baldwin will take you to the drawing room. My mother and I shall be there momentarily." Once the two younger women were gone, he said, "What did you wish to speak about?"

"The necklace your grandmother—my mother—gave me," she replied. "It has been handed down from mother to daughter through six generations." James recalled his mother wearing the beautiful silver necklace with multicolored gemstones. "Since the day I received it, I have only thought of when I would be able to pass it on. I can see the love you two share, James, for it appears to be the very same love your father and I once had. If she is your eventual choice in a bride, then it's only right that she has it."

"Mother, you're kind and generous, and I'm sure Miss Diana will be pleased on that day. But we've not discussed marriage. Not just yet. If we do, however, you'll be the first to know."

His mother patted him on the cheek. "Just be sure to do so before another gentleman steals her. 'Leave the worm lying about, and a bird will swoop in and take it away.'"

James laughed. "And who said that?"

"I did, my son," his mother said with a grin. "Even those of us lesser-knowns have good advice from time to time. It's up to you to take it."

CHAPTER TWENTY-FIVE

M rs. Rutley involved in a murder plot? Never had Diana heard such a pinheaded idea! Other rumors about her headmistress had reached Diana's ears, including romantic affairs and lovers twenty years younger. But murder? Never would she believe such nonsense!

Thankfully, Lord Barrington had put an immediate stop to the conversation. Once the topic changed, dinner had proceeded rather well. Despite the precarious beginning, Lady Barrington seemed a lovely woman, and Diana could not help but wonder what it would be like to have her as a mother-in-law.

Likely many hours of listening to gossip, she thought with a wry chuckle. She had dealt with the same during her time at the school, so enduring the rumors while Lady Barrington visited was feasible. At least in the short-term.

Since his offer of courting, Diana had trouble sleeping. Not for what he had said but rather for what was not said. Why did he not seem to trust her enough to tell her his secrets? Perhaps she could help him devise a plan to right the troubles he was enduring.

Which was precisely what she wished to ask him this evening.

What she hoped was that her worries could be laid to rest so they could move forward with whatever lay before them. But secrets could only block their path.

The evening had been wonderful thus far, although keeping her concentration on the ever-changing topics had been a struggle. The marchioness was well-trained in the art of conversation, and if Diana had not been so distracted by her own thoughts, she would have held her own. With the upcoming discussion she and Lord Barrington were to have, concentrating on the topics at hand was a struggle.

It was when Lady Barrington had inquired about the guest cottage that the hairs on the nape of Diana's neck stood up on end.

Mr. Stonebrook was staying at Penford Place? Why had neither man mentioned the other? The two being friends only complicated matters. A woman could explain that some unknown gentleman had been calling on her, a faceless man against whom the marquess would have no reason to retaliate if he so chose.

Explaining about Mr. Stonebrook had been part of the very topic she wanted to discuss. Now, however, he would believe she only wanted to tell him out of fear he would learn from someone other than her. What a tangled web this had become! She was the fly. Who the spider was remained to be seen.

"I'll send for coffee right away," the butler said as he stepped aside to allow Diana and Jenny to enter the room. "His Lordship will be with you soon, I'm sure."

Diana nodded absently as the butler left the room. Then she turned to Jenny and said, "Let's go for a stroll through the gardens. I'll explain why in a moment."

The air bit at her bare arms as they walked outside. Their coats had been taken upon their arrival and requesting them would have put the butler on alert.

"I can't believe what Lady Barrington said about Mrs. Rutley," Jenny said as she wrapped her arms around herself. "I just don't believe it."

"Neither do I," Diana said, trying to keep her teeth from chattering. "But we've a more pressing matter to see to. Did you hear His

Lordship say that Mr. Stonebrook is staying here? Why did Lord Barrington not mention it? Surely, he knows that Father approves of Mr. Stonebrook, yet he asks me to court?"

Jenny rubbed her arms. "Perhaps you're the wager in a bet. My sister knew a woman who had two men who wished to court her. Both were friends just as Lord Barrington and Mr. Stonebrook seem to be. It does happen."

Diana frowned. Usually, the stories Jenny's sister told her were outlandish, but this time, Jenny was right. It did happen.

"There is only one way to learn the truth," she said, glancing toward the house. "Tonight, we'll end this mystery while freeing myself from the inevitable clutches of Mr. Stonebrook at the same time. And if what you say is true, perhaps I should end it with Lord Barrington, as well. Why would I want anything to do with a man who is willing to court the same woman as a friend?"

"And all for the sake of a wager," Jenny added.

"Well, we don't know if that is true, Jenny. But yes, if we do learn it is the case, it's just another good reason to put an end to either man's pursuit."

Stepping onto the path, Diana wished she had forgone her worry about asking the butler for her coat. Oh, but it was cold! If only she had brought a wrap as well as her outerwear, she would have at least some sort of warmth. Jenny's chattering teeth said she was just as cold.

"We won't be long, I promise," Diana assured her friend, her breath coming in billowing clouds of vapor. "We must hurry, though. Or they'll know we've left the house."

They made their way through the garden toward the small cottage at the back. "If these men are playing games with me," Diana said, "I'll put an end to both tonight. But if not, I'll explain to Mr. Stonebrook that my interests lie in his friend, and I'm sorry, but I cannot see him anymore. Father will be angry, but I must do what is best for my heart's sake."

The sound of a pair of voices made her start, and she pulled Jenny around the side of the cottage. They peeked around the corner just in time to see the woman who was with child bundled in a heavy coat and muffler, another woman dressed similarly beside her.

"I cannot help but worry about having to hide out here like a thief, Prudence," the pregnant woman was saying. "With Lady Barrington in residence, I fear she'll find me here at any moment! Can you imagine what she would say if she saw me in my condition? I doubt even James would be able to stop her from revealing it to everyone she knows!"

"Now, Miss Amelia, you know as well as I that His Lordship will protect you and the child at any cost. Has he not already done so since learning of your condition?"

Diana glanced at Jenny, whose eyes were as wide as hers. This was no wife of a business associate but rather a young lady—an unmarried young lady!—who was hiding away because of her "condition."

An uneasiness swept over Diana. Why did Lord Barrington feel the need to protect this woman? The very same woman who had been reading the book Lord Barrington had purchased at the bookshop "for a friend." She recalled the night of the servants' party when she and this woman had spoken. When Diana had mentioned the marquess to this Miss Amelia, the young woman beamed.

Is she carrying Lord Barrington's child?

Having heard enough, Diana motioned to Jenny to follow her, and they hurried back the way they had come. She no longer felt the cold, at least not that which touched her skin. Inside was a different cold, one that threatened to leave her weeping for an untold number of days to come.

They slipped into the blessed comfort of the foyer, and Diana glanced around to make sure no one was nearby. "Something is most definitely wrong, Jenny," she whispered. "I mean, that woman. The book on Paris fashions." Tears filled her eyes. "Had he purchased it for her? Oh, Jenny, I pray that—"

"I know what you're thinking," Jenny said. "Perhaps there is a reasonable explanation for her being in the guest house. When you asked about her, did he not have a reasonable explanation?"

Diana frowned. "I suppose it was reasonable enough. When I spoke to her in the stables, she mentioned his name. I knew then something was amiss, but I refused to take notice."

"How so? Did she sound waspish or jealous? Was her reaction one that said there was more going on than what it seemed?"

"No, not necessarily," Diana replied. "But there is only one reason a man buys a woman gifts, like the book he purchased for her. To keep her happy."

She recalled her one visit home since first attending the school. That was when she had caught her father with a servant girl together in a way reserved only for the marriage bed. After sneaking away from the sordid sight, she had spent the entire night weeping.

Two days later, the servant girl received a hairpin, one that matched the ones he had gifted Diana.

Had Lord Barrington given her the white mare as a way to keep her from learning the truth about this woman? To silence her in case she learned he was keeping a pregnant woman in his guest house?

"What shall we do?" Jenny asked.

"We'll return to the drawing room. Make no mention of what we saw. I'll make an excuse that my stomach is upset so we may leave. Mr. Stonebrook sent word that he would like to call two days from now. If he's a friend of Lord Barrington's, perhaps he'll know something about this mysterious guest."

"And if he confirms your suspicions?" Jenny asked. "What will you do then?"

Diana glanced toward the drawing room. Tonight had been meant to enjoy a lovely dinner together before they discussed what secrets they were keeping from one another. Now, however, it was the night everything they shared came to an end.

When they entered the drawing room, they hurried to the roaring fire. Diana could not stop the shivering, which she was sure came from more than enduring a short time in the cold.

"I'm sorry for the delay," Lord Barrington said as he entered the room only moments later. "Mother will rejoin us shortly."

She smiled at the marquess. "You mentioned that you've a friend staying in your guest cottage. Shall I meet him sometime?"

"Stonebrook?" he asked, his grin dropping. "He's a bore. I would be forced to use disappearing magic on you."

"What do you mean?" Diana asked, her suspicion growing.

Lord Barrington laughed. "It's just an expression. There was a magician, a woman, who made someone disappear. At least that is the rumor. I would consider making you disappear to save you from enduring his excessive boredom." He glanced toward the door. "My apologies for earlier. Mother has a tendency to gossip, so you must learn to pay her little mind sometimes." He chuckled. "Perhaps hiding you would be the best solution after all!"

Diana stifled a snort. It appeared hiding women was not foreign to this man. He was hiding a pregnant woman at that very moment, was he not?

Placing a hand on her stomach, Diana said, "I'm afraid I'm unwell. We've decided to return to the school so I may rest."

"Are you certain?" Lord Barrington asked, clear concern on his features. "Can you not wait for my mother before you go?"

"Please, give her my sincerest apologies, but I'm truly not feeling well."

After donning their outerwear, the marquess walked Diana and Jenny to the waiting carriage. "What did you wish to tell me earlier?" he asked.

"We can discuss it another time," Diana said. She had not meant for her tone to be so sharp. "I do need to rest."

"I hope you feel better," he said.

Once the door of the carriage was closed, Diana leaned back into the bench and sighed. Her head swam in confusion. What was she to think about what she had overheard?

Yet as the vehicle pulled away, she peeked out the window to find Lord Barrington wearing an expression that said he was as confused as she felt.

Upon returning to the school, Diana made her way to Mrs. Rutley's office. Right now, all she wanted was someone in whom she could confide what they had learned, someone she could trust, and who had experience with life. Jenny was a good friend, but her expertise was limited to bad advice from her sister.

Mrs. Rutley sat at her desk, a glass of wine in her hand. Now, that was odd. Never had Diana seen her headmistress partake in any alcohol, not even wine. What made the scene all the odder was the small wooden top she turned in the tips of her fingers. It was the same top Diana had seen during her search for a piece of parchment in the past.

"Was that a gift from someone?" Diana asked as she walked into the room.

Mrs. Rutley did not respond. Instead, she replaced the top in the drawer and said, "You're back early. Is all well? How was dinner?"

"I'm so utterly confused, Mrs. Rutley," Diana said. "I would like to ask your advice. If you have time, of course."

"Close the door and have a seat," Mrs. Rutley said.

Diana did as the headmistress bade.

"I've been thinking of you this evening," Mrs. Rutley said. "Quite a bit, in fact."

Taken aback, Diana said, "Have you?"

The headmistress nodded. "I've seen you grow from a young girl hoping for a future of spinsterhood to a lovely young woman who has developed feelings for a certain gentleman."

Diana shifted in her chair. "Tonight, I meant to make an impression on the marchioness. I believe I was successful."

"Yet you don't look happy. Why is that?"

"Several reasons," Diana replied. "Her Ladyship was kind to me, and I do like her, but she said some things that upset me. Some very cruel things."

Mrs. Rutley gave a small snort. "She's prone to do that."

"Then you know her?"

"No, not really. Most of what I know comes from whatever gossip surrounds her."

Her headmistress did not expand. And although the comment was odd, the fact she did not wish to share more was not surprising. Mrs. Rutley taught the girls at her school that gossip came with stern consequences.

"Dinner was lovely," Diana continued. "But..." She sighed. "Lady Barrington said some very unkind things about you."

Arching an eyebrow, Mrs. Rutley said, "About me? What did she say?"

Diana dropped her gaze. Oh, why hadn't she just kept her mouth shut? She had not meant to bring up the conversation at all, yet here she was, doing just that. And now she had no choice but to explain.

"I wouldn't want to upset you, Mrs. Rutley."

"I'm sure I've heard everything said about me, Diana, so go on, tell me what she said."

"She intimated that you..." Diana swallowed hard. "That you murdered your husband."

Expecting outrage, or perhaps hearing her headmistress curse for the first time, Diana cringed. But shockingly, Mrs. Rutley laughed.

"Oh, how the rumors of the *ton* grow every day!" she said with a shake of her head.

"How did he die, Mrs. Rutley?" Diana asked before she could stop herself.

Setting her wine glass on the desktop, the headmistress leaned forward. "He fell down the stairs in a drunken stupor."

Diana gasped. "Where?"

"Right here in this very house," Mrs. Rutley replied. Diana did not miss the fact that there was no sense of pain or regret to her tone.

Everyone deals with her grief in her own way, Diana thought.

Aloud she said, "My condolences, Mrs. Rutley. And I'm sorry for telling you what I heard. I should have known better."

"There are worse fates than losing a husband, I assure you," Mrs. Rutley said. "Now, tell me what else is bothering you. Surely you didn't leave early because of a rumor you heard about me."

It was time to tell the truth. "During dinner, Lady Barrington noticed smoke coming from the chimney of the guest cottage..." She went on to explain all that occurred, including Lord Barrington's lie about Mr. Stonebrook residing there and what she had overheard from Miss Amelia.

"So, I said I was not feeling well and left. But why is he secreting away a woman who is clearly unwed and pregnant? And why did he say Mr. Stonebrook was staying there? It's a web full of lies, and I feel like a fly stuck in the middle of it! It's just an unusual situation all the way around."

Mrs. Rutley frowned. "Very unusual, indeed," she muttered.

"I had hoped to clean the slate between Lord Barrington and me. Now, I'm wondering if I should never speak to him again. What do you believe I should do?"

"I understand your concern, Diana, I do," Mrs. Rutley said. "What if he wishes to continue to court you? Would you want that?"

"Only if the child the woman carries is not his," Diana replied honestly. "If he is helping her through a difficult situation, one for which he is not responsible, that makes him a hero. But if he's the cause of that situation, that changes everything. Oh, Mrs. Rutley, I'm so frightened and confused! I feel as if I'm in a game, but I've no idea what the rules are or how it's played, leaving me destined to lose."

Mrs. Rutley rose. "Here is what I propose," she said, walking around the desk. "Mr. Stonebrook is due to call on you in a few days, is he not?"

Diana nodded. "I'm under the impression that he wishes to tell me something about my father."

"While he's here, ask him about his friendship with Lord Barrington and what he might know about this woman. Once you've done that, I would advise you to call on Lord Barrington to ask him the same question. See what he has to say about it."

Considering her headmistress's words, Diana said, "That is a very good idea, Mrs. Rutley. I'll do that. But how will I know who is telling the truth?"

Mrs. Rutley smiled. "You must allow your heart to guide you. It will reveal the truth when your eyes and ears are confused. Ignoring it will only lead to trouble."

"I fear my heart is leading me to destruction," Diana said with a sigh. "Good night, Mrs. Rutley. And thank you."

When she arrived at her room, Jenny was there waiting on the bed. Diana explained the discussion she and Mrs. Rutley had and the advice she was given.

"It will all work out as it should," Jenny said, patting Diana on the arm before leaving the bed.

Diana wanted to believe her friend, but as she lay awake that night, the memory of Miss Amelia entering the guest cottage came to mind. She was very pretty. So much so, any man would be tempted by her. Yet, if that man had been Lord Barrington, Diana knew her heart would be crushed. And she would never be the same again.

CHAPTER TWENTY-SIX

F riday morning, James perused the shelves of Mistral's
Booksellers as he waited for the proprietor to finish speaking
with another customer. The shop had always been a place of
escape, to lose himself in a world of knowledge. Although it had always
served that purpose, it had provided him something far greater. There,
he had met the lovely Miss Diana Kendricks.

He recalled the first time he had encountered her. She and her
friend had whispered his name—or rather his moniker of Marquess of
Magic. He chuckled at the memory of her grabbing the closest book
when he had confronted her. Oh, but how he had teased her so unmercifully!

The second encounter was all the more memorable, for she had
retaliated. Twice! Leading him into the dressmaker's shop had been a
successful victory for the young woman. Tenfold!

What had begun as friendship grew into something far greater, and
now James wanted to give her a special memento to always remind
them of how they met.

His mother had left for home this morning but with the promise
to return for the small party he would host for her before her journey
to the Continent. His mother had been disappointed when Miss

Diana left before she could give her the necklace, but she understood.

James, however, wondered if Miss Diana had suffered a case of nerves being in the company of his mother, especially after she had said such disparaging things about the headmistress.

"You must never mention any gossip about Mrs. Rutley while in Miss Diana's company," he had snapped at his mother. "How would you feel if someone defamed Mrs. Cleminson?" Mrs. Cleminson had been his mother's governess.

"Why, I'd give the person the sharp side of my tongue!" his mother had said before realizing the implication of her words. "Oh. Well yes, you're right, James. I'll keep a tighter rein on what I say in the future."

It appeared whatever business Mr. Mistral had been conducting was coming to an end, so James approached the front counter.

"I do hope you have a wonderful day, my lord," the proprietor said as he handed the customer a book wrapped in brown paper.

"You as well, Mr. Mistral," Lord Walcott said with a nod. Several years James's elder, the earl was a gentleman of whom James never heard an ill word spoken.

"Well hello, Barrington," Walcott said when he caught sight of James. "So you, too, have decided to brave this weather, I see. I thought I would be the only one."

A light coating of snow on the roads always had the residents hunkering down in their homes, leaving the streets of Chatsworth empty. Just as James preferred. "No weather can keep me away from books," James replied. He eyed the book in Walcott's hand. "And what has caught your attention today?"

The earl lifted the parcel. "The Confessions of William Henry Ireland," he said with a grin. "A master expert in forgery. Or purportedly a master expert. I'd say he was not as great as he believed if he was caught in the act." This had both of them chuckling. "Well, a warm fire and a nice glass of brandy are calling me. Good day to you, Barrington. Mr. Mistral." And with a warm smile, the man left the shop.

"Good morning, my lord," Mr. Mistral said with one of his friendly grins.

"Good morning. Were you able to find the book I requested?"

The proprietor nodded. "It wasn't easy, I must say. Like I said before, it's quite rare. You're exceptionally lucky that I was able to locate a copy. My man overcame the terrible conditions to find you one."

James smiled as he placed his gloved hands on the counter. "I assume he went to London and found it there but at great trouble," he said. It did not escape his notice that Mr. Mistral made searching for the book sound like a difficult quest.

The proprietor gave a nervous chuckle. "Right you are, my lord." Reaching beneath the counter, he pulled out a large tome. "As you requested."

Removing his gloves, James ran a hand over the soft brown leather. "It's truly a work of art," he said. *The Lady's Guide to Magic* was embossed in gold across the front cover. He opened the book and flipped through the pages. "Many of the illustrations are in color. I didn't expect that, but I am pleased."

"Indeed, my lord. I understand that when the book was first printed, it created a great deal of commotion. Many bookshops refused to carry it because too many men worried their wives would become interested in learning magic and end up casting spells on them."

The foolishness of some men was outrageous in James's opinion. He had heard the ruckus the book had caused, not only for the very reason Mr. Mistral had explained, but also because it was written for women. The last thing most men wanted was women who did anything beyond looking after the household and planning parties. But not James. The idea of Miss Diana wanting to learn the art of illusion pleased him greatly.

"I hope you don't think me impertinent, my lord," Mr. Mistral said. "But do you know a lady who performs magic?"

"I do," James replied. "And I can assure you she's the best England has ever seen." *After all, she was able to cast a spell over me!* That he kept to himself.

James paid the proprietor, adding a little extra to thank him for going out of his way to find the gem. He had known how difficult finding the book would be, especially on such short notice, but Mr. Mistral had done even better than expected.

Once the book was wrapped, James thanked the proprietor and left the shop. Light snow flurries fell upon the empty street, and he ducked his head as he began the trek back to the carriage. Today was a day of celebration, for he had come to realize his true feelings for Miss Diana and therefore wished to make public their courtship.

At the end of the street, he took a right to where his carriage was waiting. After a quick glance around to make sure no one would see, he nodded to the driver before opening the door and entering the vehicle.

"He was able to find the book," he said to Amelia, who was waiting inside. "And in such a short time. I do hope she likes it."

Amelia smiled. "I see no reason why she would not. It's a fine gift that comes from the heart. She'll see that."

James had felt bad that Amelia was stuck inside the guest cottage for so long. He had used the advantage of the weather to allow her a moment's reprieve. No one would be out on such a dreadful day, so there was no risk of anyone seeing them. It was also the reason he had asked the driver to park around the corner from the bookshop. But even with the curtains closed, Amelia appeared pleased to be able to go somewhere, anywhere.

"I've a request to make of you, Amelia. I'd like to celebrate all the wonderful things for which I'm thankful, including you. I know you cannot have any wine, but I'd like you to join me for dinner—as Mrs. Triton, of course, to benefit the staff. What do you think?"

She smiled. "Although your offer is kind and most welcomed, I'm not sure I should be eating at the same table as a marquess or if dining with Judith, a fellow servant, would not be more appropriate." They both laughed at this, but then she added more seriously, "You have a fine staff, my lord. They've kept their word to say nothing about my presence, even when our excuses have been abysmal at best. I can't imagine what they believe, given some know the truth while others think my make-believe husband has left me to fend for myself while he's off gallivanting in America. But they must have a great deal of respect for you not to say anything."

"They are truly fine people," James replied.

Amelia laughed. "I imagine they see you as one of them. At least on Saturday nights while they're drinking and dancing in the stable. I'd be happy to join you for dinner. And it will be a night we'll both cherish for years to come."

"I would like that," James said. "And you're correct. It will be a night I'll never forget."

⸺‿⸺

Late Friday afternoon, snow fell upon the grounds of Mrs. Rutley's School for Young Women as Diana gazed out the drawing room window. A beautiful blanket of white covered the gardens, leaving not a single blade of grass or bough of a tree untouched.

Although Diana would not be seeing Lord Barrington until tomorrow, that sense of urgency to speak to him had remained since having dinner with the marchioness two days earlier. She had to know the truth about the servant who lived in the guest cottage, the woman he had hidden away. Miss Amelia, or so the woman in her company had called her, had to be a part of the trouble the marquess had mentioned, but to what extent that trouble went was what worried Diana most.

Then there was Mr. Stonebrook. If he was friends with Lord Barrington, did he know about the woman kept hidden away? And what had her father said when Mr. Stonebrook told him they would no longer be seeing one another?

Diana could not decide which knotted her stomach more.

"I hear voices," Jenny said from where she had been keeping watch. She opened the door a few inches and peeked into the hallway. "It's Mr. Stonebrook."

With a nod, Diana walked to the middle of the room, Jenny hurrying to her side. As the voices of Mrs. Rutley and Mr. Stonebrook grew louder, Diana braced herself for whatever news he brought.

"Good afternoon, Mr. Stonebrook," Diana said when he entered the room. She dropped into a perfect curtsy, Jenny doing the same at her side.

Mr. Stonebrook responded with a bow.

"I'll be doing some work in my office if you need me," Mrs. Rutley said before leaving the room.

"I must say," Mr. Stonebrook said with a smile as he removed his gloves, "it's frigid out there, but I'll not allow the weather to keep me from seeing you today."

He was a kind man who spoke even kinder words, yet Diana felt nothing for him. Friendship, perhaps, but even that was an exaggeration. Anything they could possibly have together paled when she thought of Lord Barrington and their courtship.

"Please, sit," Diana said. "I can have tea brought up if you would like."

"Tea would be lovely," he replied.

Jenny stood. "I'll call for it."

Diana sat with her hands clutched in her lap, Mr. Stonebrook across from her. Although she had practiced time and again what she would ask him, she found the words stuck in her throat.

He saved her the trouble by speaking first. "I know some time has passed since we last saw one another, but I'd like to begin with my conversation with your father if I may."

Diana sighed with relief. "Yes, of course. I must admit that I've wondered about his response, though I thought he would write me himself."

Mr. Stonebrook reached into his inside coat pocket and pulled out a letter. "He asked me to deliver this myself."

Diana took the parchment, noticing that the seal was broken. Had Mr. Stonebrook read the letter? Surely, he knew what it contained if he had spoken to her father. Pushing aside the concern, she unfolded the letter and read its contents.

With each word, her eyes widened, and she was gaping by the end. Then she reread it just to be certain she understood its meaning correctly.

"This says that my father insists that you and I court? And you accepted? After what we discussed before you left? I thought we were friends and you understood how I felt!"

Mr. Stonebrook lowered his head. "My intentions have never been to upset you, but my hand was forced. Your father was quite adamant that this was what he wished. What choice did I have?"

"Choice?" Diana demanded, rising from her seat as she blinked back tears. "I told you what I wanted, and you disregarded it without any thought for my feelings."

"Your father asked... no, he begged me to court you. I refused because that is what you requested, but he would not accept my position. He said by courting—and eventually marrying—you, you would not need to complete your final year of schooling and thus save him money. I was stunned, to be sure, but he was insistent. I found I could not refuse him. It's no wonder he does so well. He's a very worthy negotiator."

Diana choked back a sob, and Jenny grasped her by the hand and settled her back onto the couch. How could her father do this to her? When had he begun believing her schooling was far too expensive? And when had he determined she could no longer decide her future? After all these years of making her believe that the choice was hers only to take it away from her made it all the more difficult to stomach!

"I'm sorry you've been put in this situation, Miss Kendricks," Mr. Stonebrook said. "But I promise to be a dutiful and attentive suitor if you'll have me. I would see it as an honor."

"I've much to consider," Diana said.

She paused. What was there to consider? She had no choice in the matter. Her father had every right to choose her husband and demand she marry him. Even if she did not want to do so.

But what did this all mean for the courtship between her and Lord Barrington? If that even existed anymore. That thought led to the question she had meant to ask Mr. Stonebrook.

"Are you acquainted with Lord Barrington?" she asked.

"I am."

"Are you currently residing in his guest house?"

Mr. Stonebrook frowned. "I'm not. What makes you think that?" Then he chuckled. "I see now. Is he the man in whom you have an interest?"

"I don't wish to hurt you, Mr. Stonebrook. As I said before you went to speak to my father, I do think highly of you. But Lord Barrington has asked to court me, and I accepted. I had hoped to tell Father, but I was waiting until you had spoken to him to tell him." She sighed. "It appears I waited too long."

"Lord Barrington and I are indeed friends," Mr. Stonebrook said. "I've come to see the kind woman you are, and I would never believe you would want to hurt me in any way. Nor would I wish to cause you any pain. But when it comes to the marquess, I'm afraid that is exactly what I must do."

Diana glanced at Jenny, who appeared as confused as she. "I'm sorry. I don't understand. What do you mean?"

He heaved a heavy sigh. "Lord Barrington spent a great deal of time boasting about a beautiful woman. Now I can see that woman was you."

"Me?" Diana asked, shocked. "He spoke about me to you? Then you must have already known he was calling on me."

Mr. Stonebrook shook his head. "But I didn't know, for he refused to give the woman's name. If he had, I would have warned you long ago about the things he's said about you."

Diana's heart clenched. "What things?"

"No, I cannot say," Mr. Stonebrook said, shaking his head adamantly. "I cannot repeat what he had hoped to gain in the company of a number of ladies. Even you, the young woman I intend to marry."

Bile rose in Diana's throat. "Are you saying that he sees me as a..." She could not say which word fit best, but hussy came to mind. Had his plan been to get her to give herself to him before they were married? Well, he had another think coming if he thought her that trusting! Or that naive!

"May I ask, what made you ask about his guest cottage? And how did you learn that we are acquainted? I mean, it's not as if you've seen us together."

The door opened, and Mrs. Shepherd entered with a tea tray. She eyed Mr. Stonebrook and then asked, "Do you want me to pour?"

Diana shook her head. "No, thank you, Mrs. Shepherd. I'll see to it."

The cook pursed her lips and narrowed her eyes at their guest once more before leaving the room.

"Miss Clifton and I were invited to dinner a couple of nights ago," Diana said as she poured the tea. "His Lordship made mention that you were a guest there. But I found a woman there instead."

Mr. Stonebrook accepted the teacup. "I take it you met Miss Amelia Lansing."

"How did you know?" Diana asked, nearly spilling her tea. "But of course, if you're friends with Lord Barrington, you're likely acquainted with his guests."

"Yes, well, I know Miss Lansing only in passing. Perhaps a polite hello at parties but nothing more. But I do know all about the pair of them."

He shook his head and stood. "Forgive me. It's quite evident that you have very strong feelings for Lord Barrington. After all, he's a marquess, and I'm a simple baron. Or shall be when the time comes. I can see why you'd prefer him over me. I've tried to warn numerous impressionable women like yourself about him, but to no avail. All I ask is that you take care if you choose to accept his offer of courtship over mine." He walked over to the window and gazed outside, his shoulders drooping.

Diana joined him. "Mr. Stonebrook, I promise you, my choice of Lord Barrington over you has nothing to do with title."

"You're just saying that to placate me."

She placed a hand on his arm. "Not at all. I see you as a friend. A good friend who is willing to tell me the truth, even though you know it may hurt me."

"I'm glad you see it that way, for I don't know what I would do if you came to hate me."

Diana laughed. "I can never hate you! Now, tell me what you know of this woman. And I want to hear everything, no matter how terrible it is."

Mr. Stonebrook nodded. "I don't know much, but I'll tell you what I do. Whether you believe me makes little difference, for I'll do whatever I can to see no harm comes to you." He smiled. "I only wish to protect you."

"I appreciate you saying so," she whispered. "You're a very noble gentleman."

With a sigh, Mr. Stonebrook said, "Lord Barrington and I first met a few years ago in London, and I was immediately taken in by his demeanor. Never had I met a man so kind to others, especially to his servants. As I came to know him better, however, I began to notice his eyes settling on one woman after another. Some were married, some servants. But I had no proof of wrongdoing, so I believed I was just being suspicious. As if maybe what I was seeing wasn't there."

Diana's stomach churned, but she had to know the truth. "Go on."

"Although I didn't know her name at the time, last year, I saw Miss Lansing leaving Lord Barrington's London residence. When I mentioned this to him, he confided in me that he wished to use her to assuage his carnal needs. Later, he bragged that he had succeeded in his conquest of her. I made every attempt to convince him that following through on such a plan was unwise, but he refused to listen." He shook his head. "'What kind of man wants just one woman when he can have many?' is what he told me."

"You did the right thing," Diana said, although the fist around her heart tightened. "You're a very honorable man, indeed."

"What is honor when you cannot convince a friend to turn from his terrible ways?" Mr. Stonebrook replied, his voice choked with emotion. "I heard a rumor that Miss Lansing became with child. I went to Lord Barrington to inquire if he was the cause only to find that he had fled London with her."

Diana considered all she had heard and how it worked into what she had seen with her own eyes. Something still did not seem right. "But why would he ask her to come to Chatsworth with him? Would it not be easier for him to simply run away and deny any wrongdoing? Offering his guest cottage does not seem a viable way to handle the situation."

"I asked the same question," Mr. Stonebrook said. "When your father sent me here to see you, I took the opportunity to call on him at Penford Place. When I inquired into the rumors, he came right out and said he was hiding Miss Lansing until the birth of the child, whom he plans to send to an orphanage. Miss Lansing will remain at Penford Place as a servant. I'll not say what sort of serving she will do."

Diana crossed her arms over her stomach and shuttered. "Thank you for that."

"I did all I could to make him do right by her, to put away his fool-ishness, and marry the young lady. But saying so angered him. He struck me and banished me from his home." He looked at her, his eyes filled with grief. "I've never admitted such an embarrassing encounter to anyone. Please don't think me weak for not defending myself, but I believe in peaceful resistance, not force."

A tear rolled down Diana's cheek. After all this time, this man had been kind and caring, and she had not valued that fact. "You're not weak, Mr. Stonebrook. I can assure you. I understand now how brave you truly are. Standing up to a man you believed to be your friend took a great deal of courage, and you should be proud of that." She lifted herself onto her toes and kissed his cheek. "I appreciate your honesty. Thank you."

"What would you like to do?" he asked. "We must give your father a response to his letter."

For a moment, she wondered about his smile. It was... victorious?

"I'm to meet with Lord Barrington tomorrow. I want the opportunity to confront him and to hear the truth from his lips. If he chooses not to confess, then I'll know he's not the man for me. Afterward, we can discuss my father's wishes."

"So, you'll accept my offer of courtship?"

"Yes, but—"

"Then there is no reason to delay," he said, beaming. "I've a carriage waiting outside. Why wait until tomorrow when you can learn the truth this very evening?"

Diana grasped hold of his arm as he turned to leave. "Why would you allow me to speak to him if he is as cruel as you say? And did you not say he banished you from Penford Place?"

Mr. Stonebrook rested the back of his hand on her cheek. "My sweet Diana," he whispered. "It's vital you learn the truth. For once you do, our courtship will have a chance to be something wonderful. If it requires me taking you to the lair of a rogue, so be it. All I ask is this. If you learn that what I've said is true, you'll forget him forever."

Diana considered this offer. If what he had told her was true, then yes, she would have every reason to erase the marquess from her mind. "I promise," she replied. "And thank you for telling me the truth."

His lips brushed her ear as he leaned in and whispered, "What else is there but the truth? Now, let's go and hear it."

CHAPTER TWENTY-SEVEN

A languid quiet filled the room as James took a sip of his brandy and sighed. Having forgone his coat and wearing only his shirtsleeves, he rose to refill his glass.

"I'm in no condition to help you to your room," Amelia warned him. "If you collapse into a drunken state, the floor will be your bed."

James barked a laugh. "I'll admit that my head does feel light, but I'm far from drunk. I can consume several more glasses and still remain in good standing." He went to take a step only to wobble, making Amelia laugh. "That was figurative, of course."

Dinner had been delectable and their conversation congenial, and now they were sharing in after-dinner drinks. Well, James was drinking. Amelia settled for coffee. He was not one to drink, at least not in excess, but he had reasons to celebrate, Miss Diana's agreement to allow him to court her at the top of the list.

"With Mother gone," he said as he returned to his seat, "I can refocus my efforts here. Miss Diana had wanted to discuss something important. I wish she hadn't fallen ill. I must admit that waiting to hear what she wishes to say has been difficult. But once we've shared our secrets, everything will be as it should. With you, with Miss Diana. All will be well."

Amelia set her cup on the table and leaned back in the chair, her hand on her stomach. "You're happy, as is your mother, and knowing my child will have a good home makes me happy. Life is simply... well, happy."

"I couldn't agree more. And I'm glad you've such a positive outlook on the future." He sighed and stared into his glass, the amber liquid moving back and forth like waves on a quiet ocean. "I'd like to ask you a question if I may. It concerns something Baldwin told me."

"Of course," Amelia replied. "Anything."

"When I was young, Baldwin said my parents were close. But then something happened, and as Baldwin puts it, the magic between them disappeared. I don't wish to speak ill of her, for she was a wonderful mother. Yet it was as if a chasm formed between my parents, and I don't know why. I was wondering if your parents ever mentioned anything that may help me to understand what transpired between them."

Amelia wrung her hands.

"Please, if you know something, tell me."

With a sigh, she said, "One afternoon during one of our visits, your parents were arguing. They were so loud I imagine the entire household heard them. I was perhaps eight at the time, so quite young, but from what I understood, your mother learned from the doctor that she could no longer have children. Although she was terribly upset by the news, your father didn't seem concerned. He had his heir and that was enough for him. Despite your father's arguments to the contrary, your mother felt like less a woman."

James sighed. "Father was always so forgiving," he said. "That which bothered other men had no effect on him. But this explains why they had no other children. And what drove them apart." He slapped his hands on his legs. "Enough sad talk! This is to be an evening of celebration, so we're only to discuss happy things."

A knock on the door made him call out, "Yes?"

Baldwin entered. "My lord, you asked me to inform you when I'm to leave. Is there anything else you'll be needing?"

"No, Baldwin. Enjoy your stay at your cousin's home. Just don't grow too accustomed to an easy life and choose not to return in three days as you promised."

The butler smiled. "Of course not, my lord. Constance is finishing her duties in the study per your request. You asked to inspect it before she retired for the night."

"Very good," James said. Constance was put on probation after being caught slacking in her duties. The only thing keeping her in her position was James's belief in giving people the opportunity to prove themselves. "Have a nice time, and we'll see you again soon."

"Thank you, my lord," Baldwin said with a diffident bow.

"He hasn't aged at all," James said when the butler was gone. "I wish I knew his secret."

Amelia smiled. "I assume, unlike you, he forgoes the brandy every evening."

This had them both chuckling, and then a memory came to James.

"I'll never forget the time he caught me with father's wine. He tried to convince me that overconsumption at a young age would reverse my growth. If I'd been ten at the time, I might have believed him. But as I was fifteen, I wasn't so gullible."

"Do you recall the party for Lord Plating...?"

They went on sharing stories about the past, one leading into another, until they were both weeping tears of laughter. James was pleased to see Amelia laughing again, and he reveled in the freedom he felt in her presence.

He was returning to the decanters to refill his glass in the middle of another story when a light rap came to the door. Perturbed at being interrupted, he called, "I'll be there in a moment!"

"Yes, my lord," Constance called from the other side of the door.

After refilling his glass, James walked over to his seat, nearly falling in the process. He chuckled. "Perhaps I'll not drink this last glass," he said, setting it on the table.

"And the maid?" Amelia asked with eyebrows raised.

"She can wait. She's lucky I haven't given her the sack. It's a relief to know Baldwin can go with me to London. I don't know what I would do without his wisdom and friendship." He glanced at Amelia, and a pang of guilt came over him. "I'm sorry. I didn't mean to say yours is not welcome."

Amelia clicked her tongue at him and struggled to her feet. "There's no need to leave on my account."

She laughed. "My leaving has nothing to do with you. I'm just tired, is all. And I'm pleased to hear that you welcome my company, but I'd say much has changed as of late. Would you not agree?"

James rose and took her hand in his. "For all we've endured, the bond we share, the child you carry, know that I'll always cherish you."

"You're a gentleman above all gentlemen," she said, smiling up at him. "And that's why you'll always have a special place in my heart." She kissed his cheek and left the room.

James sighed. "Constance, are you ready?"

"No, my lord," the maid said as she entered the room. Her cheeks were the color of beets. "But you've a caller, my lord. A Miss Diana Kendricks. I put her in the parlor."

"Miss Diana?" he asked, pinching the bridge of his nose in confusion. "It's Friday, not Saturday."

"Indeed, my lord."

"Then, why is she here?" he mumbled, wishing now he had heeded Amelia's warning about overindulgence.

The maid went to answer, but he waved a hand to forestall her. "It was rhetorical, Constance. That means you don't need to respond. Thank you. You may go."

The maid bobbed a quick curtsy and withdrew.

James donned his coat, took a deep breath, praying he would not stumble, and left the room. The parlor was the next room over in the corridor, so he was entering the room in no time.

Yet, what he found made his stomach clench. Her eyes were red as if she had been weeping. "Miss Diana?" he asked as he hurried to her side. "What is it?"

"I've something to tell you, my lord."

As Diana sat in the carriage outside Penford Place, she wondered what she was doing. Her desire to march into Lord Barrington's home and confront him had been fueled by hurt. Now she was unsure if she was doing the right thing. If she learned Mr. Stonebrook had spoken the truth, it would crush her heart. But if she learned otherwise, her distrust of him might crush the heart of Lord Barrington. Neither sounded pleasant.

"Are you ready, Miss Kendricks?" Mr. Stonebrook asked from his seat across from her. "You seem to be hesitating. Would you prefer to return to the school?"

Diana shook her head. "We're here, so I would like to speak to him now. Perhaps it would be best if you remain in the carriage."

Mr. Stonebrook pursed his lips. "I don't think that is a good idea. Barrington is prone to fits of anger. I worry what he may do to you if I'm not there to protect you."

"Please, I must do this alone. With Jenny in attendance, of course. I do have some sense of propriety." She frowned. "If you refuse to remain here, I'll only return tomorrow without you."

Heaving a sigh, his cheeks reddening, Mr. Stonebrook said, "If that is what you wish. But at least allow me to wait in the foyer for you. Please, I worry about your safety. You don't know what he's truly like."

"Very well," she said, pushing open the door and alighting from the carriage, Jenny following behind. She wanted the truth. No, she *needed* the truth. "But you're not to interfere unless something goes terribly wrong."

"I swear," he replied.

"I'm sorry you must do this, Diana," Jenny whispered as they walked toward the front door. "If there was any way I could do this in your stead, I would."

Each step felt as if Diana's shoes were made of lead. "Thank you, my friend, but I must do this for myself. Whatever I learn today, at least I'll know."

She knocked on the door, and a young servant girl with a pretty smile and dark hair answered. "Yes?" she said in a quiet voice.

"Miss Diana Kendricks to see Lord Barrington."

"Yes, miss," the maid said. "Please come in. May I take your coat?"

Diana shook her head. "There is no need. Is Lord Barrington available?"

The maid glanced across the room. "Well, he's in a meeting of sorts, miss. If you'd like, you can wait in the parlor while I ask if he's seeing anyone." Her voice shook, and Diana's suspicions grew.

"Yes, that is fine." She turned to Mr. Stonebrook. "You promised to wait here."

He gave a small grunt but agreed, and Diana followed the maid past the drawing room toward the parlor. Her skin grew cold upon hearing the sound of a woman's laughter, soon joined in by that of the marquess.

"I'll inform His Lordship you're here, miss," the maid said as she lit several of the candles in the room. "I'm sure he won't be long."

Once the maid was gone, Diana turned to Jenny. "Did you hear a woman laughing?"

Jenny nodded. "I did."

"Who do you think it is?"

Jenny glanced at the door. "Wait here." She peeked out into the corridor. "We can't listen at the keyhole. That maid's out there."

Diana growled in frustration but then gasped. "The hidden passageway. Let's use it to see who is with the marquess."

Remembering how Lord Barrington had opened the passageway, Diana felt with her feet for the lever. With a click, the shelf slid open. Diana grabbed one of the candles and entered the passageway. It was dark, the candle giving much less light than the candelabra had the night the marquess had shown them the hidden space.

It did not take her long to find the drawing room, and once there, she peeked through the eye holes. Her heart sank. Lord Barrington was in a state of undress, lounging with a leg hanging over the arm of his chair. Miss Amelia sat across from him.

Fighting back tears, she watched as Lord Barrington stood and took Miss Amelia's hand in his in a much too familiar way. She had to cover her mouth to stifle a gasp. He admitted to his responsibility for the child? No! It could not be! Yet it was, for he also spoke of a special bond they shared.

So, this was the personal issue with which he was dealing. It was clear the woman was not married but rather a hussy for whom he cared!

"You'll always have a special place in my heart," Miss Amelia said before kissing his cheek.

Diana could not watch any longer. "Go back!" she hissed, and Jenny returned in the direction from which they had come.

Once they were back in the parlor, Diana could not stop the flow of tears.

"I'm so sorry," Jenny said, pulling Diana in for an embrace. "I cannot believe what we heard."

"Nor can I," Diana said, sniffling. "I believed he was different, but I was a fool. At least I learned the truth before we became engaged!"

Footsteps announced the arrival of Lord Barrington, and he entered the room wearing a wide smile. He now wore his coat.

How thoughtful of him, she thought ruefully. He truly was a magician, for he had performed an illusion on her heart.

"Miss Diana? What is it? I didn't expect you until tomorrow. I even confirmed with Constance which day it was." He barked a laugh, and the odor of brandy filled the room.

Diana could not help but wonder if Constance had a special place in his heart, too.

Jenny had repeated a rumor she had heard that a dozen women had fallen in love with the Marquess of Magic. At the time, Diana had dismissed it as nonsense. Now however, she knew it was she who had been naive enough not to have believed it.

"Things have changed since we last spoke, my lord," she said, mustering all her strength, all her courage to say what needed to be said. "Father has asked that I allow another man to court me, and I've agreed. The charade in which we've participated is over."

"Charade?" Lord Barrington asked. "None of this has been a charade. Please, allow me—"

"I no longer care to hear what you have to say. The man I have chosen to court me happens to be a friend of yours. Mr. Peter Stonebrook? Ah, I see you know who he is. Well, he's proven to be a much better gentleman than you'll ever be."

"Oh, Miss Diana, you've no idea what sort of man Stonebrook his. You cannot trust him!"

Diana shook her head at how easy it was for him to lie and keep such an innocent look in his eyes. "I can and I do, far more than you. He's an honorable man who has warned me about you."

He grabbed her by the arm. "You must listen to me. Stonebrook is a terrible, terrible man. He woos and uses women at every turn. I can assure you his intentions with you are far from pure."

Diana pulled her arm from his grip. "Is he the type of man who beds women?"

"He is!"

"And what about giving them children out of wedlock? Does he do that?"

"He's done that and more. Please, you must believe me. He's no good!"

The pain of this man casting his sins on another made her feel ill. "Perhaps you can find a woman willing to fall for your illusions, my lord," Diana said, her voice trembling with anger and hurt. "One innocent enough to be lured by your playacting. But it will no longer be me."

"Miss Diana, please," he called out after her as she hurried from the room. "Please, don't go." But she ignored him.

When she and Jenny reached the foyer, she signaled to Mr. Stonebrook, who opened the door and followed them to the carriage.

"Are you all right?" he asked as he gathered her into his arms in front of the door to the carriage, holding her as she wept.

"Stonebrook!" Lord Barrington bellowed from the front door. "Get away from her this instant!"

"Don't think I'll allow you to hurt her any longer, Barrington," Mr. Stonebrook said. Then he turned to Diana. "Get into the carriage. Hurry, before he becomes violent."

With her heart racing, Diana stepped from the carriage and wrapped her arms around Jenny as the two men sized up each other.

"For the love of heaven, Miss Diana," Lord Barrington said. "This man is not who you believe him to be!"

"Don't blame me for your troubles," Mr. Stonebrook said with a snort. "Miss Kendricks is no fool. She knows who it is you hide away and why."

"You set me up!" the marquess said, reaching for Mr. Stonebrook.

Diana swatted at his arm. "Don't you attack him again!" she said.

Lord Barrington gaped her. "Again?"

"Did you not strike him before?" she asked.

"Well yes, but—"

She gave a sharp nod. "And is there not a Miss Amelia Lansing hiding in your guest cottage?"

"Yes, but it's not what it seems. I must hide her."

Once more, the tears streamed down her cheeks. "You're right, things aren't what they seem, for your magical ways fooled me. But like the illusion of the moving coin, I know how it's performed. Now you can fool me no longer."

Mr. Stonebrook placed a foot on the carriage step. "Barrington, I warned you this day would come. That you'd be ousted for the man you truly are. I swear to you, if you seek to hurt Miss Kendricks in any way, I'll do all I can to defend her."

"You'll pay for this," James hissed.

Diana wiped the tears from her eyes. "If you've any decency left, *my lord,* leave us alone."

She pulled the door closed, and Mr. Stonebrook tapped on the roof to inform the driver they were ready to leave.

With the faint glow of the lights coming from the window highlighting the marquess, an odd feeling settled over Diana. Although every indication of his guilt was clear, although all evidence pointed at him, her heart told her otherwise.

Yet that same heart had led her to him to begin with, and that had turned out to be wrong.

CHAPTER TWENTY-EIGHT

Mrs. Agnes Rutley was never one to fret, not until recently. Diana's decision to end the courtship with Lord Barrington four nights ago was jolting in itself. Yet when Agnes had pressed the girl as to why she had made such a decision, the story she told had been an utter shock.

According to Diana, Lord Barrington had fathered a child with a woman to whom he was not married. And he was hiding her away on his estate! Was that what had brought him to Chatsworth during a time most of the *ton* was setting out for London for the Season?

Other questions swarmed her mind. Who was this mysterious woman? Was she a servant with whom he was dallying and now he was helping her to ease his conscience? Surely, she would have her own family to hide her away until the birth if she came from titled stock.

And what part did Mr. Stonebrook play in all this? There was something about that young baron-to-be that did not sit well with Agnes. He was not nearly as charitable or honorable as he presented himself to be. Nor was Lord Barrington as suspect as he seemed. Yet she had no way to prove either hypothesis.

What she did know for certain was Mr. Stonebrook's sudden interest in the marquess and his female friend was far too advantageous for his own good. He would gain much if Lord Barrington was as terrible as he had been portrayed, which would only hurt Diana. And Diana was Agnes's only true concern in all this.

Time was of the essence, as some of the other pupils were returning for the next term. The last thing she needed was for any of them to learn what Diana had endured in their absence. Girls could be so terribly spiteful.

The door opened and Mrs. Shepherd entered. "Lord Walcott's here. You need me to mind the corridor in case curious ears are roamin' about?"

"Please," Agnes replied.

Mrs. Shepherd gave a firm nod as if she had expected the response and left the room. A moment later, Henry, Lord Walcott entered. Of the same age, the earl had been a longtime friend of Agnes. His dark hair was now all silver and fine lines creased his face, but he was very much the same man she had met all those years ago. One on whom she could always rely.

"Hello, Henry," she said. "Would you please close the door."

Henry smiled and did as she bade. Then he glanced around the room, an amused yet warm smile on his face. "I don't see a table set up for hazard. Have you some other need of me?"

Agnes chuckled. "Please, have a seat. Can I get you a drink? Or I can ask Mrs. Shepherd to bring us tea." She poured herself a glass of sherry before waiting for his response.

"No, thank you," Henry replied, unbuttoning his coat before sitting in the chair she indicated. "Has there been any word from Miss Hunter?"

Miss Emma Hunter was a former pupil who was now planning her wedding to Baron St. John, and the earl had been an integral part in their coming together. As had Agnes. Seeing those two brought together had been just as difficult as bringing together Miss Julia Wallace and the Duke of Elmhurst, but by the time both couples had announced their engagements, all knew each pair was right for each other.

"I received a letter three days ago," Agnes said. "All is well and the first of the banns have been read."

"Excellent. They will make a wonderful couple. I know St. John is looking forward to the wedding." He shook his head. "The boy's changed so much, and I see nothing but improvements in his estate. And his life. I see a great future ahead for him." He tilted his head. "But we're not here to speak of the St. Johns. Something is clearly bothering you, my friend."

Agnes sighed and shook her head. "You've always known me far too well, Henry. It's concerning the request I made of you. Did you learn anything in your inquiry of Mr. Stonebrook?"

"I received a reply from two friends whom I recall mentioning his name on occasion. Both hold him in high regard. Neither is well acquainted with him, however, so I cannot be certain their opinion of the young man is of any great value."

Agnes took a sip of her sherry, and Henry frowned. "It's not like you to drink, Agnes. What's wrong?"

"It's not as if I'm against a drink or two. And if you're concerned that I'm drinking to excess, you've no need to worry. I know my limits."

"True," Henry said, crossing one leg over the opposite knee, "but I've never seen you consume any sort of alcohol outside of the occasional glass of wine at dinner. So again, I ask you. What's the problem? And don't give me that balderdash that nothing is troubling you. I know you far too well for that."

Agnes sighed. "Very well. I've a student here, Miss Diana Kendricks."

"Oh, yes, I'm acquainted with her father. Unfortunately. He's a tendency for wandering eyes and hands."

"Yes, I understand that is the case," Agnes said. "Well, it turns out that Diana has been seeing Lord Barrington. She's come to admire him a great deal, or rather did."

"Did?" Henry asked with a raised eyebrow.

Agnes nodded. "Apparently, he's been keeping a woman in a cottage on his property, and she's now with child. By all appearances, the marquess is the father. But I've a feeling it's not what it seems."

"Are you saying that you believe he's not the father?"

"That is exactly what I'm saying."

"But have you any proof? How can you know for certain?"

With a heavy sigh, Agnes leaned back in her chair. "That is where my problem lies. I've no proof whatsoever. But you're acquainted with the boy. He's a respectable, soft-spoken man with an impeccable reputation. Why would he ruin all he has built by getting a woman to whom he's not married with child? It makes no sense!"

To this, Henry snorted. "He may be as reputable as you say, but he's still a man, Agnes. What makes you think that he's immune to the temptations of the flesh?"

"Of course, he's not," Agnes said. "But his head is better placed than most. And I've such a strong feeling that there is more to this story than what's been presented."

"Has he admitted or denied his involvement in this situation?" Henry asked.

"According to Diana, he has taken responsibility."

Henry stood and buttoned his coat. "Then there is nothing that can be done. He's guilty by his own admission." He shook his head. "You're trying to make innocent one who is guilty. Life is not a court of law, Agnes. You've always done more than your fair share for your students, and in most circumstances, you're correct. But if he's already taken responsibility, he must suffer the consequences. Either way, I don't know how I can be of help."

Agnes leapt from her seat. "But you can help," she said, hurrying to his side. "I'm rarely wrong when it comes to a person's true character, and Lord Barrington is not at fault. I'm certain of it. You received an invitation to the party he plans to throw for the marchioness next month, did you not?"

Henry frowned. "I did, but what does that have to do with anything?"

"Have Diana and Mr. Stonebrook accompany you as your guests. I'll go as Diana's chaperone." She placed a hand on his arm. "Please, Henry. I'm sure the Barringtons won't mind, especially if what I've planned proves what I believe to be the truth."

"Even if I do this, how do you know Mr. Stonebrook will agree?" He gave a great snort of derision. "And what about the marquess? If he has an interest in Miss Kendricks, why would he allow her to attend his party in the company of another man?"

"Oh, he'll agree," Agnes said. "I sent word to Baldwin—" Her voice caught in her throat mid-sentence when Henry narrowed his eyes at her.

"Agnes, what did you do? You promised to keep your distance from the Barringtons, to never interfere with their lives again. Will you go back on your word after all these years?"

"I've kept my promise, as you know quite well," Agnes said. "I've kept their names from any conversation when possible. I cross the street whenever I encounter the marchioness in the village, just as I promised. But one of my students has become involved with the son, so I've no choice but to at least name him. I don't give my word only to break it without good cause. And I'd do nothing to jeopardize the part you played in that promise, either. You know me better than that."

"No," Henry snapped. "I'll have nothing to do with whatever scheme you've cooked up."

Agnes grabbed his arm. "I can no longer keep my promise, Henry. The boy's happy, and Diana's so full of life for the first time since she arrived at the school. But I cannot in good conscience allow Mr. Stonebrook to have her. There's something wrong with that young man. I'm as sure of that as I am of Lord Barrington's good character. What sort of life will Diana have if I don't intervene? Or what could become of the marquess? They must be given the opportunity to speak in private, to reach the truth. What better place than a party?"

He let out a heavy sigh. "You of all people know how sacred one's word is. I, too, gave my word that day. *We* gave our word. I refuse to go back on it for any reason. I'm sorry."

Agnes's eyes grew misty, but she blinked back the tears. She was not one to give into hysterics, and she would not do so now! "That pact we made then was best for everyone. Now is a different time, and I need your help if Diana and the marquess have any chance at happiness. I'm telling you. They belong together."

For a long moment, Henry stood looking down at her, his lips pursed and appearing as ready to refuse as he had earlier. Finally, he said, "I'll do this. But even if we manage to get them together, what then? It changes nothing about the fact her father has chosen Mr. Stonebrook for her. Will you be able to rely on a missing pocket watch or another game of hazard to pave the way for them?"

Agnes smiled. "No. I think magic will play a part this time. I've not worked out how exactly, but I'm confident it will."

Henry shook his head in wonderment. "Your hope in the lives of others has always been far greater than mine. But understand one thing. I do what you ask because we're friends. Once I've made the offer to Mr. Stonebrook, and he's accepted, I'll no longer have any part in whatever scheme you devise. Lady Barrington is my friend, no matter what she thinks of you."

"And I respect—"

Henry held up a hand, and she closed her mouth. "I only wish to warn you to be careful what you plan. The good you're trying to do may prove to be in vain if the wrong secrets are revealed."

"Henry—"

"Lives will be destroyed, Agnes," Henry said. "Wounds may open that can never be healed. All I'm saying is, whatever you do, please take care."

Agnes dropped her gaze. "I understand," she whispered. "I appreciate all you've done for me, past and present. You've always come to my aid, and I cannot thank you enough. And don't worry. I'll not ask you to go beyond the invitation. You have my word."

Henry nodded. "Just see that you keep it." Then he was gone.

Agnes returned to the chair behind her desk. Opening the drawer where she kept her greatest treasures, she removed the wooden top and placed it upon the desk.

A single tear rolled down her cheek as she ran a loving finger over the toy. One's word was her bond, or so went the saying. But circumstances changed, making the breaking of vows necessary for the good of others. And she prayed that by doing so, the result would be happiness and not the destruction Henry predicted would come.

CHAPTER TWENTY-NINE

Christmas and the New Year came and went, and in that time, Diana had received four letters from Lord Barrington, all of which she chose to ignore. Students began returning to the school over the week following Twelfth Night, and tales of parties, gifts they had received, and the rumors they had heard filled the corridors and bedrooms.

Louisa switched rooms with Jenny—a common practice every year as girls came and went—to share a room with Ruth. What those two could be up to only meant trouble, but the move allowed Jenny and Diana to be together. As much as Diana adored Jenny, however, all she wanted now was to be left alone.

Glancing down, she moved a coin from one hand to the other, just as Lord Barrington had shown her. She had practiced the illusion a hundred times and was pleased at how quickly she had mastered it.

Yet that happiness fell and the now-familiar sadness took its place once more. Never had she felt such melancholy in all her life. That which had once brightened her day now was as dormant as the winter grass. Everything she ate had no flavor. She tossed and turned throughout the night, making rising in the morning all the more difficult. After learning what she had about Lord Barrington, she no longer cared.

About anything.

Although she and Mr. Stonebrook had become fast friends, she could never care for him in the same way she did the marquess. He had called on her once before returning to London, but Diana had to force her attention on him or it would wander back to Lord Barrington. The familiar feelings she had for the marquess refused to leave her, much to her irritation.

As she peered out the bedroom window, she thought of the kisses she and the marquess had shared. They had evoked strong feelings in her, feelings that were far from proper. Had he felt the same or had it all been a part of an intricate plan? What she had seen as pure and beautiful was likely nothing more than a means to woo her to his bed.

Diana was uncertain which hurt more. The thought of being tricked and used or being left with a heart that ached worse than any wound she could have received. For when a woman's heart was wounded, did it ever truly recover?

A light knock at the door made Diana turn as Mrs. Rutley entered the room, a parcel in her hands. "This just arrived for you," the headmistress said as she closed the door behind her.

Diana took the package. It had the shape and size of a book, something her father would never offer her. On top lay a letter. "Have you any idea who sent this?" She glanced at Mrs. Rutley. "If this is from Lord Barrington, I don't want it. Return it without a reply. I want nothing to do with him again."

"I believe you should open it," Mrs. Rutley said. "And read the letter. Perhaps he wishes to apologize."

Diana shook her head and turned her attention once more to what lay outside the window. "Even if he does, I won't accept it. Nor any gifts he wishes to give me. I'll not be bought."

"I think it's important you at least read what he has to say."

Anger raged in Diana, and she turned to glare at her headmistress. "Why? Why should I allow him to apologize for what he's done?"

Mrs. Rutley placed the parcel on the bed. "You don't know—"

"Perhaps there is much I don't know. But what I do know is that I spoke from my heart and he stomped on it! I was beginning to believe he was different from other men, but he's not. They are all the same." She motioned to the package. "Gifts. They all think that gifts can erase whatever pain they've caused. Were you aware that he gifted Miss Amelia a book, as well?"

Mrs. Rutley shook her head. "I was not."

"Lord Barrington uses books to make amends, it seems, and they're accepted with smiles and fawning by all the foolish women who've fallen under his spell. If you see a dozen women walking into the village, each with a book clutched in her hand, you'll know they're all his!"

Mrs. Rutley drew in a deep breath. "Diana, I know you're hurt-ing, and you've every right to feel as you do. But when we act in anger rather than with our hearts, our thoughts tend to be clouded."

Diana shook her head in disbelief. "You told me that a woman should listen to her heart. And I was hurt because I took your advice. So, allow me to make my last request of you. Don't help me again, for all it will lead me to is a life more pitiful than the one with which I began."

With a sad nod, Mrs. Rutley withdrew, leaving Diana alone.

Frustrated with her outrage, with her disrespect for the one person who cared for her, Diana sat on the edge of the bed, eyeing the parcel as if it contained a viper or some other dangerous creature. Her heart urged her to open it, but her mind advised against it. A war waged between the two, but in the end, her heart won. At least for opening the letter.

Dear Miss Diana,

There once was a woman who was considered the best magician to ever live. I had believed it a myth until I met you. My sorrow for the lies, the deceit I inflicted upon you, are more than I could have ever imagined. You may not be willing to believe me, but I am not the rogue you think me to be. I'm not ashamed of any action I have done save one. When I wished to express to you how much I care for you, I did not.

Please accept this token of my affection.

Sincerely,
    James Barrington

Wiping at her eyes, Diana set aside the letter and stared at the brown paper-wrapped parcel.

What if this is an attempt to trick you again? she thought.

Then again, what if he was not the rogue she believed him to be?

She placed the parcel in her lap with a sigh and pulled off the paper. Her eyes went wide as she traced a finger over the gilt lettering. *A Lady's Guide to Magic.*

With great trepidation, she opened the book, and a smile crossed her lips. It was a collection of illusions a lady could perform. Some were depicted in lovely colored plates while others were mere sketches.

Scooting so her back was against the headboard, she turned to the first page and began to read.

When the legend of Miss Clara Moonlight, which of course is not her true name, began to surface nearly two hundred years ago, it caused fear in many throughout England. All sorts of valuables went missing, from jewelry to coins, and even horses, never to be seen again. None could be connected to the mysterious female illusionist, but that did not stop people from placing blame on her.

As her legend grew, so did the raging debates within the circles of practicing illusionists. Yet one question always rose above the rest: Did Miss Clara Moonlight perform the greatest act of any magician of her time? Did she make a person disappear? If so, how had she accomplished such an illusion? Making a coin disappear was one thing, but to make a prominent gentleman vanish from the company of his peers was quite another.

This was the case in regard to..."

So engrossed in the book was Diana that she not only read the introduction, but she also went on to the first illusions offered within its pages. Each was fascinating in its own way, and she would learn every one of them!

How much time passed, Diana was unsure, but when she got up to stretch, the tiny bones in her back and neck cracked with her movements.

The door opened, and Jenny entered. "Mr. Stonebrook is here to see you. I didn't know he was calling this evening."

Diana frowned. "Nor did I. I wonder why he's here."

Jenny shrugged. "Mrs. Rutley said to meet them in her office. Would you like me to go with you?"

"No, you wait here. Mrs. Rutley will be there with me. I shouldn't be long, but I'll tell you everything as soon as I'm done."

Curiosity filled Diana as she made her way downstairs and into Mrs. Rutley's office. Her headmistress sat in her chair behind the desk, giving a polite laugh as Mr. Stonebrook finished speaking.

"Ah, here she is," Mrs. Rutley said. "Diana, Mr. Stonebrook has some wonderful news for you."

Mr. Stonebrook stood and smiled at Diana. "It's lovely to see you again, Miss Kendricks."

Diana dropped into a curtsy. "And you, as well. This is a pleasant surprise."

His grin widened. "It's my wish to only bring you more pleasure. As I was telling Mrs. Rutley, I've been extended an invitation to a party, and you are to attend with me."

The last thing Diana wanted was to be around others. "Oh? And what party is this, pray tell?"

"It's to be held at Penford Place," he replied, and Diana's heart skipped a beat. "I thought it would be a wonderful time to announce our courtship. Yes, yes, I know courtship is not typically given the same emphasis as an engagement, and couples don't usually *announce* a courtship, but really, is one not a means to achieve the other?"

Diana was stunned. He had made it clear that he wanted to wait to announce any intentions at a later time. Panic overtook her, and breathing became difficult. But he gave her no time to respond.

"Mrs. Rutley suggested that I ask your father to attend, as well. Isn't that wonderful?"

With a glare for Mrs. Rutley, Diana filled with rage. How dare her headmistress suggest such a thing! And Mr. Stonebrook was no better. Diana was not ready to make any announcements just yet.

Diana walked up to Mr. Stonebrook. "I thought we were going to wait until we made a final decision before making any announcements."

Mr. Stonebrook frowned. "But why delay the inevitable? You promised me, once Barrington was out of the way, we would proceed."

Diana shook her head. She had said no such thing! "But why do you wish to make such an announcement at the home of Lord Barrington? Surely, there is a more appropriate time and place?"

The smile Mr. Stonebrook wore made Diana's skin pebble, and she clutched her skirt to keep her hands from shaking.

"He must learn that he's failed," he replied. "That those who practice patience will ultimately emerge the winners." He sighed. "You've seen Lord Barrington for who he truly is. Does he not deserve to be brought down a peg or two? Plus, you made me a promise, Miss Kendricks. Don't tell me you wish to go back on your word. Not after all I've done for you."

She was stunned. What exactly did he believe he had done for her? Spoken to her father? He had done so on his insistence, not hers. She could have done just as much on her own, but in writing rather than in person. Was that what he meant?

What could she say, really? She had wallowed in her sorrow day in and day out rather than considering what could be. It was clear Mrs. Rutley would do nothing to stop this fiasco. If anything, her headmistress appeared excited about the prospect of Diana attending this party. Diana was left with a sense of helplessness. No matter how hard she tried, the words would not come, so she nodded her agreement.

Excellent!" Mr. Stonebrook said, grinning widely. "I'll be away for a few days, but I'll write to you before the party."

"Wait," Diana said. Although Lord Barrington had broken her heart, she could not allow him to see her with another man. "Perhaps we can miss the party and find another time to make our announcement."

He tapped his chin as if giving her idea thought, but responded with, "No, you'll find humiliating him is in my best interest. Once we've left the party, we'll never speak his name again." He turned to Mrs. Rutley. "I appreciate your kind words of hope, Mrs. Rutley. And thank you for recommending I send for Mr. Kendricks. It will make for a very interesting evening, indeed."

Mrs. Rutley stood. "You are most welcome, Mr. Stonebrook. May I see you to the door?"

Mr. Stonebrook waved a dismissive hand. "There is no need. I can see my way out." He turned to Diana. "We'll speak soon, I promise." And with that, he was gone.

Diana had no idea what to say. Confusion, anger, and hurt coursed through her. What would the guests think when this announcement was made? What would the marchioness think? She took a sudden inhale of breath.

What will Father think?

She rounded on her headmistress. "Oh, why would you suggest my father attend this party, Mrs. Rutley?" she demanded. "I cannot believe you are willing to allow Mr. Stonebrook to humiliate Lord Barrington in such a terrible way! I mean, I suppose he deserves it given what he's done, but I've no heart for revenge. And what this will do to me? Have you taken that into consideration? It will only make my heart ache more than it already is."

"I couldn't agree with you more," the headmistress said, giving a light chuckle. "Yes, I know exactly what it will do to you."

Diana's jaw tightened. "I thought I could trust you," she said, seething. "That you and I were friends. But now you laugh as I ready myself for the most humiliating experience of my life! You know quite well I've no interest in allowing Mr. Stonebrook to court me, but you want my father there to bear witness to my shame? This is ludicrous!"

"You can trust me," Mrs. Rutley said. "I believe we are friends, but more importantly, I'm your headmistress. You'll stop acting like a child and behave like the proper young lady you are and do as you're told. Now, I expect you to attend this party and accept whatever occurs there. Am I making myself clear?"

Diana felt sick. If her life had been bad before, now it was far worse. Not wishing to set eyes on Mrs. Rutley again, she stormed out of the office and ran to her room. Once there, she threw herself onto her bed to weep soundlessly into her pillow in hopes of never rising again.

CHAPTER THIRTY

A silver coin rolled across James's knuckles without much thought as to what he was doing. Magic had been a part of his life since he was young and had earned him a moniker because of it. But he would rather never perform an illusion again now that the magic in his world was gone.

How could two people feel invincible one moment and vulnerable the next? Without Miss Diana in his life, nothing would be the same again.

He glanced at Amelia, who sat reading in one of the chairs beside the fire. She had come to spend time with him, to help ease his pain. But he was not up for a chat, so he offered her a place to relax away from the cottage.

It would be so easy to place blame on Amelia for all that had gone wrong in his life, but doing so was unfair. She had done nothing wrong.

No, the fault lay with him. It had been his actions that led to the parting of ways between him and Miss Diana, and there was nothing he could do to rectify the situation.

Over the past weeks, he had written her several letters of apology and sent her gifts to express how sorry he was. Yet he received not a single reply. Baldwin encouraged him to not give up hope, but it was becoming harder with each passing day.

His mother was due to arrive Friday, two days from now, just in time for the Saturday evening party he had planned as a farewell to her and her friends. He had hoped to add to the celebration with an announcement of his courtship with Diana, but now it would be nothing more than an excuse to pass the time. And as the farewell party, of course.

"You've become quieter as the days pass," Amelia said. "I can't help but think that I've brought on these troubles."

James shook his head. "You mustn't say that. You've done nothing wrong. This is my doing. If I'd only been honest with Miss Diana, all this could have been avoided. But no, I had to have my secrets. Now I'm paying the price for my foolishness."

"Don't give up hope, James. Women can be stubborn, especially when they've been hurt. Just give her time. She'll see reason."

"Time is exactly what I lack," James said. "Miss Diana will be forced to marry that cad Stonebrook, and there is nothing I can do about it. Not without exposing you, and I shan't allow that."

A knock on the door made them both turn as Baldwin entered the room.

"Doctor Humphreys for Mrs. Triton."

James leapt from his chair to offer his hand as Amelia rose from her seat, a hand on her back. "Ask him to meet me in the cottage." She turned to James. "If there is anything I can do, please let me know."

"I appreciate it," he said, giving her a small smile. "And do be careful."

James watched her walk away, more an ambling movement than walking. It would not be long before the child was born. He hoped she would find an honorable man in the new life she would lead.

The butler entered the room. "The kitchen staff has received their final instructions. The maids will see that all the rooms are given a second cleaning to insure they are at their best with the help of the footmen. Have you any last requests, my lord?"

"No, Baldwin. And I've considered what to do once Miss Amelia leaves."

"Oh? And what is that, my lord?"

"I'd like to go to the house in Yorkshire and escape these memories. I've no reason to return to London. If anything, I'd rather stay as far away from there as I can."

Baldwin frowned. "You speak as if a life of solitude awaits you, my lord. I may not know what the future holds, but you're far too young to hide away. And I doubt you would enjoy the life of a monk."

James gave a wry chuckle. "I appreciate you saying so, but it's fruitless to waste time on hope. Miss Diana has ignored all my attempts to apologize. It appears Stonebrook has somehow convinced her that he is better suited for her. And there's not a deuced thing I can do about it."

"Forgive me for disagreeing with you, my lord, but you're wrong. I believe you can do something." James frowned, but the butler continued. "I heard Lord Walcott will be attending."

James snorted. "Of course he is. He's been a family friend for longer than I've been alive. But what does that have to do with anything?"

"Well you see, I saw Lord Walcott on my way into the village, and he asked if I thought you'd mind if he brought a guest with him. I told him I didn't see that it would be a problem."

Arching an eyebrow, James pushed down a sudden wave of anger. "Who will the guest be?"

"Mr. Stonebrook."

The dam that had been holding back his anger burst. "How dare you!" he shouted, pointing an accusatory finger at his butler. "You had no right to speak on my behalf. And Stonebrook of all people! You'll go directly to Walcott's home and tell him you were mistaken. If he disagrees, disinvite him... and his blasted guest! You're lucky I don't throw you out for your insubordination, Baldwin."

The butler swallowed visibly. "But don't you see, my lord? Miss Kendricks will also be attending. On his arm, yes, but she'll be here. When I heard this, I couldn't help but applaud Lord Walcott's wisdom."

In two long strides, James was glaring down at Baldwin, his breathing coming in short gasps, he was so angry. "Have you lost your mind? Why would I want to watch him parade her about? And in my home, no less!"

Baldwin, however, did not even flinch under James's harsh gaze. "So you can speak with her, my lord."

For a moment, James was dumbfounded as he walked over and leaned against the desk. "I must admit it does make for a most opportune moment," he said thoughtfully. "But I'm afraid of what I'll do if Stonebrook is anywhere near me."

Not to mention the risk of Stonebrook letting slip what he knew about Amelia. It would ruin her, tarnish his mother's name, and dishonor the reputation of any future wife.

He knitted his brows. No one outside of his staff was aware that Amelia was at Penford Place, and few of them knew who she truly was. Although Stonebrook had intimated his suspicions, he did not know for certain. If he did, the rumors would have circulated throughout the country by now.

Granted, Miss Diana and her companion knew, but he was confident neither would reveal this secret to anyone. Miss Diana had a heart of gold. He trusted her to be discreet no matter what disagreements they had.

It was not as if Amelia would be in attendance at the party. He had already made plans to send her away, so the evidence would be nowhere to be found.

"I'm sorry, my lord," Baldwin said, hanging his head. "I thought I was being helpful, but it's clear I overstepped my position. If you'd like me to go, I'll pack right away."

James sighed. Baldwin had angered him, but now he saw the opportunity he would not have had otherwise. "Have you any other confessions to make, Baldwin?"

The butler nodded. "I lied to you, my lord."

James pushed away from the desk, taken aback. "Lied? About what?"

Baldwin blanched. "You... you asked me about your parents, what had caused the chasm between them, and I said I didn't know. But that was untrue."

Something tightened around James's heart. "Go on. Explain yourself or so help me, you'll be out on your ear within the hour, party or no party!" When the butler flinched at his harsh words, he sighed. "Please, tell me. I must know the truth."

"They gave up, my lord," Baldwin replied. "I could see it in their eyes. Early on, they were happy. They were filled with joy. Just like you, my lord, your father had a love of magic, and practicing his illusions on her was one of their favorite pastimes."

Stunned, James said, "I never knew. So, what happened?"

The butler sighed. "I'm not sure exactly, my lord, but early in their marriage, Her Ladyship began berating herself. On more than one occasion, she could be heard shouting that he should seek a divorce and find a more suitable wife. I never knew why, nor did I feel it my business to know. His Lordship went out of his way to appease her, made every attempt to make her feel worthy, but to no avail. It finally came to a point when he simply gave up."

Baldwin shook his head. "It's your choice whom you allow in your home, my lord. But if you want one last chance to speak to Miss Kendricks before she's engaged to Mr. Stonebrook, I'd advise you to take it. What I fear is, like your father, you'll never be able to enjoy what could have been."

James considered this. "Perhaps you're right, Baldwin. If I have just a few moments alone with her, perhaps I can untangle all of this."

"Then I haven't gotten the sack, my lord?"

"Not this time," James replied. "But don't let it happen again." He added a smile. The butler meant well.

Baldwin bowed. "Never, my lord." He turned to leave just as Doctor Humphreys entered. He was a stout man with a round stomach that stretched his coat to its limits. "Can I get you anything, doctor?" the butler asked. "A drink or something to eat?"

"No, no," the doctor replied offhandedly. "I can't stay long. I must leave soon to see another patient back home."

Baldwin bowed and left the room.

"Welcome, doctor," James said, shaking the man's hand. "Thank you for coming. How is my cousin faring? She was complaining of pains in her back. I just want to be sure everything is progressing well. I wouldn't want her husband to return to bad news."

"She's progressing just fine, my lord," Doctor Humphreys replied as he removed the spectacles from his bulbous nose and placed them inside the pocket of his coat. "Both mother and child are well. Back pain is a common ailment in women, but I did notice swelling in her ankles that causes me a bit of concern." He puckered his lips in thought. "She mentioned the possibility of traveling home tomorrow. Is this true?"

"Indeed. Her husband is due to return from America soon, and she's eager to be there when he arrives."

The doctor shook his head. "I don't think it wise, my lord, not yet. My recommendation is that she remain here until the child is born. Surely, her husband can come here?"

"She's adamant," James said. "Is there any chance she can make the journey? What if I instructed the driver to go at a slow pace?" He knew he was clutching at straws, but he had to do something!

Doctor Humphreys sighed. "If she remains in bed for the entirety of next week, then perhaps she can travel. And only if the swelling in her ankles recedes. But I must warn you, it's not likely to happen. If she wants to give birth without any complications, she should not travel at all until after the babe is born."

James sighed. What choice did he have? "Thank you, doctor. I'll do my best to convince her to remain here."

"I'm curious, my lord," the doctor said. "Why didn't you send for Doctor Mosley? After all, he's local. Why send for me when I must travel over an hour from Larkston?"

James was prepared for this question. "Although I respect Doctor Mosley, his reputation pales in comparison to yours. Mrs. Triton's husband requested that I have the best doctor see to her needs, and I heard that man was you. I hope the payment is adequate to cover any inconvenience."

Doctor Humphreys chuckled. "Quite adequate, my lord. And I'm pleased to hear that my name holds such weight. You made the right choice."

Once the doctor was gone, James considered this new problem. He could not ask Amelia to sit in the cottage without lighting the fire. Yet, Mr. Stonebrook would notice the smoke coming from the chimney, which would only give him cause to bring up his suspicions about her being in residence.

"This will be a disaster!" he growled as he dug a fist into his thigh.

And there was nothing he could do to stop it.

CHAPTER THIRTY-ONE

Although Diana would have preferred to remain home wallowing in her sorrow rather than attending any party at the home of Lord Barrington, she had little choice. Her father would be irate if she refused Mr. Stonebrook's invitation, and she would not give him yet another reason to despise her.

Therefore, she and Jenny had spent the better part of this Saturday morning in preparation. She chose a violet ball gown with puffed sleeves and lace across the bodice. Her hair was pinned into an intricate chignon with more than a dozen amethyst-encrusted hairpins. She wore a gold necklace with three large amethysts accented by yellowish beryls and matching earrings and bracelet.

If only she were dressing for Lord Barrington and not Mr. Stonebrook. At least Mrs. Rutley would be her chaperone. Jenny was lovely, but she did not have the experience and words of encouragement of their headmistress.

Plus, Jenny could be quite lax in her chaperoning, one thing Diana did not need now. It was one thing to be alone with the marquess, that she could endure. But Mr. Stonebrook was another matter altogether.

She sat on her bed, clutching the book of magic in her hands as she awaited the arrival of Mr. Stonebrook. Her father had sent word that he was in Chatsworth and would be attending the party but would not arrive until later in the evening.

She sighed. Even on a night as important as this, he could not be bothered to stop by to see her beforehand.

And this party! Whatever Lord Barrington was celebrating would be turned onto its head. How dare Mr. Stonebrook commandeer someone else's party for his own announcement? An announcement in which she wanted no part!

From tonight, she was as good as engaged to Mr. Stonebrook, which sickened her. Eventually, they would be married, and she had no say in the matter.

"Diana?" Jenny said. "It's time for you to tell the others what happened over the last few weeks. And don't give me that look. It's not for me to tell."

Diana set aside the book and smiled as her friends entered behind Jenny, the very same girls who had pledged to be there for one another. Unity and Theodosia, both inseparable, crawled to the far side of the bed. Ruth sat next to them, her bright hair as wild as she. Then came Louisa, her honey-blonde hair hanging loose down her back.

They were seven when the vow had been made. Well, eight when one counted in Mrs. Rutley. But Julia and Emma were now gone, leaving only these five. Soon, there would be four.

"So much has happened while you were away," Diana said. "And because I have time before Mr. Stonebrook collects me, I'll start at the beginning."

And so she did.

Diana explained how she had made certain that she and the Marquess of Magic crossed paths at the bookshop. How they met again, this time unplanned, in the very same spot. She told of going to the servants' party in the stable and meeting Miss Amelia, believing she was a servant only to learn who she truly was. Of the final encounter with Lord Barrington and her father's insistence that she allow Mr. Stonebrook to court her.

By the time she finished, her jaw ached. "Which leads me to tonight's party."

Unity shook her head, her high cheekbones red with anger. "Let me see if I understand this correctly. Lord Barrington has upset you, hurt you even, yet when you speak of this other woman, you make it sound as if he did nothing wrong!"

Ruth snorted. "I agree. It's clear he's the cause of Miss Amelia's 'condition.' Why else would he hide her away?"

Diana sighed. "Mrs. Rutley told me that my heart will always lead me to the truth, and it tells me that something about all this doesn't make sense. The question is, can I trust it?"

"And what about Mr. Stonebrook?" Theodosia asked. "You don't seem happy that he wishes to court you."

Diana sighed. "At first, I believed I could be happy, but each time he calls as of late, he seems... I don't know... different, somehow. He's no longer the kind gentleman as when he first called on me. Now, I see lust in his eyes and something sinister in his demeanor. He frightens me."

All too often, she had caught his eyes lingering on her for far too long. His smile made her look away in shame.

"My sister says all men are that way," Jenny said. The others groaned. "Well, it's true! It doesn't make him a bad person. Men are always full of lust, and it's our responsibility as women to tame them. And to do that, my sister says—"

"Yes well, you may be correct," Diana interrupted, not wanting to hear what Jenny's sister had to say about taming men. "But it's as if Mr. Stonebrook has become a different person." She blew out her breath in frustration. "Oh, but what does it matter? Father will be there tonight, and Mr. Stonebrook will make our courtship official. Everything is out of my control."

"It's not too late to run away," Ruth said. "I've become friends with the cobbler's son. I'm sure he'd be willing to hide you for the night. Then you can steal away tomorrow."

Diana shook her head. "I can't do that. I've never been one to run away from my problems."

Louisa pressed a finger to her lips in thought. "You know, you should go and talk to the marquess."

Ruth frowned. "And why would she do that?"

"To learn the truth," Louisa said. "It's clear it still bothers you,

Diana. Don't you want to put all this behind you? What harm can come by talking to him?"

Ruth clicked her tongue and stood. "Why ask for the truth if you already know it? All you'll do is make yourself even more miserable. Trust me, I know. Besides, how will you find time to speak to him when your father and the man you're to court are there? Do you think either of them will let you out of his sight? I'm telling you, running is your only true option. But don't take my word for it." And with that, Ruth left the room.

"Oh, what does she know?" Theodosia asked. "It's not as if she's had much experience with love."

But Diana was not so sure. Ruth was right in one respect. No, two. Why take the risk of being hurt again? And even if she wanted to take that risk, how would she get a chance to be alone with the marquess?

Whatever decision she was to make, it would have to come later. For Mrs. Rutley knocked on the door to announce that the carriage had arrived to collect them.

"The rest of you, enjoy yourselves. Mrs. Shepherd has promised to make you some chocolate to drink in an hour as a special treat."

It was with a heavy heart that Diana said goodbye to her friends. There was a sense of finality in this evening, and it increased her melancholy.

As she donned her coat, a wave of guilt washed over her. "Mrs. Rutley, I want to apologize for the cruel words I spoke to you the other day. You've always been there for me, and I appreciate all you do."

Mrs. Rutley smiled. "We often say what we don't mean when we're angry. But I appreciate your apology, for that is how relationships are healed." She hugged Diana. "Are you ready for tonight?"

Diana sighed. "I suppose so. But this is not what I expected my future to be. I had hoped that I would be celebrating with Lord Barrington, not with Mr. Stonebrook. But it was not meant to be."

"There is always hope," Mrs. Rutley said. "It's during our darkest days when we must remember that the storm always clears. That what we see now may not be what remains tomorrow."

"I don't know. I would like to speak to Lord Barrington, but I'm not certain I should. Even if I do, who knows what tomorrow will bring?"

"But that is the beauty of it, Diana. It could be clear for all we know. But I'm sure that, of all people, you can find a way."

Diana's confidence rose. Perhaps there was a way to change tomorrow by changing something tonight.

A knock on the door announced Mr. Stonebrook. He looked dapper in his dark tailcoat and beige breeches that buttoned just below the knees. His red hair was brushed forward in the latest fashion, and he wore a wide smile.

"Good evening, ladies," he said with a bow. "My, but don't you both look lovely? Tonight will be wonderful. Do you not agree?"

"Indeed, Mr. Stonebrook," Mrs. Rutley replied with far more enthusiasm than was warranted. After all, Diana felt more as if she were on her way to the gallows rather than a party. "Have you received word from Mr. Kendricks? He is coming, is he not?"

Mr. Stonebrook sighed. "I did, and he sends his regrets, but he will not be able to arrive until much later. Something about a meeting to discuss the purchase of several milk cows for one of his properties. That means we'll have to delay our announcement until then, but it will be well worth the wait."

Diana smiled. If she was lucky, her father would forget about the party altogether. Then they would not have to make an announcement at all!

"It's always been my opinion that these sorts of announcements are best served later, anyway," Mrs. Rutley said, smiling broadly. "The guests are cheerful and much more relaxed. Let them leave with a smile rather than allowing time for other gossip to dim your evening."

"I hadn't considered that," Mr. Stonebrook said thoughtfully. "That's an excellent idea." He offered his arms to both ladies. "Shall we?"

As they made their way to the carriage, the doubts continued to multiply. Although she had promised to make the most of their courtship, something still did not sit right with her. Did the surrounding darkness give Mr. Stonebrook's features a sinister look?

"I know this night is very important to you, Miss Kendricks," he said before handing her into the carriage. "I've a sense that you're worried about the future that lies ahead of you."

Perhaps her concerns had made her see what was not there, for now all she saw was a kind smile. "I admit that I am."

"Well, I can assure you there is nothing with which to concern yourself. Every decision I make, I have your best interests in mind. All I ask is that you trust me."

Two months ago, Mrs. Rutley had given Diana some advice that she had chosen to ignore. But as Mr. Stonebrook asked her to trust him, her heart screamed with the truth. One single word appeared in her mind.

Run!

CHAPTER THIRTY-TWO

J ames had done his best to keep his eyes averted since Miss Diana arrived ten minutes earlier. Yet he failed miserably. She looked more stunning than he had ever seen her. No other woman matched her beauty. He longed for a single moment alone with her, to ask if she was practicing any of the illusions found in the book he had sent her.

Yet he could not approach her, not while she was in the company of Mr. Peter Stonebrook. Seeing them together made him grind his teeth. Mr. Stonebrook wore a warm, welcoming smile, but James knew the lying tongue that hid behind it.

He would bide his time and wait for the perfect moment to steal her away. He had to talk to her, had to explain the truth, but when remained to be seen. The host did not leave the party so early in the evening, not when he had guests to greet. His mother had taught him better than that.

Close to two dozen people were in attendance, which was more than he had expected. Most of the guests were older. Lord and Lady Montgomery were stooped and white-haired. Lord Bannerman stood tall but his mumbling made him appear older than his five and sixty years. Those closer to his age had already left for London to get ready for the

Season. His mother had insisted no one was to know why they were throwing the party. She wanted to make the announcement herself.

His mother had asked earlier about Miss Diana, and he had lied to her. "We've postponed our courtship," he had explained.

To his relief, she had not asked why, and he did not offer an explanation.

"What a wonderful party, Barrington," Lord Crigons said. "The wine is tasty, and I cannot wait to see what you have planned as refreshment." A spindly man with a beak of a nose and speckled dark hair, the viscount spoke so quickly, one struggled to understand him. "I'm curious as to why you're throwing this event. Your mother says she plans to make an announcement. Is there a woman you're interested in that I don't know about? I heard you left London in a rush."

"Does one need an excuse to return to Chatsworth?" James asked. "And you'll just have to wait for the announcement. I'll not ruin her fun." He easily caught sight of Lord Wellington, who was wide as he was tall with a pudgy, youthful face, though older than James. They'd conducted business together in the past. "Enjoy yourself, Crigons. If you'll excuse me."

When he turned away, his heart skipped a beat to see Miss Diana alone. Now would be the perfect time to speak with her.

No sooner had he thought this, however, and Mr. Stonebrook's voice whispered in his ear, "Where are you headed, Barrington?"

James turned to face his nemesis. When this party was over, he would have nothing to do with this man. No number of prospects were worth the trouble he caused. "To speak to my guests, of course. Is that not what hosts do?"

"They may, but you'll not speak to Miss Kendricks," Stonebrook growled. "The woman is mine. She may not know it yet, but I'll have her in my bed by the end of the month." He leaned in and lowered his voice further. "And there is nothing you can do about it. If you try anything, especially on this night, I'll reveal to everyone who you have hidden away in that cottage of yours. Oh, and Miss Kendricks's father will be arriving this evening."

James frowned. "What? I didn't invite him."

"But I did," Stonebrook said. "And it was Mrs. Rutley who suggested it! At first, I thought her a blathering fool, but then I saw the wisdom in her suggestion. I cannot wait to see the look on your face when I announce to everyone here that Miss Kendricks and I are courting. But the greatest pleasure will come in knowing there is no way for you to stop me! For if you say anything, I'll see you and Miss Lansing both ruined before night's end."

"Miss Lansing is gone," James said through clenched teeth. It was a lie, but this man did not need to know that. "So, now what will you say to ruin me?"

Stonebrook laughed. "I'll say nothing, but I've no doubt I can convince Miss Kendricks to tell what she's witnessed." He motioned to the far wall. "Do you see that man?"

James nodded. "That's Walcott. What about him?"

"He, too, knows about your little secret."

James paused. Stonebrook had to be lying. How would Walcott know about Miss Lansing?

"From what I've gathered," Stonebrook continued, "he's one of the most respected gentlemen outside of London. What he heard about you and Miss Lansing disgusted him, and he's agreed to admit to what he learned if he needs to do so."

James had to force his fists at his sides. He would help no one if he chose to strike this man!

"But don't worry, old friend," Stonebrook continued. "I'll take very good care of Miss Kendricks. Did I mention, her father has given his blessing to stay at their home while he goes to London on business? I'm sure her mother won't hear me slipping into Miss Kendricks's room late at night."

Rage rushed through James, and he grabbed Stonebrook by the arm. "It may not be this night, but I'll come for you. And when I do, you'll regret everything you've said and done!"

Stonebrook looked at James's hand as if a ladybird had landed on his arm. With a snort, he pulled his arm out of James's grip. "You know as well as I that you'll do nothing. You've a reputation to uphold, after all. Now, I've had several people who've been searching for me since learning I was in Chatsworth." He laughed. "It seems my reputation grows by the hour."

James glared at Stonebrook's back. Was there any excuse to end this party and send everyone home? Or was there a scheme he could devise that would have this man removed from his home without their secret being revealed?

Well, James had not lied. He would find a time to exact his revenge, and time would allow him to make it all the sweeter.

His gaze fell on Miss Diana. She looked at him for several moments before turning away.

"Blast you, Stonebrook!" James cursed under his breath. He was being blackmailed in his own home, and there was little he could do about it.

"I beg your pardon, my lord."

James turned to face Baldwin. "Yes?"

"I've bad news, my lord."

Pinching the bridge of his nose, James said, "Baldwin, there's nothing you can tell me that will make matters any worse than they already are. What is it?"

The butler leaned in and lowered his voice. "It's the wine room, my lord. I'm not sure what happened, but Judith is adamant that she speaks to you about it."

"Judith?" James said with a frown. Indeed, the red-haired servant stood just outside the door to the ballroom, her hands clasped together and a fervent look on her face. "Why can she not simply tell you?"

"I'm not sure, my lord," Baldwin said. "But she insists on speaking only to you."

James rubbed his temple. He had a headache coming on. Baldwin extending invitations without consulting James first. Judith refusing to use the proper channels to report a problem. His servants had been unruly as of late, and he had no one to blame but himself. Perhaps he had pushed things too far by joining them in their fun.

"I'll deal with this. Make sure everyone is doing what's required of them and not off writing letters to invite more people to my parties!"

Moving through the guests, James drew closer to where Diana

stood. Like before, she looked at him for several moments before turning away.

"My lord!" Judith bellowed, drawing a few curious looks.

"Hush!" James said. "Now, what's wrong?"

"A man, my lord!" she replied, her voice lowered. "In the wine room. I saw him take two bottles, and then he went back for more!"

"A thief?" James said. "Who was he?"

Judith's eyes filled with tears. "I don't know, my lord. When I asked, he scolded me!"

"I'm sure you can describe him, Judith. Was he a guest or a vagrant?"

"I don't know, my lord."

James sighed. "I'm sure you at least saw how he was dressed. Did he wear a tailcoat or something more suited to servants?"

"Oh, he was finely dressed, my lord. That's why I knew telling Mr. Baldwin wouldn't do any good. Only you can rebuke a gentleman."

With a shake of his head, James pushed past the maid. "I'll take care of this. If I'm lucky, he'll still be there."

"I... I can go out front and see if he's gone to one of the carriages, my lord."

"Yes," James said offhandedly. He preferred to deal with this alone, anyway. The girl would only get in his way. "If you do find him, don't approach him. Come find me. I'll not have you putting yourself in danger. If he's not there, get back to work and leave this to me."

"Yes, my lord." She hurried away.

James turned to find Baldwin joining him. "If you see someone making off with my wine, stop him. Judith says he's well-dressed, so he's either a guest or someone pretending to be one. It's outrageous that someone would wish to steal from me!"

"Indeed, my lord," Baldwin replied. "It's a shame, and tonight of all nights. If anyone inquires after you, what shall I say?"

"Inform them that I'm in a meeting," James said. "Because if the thief is not there, I'll lay in wait." He could not have asked for a more perfect excuse to leave his own party!

"Most excellent, my lord," Baldwin said, giving him a rare smile. "And have no worries. I have everything under control."

James grabbed a candle holder. "I'm glad someone does."

He made his way through the kitchen and down the short corridor that led to the room where his wine collection was housed. The extra key that hung just inside the door was missing.

So, he thought he could return later and finish the job, did he? Well, he'll learn that I'm far more intelligent than he'll ever be!

The wine room was a large, stone room with lines of crates filled with various vintages. Tall columns broke up the space and allowed places to hide, so James set down the candle, grabbed an iron rod that sat beside the door, and crept into the room.

"Hello?" he called as he took a step forward, holding the bar above his shoulder. "Who's there? Show yourself!"

There was no response.

"If you think you can get away with stealing from me, you'll soon learn I'll not allow it!"

Still no response.

The farther into the room he moved, the quieter became the music from the ballroom and the more his voice echoed. By the time he reached the far end, he realized no one was there.

"James Barrington," he said aloud, "you're nothing but a fool!"

He drew up a crate and sat upon it, and thoughts of Miss Diana came to mind. What had his life become? One lie after another filled his days. His intentions had been good, but no lies went unpunished.

"Never doubt how much I've cared for you!"

A sudden cry made him leap from his seat. Then came the harsh sound of the heavy door closing and the lock being turned into place. He hurried to the entrance of the wine room and found a woman lying on the floor.

When she turned to look up at him, he gasped, "Miss Kendricks? What are you doing here?"

CHAPTER THIRTY-THREE

Diana's stomach knotted as she watched Mr. Stonebrook and Lord Barrington with their heads together. They looked like two children amidst a confrontation over a toy, and Mr. Stonebrook was the victor and the marquess the loser. Surely, they weren't discussing her, were they? She did not like the idea of being seen as a toy.

"I'm surprised at the number of people at this party," Mrs. Rutley said from Diana's side. "And the odd array of guests. It appears many of the landed gentry were invited. Perhaps it's because so many of the *ton* have already left for London for the Season. Ah, but there is Lord Walcott. He's a most wonderful friend."

Diana gave a polite nod, but her mind was still on the marquess.

Mrs. Rutley must have realized this, for she asked, "Have you given any more thought to how you'll create an opportunity to speak with Lord Barrington?"

With a heavy sigh, Diana turned to her headmistress. "I've thought of little more as of late, I'm afraid. Although there is wisdom in discussing... whatever it is we must discuss. But what good can it do? There has been too much hurt and—"

"My lord!"

All heads turned, Diana's included, to find Lord Barrington hushing the young redhead Diana had seen dancing the night of the servants' party. What was her name? Oh, yes. Judith.

"How very interesting," Mrs. Rutley whispered. "Why would he be speaking with his servant?"

Diana frowned. "Don't all masters speak with their servants from time to time?" she asked. Yet she could not say why, but her curiosity was now piqued. When they both disappeared together, him in a huff and her nearly in tears, Diana found herself wanting to follow.

It's none of your concern! she chastised herself. Who did she think she was? Louisa?

"How very strange," Mrs. Rutley said, seeming to ignore Diana's point. "Now they've wandered off together. Where would our host be going with a servant girl, do you think?"

Diana stared at her headmistress. What was wrong with the woman? Yet her questions now had Diana wondering. Then a thought occurred to her. Perhaps this was her opportunity to catch him out of the prying eyes of the other guests. And more importantly, those of Mr. Stonebrook, who was across the room in deep conversation with two older gentleman whose names she could not recall.

No time like the present, she thought. Aloud she said, "I must... speak to someone, Mrs. Rutley," she said, thinking of the first thing that came to mind that would allow her to leave unaccompanied. When her headmistress turned as if to follow, she quickly added, "Oh no, I'm sure I can manage alone. I'll return shortly, I promise."

Mrs. Rutley patted her hand. "Yes, I'm sure you can manage alone. And this will give me a moment to speak to Lord Walcott. You may find me with him when you return."

Seeing that Mr. Stonebrook's back was to her, Diana hurried from the room. She soon encountered the old butler in the corridor with his hands clasped in front of him.

"May I be of assistance, Miss Kendricks?" he asked.

"I must speak to His Lordship. Do you know where he's gone?"

Baldwin nodded. "He's in the wine room. If you follow this corridor to the end, you'll find the staircase that leads to the kitchens. The wine room is located down a shorter corridor on the opposite side of the kitchen. It has a heavy unpainted wooden door."

"Thank you," Diana said. He really was a good butler, so helpful.

With hurried steps, she found the staircase to the kitchens, ignored the staring staff as she walked past them as they worked, and found the wooden door. It was open.

She tiptoed toward it, straining to hear the voice of Lord Barrington or the maid. Finally, his came to her ear.

"Never doubt how much I've cared for you!"

Diana scowled even as tears sprung into her eyes. He was wooing his servant? Well, she was not about to witness such an atrocity!

Yet her decision to leave was short-lived, for as she went to turn back toward the kitchens, she cried as an unceremonious shove sent her sprawling to the floor of the wine room. The door slammed shut, and the lock turned into place.

The room was dark except the single candle that moved toward her, and she uttered a shocked cry upon seeing the face of Lord Barrington.

"Miss Diana? What are you doing here?" He set down the candle holder and helped her up from the floor.

"I should ask you the same thing," she snapped, pulling herself from his grip and swiping at her skirts. She glanced toward the back of the room. "Is Judith decent?"

Lord Barrington frowned. "Judith? Judith isn't here. I'm here alone."

"I don't believe you!" Diana said, pushing past the marquess. But no one was there. "Is there an entrance into the secret passageways from here?"

He shook his head. "Why did you fall?"

Diana straightened her back indignantly. "I didn't fall. I was pushed."

Lord Barrington hurried to her side. "Are you hurt? And did you see who? I'll have him tossed out on his ear!"

"I didn't have the opportunity to make out who it was," she said. "But I should leave. I cannot be found alone here with you."

She marched over to the door, grasped the handle, and tugged. "It's locked," she said, her heart rising to her throat.

"Here, allow me," the marquess said.

Diana scowled. "I'm quite capable of opening a door, my lord," she said, crossing her arms and stepping aside.

As expected, he pulled on the handle and the door did not budge.

"It's locked."

"I said as much. What? Did you think I lied?"

He sighed and pulled a crate into the middle of the room. "Please, sit. This is likely some cruel prank. Whoever locked us in here will return soon enough. If not, I'm sure Baldwin will come in search of us. He knows we're here. Or rather he knows I'm here."

With no other choice than to oblige, Diana sat on the offered crate. The cellar was dark except the single candle that was just bright enough to create a circle of light around them.

"To whom were you speaking?" Diana asked, remembering what she had overheard upon her arrival.

"Myself," Lord Barrington snapped. Then he sighed and pulled up a second crate. "I was thinking of you. And what I said is true. I do care about you. Greatly."

Diana dropped her gaze, her heart even heavier than it had been as of late. Perhaps speaking to this man was unwise after all, for doing so only increased her melancholy. And that she had in bushels already.

"I... I had thought you were speaking to Judith. Or that woman, Miss Amelia," she said.

"Why would you think that?"

She heaved a heavy sigh. "The evening I came to inform you about Mr. Stonebrook and me, I used the hidden passageway and overheard you speaking to her. I didn't mean to eavesdrop, but I just could not help myself."

"And what did you hear exactly?" he asked.

"You spoke of a bond of sorts, of your responsibility for the unborn child, and... and how you have a special place in her heart." And just as Ruth had predicted, the old wounds surfaced as easily as if they had emerged from a newly dug grave. "I was overwhelmed by what I heard, for you had told me that what we shared was special. That I was special. That we shared a certain magic."

"And I didn't lie, Miss Diana." Lord Barrington reached out and took her hand. "I meant what I said to you. And I still feel the same."

His hand was strong, and she felt safe for the first time since their separation.

"I want to believe you, I truly do. But I know what I heard, and I cannot simply forget it."

Lord Barrington nodded. "And I would never deny that you did. But you only know a part of the story. If you're willing to give me this one chance, I believe I can clear up this entire matter."

The candle flickered, and Diana removed her hand from his. They were stuck in this dungeon of a room for the time being. Perhaps she should allow him to clear his conscience, although it would be at her expense.

"I'm listening."

He shifted on the crate. "I've known Miss Amelia for as long as I can remember. Our parents were close, and she spent a great deal of time at Penford Place until I left for school. We grew up together, and our parents believed we would eventually marry. That, of course, did not come to pass, for our feelings for one another do not go beyond friendship. It would be like... like marrying my sister."

Diana's eyes widened. "Then the child she carries is not yours?"

"No," Lord Barrington replied. "A little more than a year ago, I became acquainted with a young man who was charitable and kind. At least, according to him. I didn't realize until much later—when it was far too late—that most of his stories were fabrications. But in the interim, he mentioned that a certain woman had caught his eye, one with whom I was acquainted, and he asked if I would introduce them."

"Mr. Stonebrook and Miss Amelia?" Diana asked in shock.

"Indeed. Because I believed his tale, I happily introduced them. I vouched for him, you see. I told her that his intentions were pure, and it was her faith in me that led her to accept." He looked down at his hands, which were clasped so tightly, the knuckles where white. "But his intentions were not pure. He convinced her that he wished to marry her so he could take her to his bed. Which is how she came to be with child. His child."

"But how could any of this be your responsibility?"

"I was the one who introduced them," Lord Barrington said as he pressed a fist into his thigh. "I convinced Miss Amelia to allow him to call on her. If I had not, she might have refused and therefore would not be in her current situation. I tried to make amends as best I could, even going so far as to concoct a story about her going to Paris for a year. We even sent a woman in her place so she could post pre-written letters to keep up the ruse. Once the child is born, a family will adopt it, and Miss Amelia will return to her previous life, and no one will be any the wiser."

"I hadn't realized," Diana said in awe. "With only the bits of conversation I overheard coupled with what Mr. Stonebrook told me, I never considered what I knew to be false." She looked up at him, her eyes swimming in tears. "I should have asked you before making a final judgment. I'm sorry."

Lord Barrington offered his hand and helped her stand. "I should have been truthful with you from the beginning rather than hiding it. But I swear to you, all I've told you is true. But I've not told you everything."

Diana braced herself. She was not sure she could handle more news. "Go on."

"From the moment I first laid eyes on you, I've been under your spell. Yet I still could not bring myself to trust you, even when my heart told me I could. And that was unfair of me. What I've understood as strong feelings for you have developed into what I can now name as love. If you ever believe one thing I've ever told you, believe this. I love you, Miss Diana. And I always will."

A tear rolled down her cheek, and the marquess wiped it away. She placed a hand on his broad chest and smiled up at him. "I was told that if I listened to my heart, all would work out as it should. I doubted that advice at first, but I'll no longer do so. For my heart tells me that what you say is true, both about what you feel for me and your situation with Miss Amelia."

She took hold of his hand. "That first time you kissed me, it was as if everything I ever wanted, that life as I knew it, had changed. You truly are the Marquess of Magic, for on that day, I, too, came under your spell. And my heart tells me that I share your love."

When they kissed, a hunger grew inside Diana, a desire to be held, kissed, loved. And she knew Lord Barrington should be the man she trusted with her future.

"I'll have words with Baldwin later," he said as he looked down at her, love smoldering in his eyes. "Although I'm thankful for what he's done, he should not have pushed you."

"Are you certain it was he?"

He smiled. "Oh, I'm quite certain. He's been acting odd lately..." He shook his head. "Well, it doesn't matter now."

The sound of people talking in the corridor came to Diana's ears. "What are we to do about tonight?" she asked, her previous despair from earlier returning. "Father will be arriving soon, and Mr. Stonebrook wants to make his announcement. I wish there was a way to stop him, to expose him for the scoundrel he is." Any sane man would wish their daughter to marry a marquess rather than a baronet. But Diana feared her father simply would not care.

"Even if Miss Amelia were to confess the truth to your father, he'd likely pay her no heed. She may be the daughter of an earl, but she's unmarried and with child. All we've done would be nothing more than wasted time. Plus, there is no way to prove Stonebrook's the father."

Diana worried her bottom lip. "There must be a way to expose him for the vile man he is," she murmured as she began to pace. Then she paused and looked up at the marquess. "We're like those etchings on the bridge to Spelling. We've confessed our love, and now you're ready to wage war." She squeezed his hand. "To protect me. And Miss Amelia. You're a great magician and an even better gentleman. I trust you can devise a plan."

"If only I could make him disappear," Lord Barrington said. "That would take care of all our worries." He walked over to the far wall. "But no magician has that capability, not even me. Oh, we can certainly create an illusion, but he'll return soon after, laughing all the while. But I cannot allow you to become a victim to his ways. I'll do whatever it takes to save you and see you're at my side where you belong."

Diana's heart soared with admiration for him. The love in her heart grew tenfold.

Then she let out a shriek as he grasped hold of her. "Miss Clara Moonlight!" he said. "From the book I gave you. Have you had a chance to read it?"

Diana nodded. Why had she not considered Miss Moonlight? "I studied several of the illusions and her notes throughout. It was said her greatest illusion was to make a person disappear."

"I think I now understand how she did it!" he said, smiling broadly. "And you'll do the same!"

She stared at him. Had he gone mad? "But her performances are nothing more than legends. No one can make anything, let alone a man, disappear. Even if she could, she's long dead. Even her book never revealed how the illusion was performed."

Lord Barrington ignored her. "It's been right in front of me the entire time! How could I not see it?" He shook his head. "I'll need your aid if I'm to see this through. Will you help?"

Diana tried to make sense of what he was saying. "I've learned to make a coin move from one place to another, but that is about all. What can I possibly do?"

"You, Miss Kendricks, are a great magician," he said, his grin cutting his face in half. "I've no doubt you'll be helpful. Together, we'll perform the greatest illusion ever! One that will be discussed for years to come."

"I still don't understand," she said. "How can we possibly make Mr. Stonebrook disappear without him returning to call us out as frauds?"

The sound of a key turning in the lock had him grasping her arm. "Don't you see? You'll be as great as Miss Clara Moonlight! You're going to make Miss Amelia disappear. And Stonebrook will disappear right after."

CHAPTER THIRTY-FOUR

P eter Stonebrook considered the victory he was about to win, and it would be sweeter than the wine in the glass he held. Mr. Kendricks had arrived ten minutes earlier, and soon, Peter would announce his courtship to all the revelers in attendance.

He would have preferred more attendees, but the stage was far more important than the audience. A better setting could not have been had. He would put that judgmental marquess in his place once and for all, and in his own home, to boot!

Even if Barrington and Miss Lansing made known who the brat's father was, they had no proof. The fact the girl had been in residence at the guest cottage made the marquess appear far more guilty than Peter ever would.

How fortunate that Lord Walcott had extended his invitation to Peter and Miss Kendricks. He had also offered several appealing contracts that included an agreement with Lord St. John in a farming scheme.

Being Londoners, the Stonebrooks had yet to add any sort of farming interests to their vast enterprises. Perhaps it was about time he convinced his father to expand beyond the boundaries of London, for Walcott certainly weaved a great tale of profit.

But that was just icing on the cake. Peter's main interest lay in the lovely Miss Kendricks, a prized beauty he had stolen right under the nose of the oblivious marquess.

His gaze turned to Lady Barrington, who was to make an announcement soon. Perhaps the old mare had found a new husband. Well, let her believe she would be the center of attention, for he would be pulling that rug right out from under her.

"Where's my daughter, Stonebrook?" Mr. Kendricks asked, breaking Peter from his thoughts. "You said she shouldn't be long, but I've yet to see her."

Peter scanned the crowd. So caught up in his impending victory was he that the girl had slipped his notice. Well, she could not have gone far.

Hmm. Barrington's gone, too. He clenched his hands into fists. If those two were making plans...

Ah, there you are, Peter thought as he spotted the marquess moving along the far wall like a panicked rabbit. What had he been up to? Had he found an opportunity to meet with Miss Kendricks in private? And if so, what sort of plan had they concocted?

Then Peter gave a sigh of relief as Miss Kendricks joined him and her father. "Here she is," Peter said. But something had changed in her demeanor. Gone was the straight back and confident air. Was she hiding something? Guilt perhaps?

"Where have you been?" Mr. Kendricks asked his daughter. "I've been here nearly a quarter hour, and you were nowhere to be seen. Well, child, speak."

"There you are," Mrs. Rutley said as she approached the group. "Is Mrs. Winewood settled down now?" She turned to Peter with an apologetic smile. "The poor woman is far too old to attend these functions. Miss Kendricks was kind enough to help her to one of the guest rooms so she could lie down and rest for a while."

Peter did not recall meeting a Mrs. Winewood, but given she was not of the aristocracy, he likely had forgotten her as soon as they were introduced. Those of the gentry were not worthy of remembering. Except Mr. Kendricks, and only because of what Peter could gain from recalling his name.

268

"Yes, Mrs. Rutley," Miss Kendricks replied. "She is doing much better. I stayed with her until she fell asleep, which was almost as soon as her head lay on the pillow, poor thing."

"So when will this announcement take place?" Mr. Kendricks asked as he pulled out a pocket watch. "I've plans this evening."

Peter smiled. Mr. Kendricks was a man of little patience, who did not bother to greet his own daughter. If Miss Kendricks was accustomed to such treatment, it would only make their marriage that much easier.

"I believe now would be a perfect time," Peter replied. "Besides poor Mrs. Winewood, it appears everyone is well into their cups. An announcement such as this will only give them more reason to celebrate."

And on Barrington's pound, he thought wryly. He was saving a great deal of money using the marquess's party for his needs.

"Before we make our announcement, Mr. Stonebrook," Miss Kendricks said, "may I have a quick word with you first?"

Peter frowned as his suspicions returned that she and Barrington had somehow met. Surely, she would not try to break off the agreement they had made.

"Mr. Kendricks," Mrs. Rutley said, "may I get you a glass of wine? You must have something with which to toast. That will allow these two to speak, likely to go over what they've planned to say one last time before the announcement is made."

"Yes, wine would be appropriate," he replied, and the two walked away.

Peter narrowed his eyes. "We really should make this quick, Miss Kendricks. If we wait too long, the guests will be drunk and not remember a thing we've told them."

She looked up at him, her hands clasped at her breast. "I've the most wonderful news, Mr. Stonebrook!"

"And what would that be?" Peter asked, scowling.

Miss Kendricks leaned in closer and lowered her voice. "When I was returning from taking Mrs. Winewood to her room, I saw Lord Barrington leading that girl to the parlor." She lowered her voice further. "You know which I mean. The one who is in a delicate condition?" A faint smile crossed her lips. "If we're to eventually wed, which is what I assume you have in mind, I'd like to request an early engagement gift."

Peter's scowl deepened. "Speak plainly. What gift could you possibly mean?"

"For the hurt Lord Barrington has caused me, I want you to expose him for the rogue he truly is. And what better place to exact revenge on my behalf than in front of a room full of people who hold him in high regard!"

The thought made Peter smile. Ruining Barrington's name here and now would be a great form of retribution. Yet the request seemed out of character for the lovely Miss Kendricks.

Then she rose onto the tips of her toes and whispered in his ear, "Do this for me, and I'll give you your marital rights tonight and every night hereafter."

His intake of breath was sharp, and desire washed over him as she bit her bottom lip. So, she was not as chaste as she had pretended to be. He would make good use of that information this very evening.

With his blood pumping, licking his lips in anticipation, he said, "Let's go to catch them together."

Miss Kendricks snaked an arm through his, and together they walked to the parlor. When he opened the door, she said with glee, "See! I told you she was here. She's likely waiting for Lord Barrington so he can indulge himself with her again."

Peter smiled. Miss Kendricks had not been lying. There, on the couch, sat Miss Lansing, the evidence of her pregnancy bulging beneath the skirts of her dress.

Miss Lansing pulled herself from her seat with a gasp. "Please," she begged, "please don't reveal anything about Lord Barrington and me!"

"Silence, woman!" Peter barked, hiding his glee. But oh, but how he loved to hear her beg! "Remain seated, and don't move from that spot while I decide your fate."

Her eyes were filled with tears, just as they had been when she showed up on his doorstep all those months ago, insisting the child was his. He had no doubt she spoke the truth, but he would never admit that to another soul. He would not associate himself with a bastard, even if it was his. Miss Lansing had been a pleasant diversion, but her father had nothing to offer. Even if he was an earl.

The evening could not have gone better! Here before him sat the very thing he needed to grant Miss Kendricks the gift she requested. No one would believe Barrington had nothing to do with the girl, not after finding her in his parlor and in her current condition.

Not only was this a wondrous gift for Miss Kendricks, but so was it for himself. He could not allow this opportunity to pass!

"You'll remain here until I return. Don't think of leaving or I'll see you pay in ways you cannot imagine."

Taking Miss Kendricks by the arm, he led her out into the corridor, closing the parlor door behind them. "Here's what we'll do. I'll gain the attention of those at the party and ask them to follow me here."

Miss Kendricks nodded. "May I wait in the drawing room? When you've revealed your secret, I can sneak out and join the others. No one will know my involvement in your plan. If not, my father will surely make me remain behind, and I'll not be present to see you at work." She placed a hand on his arm. "I like watching you work," she said in a husky voice that spoke of the eventful night ahead.

"I think that a wonderful idea," he replied. Lord Walcott approached, and he whispered, "Go, now!"

She gave him a provocative smile that made sweat bead on his brow. "I'll wait for the right moment," she whispered as she ran a fingernail down his cheek and hurried away.

"Is all well with you, Stonebrook?" Lord Walcott asked.

Peter forced a sigh. "Unfortunately not. Do you remember the terrible secrets I told you about Barrington and Miss Lansing? Well, she's here right now inside the parlor! Can you believe he would be so bold as to parade her around in this way?"

Lord Walcott frowned. "So, that is why you left the ballroom in such a hurry. I can only assume Miss Kendricks saw the woman, as well?"

"Indeed, she did," Peter replied, shaking his head with dismay. "It upset her terribly, I'm afraid."

During the carriage ride to the school with the earl, Peter had explained his version of the Barrington and Lansing tale. The old man had been full of talk about morals and respecting women and had expressed anger at being invited to a "house of loose morals" or so he had termed it.

"But it's too late to refuse now," Lord Walcott had said with a regretful sigh. "After all, we're quite literally on our way. I do pray Miss Kendricks recovers from this terrible news. Young ladies, those with weak countenances, they can take days—weeks even!—to recover from exposure to this type of wanton behavior."

And now Peter had an ally to see through his plan! After explaining to the earl his intentions, he said, "I would usually turn a blind eye to behavior that is so outrageous. After all, what concern is this of mine? But Miss Kendricks is now involved. I simply cannot ignore such wickedness. I've come to love Chatsworth and its people, so I do this for them."

"I admire your integrity, Stonebrook," Lord Walcott said, clasping Peter on the shoulder. "What can I do?"

"Would you be willing to guard this door in case the woman tries to make her escape?"

The earl frowned. "But what if she tries to climb out a window?"

Peter chuckled. "Trust me, she's in a delicate condition, far too delicate to be climbing in and out of windows. She's no other way of escape but through this door. But if you're here, she cannot leave."

Lord Walcott smiled. "What a marvelous plan. Of course, I'll remain here. Men the likes of Barrington should get his just dues, wouldn't you say?"

"I couldn't agree with you more," Peter replied. "I'll return soon, and everyone will get his just desserts!"

Peter doubted he had ever moved so quickly as he did this night. Upon entering the ballroom, he looked around before clearing his throat and saying in his loudest voice, "May I have your attention, ladies and gentlemen?" The music stopped abruptly, and he waited for the conversation to wane before continuing. "I would like you all to follow me, please."

Mr. Kendricks broke through the crowd of confused guests. "What's this all about, Stonebrook. Are you drunk?"

"No, sir," Peter replied. "Trust me." He raised his voice once more.

"I'm about to reveal a secret our grand host has been keeping from all of you. Please, follow me if you'd like to learn the truth about the man you've always held in such high regard."

"This had better be good," Mr. Kendricks murmured. "I don't appreciate foolish acts."

"You'll see," Peter said, grinning as the guests gathered around him. He turned and led the group down the corridor to where Lord Walcott stood in front of the parlor.

Just as they arrived, Lord Barrington came running toward him. "Please stop, Stonebrook. I'd hate for you to embarrass yourself."

Peter laughed. "Walcott, only moments ago, I asked you to guard this door. In that time, has anyone entered or left the room?"

Lord Walcott shook his head. "No one."

Peter licked his lips in anticipation of the shock that would carry through the crowd. "Then behold. Inside this room is a woman of such vileness, of such immorality, she should be shunned by every decent man and woman in this country. She is a woman who gave herself freely—without benefit of marriage vows, mind you!—to our host, our very own Lord Barrington. And the proof of that union will be evident by the swelling belly in which she carries his child. His *bastard* child!"

The corridor filled with disapproving murmurs. Mr. Kendricks grabbed hold of Peter's arm. "What is this all about, Stonebrook? Don't embarrass me with mere gossip. I don't abide it in any form."

Ignoring his future father-in-law, Peter said, "As you all heard, Lord Walcott, whom you all respect, guarded this door. And by his own word, you can be certain no one has come or gone from this room. Now, I'll open the door so you may all see the object of Lord Barrington's lust, a woman of loose morals who carries his child and should be ridiculed as much as he!"

He opened the door and stepped into the room with a flourish... only to come to an abrupt halt. Those behind jostled him, cursing as they stepped on one another's toes and barreled into each other's backs.

"Where is...?" His voice trailed off as he looked behind the door and rushed to peer behind the couch. He went so far as to pull up a cushion and check beneath it. But Miss Lansing was nowhere to be found.

Instead, there sat Miss Kendricks, a book open on her lap, and staring up at the group in alarm.

"What's this?" she asked, a look of fright on her face.

"How dare you accuse my daughter of loose morals!" Mr. Kendricks roared as he took hold of Peter's coat. "I should call you out right now! Do you prefer swords or pistols?"

"But..." Peter glanced around the room, panic filling him. "But she was here!"

"Who?" Mr. Kendricks demanded. "The only person I see here is my daughter."

"No, not her! I mean Miss Amelia Lansing. She was here!"

"That's not possible," Lady Barrington said, and all eyes turned to her. "She's in Paris and has been for some time. Her mother received a letter from her just last week. Surely, you don't think she's made the return journey from Paris already without informing her mother?" She clicked her tongue in vexation and turned to glare at Peter. "These rumors about Miss Lansing have been circulating around for months, and now I know who started them!"

All eyes were on Peter, every single person glaring at him as if he were taking that final walk to the gallows. The room began to spin.

"Are you drunk again, sir?" Miss Kendricks asked, concern blanketing her tone.

Peter's heart was beating so hard, it nearly broke through his chest.

"What do you mean 'again'?" Mr. Kendricks asked, his glare so hot Peter should have melted like snow in the sun. "Is this common? You know what I think of men who waste their lives on drink!"

"Mr. Stonebrook is drunk quite often, Father," Miss Kendricks said sadly. "It's why I came here—to read scripture and pray that he stops." She held up the book she had been reading. It was a Holy Bible.

"What kind of father allows such a man to call on his daughter?" one of the ladies asked. Another echoed an agreement.

Anger rose in Peter. Everything had gone wrong! "You're a liar!" he shouted as he pointed at Miss Kendricks. "You tricked me! Where is that other woman?"

Miss Kendricks broke out in sobs, and Lady Barrington hurried over to gather her into her arms. "That is quite enough, Mr. Stonebrook. James, do something!"

A hand gripped Peter by the shoulder. "I cannot, and will not, allow you to spew your lies in front of my guests. And your drunken behavior can no longer be tolerated."

Peter tried to wriggle from his grip, but it was too tight.

"My friends," Barrington said, "I'm afraid that Mr. Stonebrook is a vile man, and I apologize you've been forced to endure such brazen behavior. You see, when he learned I wished to request permission to court Miss Kendricks, Mr. Stonebrook became enraged. This is what jealousy and drink has done to him."

"He's lying!" Peter shrieked. "I was supposed to court her, not you. Her father already agreed! Tell them!"

"Mr. Kendricks?" Barrington said, turning to Miss Kendricks' father. "Surely, you would not give a man who spends most of his time looking into the bottom of a bottle permission to court your innocent daughter rather than me?"

Every guest looked on with anticipation. No one breathed, no one spoke, as they all awaited the father's reply.

"No," Mr. Kendricks said after several moments of thought as he rubbed his chin. "No, I would never trust my daughter to a drunkard. What is true is that Lord Barrington did come to me and ask my permission to court my daughter. And I granted it." He turned to Peter, his face pinched as if he smelled something foul. "I've only met this fool an hour ago."

Peter's eyes went wide. Just met him? Yet another lie! Glancing around, the panic now turned to horror, and he pointed at Lord Walcott. "He lied! There was a pregnant woman here, and he helped her escape!"

The earl's face darkened. "Where to, man? I was here in the hallway speaking to Mr. Slate. I saw no one leave the room, just as I said."

A squat, balding man in his later years took a step forward. "He speaks the truth. We were discussing the outrageous price of tobacco right outside the door. Unless you wish to call me a liar, as well."

"Walcott is known for his integrity," Lord Mallings said in a voice that quaked with age. "I think you've embarrassed yourself enough for two lifetimes, young man. Perhaps you should leave."

A murmur of agreement filled the room, and two dozen pairs of disapproving eyes were settled on Peter.

All was lost. He had been duped. If he did not leave Chatsworth this very night, his crumbling reputation would reach London long before he did.

Therefore with his head low, Peter Stonebrook, the future Baron of Forthington, pushed through the crowd. Without waiting to collect his overcoat and hat, he made his way to his carriage, promising himself never to step foot in Chatsworth again.

The crowd had dispersed, returning to their gossip. Diana was certain what would be at the forefront of their discussions.

Ready to return to Lord Barrington, she stopped and tilted her head with curiosity. What could Mrs. Rutley and her father be discussing?

Then her heartbeat quickened as her father walked up to her. Would he now say that his agreement to allow the marquess to court her was all a ruse? That somehow, she had once again disappointed him?

"I've come to realize that my ways..." He sighed. "Yes, that is the only way to describe my atrocious behavior... that my ways almost led to you marrying a fool of a man. It's been brought to my attention"—he glanced toward Mrs. Rutley—"that you believe I don't care about you, but that cannot be further from the truth. It's because of you that I work so hard, so you can have everything I did not have when I was younger. My father often gave gifts as tokens of love and admiration. I only wished to do the same. But in all of this, I see I've taken it too far, and for that, I'm sorry. Do you have it in your heart to forgive me?"

A wave of emotion washed over Diana, and she threw her arms around her father. "You've no idea how much that means to me, Father."

As she pulled away, she glanced at Lord Barrington, and a new thought came to mind. Her future was now secure, but she knew another woman whose future was not.

"Father, I would like to make one request before we join Lord Barrington."

"Have you already spent your allowance?" he asked, chuckling. "If you need more, simply ask."

"No," she replied, smiling. "It's just that there is a particular woman who misses her husband. From my understanding, he's been far too busy to spend any time with her. Busy with 'his ways.' You've restored the bridge to me. Do you think you can do the same with Mother? I think she would be pleased to have you returned to her."

Her father gave a heavy sigh, his cheeks a deep crimson. "Yes well, perhaps he's just an old fool who has no idea what he's lost. Maybe it's about time he tries to rebuild what they once shared. After all, the fault lies with him."

"I think she would like that," Diana said, her heart filled to bursting.

She and her father went to join Lord Barrington, and the two men she loved fell into an instant discussion. They would become fast friends, she was certain.

As the men spoke, Diana searched for her headmistress, who had somehow disappeared from the party. Just as she was about to give up hope in finding her, she spotted Mrs. Rutley along the far wall. When Mrs. Rutley noticed Diana staring at her, she gave a simple nod and a small smile.

And like a great magician, the headmistress disappeared into the crowd.

CHAPTER THIRTY-FIVE

"I still cannot believe our plan worked," James said as he strolled beside Diana in the gardens behind his house six days after the party. "It was a brilliant idea. Truly, you are the greatest magician in all of England."

Diana smiled as she thought of that evening. Not a single flaw marred their plan, and Lord Walcott inadvertently being asked to guard the parlor door only made the illusion all the more successful.

Once the marquess had led Miss Amelia to the parlor as—for better lack of a word—bait, Mr. Stonebrook entered the trap as easily as any hare. Once they were certain he had seen Miss Amelia, he had acted as expected. Men such as he could not resist a chance to embarrass his betters.

All that was left to do was have Miss Amelia use the secret passageway to reach the drawing room, where Baldwin waited to sneak her down to the kitchens where she would hide for the remainder of the party.

"Shall I become the Marchioness of Magic once we are married?" Diana asked.

James laughed. "I think that would be most appropriate. You've certainly proven yourself worthy of such a title."

They continued their walk, Jenny following behind them. In three days, Diana's mother would come to collect her from the school, and the next phase of her life would begin.

"Here she comes," James said.

Diana smiled as Miss Amelia walked up to them, bundled in many coats and a thick, gray muffler.

James bowed. "Allow me to formally present to you Miss Amelia Lansing. Miss Amelia, this is Miss Diana Kendricks, my fiancée."

Miss Amelia grinned. "It's so nice to officially meet you, Miss Diana. And under much better circumstances."

Setting aside all propriety, Diana threw her arms around Miss Amelia. "I'm very glad we've met now, knowing who you are and the friendship you share with James." Using his Christian name still tasted wonderful on her tongue and sent a mischievous thrill down her spine.

"It makes me happy knowing the two of you are together," Miss Amelia said. "I told James that your smiles told me well before your tongues the future in store for you."

"And are you well?" Diana asked.

Two days earlier, Miss Amelia gave birth to a child, a boy who was given to a family unable to have one of their own. A much better place than some children born in similar situations. In Diana's opinion, it said much about the woman before her. Despite what fate had given her, despite the decisions she had made, she cared what happened to her son.

"I am," Miss Amelia replied. "Quite well, indeed. I won't lie and say I'm not sad, but knowing my child has a good home and will be raised without the stigma of being born out of wedlock eases my sadness. And I'll be returning home today. My parents believe I became home-sick and could not remain in Paris a moment longer and wanted to go home. Or so said my last letter. After all, they warned me I would do just that."

She gave a mischievous grin, and Diana could not have been more pleased for her. All had worked out as it should. Granted, it had nearly led to disaster, but knowing she played a part in its success filled her with pride.

Miss Amelia tilted her head and gave Diana a thoughtful look. "You know, what you two share is magical. I can see why James loves you. You're different from other young ladies."

"Oh?" Diana said. "How so?"

"Most would turn and run, seeing me, knowing what I've done. But not you. You treat me with honor and respect. And I appreciate that."

With a small smile, Diana responded, "I've no idea what you mean, Miss Lansing. We only met today, and I know nothing about you. Perhaps a few rumors, granted, but I don't listen to gossip."

Miss Amelia wiped a tear from her eye and embraced Diana again. "Thank you," she whispered. "For everything."

"You're most welcome."

Miss Amelia pulled away. "I suppose the next time we meet will be at your wedding," she said. "Surely, I'll be invited?"

Diana laughed. "Of course you will be."

"Well, I'm off to pack." She hugged James. "Thank you again. I could not have done any of this without you."

"Just go and have a happy life," James said. "And do be careful of future suitors, will you?"

After a playful slap on his arm, Miss Amelia walked away.

"So, that now leaves us," James said.

"Us," Diana repeated. "I like the sound of that. It's far better than the cruel words you said to me at Mistral's Bookshop."

James gave her a mock indignant look. "I? Perhaps I should remind you of who selected a most improper book!"

They laughed, and Diana knew her life was destined for love. They planned to marry in June. What would happen from there remained to be seen. But one thing she knew was that Miss Amelia was correct. What she and James shared was truly magical.

Diana stared up at the ceiling of the foyer in the school that had been her home over the past three years. Her mother had brought her to Mrs. Rutley's School for Young Women when she was but fifteen, and today, at the age of eighteen, the same woman waited in the carriage to take her away. Once home, they would make preparations for the wedding. And the start of Diana's new life. A life she would share with James.

"Diana," Mrs. Rutley said from the corridor, "it's time."

With a nod, Diana followed Mrs. Rutley to the drawing room, where her friends waited to say goodbye. Momentary sadness filled her as she looked at each of the faces with whom she shared a special bond. And although she was pleased with the life that had been set ahead of her, she could not help but worry for those she was leaving behind.

Ruth, who had been unusually quiet as of late, was the first to bid her farewell. "You're happy," she whispered in Diana's ear. "Always remain so."

It was a strange message, at least from Ruth, but Diana had no time to consider it as the twins, who were not twins, pulled her in for a hug.

"I'll miss you both," Diana said. "Do remember to write."

"Oh, we will," Unity said. "No matter what happens, we'll always write."

Theodosia nodded. "Yes, no matter what."

Louisa was next. "Be careful," Diana said to her. "Your curiosity may lead you into all sorts of trouble. Remember what Mr. Johnson warns. 'Helter skelter, hang sorrow, care'll kill a cat, up-tails all, and a louse for the hangman.'"

Louisa gave a laugh as she wiped a tear from her eye. "I'll do my best to keep my curiosity under control, I promise. But it will most certainly take all the fun out of things."

Finally, Diana came to Jenny, to whom she felt the closest as of late. "Thank you for encouraging me when I believed all was lost. And promise me you'll not drop any more handkerchiefs."

"I promise," Jenny replied as she wrapped her arms around Diana. "Goodbye, my friend."

With one last look at the girls who were her sisters, Diana left the room. Mrs. Rutley waited at the front door.

"You were right, Mrs. Rutley," Diana said. "If I listened to my heart, it would lead me to happiness, and that is exactly what happened. Thank you for giving me such wise instruction and for teaching me not to give up hope. That a better day would come tomorrow. For it truly has."

Mrs. Rutley smiled and adjusted Diana's collar to guard against the cold winter breeze. "There is no need to thank me. You arrived here a girl and leave as a woman, and that is good enough for me. But I do have one more request. Not as your headmistress but as a friend."

"Of course," Diana said. "Anything you wish."

She pulled out a small wooden top, the very one Diana had seen in the study, and placed it in Diana's hand. "The next time you see Lord Barrington, give him this, will you? I know it's an unusual gift, but I would like him to have it. One day, you'll have a son, and I think it will make a fine present for the boy."

Diana smiled. How thoughtful that her headmistress was already thinking of the children she and James would have one day! "I'll see that James receives it and knows it's from you."

Mrs. Rutley's eyes misted, but just as Diana went to ask what was wrong, the woman said, "It's time for you to go. Goodbye, my dear."

With a mixture of elation and a heavy heart, Diana hugged her headmistress once more. "Goodbye, Mrs. Rutley. And thank you. For everything."

She made her way to the waiting carriage but stopped halfway to turn back to Mrs. Rutley. "And don't worry. The marquess is a good man, and both of us will always be happy."

"I know."

Once inside the carriage, Diana looked out the window toward the school. Her friends were at the windows, and she returned their enthusiastic waves with her own. As the carriage pulled away, she gave one final wave to her teacher, her friend, and the image of Mrs. Rutley returning the gesture was one Diana would always remember.

CHAPTER THIRTY-SIX

Mrs. Agnes Rutley was unsure if an hour or three had passed since Diana had left, so lost was she in her thoughts. She paid little heed to the chill of the cold winter wind, which played with the end of the muffler wrapped around her neck. Sadness filled her heart as memories filled her mind, memories she had hoped would never see the light of day. She should not have been surprised, however. Chatsworth was a small village, after all.

Agnes's mind went back to a time many years earlier. Her husband's death had left her shattered, and she was in no mind to watch over herself, let alone the newborn boy bundled in her arms.

It had been Henry Walcott on whom she had called and who had stood beside her and Mrs. Shepherd outside the tiny cottage an hour's ride from Chatsworth.

Under the guise of mourning, Agnes had stolen away to the cottage to wait out the birth of her child. There she could keep out of the prying eyes and the inevitable whispers of those who knew her.

The carriage came to a stop, and a lord and lady alighted. Unable to have her own children, she had entered into an agreement to adopt Agnes's son and raise him as her own. Although the thought clenched her heart, she knew it was what was best for the boy.

Tears filled her eyes as the couple drew near. She said a silent prayer and kissed the newborn on his forehead.

"You'll be far better off," she whispered *as a way of explanation.*

"Remember, Agnes," Henry said in just as quiet a voice, "we've all given our word. None of us will speak about what takes place here today. Nor shall you ever speak to them again. The child will no longer be your son."

"I know," Agnes said.

"Walcott. Mrs. Rutley," Lord Barrington said. Then with a wide smile, he looked at the bundle in her arms. "Hello, my son."

As Agnes handed Lady Barrington the child, her heart shattered into a thousand pieces. She was tempted to turn and run away with the babe, but she did not. This was the right thing to do. Her son would thrive in a loving home. He would become a marquess. What could she offer him other than a fatherless home and a mother whose mind was no longer sound?

The marchioness smiled. "James," she said. "We'll name him after your grandfather."

Doing all she could not to begin weeping, Agnes reached into the pocket of her coat and took out a small wooden top. "A gift for when he's older," she said.

Lady Barrington sneered and pulled the child away. "I'll buy my son what I deem proper," she snapped. "And he'll certainly not receive gifts from a woman like you. Don't forget our agreement. Never look our away again. Never ask to see the boy for any reason. He's no longer your child. He's now a Barrington."

Without waiting for Agnes to reply, she turned on her heel and returned to the carriage.

Lord Barrington gave a small nod and followed his wife without comment.

Once they were gone, Henry said, "You did the right thing, Agnes. Always remember that." And with that, he was gone as well, leaving Agnes and Mrs. Shepherd alone.

"What do I do now?" Agnes asked. "My heart is broken. I fear it will never heal."

The cook pulled Agnes into her arms. "We'll rebuild you, Mrs. Rutley. Every little bit of you that's broken, we're going to put back together. Just you wait and see."

"And how will we do that?"

"We'll begin with a cup of tea," Mrs. Shepherd replied. "And a bit of a chat. That's how we'll start, anyway. The rest'll just fall into place, won't it?"

The creak of the door pulled Agnes back into the present, and she did not turn as Mrs. Shepherd joined her. The cook said nothing but instead remained at Agnes's side, just as she had all the years they had known one another. Agnes had no better friend than Mrs. Shepherd.

A leaf that had clung to the limb of the ancient tree fluttered toward the ground, only to be sent flying with the wind. A new season would soon arrive, then another. Days would become weeks, winter would become spring. Girls would become women.

"Tell me, my friend," Mrs. Shepherd said. "What are you thinking about?"

Agnes gave a weak smile. She had never been one to weep, but when the tears came, they were sometimes difficult to keep back. But she had shed enough tears over this particular subject to last her entire lifetime.

"I was thinking of a young girl who carried a child," she whispered. "Fearful of the days ahead of her. Of all her choices, she was unsure which to make, for her world was ruined, a veil of innocence was taken away, and she was lost."

She wiped at the treacherous droplets that rolled down her cheek. "Then believing she was doing what was best, she gives the child to a family who will love him and raise him to be a strong man, for she is too weak to do it properly. So she made a choice, using her love for him, to place him with a family who would give him all she could not."

She turned to Mrs. Shepherd. "Did I make the right decision?"

"Most definitely, yes," the cook replied. "And the boy you gave to that loving home has prospered. He's turned into such a fine gentleman. Anyone can see that. Now you'll not have to worry about him anymore. Miss Diana will see he's taken care of and that he's loved. He'll be happy, and that's what you wanted from the very day you gave him away, isn't it?"

Agnes nodded, the tears falling unchecked. "I should be grateful that I was able to watch him grow, even if it was from afar." She shook her head and pulled a handkerchief from the sleeve of her coat. "I don't know what's come over me. That was a long time ago, and I've made peace with my past."

Mrs. Shepherd wrapped an arm around Agnes's shoulders. "You still love your son. And there's nothing wrong with that. You're allowed a few tears from time to time. We all are. Will you ever tell him, do you think?"

Agnes shook her head. "I promised Lady Barrington that I would never reveal the truth, and I always keep my word. Plus, what would be gained from revealing such information?"

"It could ease your heart," Mrs. Shepherd said.

"No, my heart is at peace now."

Mrs. Shepherd smiled. "Come on, let's get you inside, and I'll make you a nice pot of tea to warm you up. Tea and a bit of chat always brightens even the darkest days."

And Mrs. Shepherd was right, for sharing a cup of tea and talking about days long past left Mrs. Agnes Rutley feeling much, much better.

CHAPTER THIRTY-SEVEN

L ady Diana, Marchioness of Barrington, walked through her Yorkshire Estate, the skirts of her day dress flowing around her ankles. In her arms, she held her sleeping son who was just four months old. Her love for the child—and the man who had helped her create him—knew no bounds. She stopped in the doorway to the study, where her husband sat hunched over a ledger. Love was a beautiful thing, and Diana paused to reflect on her life since it began upon her marriage two years earlier.

"A penny for your thoughts," James said as he rose from his desk.

Diana joined him, and he placed his hand on her arm. "I was just thinking about what my prospects were before you entered my life. I cannot imagine what life would have been like living as a spinster. And living alone." She smiled up at him. "But then I met a certain man who cast a spell on me."

"That is a very interesting tale, Lady Barrington," he said. "And I, too, was unsure what my life would be like. I can say with certainty that marriage was not a priority. Then a woman enchanted me with her beauty and wit. Not to mention that she made a fool of me by making me enter a dressmaker's shop. But rather than pushing me away, it only drew me closer to her."

"I did not make you do anything, my lord," she said. "It was you whose pride was hurt and chose to chase after me." Their son, named after James, stretched and yawned before falling back to sleep. "You see, even he knows the truth."

James laughed. "Denying it would be futile," he said. "But I'm glad I did follow you." He brushed one of her long curls over her ear. "For I learned about a new type of magic, one which I believe we have both experienced every day since."

Diana nodded. "And together, we've made the most wonderful magic the world has ever seen."

In the past, her meaning would have been the illusion of riffling through a book or making a coin or even a person disappear. Yet this was even better, for it had the ability to break barriers of one's heart and bring together two very different people, just as it had them. A man who felt guilty over the introduction of a young woman, who was a dear friend, to a man who was a cad, and a woman who would have preferred spinsterhood to marriage.

And unlike the simple illusions shown in books, their magic was real. A feat Diana hoped one Miss Clara Moonlight had learned, as well.

EPILOGUE

Chatsworth, England 1825

Diana, Lady Barrington, wiped at her eyes. "And that is the story of how I came to know, and later love, a man known as the Marquess of Magic."

"And what a lovely story it is," Mrs. Rutley said. "One I've always cherished as much as the others shared thus far."

"They are all such beautiful stories, Mrs. Rutley," Diana said. With a smile, she looked at Julia and Emma, who sat in chairs across from her. "And to think that I witnessed both your stories unfold right here in this school, too." She let out a small laugh. "But what I find strange is that I think often of that night at the party, when James and I became trapped in the wine room. Until the day he died, Baldwin refused to admit he was the one who pushed me into the room. James threatened to give him the sack and even offered him a bonus if he would only confess, but to no avail."

"That is because it was not he who pushed you," Mrs. Rutley said.

Diana gasped. "But if not he, then who?"

The headmistress smiled. "I did." Her hand opened, and upon her palm lay a large iron key.

"That is not—"

"The key to the wine room?" Mrs. Rutley asked. "Of course it is. And now it's yours."

Diana took the key, staring at it in wonder. "I don't understand. That night... how did you know? Why would you push me into that room?"

Mrs. Rutley gave a weak chuckle, which turned into a hacking cough. Julia poured her a glass of water, and once the headmistress had drunk her fill, she continued. "There were many schemes afoot that night. I knew you simply needed time alone with Lord Barrington, and all would be right. So, I instructed Mr. Baldwin to inform the marquess there was a thief who was stealing the wine. There was none, of course. It was also I who convinced Lord Walcott to invite Mr. Stonebrook and you to the party, using Mr. Baldwin to inform His Lordship. We also used the maid because I knew you could not resist learning what the man you loved was up to."

"You knew I'd follow James?"

Mrs. Rutley smiled. "Of course. It was all a part of my plan. But I can only take credit for what happened up until I pushed you into the room and locked the door. You and your husband were the ones responsible for the grand illusion. A magnificent performance, indeed."

With a laugh, Diana wiped tears from her eyes. "I'm glad you did push me in because my life would have been far different today if you had not. So, thank you. You knew me better than I knew myself, it appears. But I do have another question. You gave me a toy, a wooden top, the day I left the school. Why?"

Mrs. Rutley smiled, her eyelids fluttering. "That is a story for another day. For now, I must rest."

With a small nod, Diana stood and walked to the door with Julia and Emma. "Now we must wait for Jenny and Louisa," Julia said. "I'm sure they'll be here soon. I see no reason they would not come."

Emma gave a nod of agreement. "They must come. Unlike Unity and Theodosia, they are in England. There is no excuse for them not to do so."

Diana nodded. She had been sad to learn they would not be coming, and sadder still to learn about Ruth's death. "No matter what happens, I'll remain here until our next sister arrives. I just wish I knew who it will be."

As soon as she said this, a soft knock came to the door. Diana opened it, and all three smiled.

"Oh, Jenny, it's so good to see you!" Diana said as she hugged her dear friend. "Mrs. Rutley is resting, but soon, she would like you to tell her a story. And I know I'm not the only one who wishes to hear it."

THE END

Thank you for reading *Marquess of Magic*!

Lord Dowding comes to collect on the promise Miss Jenny Clifton made in the next book of the series, *The Earl of Deception*. Coming in August 2022!

In the meantime, have you already read Julia's and Emma's story in *Duke of Madness* (book 1) and *Baron of Rake Street* (book 2)?

SISTERHOOD OF SECRETS

While waiting for book 4 to be released, check out other books by Jennifer Monroe or dive into one of the latest releases by WOLF Publishing: *Once Upon an Accidentally Bewitching Kiss* by *USA Today* Bestselling Author Bree Wolf.

THE WHICKERTONS IN LOVE

ALSO BY JENNIFER MONROE

ABOUT JENNIFER MONROE

 Jennifer Monroe writes clean Regency romances you can't resist. Her stories are filled with first loves and second chances, dashing dukes, and strong heroines. Each turn of the page promises an adventure in love and many late nights of reading.

With over twenty books published, her nine-part series, The Secrets of Scarlett Hall, which tells the stories of the Lambert Children, remain a favorite with her readers.

Connect with Jennifer:

www.jennifermonroeromance.com

f facebook.com/JenniferMonroeAuthor
instagram.com/authorjennifermonroe
BB bookbub.com/authors/jennifer-monroe
a amazon.com/Jennifer-Monroe/e/B07F1MRXDN

Made in the USA
Middletown, DE
24 May 2022

66198063R00182